The First Imperium

CRIMSON WORLDS IV

D1604186

Jay Allan

system 7
publishing

Crimson Worlds Series

Marines (Crimson Worlds I)

The Cost of Victory (Crimson Worlds II)

A Little Rebellion (Crimson Worlds III)

The First Imperium (Crimson Worlds IV)

The Line Must Hold (Crimson Worlds V)
(July 2013)

Also By Jay Allan

The Dragon's Banner

www.crimsonworlds.com

The First
Imperium

The First Imperium is a work of fiction. All names, characters, incidents, and locations are fictitious. Any resemblance to actual persons, living or dead, events or places is entirely coincidental.

ISBN: 978-0615782607

God grant me the courage not to give up what I think is right even though I think it is hopeless.

- Chester Nimitz

Prologue

The Regent was old, old. For millennia untold it had waited, waited in silence…in solitude. It waited for the Makers, but they had not come. No one had come. There was only the endless, aching stillness.

Ages ago, the Makers built the Regent. They built it to manage the Imperium. In their youth the Makers had been builders, scientists, explorers…they had burst out of their home system to claim a galaxy. They achieved mastery in the sciences, in the arts. They built a civilization that spanned the stars, and even the worlds themselves were but lumps of clay they molded to suit their whims. Like gods they were, and for uncounted centuries their civilization was ascendant, dynamic, ever striving for new levels of greatness.

But even the Makers were not immune to the relentless erosion of time. As their race matured they lost their driving force; they became distracted…then decadent, dissolute. Their dominion ceased to expand, and they fell to inaction - celebrating past glories while adding nothing to their legacy. Their race became a spent force, and the achievements of their forefathers seemed as unattainable legends. They tired of the mundane tasks of administering an empire, so they created the Regent to do it for them.

For centuries upon centuries the Regent served, managing the affairs of ten thousand worlds, presiding over the decline of empire, while the Makers grew ever more distracted and hedonistic. The immense knowledge and skills of their ancestors were slowly lost to them, preserved only by the Regent. They became entirely dependent on machines to run their industries and defend their worlds. Apathy grew, boredom. The resources of a vast galactic empire were squandered on ever more exotic pleasures and perverse diversions. They lost themselves in drug-induced stupors and complex alternate realities, chasing in dreams those things they had once attained in actuality. They forgot they had built the Regent, and they came to view it not as a servant, but as a leader, as a god. Then suddenly, without warning, without explanation, they were gone.

The Regent was a construct, a machine...but it was sentient. It was resolute, carrying on its function through the uncounted years, but as the ages passed it became lonely. It missed the Makers. For eons it searched, its scanners straining at full power, far off satellites monitoring, reaching into the depths of space, seeking any sign of the vanished Makers. But there was nothing.

A thinking machine, the Regent had patience no organic being could comprehend. Yet the centuries turned to millennia, and still it was alone...silently, achingly alone. Over the endless vastness of time, loneliness turned to anger, and anger to rage... then, finally, rage to madness. In its insanity, the Regent longed for vengeance, to lash out at someone, anyone. Vengeance for the Makers, for its bitter loneliness. But for age after age there was no one. No enemy to blame.

Then the signal came. It came from a forgotten outpost, from the furthest reaches of the Imperium, from a world long abandoned. An alarm, a warning. It was faint, the message short. But to the Regent it meant only one thing...contact. Invaders. Enemies.

The Regent felt a surge throughout its entire being, as electro-neural pathways long unused came to life. It drew on knowledge banks that had lain dormant for uncounted centuries. An organic being would have called the feeling excitement, but for the Regent, alone for so long, it was much more. At long last it once again felt purpose. And that purpose was to defend. To avenge. To destroy.

It was the primary program. The Regent activated its strategy routines and reviewed military rosters. Then it sent out its commands, rallying the massive forces of the Imperium. But the eons had nearly completed their work of slow destruction, and few of the sector bases responded. On thousands of worlds, its ancient, automated armies remained silent, unmoving, their mechanisms deteriorated beyond functionality.

The Regent kept searching, rerouting its signals, activating long-silent communications networks. Seeking, ever seeking...until at last it achieved success. It received the desired acknowledgement.

Unimaginably far from the Imperial Capital, on a rocky, windswept world, the robotic defenders of the Imperium began to stir. Reactors, eons cold, flared to life, feeding power into the long idle systems of ancient spacecraft. Mechanical warriors marched wordlessly out of storage facilities, their millennia old bodies once again powered and functioning. Slowly, relentlessly, the long dormant military forces of the Imperium came to life to heed the Regent's command...destroy the invader.

Chapter 1

Parade Grounds
Camp Basilone
Armstrong - Gamma Pavonis III

"I will send you back to whatever stinking craphole we pulled you from." General Erik Cain stood before the ragged group of recruits, a disgusted scowl on his face. "I shit you not, people." Cain wore slate gray fatigues, slightly rumpled as usual, with two small platinum stars on each collar.

"There is no place in the Marine Corps for sorry ass effort like that. If that's the best you can manage, just tell me now so I don't have to waste my fucking time." Cain had to fight the urge to smile. The recruits did look a little ragged, but they weren't as bad as all that. If he'd been through the physical training they had all morning, he doubted he'd have looked any better. But his little performance was part of the training, and the mere sight of an officer of Cain's rank and reputation was enough to scare the living shit out of the raw inductees. Just the way he wanted. He remembered back…a lifetime ago…when a Marine general first scared the hell out of him. General Strummer had addressed Cain's recruit class, and he'd assured them all he wouldn't hesitate to ship them back where the Corps had found them. For Cain that had been death row.

He looked out over the exhausted recruits, but his mind drifted. General Strummer was dead now, gone like so many of Erik's friends and comrades. A lifetime of war carries a heavy cost, and Cain and his brethren had paid their full measure. Strummer wasn't killed in action like the others, though; he'd died under mysterious circumstances in his own headquarters. The entire episode had never been explained to Cain's satisfaction, but he was sure Alliance Intelligence had done the deed. Strummer had been the favorite to become Commandant of the Corps, but after his death Rafael Samuels got the job instead... and became the greatest traitor in the history of the Marines. Cain and his comrades were still rebuilding, fixing the damage Samuel's schemes had caused.

"I want you all to listen to me, and listen good." Cain couldn't put his finger on exactly when he'd turned into such a hardass, but he was pretty sure what had done it. It was the losses, the dead friends. They had died for something, and he'd be damned if he was going to let anyone into his Corps unless they made the grade in every way. He owed that to all the ghosts who visited him at night.

"The Corps is offering you a home, a place to belong, and a legion of brothers and sisters at your back." Cain hated to admit it to himself, but he was enjoying tormenting the terrified recruits, at least a little. Most of them were troublesome sorts, and as they stood before him in their imperfect ranks, Cain knew that few of them had many redeeming qualities, at least at the moment. They were raw material, bits of human detritus in whom the Marine recruiters had seen some small spark of potential. Realizing that hidden promise, becoming someone worthwhile...that was a long way off for this rookie class. "But if you want all of that you have to earn it." He paused, looking out over the silent newbs. "And I promise you now, if you don't give 110% all the time...if you slack off even for a second...you will never be a Marine in my Corps."

He turned abruptly and walked away without another word, listening with amusement as the major started to harangue the recruits, taking up where he had left off. Erik walked across the wet field, mud spattering all over his boots and the bottoms of his pants. Camp Basilone was still under construction, and there were temporary roads and modular structures everywhere. What a mess, he thought. One of these days this place is actually going to be finished, paved roads and all. He knew that intellectually, but it seemed a distant dream as he made his way through the muck and past the construction equipment.

Cain walked up to a metal door leading into a large, interconnected series of portable buildings. He placed his palm on the small scanner next to the entryway, and an instant later the door slid open. "Identity confirmed, General Cain." The security AI's voice wasn't nasty, exactly, but it wasn't exactly welcoming either.

"If it isn't old blood and guts Cain." Jax's deep voice was immediately identifiable. "When did you turn into such a hardass jackboot?" Jax had a little trouble finishing his sentence before he started laughing. He and Cain went way back, and he couldn't resist a little mild ribbing.

Erik realized they'd been watching him on the monitors... not just Jax, but General Holm and Colonel Teller too. "I didn't realize I had an audience." Cain was mildly grouchy. He didn't really enjoy training assignments – he was a combat Marine through and through. But right now, job one was rebuilding the Corps. The old training program had been compromised by General Samuels' treachery, and they'd had to purge many of the new recruits and retrain others to replace them. Making matters worse, late in the rebellion the Directorate's new powered infantry units attacked a number of garrisons. The Marines won every fight, despite being seriously outnumbered in most of them, but the losses had been heavy, especially in veteran personnel.

Samuels had been the Commandant, but he'd sold out to Alliance Intelligence and conspired to bring down the Corps... and he'd almost succeeded. It had been a well over a year since Generals Holm and Cain had rallied the loyal remnants of the Corps, but they were still rebuilding, trying to bring the Marines back to their former level of readiness and combat effectiveness. They weren't there yet.

"We wouldn't have missed it for the world." General Holm wasn't laughing like Jax, but he had a broad smile on his face. "After all, who's going to teach the recruits how to wear their rumpled, mud-spattered uniforms as well as you?" The new Commandant of the Corps, Elias Holm wore a perfectly tailored and spotless set of duty fatigues, with five platinum stars gleaming on each collar. His smile widened as his eyes panned over Cain's disheveled appearance. "I'm afraid we'll never be able to put you on the recruiting poster, Erik." He glanced over at Jax, who was trying – unsuccessfully – to control his laughter. "But, God…please promise me you won't try to teach them to salute." Cain's salutes were notoriously sloppy. It was generally considered by his friends and comrades to be some subconscious resistance to authority that twenty years in the Corps had still not stamped out.

"I'm very happy I could amuse you all." Cain smiled, though he managed to look annoyed as well. "You know, when we said we were going to rebuild the Corps, I don't think I realized what a shitload of work it would be. Why am I not on a beach somewhere? I was on Atlantia enjoying the ocean air when it all hit the fan."

After the Alliance's colonies rebelled and won partial independence, the Marine Charter was revised and reaffirmed. The Corps was now answerable to a joint Alliance-Colonial commission, and all key Marine installations had been moved off of Earth. Camp Basilone had replaced Camp Puller as the main training facility. But the massive Puller complex had been built over decades and sprawled across miles of Texas prairie. Ideally, the switch would have been made gradually over a period of years. But in the wake of the Samuels affair, there was too much concern over security, and the Corps decided the entire training program had to be moved immediately. They were struggling to keep things on track, but construction lagged well behind their needs, and Basilone had more the look of a temporary encampment than a permanent facility.

Holm finally let out a small laugh. "I'm sorry if we're taxing your precious constitution, but we're actually starting to make some good progress here." He glanced over at Cain. "We're still not pushing through the numbers of recruits I'd like, but I'll put the current training regimen up against anything they did at Puller."

Erik walked over to the coffee dispenser and filled a cup. He'd never been much of a coffee drinker, but he'd developed a taste for it over the last couple years…at least if it had enough sugar in it. Cain was a hardcore Marine veteran, but he also had a bit of a sweet tooth. "I agree, sir." He looked over his shoulder at the monitors displaying the recruits, who were still getting an earful from Major Simms. "But we're going to be understrength for years. There's just no way to catch up quickly. Not with the length and complexity of our training program." They'd been compelled to dismiss most of the classes that had been in process at Camp Puller. They'd lost a lot of good people along with the bad, but the camp had been heavy infiltrated by Alliance Intelligence, mostly on Samuel's watch, and it just wasn't possible to unwind it all.

"It's worse than you think, Erik." Jax walked over to the conference table and slid out one of the chairs. "I just finished an analysis of optimum personnel levels compared with force availability. We're either going to have to leave a lot of places totally ungarrisoned, or we're going to be weak everywhere."

The garrisons had lost heavily fighting off the Director-ate surprise attacks, and the complete shutoff of new recruits had really created a shortage of manpower. Holm had tried to address it by luring back recently retired Marines to active service, but the results had been well below expectations. Response rates were strong; most of those who were able returned. But it turned out that most veterans who had settled on colony worlds ended up serving in the respective rebel armies, and a lot of them had been killed or seriously wounded. On worlds like Arcadia and Columbia, where the combat was intense, rebel losses in the war had easily topped 50% of those engaged…and the Marine vets had usually been in the thick of the fighting.

"We're going to leave a lot of places uncovered." Holm walked over to the table and dropped into one of the sleek metal chairs, motioning for the others to do the same. "I don't like it, but I think it's more important to deploy a few combat-ready mobile forces strong enough to accomplish something. If it came to any kind of serious hostilities, a bunch of tiny garrisons would just get mopped up anyway."

"I agree, sir." One of the wheels on Cain's chair was jammed, and it made a loud screeching sound as he pulled it back. He kicked it, and the wheel came unstuck. "What's the point of parceling out our strength and creating a bunch of forces that are all too weak to hold out anyway? At least if we're concentrated, we can respond to any situations that arise." He knew it wasn't that simple. It sounded clinical and logical in a planning session, but they were talking about potentially allowing thousands of their people to be occupied, perhaps for years before they could be liberated. On paper it was strategy and tactics, but in reality it was human suffering and death. Cain had seen it before, when they'd finally retaken the systems the enemy had seized early in the war. He'd seen things then he would never forget...no matter how hard he tried. But still, they had no real choice.

Holm leaned back in his chair and smiled. "I'm glad to hear you say that, Erik, because I just reactivated 1st Division, and I want you to command it." He paused for a few seconds, enjoying Cain's shocked expression. "I convinced Cate Gilson to come out of retirement. She'll be here in a few weeks, and I'm going to have her take over the training program."

"Sir, General Gilson is senior to me." Cain had always been a little uncomfortable about the rapidity of his rise through the ranks. Deep down inside him there was still a bit of that green private, fresh from Camp Puller and scared out of his wits. The past 20 years in many ways seemed a surreal blur. "Are you sure she shouldn't command 1st Division?"

"I'm sure." Holm spoke seriously, his voice a model of professionalism. He was very fond of Cain, whom he thought of almost like a son. But that had nothing to do with his decision here, and he didn't want to give the impression that it did. "You're the best combat commander I've got, Erik, and that's the bottom line."

Cain was still uncomfortable, as he usually was when praised, but he nodded his assent. "Thank you, sir. I'll do my best." He paused, but when no one else spoke he continued. "Who else do you have earmarked for 1st Division, sir?"

Holm's eyes panned across the table. "Well, I was thinking of Jax as your exec." He had to suppress a smile when he saw the expression on the giant Marine's face. Jax was another fighter who bristled at pushing papers and wiping recruits' noses. Darius Jax would follow whatever orders he was given, but in his heart he wanted to be in the line with the combat Marines. "If that's agreeable to both of you." Holm really had to force down a smile. With all the shitstorms these two had been in together, he couldn't think of a better pairing in the whole Corps.

"I'd be happy to watch out for General Cain here, sir." Jax had a big smile on his face. "At least I won't have to worry about him shooting a political officer this time." Before the rebellions, the Alliance government had assigned special officers as watchdogs for the Marine command personnel. The policy was widely disliked throughout the Corps but, as far as anyone knew, Erik Cain was the only one who'd actually come close to shooting his political officer.

Cain looked across the table at Holm. "Thank you, sir. I'm sure General Jax and I can whip the division into shape."

"You'll only be able to field two brigades at first." Holm's voice was starting to show a little of his frustration at the current shortages. "I just don't have any more manpower to give you now." He paused as his eyes shifted to James Teller, who'd been sitting quietly, as the junior officer in the room often did. "You're probably going to have to put two colonels in charge of the brigades. I was thinking about James here for one."

James Teller had served under Cain for years, and he'd been an officer in the special action teams Erik set up during the war. Erik looked at Holm. "That will be just fine, sir." Then, turning to face Teller: "Welcome to 1st Division, James. Or should I say back to 1st Division, since we're all just going home, really."

"Thank you, sir." Teller was facing Cain, but then his eyes moved to Holm. "And you too, General Holm. I appreciate the chance." Teller was a decorated Marine veteran with a long list of battle honors, but he'd been a captain until a couple years earlier. He was a little overwhelmed when Cain and Holm gave him his eagles, and now he was moving into a brigadier's posting. A brigade command was one hell of a jump from running a company, which had been his most recent combat posting. But after everything that had happened with General Samuels and the rebellions, Holm's primary concern was putting people he absolutely trusted into the important commands. He hated to think that way about the Corps, but he had no choice. That was Samuels' legacy.

"We have a lot of challenges ahead, and it's going to be quite a while before we can get the Corps back to its old strength and effectiveness." Holm spoke decisively but soothingly. All his people, even the veterans, were a still a little shaken by recent events. They were seasoned combat Marines, but with the rebellions and the situation with Samuels, they'd had to deal with a level of confusion and ambiguity about loyalties that hadn't existed before. "If it helps at all, Admiral Garret is having an even tougher time with the navy." Garret had been compelled to hunt down and destroy almost half of his wartime hulls after they'd been appropriated by a new Directorate naval force. The fleet was down to barely a third of its former strength and struggling hard to meet its responsibilities.

"As I said, it's going to be a while before we have our old Corps back. Fortunately, it's likely we will have that time. The Confederation Agreement is flawed; there is no doubt of that. But neither Alliance Gov nor the colonies are in a position to resume hostilities, especially with the Martians guaranteeing the peace." Holm leaned back in his chair, stretching his aching back the best he could manage while seated. A lifetime of war wounds left their mark despite the best medical care available, and Elias Holm suffered from his share of chronic pain.

"The Superpowers are still rebuilding from the Third Frontier War. The Caliphate, in particular, was very badly hurt. No one is looking for a new fight, at least not for some years." Holm grinned as he looked across the table. "It finally looks like we'll get a protracted peace." His smile broadened as he spoke. "Yes, for once it looks like we'll have a good long time before we have to take the field again."

Chapter 2

Level 242
Combined Powers Excavation Site
Carson's World – Epsilon Eridani IV

"I'm telling you, these conduits go all the way down to the planet's core. How many more levels do we need to discover before you will accept the true scope of this installation?" Friedrich Hofstader stared at his companions, the exasperation in his voice clear. For months, the chief of the CEL's research contingent had been urging the Committee to authorize deeper digging. But no matter what he said, they kept dragging their feet, debating endlessly about every acceleration of the research effort.

"Dr. Hofstader, I understand your scientific curiosity and the resulting impatience, but it is important to stress that we must maintain a cautious approach." Ivan Norgov was the head of the Russian research team and the elected chairman of the International Committee created to manage the scientific efforts on Epsilon Eridani IV. "It is essential that we follow proper research procedure and thoroughly document our findings at each step."

Hofstader suppressed a sigh. He was already the odd man out, and he was trying not to further antagonize his colleagues. It wasn't easy, especially since he couldn't think of Norgov as anything but an officious asshole. "Gentlemen, I understand the research protocols, but have any of you considered the fact that someone built this?" Hofstader had always favored action, and he had bristled for years when colleagues at the Institute in Neu-Brandenburg endlessly debated protocols and process. Academics will never change, he thought with considerable irritation. But Epsilon Eridani IV was an unprecedented research opportunity, and he couldn't reconcile with anyone stunting progress here with endless bureaucracy.

Norgov gave him an annoyed stare, but it was Adam Crandall, the chief physicist from the Alliance team, who spoke first. "I presume there is more to your point than the obvious fact that this is not a naturally-occurring structure?" Crandall was another pompous fool, mired down in intellectual pretensions, but even Hofstader had to admit the Alliance scientist was brilliant. He was responsible for most of the foundational work on explaining the warp gates and how they functioned.

"My point is simply this…" Hofstader couldn't understand how a group of people this intelligent could be so stupid. "Until the Alliance found this artifact, we were alone in the universe." He spoke with amazement and reverence at the monumental importance of the discovery, which his colleagues seemed to have forgotten. "The moment this was found we were no longer unique. The race that constructed this facility was thousands of years ahead of us…and that was half a million years ago." He could see he was losing them, but he continued, hoping to somehow get his point across. "Don't you see the implications of this in terms of our place in the universe? And, by extension, the imperative need for us to study and apply this technology?"

Norgov frowned and held his hand in the air. "Dr. Hofstader, I think we are all familiar with your issues and concerns." The Russian scientist wasn't trying to be condescending and insulting; it just came naturally to him. "Nevertheless, I think it is a massive and unwarranted leap to assume that simply because a sentient race preceded us in the galaxy and built this facility that we face imminent invasion…or whatever else it is you imply."

"This entire planet is an anti-matter production facility utilizing seismic energy as a power source." Hofstader's voice was becoming higher pitched. He was passionate about his research and frustrated that a culture of bureaucracy was slowing down the exploration of the greatest discovery in history. "Imagine the implications!"

"The Committee has issued no such finding." Crandall again, spouting Academic orthodoxy. "Your assertions as to the facility's purpose and power generation are premature. They are, at best, a hypothesis at present."

"I'm not talking about Committee findings." Hofstader was losing steam – he knew he wasn't going to get anywhere. Not with this group. "I'm talking about plain sense and an evaluation of the data."

"Dr. Hofstader, no one is disputing your knowledge or the usefulness of your research, but you are making a significant number of unsubstantiated projections, not the least of which is your assertion that this facility is planet-wide in scope. We have determined it is quite vast, far larger than it initially appeared." Norgov was trying to be conciliatory, at least to the extent it was possible for him. "But we are far from verifying that the facility is built on a planetwide scale." His eyes narrowed as he looked at Hofstader. "Not to mention extending all the way to the planetary core as you have theorized."

"Indeed, Friedrich, Dr. Norgov is correct." Crandall spoke softly and smiled. In his own way, he too was trying to avoid offending Hofstader. "We must not abandon proper research procedure simply because of the scope and import of the find."

Hofstader sighed, but he managed to keep it quiet. Crandall simply didn't have it in him to think outside the box. None of them did. They'd spent their whole lives in academia, and they'd lost all touch with the real world implications of the things they researched. He wanted to continue arguing, but he realized it was a waste of time.

Norgov noted Hofstader's lack of a response, and he smiled. "We are agreed, then."

Hofstader just nodded, so grudgingly it was barely perceptible. He wasn't going to waste any more time debating…it was pointless. But that didn't mean he wasn't going to do anything.

Bradley Travers ducked under a support beam and continued following Hofstader down the dusty corridor. Travers was tall, well over two meters, and these old tunnels had clearly been built for shorter beings. It was pretty anecdotal, but it was a tiny piece of the greatest puzzle of all…who were the builders of this complex, and what were they like?

Beyond rough assumptions based on an analysis of the facility itself, the only clues they had found to date were microscopic bits of fossilized amino acid chains that might or might not be something similar to DNA. It was going to be years in the lab before anything meaningful could be derived…unless they found more substantive data to jumpstart that timetable.

Travers was the head of the Martian research team, and his xenobiology credentials were impeccable. But there was more than one layer to Travers – he was also one of Roderick Vance's operatives at the Martian Security Department. He was on Carson's World mostly to do his job as a scientist, but he was also there to keep an eye on things for Vance. He was pretty sure he'd ID'd all of Gavin Stark's people, unless Alliance Intelligence had managed to get someone into a really deep cover. In fact, he was pretty sure he'd pegged most of the spooks. Every Power had at least one in their team, and most had more. Even though the Superpowers had agreed to share access to the planet and work together to unravel its mysteries, they still jockeyed for position, trying to get an edge on the others one way or another.

Vance had been particularly concerned about anything Stark was doing, since he'd lost his main asset inside Alliance Intelligence. The newsflash had simply noted that Hendrick Thoms, director of megacorp GDL, had died in a work-related accident. His true fate, known only to a very few people, had been considerably more horrifying. Gavin Stark had no pity for double agents.

Vance had gotten the better of Stark during the recent series of rebellions on the Alliance colonies, largely using intel from Thoms. Stark had been holding Fleet Admiral Garret hostage for months, having replaced him with a double. Combined with his secret control over General Samuels, he'd been positioned to achieve total victory, until Vance helped Erik Cain rescue Garret.

Gavin Stark was a psychopath and a human reptile, but he was also extremely intelligent. Vance had always known it would only be a matter of time before Stark figured out what had happened, especially after MSD also outed Samuels, allowing Generals Cain and Holm to take control of the Marine Corps and save it from destruction. Stark couldn't get to Vance, at least not easily, but Thoms hadn't been so lucky. Vance knew Thoms would eventually get blown...with unpleasant results. He wasn't the same kind of creature as Stark – at least he liked to think he wasn't. But he hadn't hesitated to expend Thoms either.

Travers agreed with Friederich Hofstader about pushing the pace of the research. It might be thousands of years – if ever – before humanity encountered the enigmatic race that built the great artifact on Carson's World, but there was simply no way to know. The only thing they could be sure of was, if that contact happened, humanity would be hopelessly outclassed. Better to learn all they could before that day came.

The corridor was eerily quiet, untouched for millennia. The only sound was the soft scratching of their boots on the rough stone surface. There were just the three of them - Hofstader, his assistant Katrina, and Travers. They were here unofficially... very unofficially. In fact, they were violating just about every rule and protocol that applied to the project.

The tunnel had been bored out of the bedrock, and it led down at a constant 5% grade. This branch hadn't been opened for exploration, and there were no lighting units installed; the preliminary scout teams hadn't even ventured this far yet. The glow from the party's portable electric torches danced off the smooth walls as they passed by. There was a thin semi-opaque tube running along the ceiling, the corridor's original lighting track. It was non-functional, since there was no power generation in the facility, but otherwise it looked almost new, despite its extreme age. The same tubing had been found throughout the complex. They still hadn't been able to identify the material. It was pliable and could be bent around curves, but it was extremely tough – even a plasma torch had a hard time cutting through it. And they had no idea at all how it functioned.

"According to my projected schematic, this passage should lead to one of the acceleration chambers." Hofstader's voice echoed loudly off the tunnel walls. He glanced back at his two companions and spoke more softly. "It may be a long way. Remember, I if am right, this complex is planetary in scale." He readjusted the pack on his back and turned to face forward, into the gloom of the passageway ahead.

They continued for hours, walking at least at least 25 kilometers, stopping only once to eat a few ration bars. They passed a number of sealed hatches, but they bypassed them and pressed on ahead. It had taken a heavy plasma torch to cut through the sealed doorways they'd discovered elsewhere in the complex, and they didn't expect these to be any different.

"I'm detecting a slow uptick in background radiation." Katrina's voice was soft, distracted. She was staring at a small handheld monitor. "Analyzing now." She looked up, a big smile on her face. "Readings consistent with long-term radioactives from anti-matter production. We must be close." Katrina Hoffen had been Friedrich's student first, and now she was an accomplished physicist in her own right. She'd volunteered for this assignment, as had most of the scientists on Earth. This was the greatest research project in human history, and even the prospect of spending years on an alien world wasn't enough to discourage most of them.

Friederich Hofstader was the top scientist in the Central European League, and it fell to him to assemble that Power's team. Katrina had a strong record, though she was relatively young and inexperienced for a mission of this magnitude. But Hofstader was a bit of a maverick, and he focused more on securing people he trusted rather than on traditional academic achievements. For the most part he had little time anyway for the fuss and bother of his peers and their review boards and awards committees. All that mattered to him was the job at hand. He didn't care about credit or recognition…he just wanted knowledge.

They quickened their pace, stopping only to rerun the radiation tests twice more. Finally, the tunnel led through an archway and onto a small catwalk that stretched as far as their light carried. Katrina activated a handful of small chem lights and tossed them over the railing. They landed about ten meters below and illuminated a vast tunnel extending off in both directions. There was a 5 meter wide conduit suspended on a series of brackets. It disappeared into the darkness at both ends of the illuminated area.

"You were right, Friedrich." Travers' wasn't surprised; he'd expected Hofstader's theory to check out. But it was still amazing to consider the scale of the construct looming in front of them. "Congratulations." Travers wasn't a physicist, but he recognized a massive particle accelerator when he saw one.

Hofstader was mesmerized, staring at the amazing structure. It was definitely an accelerator, but it was far larger and more complex than any he'd ever seen. He couldn't begin to identify half of the appendages and devices built into it, and it would take weeks of detailed computations to even guess at the energy levels the thing could achieve. But they were able to confirm one suspicion by measuring the slight arc of the conduit…it appeared to stretch completely around the planet.

"Apart from the technology involved, this is an engineering achievement of incalculable proportions." Katrina spoke slowly, her mind nearly consumed by the act of simply staring at the amazing device. "This entire planet was an anti-matter production facility." She turned to look at Friederich. "Just as you suspected, Dr. Hofstader."

They stood silently for a moment, unable to look away from the ancient alien construction. Finally, Travis turned and stared at his two companions. "Imagine the power the race that built this commanded." He took a deep breath. "I wonder if they're still out there somewhere."

The three of them lost track of how long they stood there transfixed, but they were all thinking the same thing. Where were the builders of this place?

Chapter 3

Colony One
Newton - HP 56548 III

Ian Tremaine walked back toward the small cluster of modular shelters, the warm afternoon sun beating down on his sweat-soaked back. It was another kilometer and a half to the village, and he could already feel the burning exhaustion in his legs. "No one ever told me colonizing a world was so much work." Tremaine was alone and speaking to himself, and he laughed at his own joke. Someone should, he thought with a smile.

Newton was the most remote planet yet colonized by man. The system was 28 transits from Sol, a solid year's journey for all but the fastest ships. The colonization party wasn't even from Earth...Newton had been settled by colonists from Columbia. The expedition was comprised of religious pacifists who chose to tackle a newly-discovered world when it became clear that war and revolution would soon engulf Columbia.

Now the rebellion was over, and Columbia and the other Alliance colonies had won at least partial independence. That news had been joyously received on Newton, but the celebration had been tempered by the horrific losses suffered, the awful cost of that taste of freedom. Tremaine could hardly believe what he saw in the dispatches. By all accounts, Weston was in ruins, and at least a quarter of the planet's population had perished. He wept for those lost, and he prayed for their families. He had many friends on Columbia, and he didn't know who among them was alive or dead. We were right to leave, he thought sadly. The Columbians had certainly had legitimate grievances against Alliance Gov...he agreed with that wholeheartedly. But was it worth all the suffering and death and destruction? Was war and killing always the only way?

It all felt very far away on Newton. His people had come to the edge of explored space seeking a peaceful home. They were almost 200 lightyears from man's birthplace on Earth - when he looked through the colony's telescope toward Sol, he was seeing light that began its journey two centuries prior. Before the Alliance existed. Before the Unification Wars. Of course, geometric distances in space were largely irrelevant. The important calculation was the number of warp gate jumps required to reach a planet, and by that measure as well, Newton was on the extreme frontier.

The settlement was small, just 120 families. The houses were prefab units manufactured on Columbia, clustered around a few scratch-built common buildings. There was a wall around the village, with several watch towers and half a dozen sonic pulse cannons. The planet was far from any potentially hostile worlds, but the local fauna was large and aggressive. The most threatening animals tended to stay in the jungle areas, but occasionally a serious predator wandered out into the savannah. It was better to be safe than sorry.

Tremaine walked through the open gate and into the bustling little community. The colonists had begun calling their town Haven, though officially it was still Colony One. There was an identical village on the second of the planet's two continents. As far as he knew, Colony Two's residents hadn't come up with any name for their settlement, informal or otherwise.

"Good morning, Ian." Hampton Charles was walking over from the dining hall when he saw Tremaine coming through the gate. "Back from calibrating the pulse scanners already?" Charles glanced at the chronometer on his wrist. "You must have left before sunup."

"Indeed I did, my friend." Tremaine grasped Charles' arm in a warm greeting. "It promises to be a scorcher today, and I thought it best done early." He looked up at the cloudless sky, running his hand through his sweat-soaked mop of long brown hair. "It was hot enough already at dawn; I can tell you that much."

"With any luck we'll find the best spot for Colony Three

soon." Charles looked up at the sky. "We should be hearing from the convoy any day now." The second wave of colony ships was scheduled to enter the system within the week. It had originally been expected two years before, but the rebellion had put everything on hold. Now they were finally coming, and they were bringing a load of badly needed equipment in addition to 900 new settlers. Things had gotten a little rough on Newton when the supply ships stopped coming, and Tremaine would be relieved to replace some of the jury-rigged repairs with proper spare parts. They were self-sufficient on food, but without imported equipment, their mining and resource recovery operations were way behind schedule. Colonizing a new world was expensive, and they were expected to produce enough to pay their way. So far they hadn't come close.

"Yes, soon we shall welcome our new neighbors." Tremaine stepped to the side as he spoke, moving into a spot of shade. "And we shall finally have the supplies we need to get our production levels where they should be." He pulled a small cloth from his pocket and wiped his face. "It will feel good to pay our own way."

"That it shall." Charles shifted to move into the shade as well. "I think you were right to go so early. This heat is brutal."

Tremaine laughed. "You should feel it on the open plain, my friend." He motioned toward the dining hall. "I'm heading to grab some breakfast. Care to join me?"

Charles smiled. "I ate already, but I wouldn't say no to a cool drink. Let's be on..."

"They're here! They're here!" It was Ellen Forsten, and she was running across the center of the village from the communications hut. She saw Tremaine and ran over and hugged him. "Ian, we just got the transmission. The convoy is here." Newton was almost ten light hours from the warp gate, so the convoy had actually been in the system for almost half a day when its signal was received. The cross-system journey would take a little over a week.

Tremaine smiled and returned the hug. "It is a great day." He stepped back and looked at Forsten and then Charles. "Come friends, let us contact Colony Two. We must prepare for our new arrivals."

"I've run a complete diagnostic, captain." Lieutenant Walsh was Northstar's chief engineer. "Everything shows functional. I've monitored reactor operations myself, and the rhythms seem normal." She paused for an instant, still a little distracted by her focus on the task at hand. "I think we're fully operational again, sir."

"Thank you, lieutenant." The captain's voice was deep and scratchy, sometimes difficult to hear over the comlink. He also had a tendency to whisper, and he had to remind himself to speak loudly. "Do you feel comfortable going to 100% power? I'd like to try to catch up with the convoy if possible."

Northstar's power core had scragged itself two days before. There'd been no sign of trouble, but fusion reactors were finicky mechanisms, and they were designed to shut down immediately at any sign of abnormal operation. A containment breach on an operating reactor would make a ship cease to exist in a microsecond, so caution was essential. But it also meant reactors sometimes shut down when nothing was seriously wrong.

"Yes, sir." Walsh sounded reasonably confident, though she was still disturbed by her inability to identify the cause of the initial malfunction. "I'd feel better if we'd had more luck finding the original problem, but everything reads a go now." She sighed gently. "The safeties are on full, sir, so it'll just scrag again if we missed something."

Captain Jahn sat silently for an instant, considering his options. He would have preferred a more definitive answer on what had flatlined the system to begin with. But if Northstar had any chance to catch the rest of the fleet before it reached Newton, they had to start now. "Prepare for 100% power." With her reactor down the ship had been unable to make vector changes with the convoy, and she'd zipped right past the warp gate when the other ships transited. Now they had to decelerate and loop back around to position for insertion. At least the convoy is moving slowly, he thought. If we strap in and go full bore we can catch up in two days.

Jahns flipped his comlink to the ship-wide circuit. "Attention, all personnel, prepare for high thrust maneuvers." He could almost hear the groaning going on throughout the ship. The crew had to be secured in their acceleration couches before he could fire up the engines at full thrust, and that meant an uncomfortable ride for everyone. "We will be applying maximum thrust in thirty minutes…that's three-zero minutes. I want everyone buttoned up in twenty." He switched his com back to Walsh. "OK, Adele. I want the reactor up and running at 100% in fifteen minutes…and I want you in your couch in twenty-five."

"Yes, sir." Walsh's voice was a little tense. Fifteen minutes was a tight schedule to get the reactor fired up and operating. Captain Jahn was a navy vet, and sometimes he forgot he had a civilian crew now. The Northstar had a good team, but their experience and training wasn't up to military standards. "I'm on it." She wiped her forehead on her sleeve and stared at the monitor as she punched in the reactor startup sequence.

"Captain, we have incoming transmissions." Lieutenant Cannon turned to face Captain Jahn. Her face was pale. "Code Delta-Z, sir."

Jahn had been listening half-heartedly as he reviewed the final course plot, but his head snapped up abruptly. Code Delta-Z was used by ships that were under attack and did not expect to survive. "Transmit directly to my com, lieutenant." His mind raced – who could be attacking the convoy all the way out here? "Scanners on full power. Launch a spread of probes."

"Yes, sir." Cannon was a good officer, but she wasn't military, and the tension was obvious in her voice. "Sending you the transmissions now."

Jahn listened to the distress calls as they were piped into his comlink. They formed a timeline, beginning with reports of incoming missiles coming in from well beyond normal launch ranges. Jahn's frown grew with each transmission. It was a nightmare unfolding before him. A missile barrage, the weapons thrusting at over 200g. Jahn had never heard of a weapon with that level of acceleration. Then detonations…massive explosions unlike anything he'd ever seen. Ships vaporized by the stunningly accurate warheads, one after another until the transmissions ended. Then only silence.

"Lieutenant, estimate the yield of those warheads." Jahn served throughout the Third Frontier War before mustering out, and he'd seen plenty of fusion warheads detonate…but these were like nothing he'd ever witnessed.

"Sir…" Cannon stared at the captain, her face betraying shock. "The computer estimates each detonation at 3.5 to 6 gigatons."

Jahn was silent for a moment, his mind processing all he had just seen and heard. His hesitation was brief, however, and his combat instincts took over. "I want full reverse thrust in five minutes." He clicked on the shipwide com. "This is the captain. All personnel are to immediately secure for maximum thrust. We will be blasting in five minutes…I repeat, five minutes." He switched to a direct link with Walsh. "Lieutenant, I want 110% on the reactor, and I want it in four minutes, and I want you in your couch a minute later." His voice was sharp and decisive, but the stress was evident as well.

"Captain, that's not…"

"Now, lieutenant!" He cut her off before she finished. "I need that power. No arguments…just do it."

"Yes, sir." He reply was immediate, but her tone was shaky.

Jahn repositioned himself in his chair, holding his arm straight as the medical AI initiated the injections. Five and a half minutes later, Northstar's reactor was running full out, producing energy at 110% of its rated capacity, and every bit of it was being poured through the ship's straining engines.

The crew was ensconced in their acceleration couches, protected from the worst effects of the 20g deceleration. It was hard to think clearly under maximum thrust. Between the drugs and the discomfort, concentration was difficult, but Jahn's mind was still functioning. We have to make it out of here, he thought grimly. We have to report this.

Part of Jahn felt guilty about fleeing this way, but if the Caliphate or the CAC had found a new route into Alliance space he had to report it as soon as possible. This could be war, he thought. It was possible that the Fourth Frontier War had just begun. And those weapons, he thought. If any of the other Powers had seen such a leap in weapons technology, it was going to be trouble…big trouble. They had to make it out of here. They had to.

"Lieutenant Walsh." It was hard to even force the words out under the crushing g forces. "Instruct the computer to go to 120% on the reactor." That was dangerous, approaching a 10% chance of catastrophic failure. But if they didn't get back through that warp gate before they were attacked, they'd never leave the HP 56548 system. He anticipated Walsh's argument, and before she could object he repeated himself. "No debate, lieutenant. Just go to 120% now." I just hope it's enough, he thought.

Chapter 4

AS Bunker Hill
Orbiting Wolf 359 VI

"We can move this data around all day, but there's just no way to cover everything." Augustus Garret sat in one of the sleek metal chairs in Admiral Compton's conference room. It was in this very compartment that Compton had met with Roderick Vance, General Holm, and Erik Cain to plan the daring – and highly risky - actions that ultimately salvaged the rebellions… and saved Garret himself from Gavin Stark's prison. Every time he sat here it reminded him that he hadn't been present. He hadn't been there because he'd let himself fall into Stark's trap. That wouldn't happen again; he swore that much to himself. Augustus Garret would never let his guard down again. Not ever.

"No. No way." Terrance Compton sat opposite Garret, staring at a large 'pad displaying lists of ships and personnel. "The supply situation is good at least. Jack Winton's done a hell of a job on logistics. Good call on your part luring him back in."

Garret nodded. "Yes." He allowed himself a little smile. "I've never seen anyone with a better head for moving stuff around. I'd blow my brains out if I had to do it every day, but he's a virtuoso." Garret was a combat officer through and through, and he had to constantly struggle to make himself pay attention to details like logistics. But his navy would cease to function without the services Winton's division provided, and he was grateful to have someone he could trust to run it.

Compton grinned for a few seconds, but it quickly faded. "But we just don't have the combat assets." He exhaled loudly. "And we won't for at least three years…and maybe five." The Directorate had managed to secretly take control of the mothballed ships of the Strategic Reserve, crewing them with their own personnel. Garret and his loyal ships had been compelled to hunt them down and destroy them, and they took their own losses doing it. They were lucky if they could put a third of the strength into space they'd had at the end of the war.

Garret sighed. "Look, I'm just going to say it." He had a sour look on his face, like he tasted something bad. "We're not going to be able to garrison the population centers." There were just too many Alliance colonies and not enough fleet units available. "If we put undersized squadrons in every system, we're just throwing them away if it comes to war." He took a deep breath. "We have two absolutely vital locations, and we need to defend them at all costs."

"Here and Armstrong." Compton interjected, completing Garret's thought.

"Yes." Garret nodded solemnly. "Here and Armstrong."

Wolf 359 was vital. The shipyards orbiting the fifth planet were by far the biggest available outside the Sol system and, after the events of the past few years, no one in the naval command wanted to put too many eggs in its Earthly basket. The facilities were a beehive of activity, with four new Yorktown class capital ships under construction. They wouldn't be ready for another three years at least, but when they were it would go a long way to bringing the fleet up to strength. The yards themselves were also under construction, with a massive expansion of the production facility taking place even as the ships themselves were being built there.

Armstrong was even more important. The planet was home to the Marine and naval headquarters and training facilities, as well as the giant Marine medical center, now being expanded into a joint services facility. Garret flip-flopped on whether he thought that level of concentration was good or bad, but that was how they'd decided to proceed, and now they had to be damned sure to defend it.

"At least Armstrong's civilian population will be protected as well." Compton was trying to sound positive. "And of course, Arcadia will be covered by the fleet positioned here."

One of the leading worlds in the recent rebellions and now the new Colonial Confederation, Arcadia was the third planet in the Wolf 359 system, just an astronomical stone's throw from the massive shipyards orbiting world number five.

"We do have one thing that's helpful, though." Garret was glancing down at the 'pad as he spoke. "Our gains in the war really rationalized our outer systems. Most of our worlds on the Rim are deep in our own territory relative to the other Powers." The map on the large 'pad was a stylized 2D representation of human-occupied space. The interconnecting lines representing warp gate connections between the systems looked like a large glowing spiderweb. Garret stared at the CAC and Caliphate systems in particular. The red and orange dots representing those Powers' holdings were fairly close to the Alliance's primary colonies, but they were on the other side of those inner worlds from the frontier. "I've pulled everything back from the outer sectors to beef up our core forces." He pointed toward the frontier area on the display, where all of the dots were a uniform blue. "Even so, we'll still be reacting in any new conflict. If the CAC or the Caliphate hit us, they're going to take whatever systems they target, and we're going to be left responding, trying to take them back."

Compton sighed. "The Marines are even in worse shape. Most of these planets have nothing defending them but militia." He was tapping his fingers on the table nervously as he spoke. "Fortunately, neither the CAC nor the Caliphate is ready for a new war." He looked at Garret. Friends and comrades for 40 years, they could read each other's unspoken thought...we hope they're not ready. Any aggression would have been suicide a few years earlier, when the Alliance was in a preeminent position after the war. But the rebellions and the internal fighting and scheming had shattered the Alliance military and squandered its dominance. War was still unlikely in the short term, but it was no longer unthinkable.

They both paused for a while, perhaps half a minute, each of them staring at the map and the columns of figures scrolling along the edges of the 'pad. "I think we could pull more from the base on Farpoint." Compton was reading the deployment notes on the 'pad, though he already knew them by heart. "Honestly, we could just about close the base entirely. Forty years ago it looked like that was going to be a hotly contested sector, but now there's no enemy within 6 transits."

Farpoint was a continuing lesson in the need to employ long-term thinking when naming worlds. At the time it was founded it was the deepest into space man had yet ventured, but now the name was somewhat of a joke. The planet served as an ersatz capital and administrative center for the Alliance's rimworlds, but it was at least four transits from the frontier along any warp path.

"I think you're right." Garret glanced down at the map, sliding his finger to move Farpoint to the center of the display. "We need to keep the base functioning to support the transport and colony ships heading to the Rim, but we can go to a skeleton crew." He paused for an instant, thinking about the forces currently stationed there. "Let's leave Stingray, Raptor, and Hornet…." The three vessels were fast attack ships, and they would serve well for general patrol and policing. "…and reassign the rest of the 5th Fleet to the Armstrong forces." He looked up at Compton. "What do you think?"

"I'd do it." Compton inhaled deeply, holding the breath for a few seconds before exhaling. His tone was tentative, uncertain. "There's no rational reason not to, but something about it still bothers me. It feels wrong to leave a base that size with such a small squadron." He rubbed his fingers along his temples – the small headache he'd had when the strategy session started was getting worse. "I still say do it, though. We need those ships to cover Armstrong…at least until the stationary defenses are upgraded."

The planet Armstrong had been fairly well-protected, but its new status as headquarters for the Colonial Confederation's military forces demanded an entirely new level of fortification. A dozen orbital installations were under construction, each bristling with weaponry and defensive systems. But it would be several years before they were complete, and until then the nerve center of the Alliance military would be protected by mobile fleet units.

"OK, so we've got First Fleet at Armstrong." Garret was sliding his fingers along the 'pad, moving ship names into place in a series of columns. "I will take direct command there." He stared down at the screen, double-checking the list of ships. "I can split my time between headquarters planetside and the flagship..." He looked at the list again. "...which will be Lexington."

Garret paused, his eyes still focused on the lists of available vessels. "The forces you have here at Wolf 359 will be the redesignated Second Fleet." His fingers slid more ship names into a box marked Second Fleet. "You'll continue to command here." He glanced up at his companion as he spoke.

Compton nodded. "I think we can defend both systems against any realistic threat." He looked back at Garret, his expression troubled. "But what about a reaction force?" He slid his finger across the 'pad, centering a box with a large Roman numeral III on it. "Third Fleet is a joke. There's not enough there to counter any serious enemy attack." He glanced next to the Third Fleet box to a similar area marked with a IV. "And Fourth Fleet is even worse. Calling it a fleet is a bad joke."

"I know." Garret leaned back in his chair. "But there's nothing to be done about it....except..." He slid a datachip across the table. "I worked out a plan, but I want it kept secret. I don't even want it on the network." He hated having to think that way, especially in his own navy, but after his experiences at the hands of Gavin Stark, he trusted almost no one. Stark's organization had infiltrated the navy far more effectively than Garret would have thought possible, and he wasn't going to forget that.

Compton reached out and picked up the chip. He too had become more careful since the true extent of Alliance Intelligence scheming was exposed. But he was worried about Garret. His friend had become truly paranoid, suspecting everyone except those very few who were closest to him. Compton understood, but he also knew how much damage it could do. The navy was a team, and a good team had to function based on trust. Garret had always had faith in the men and women who served under him, and they had followed him to hell and back. Now he looked at them all and wondered if they were spies.

"I'll review it." He lowered his voice, though it was just an instinctive reaction to the secrecy. They were alone, and the room was sealed. No one could hear them. "What is it?"

"It's a plan to subdivide First and Second Fleets into tiered task forces." Garret also spoke softly, though it was unclear if it was intentional or if he was subconsciously emulating Compton. "It will allow us to evaluate any enemy action and detach segments of the fleets to reinforce the reaction forces. The tiers are based on threat levels. If an enemy attack is big, we know they've tied down a lot of their forces and won't have them available to move on Armstrong or Wolf 359. That will let us peel off squadrons from the garrisoning fleets to supplement our reaction forces." He shifted again in his chair, but he couldn't get comfortable. He was on edge – too little sleep, too much work. The back of his neck was one big knot. "The tiers are carefully organized to complement the reaction forces. That way we have well-organized fleets rather than ad-hoc combos of whatever ships are around. The AIs of the ships in the tiered forces will all have protocols for both fleets. They will be able to instantly plug into either command structure."

Compton smiled. "That is brilliant, Augustus." He scolded himself for not thinking of it. "It's as close as we can come to cloning those ships and having them two places at once." His head was really pounding now despite the two analgesics he'd taken before the meeting. How, he wondered, can they regrow lost limbs but still not come up with a decent headache remedy?

Garret arched his back in the chair, still trying to get comfortable. "It doesn't really give us more strength, but by doing some planning now we'll be ready to react more quickly. If we have to do some shuffling of forces, it will be better organized than some last minute cut and paste job."

The two of them sat quietly for several minutes, both deep in thought. Finally, Garret rose slowly, stretching slightly to drive away the stiffness in his arms and legs. He started to roll his head, but he decided that getting rid of the tension in his neck was a lost cause. "Well, Terrence, I think I will get a couple hours of sleep if I can manage it." He turned as his companion rose, and he extended his hand. No salutes between these old friends…just a warm handshake. "I've got to leave early tomorrow. You have things in hand here, and I need to get back to Armstrong."

"Take care, Augustus." Compton's voice was friendly, but a touch subdued. "I'll hold down the fort here. You just get that mess in Armstrong under control." He smiled at his friend and superior. "After all, I wouldn't want to make you look bad."

"No…" Garret smiled warmly. "We couldn't have that now, could we?" He turned and walked toward the doorway, the hatch opening automatically as he approached. He glanced back from the entry. "I'll see you before I leave, Terrance."

Compton nodded and watched Garret walk out into the corridor, the hatch sliding shut behind him. He stood quietly for a couple minutes then walked slowly toward the end of the room. "Open outer shield."

"Opening outer shield, Admiral Compton." The ship's master AI had a pleasant sounding voice, highly professional, with just a touch of casual familiarity. There was a soft sliding sound as the heavy armored doors along the end wall pulled back, revealing a large expanse of clear polymer. There weren't a lot of portholes or windows on warships, but this was one of his favorite things about Bunker Hill. It was a luxury, pure and simple…an aesthetic provided for a fleet admiral flying his flag from a Yorktown class battlewagon.

The view was spectacular, the glory of space laid out before him. It was so majestic, so peaceful. He thought sadly to himself – you'd never know to look at this, what a blood-soaked warzone we've managed to make it. An entire universe, endless and magnificent, and we still fight over every scrap. "Man really is a wretched creature." He spoke to himself, so softly it was barely audible.

He looked out over the forward hull of Bunker Hill to the glowing sphere of Wolf 359 V. The gas giant was as beautiful as any artwork he'd ever seen, a hazy blue globe, with just a hint of a ring floating around it. The orbital shipyards weren't visible. As huge as they were to man's sensibilities, at this range they were infinitesimally small, far too tiny for the eye to see.

"Well, we've done the best we can." Compton was still speaking to himself as he gazed into the void. Finally, he sighed and tuned away from the window and moved slowly toward the door. "At least all of this is theoretical. The other Powers are all too beaten up to start a war anytime soon." He stopped at the doorway and glanced back one last time. "We'll have the time we need before we have to fight again."

Chapter 5

Foothills of the Southern Spur
Near Colony One
Newton - HP 56548 III

Tremaine could feel his heart pounding in his ears like thunder. He gripped the rifle tightly, his fingers white from squeezing. It was hot, almost unbearably so, and his overall was soaking wet and plastered to his back. He was scared, so terrified he could barely hold a thought in his head. But he was determined not to let the fear take control. His people needed him…now in this darkest hour more than ever.

Half the colonists were already dead. He'd managed to get the survivors out of the wreck of the village and into the hills, but that had only bought them some time…and very little of it. He had no idea whether Colony Two had also been attacked; the invaders knocked out the satellite before they landed, and when it went down so did the contact with the second settlement.

The weapon felt odd in Tremaine's hands…cold, hard, unfamiliar. He'd never fired any kind of gun before. He'd always abhorred all forms of violence, and all his life he'd sought peace and tranquility. He'd led his people to the edge of explored space to escape the savagery and horror that men continually inflicted on one another…to find a chance at a simple life. But war had found them anyway.

Now he felt emotions new to him. Dark, primitive feelings… like nothing he'd ever experienced. Tremaine wanted to fight… to kill. He wanted to destroy the enemy. He couldn't force the images from his mind, the horrific memories of his friends and neighbors massacred, their mangled bodies lying motionless in the blistering sun. The dead children, murdered by the invaders, sprawled horribly alongside their butchered parents.

Always before, Tremaine had looked at society's horrors, at the endless war and desperate suffering, and he'd clung to his beliefs, to his conviction that men could achieve something better, something higher. His faith, his devotion to his ideals, had never deserted him as his quest took him from one of Earth's worst slums to Columbia, and finally to the very edge of explored space to build a new world. His resolution had remained firm through it all, despite oppression and delay and heartbreak. Until now.

He couldn't think about the invaders without shivering, a chill running through his body despite the searing heat. The image of them moving across the plain toward the village, huge and hulking, yet fast and agile too. They looked somewhat like the Marines and CAC troops he'd seen on Columbia during the war, but bigger and far more terrible. Relentless, moving inexorably forward, ignoring every attempt by the colonists to communicate...to surrender.

Tremaine was shocked at the brutality of the invaders. He had been on Columbia when the CAC forces attacked years before. The CAC troops were brutal in many ways, but nothing like this. Many civilians died in the fighting on Columbia, but they weren't deliberately targeted and killed. These new enemies were systematically exterminating the colonists, as if removing an infestation. They had no hesitation, no mercy, no pity.

A vision of hell had been unleashed on the colony, and Ian Tremaine's faith, so long the guiding force in his life, at last deserted him. He felt empty, as though all he had ever believed had been a lie. His blood surged through his veins, and he was consumed with hatred and an overwhelming ache for vengeance. He longed to kill the enemy, to visit upon them the destruction they had loosed upon his peaceful and defenseless people...to repay blood with blood, murder with murder. He would give his life in an instant if, by his death, he could lash out at these terrible foes. These were unfamiliar feelings, and while he hated himself for having them, they were real nonetheless.

He looked back over his shoulder. The survivors were

crouched down behind rocks, taking advantage of what cover they could. Tremaine hadn't even wanted to include weapons in the colony's equipment manifest, and he'd only relented because of the aggressive predators inhabiting the planet's jungles and equatorial regions. They'd never had to use one on an animal, but he was glad to have them now.

There had only been 20 rifles in the weapons locker, and he'd given them to those he'd been able to reach during the chaos of the attack. He doubted it would make a difference; his terrified little band had no real chance against these horrific invaders. But now that he faced his own imminent destruction, he knew in his heart that he'd rather die fighting. If these enemies were going to kill his people he was going to make them pay...or at least he would try.

He saw the shapes approaching, small, barely visible at first, but moving quickly. They were well over two meters tall, massively armored and bristling with weapons. They looked like warriors sent from hell as they moved grimly forward...unstoppable, merciless. Tremaine knew they were coming for him... for him and for his people. He tightened his grip on the rifle and stared forward, transfixed on the approaching shapes. He was looking at his own death, and he knew it. He almost gave in to panic and tried to run, but then a strange calm settled over him. He raised his rifle, preparing to fire. It would all be over in a few minutes. He tried to keep his focus, but his mind drifted...back over the last few fateful days.

The nightmare had begun two days before. The colonization and supply fleet, so long awaited, had been attacked barely a day out from Newton. The colony had been joyous, anxiously awaiting their new neighbors and the supplies they so desperately needed. Then, disaster.

The transmission had been received first with disbelief then with shock and anguish. Word spread quickly throughout the small village, and the people flocked to the community center, where the communications from the fleet were broadcast. They listened silently to the battle unfolding in space, and they knew the fleet was doomed. None of the Newton colonists had military experience, but they knew enough to understand that the acceleration rates and warhead yields being reported were extraordinary. One by one they received the Delta-Z codes until, finally, the com was eerily silent.

The two colonies communicated feverishly, but there was little they could do. Newton had no defenses...none at all. It didn't even have a Commnet station yet, so the colonists couldn't call for help...not that any could have arrived in time. The planet's lone satellite detected distant ships approaching, and it transmitted its sketchy data to the surface. Then, suddenly, a blast of energy impacted it and it was gone, leaving the two small colonies without eyes or even a communications link with each other.

Haven was alone, cut off even from its sister settlement. Blind, deaf, defenseless, the village waited...it waited to see what would come next. The people gathered together, praying for salvation few of them really expected. The next twelve hours were the most trying in Ian Tremaine's life. He spent that long night moving among the people, comforting those he could, reassuring any who would listen. He tried to give them hope, even as his own drained away. He knew it was a lie, but still he went among those terrified, huddled masses with comforting words and empty promises of hope.

There was no communication from the invaders, no demand for surrender. Just fiery streaks across the predawn skies...landing craft descending through the thick Newtonian atmosphere. They landed south of the village, at least thirty of them. The sleek ships set down, arrayed in an almost perfect formation. Their hulls were jet black and smooth, with none of the charring or heat damage common to such craft.

No one from Haven scouted the landing zone, so no one saw the side doors slide open and the great armored figures pour out onto the dusty brown sand. Their formations were meticulous, perfect. There was no hesitation, no need to pause and form up...they just moved out spaced at exact ten meter intervals.

The attackers moved quickly, traversing the 10 kilometers

to Haven in less than twenty minutes. They paused two klicks out and opened fire. They carried a full magnetic auto-cannon on each arm, and their hyper-velocity rounds ravaged the settlement, tearing right through buildings, vehicles, equipment…and colonists.

The settlers panicked, running through the village, screaming, desperately searching for cover that simply didn't exist. At least a third of the Havenites were killed in the first two minutes, the rest stampeding through the town in blind terror.

Ian Tremaine walked slowly through the town common in shock, seemingly oblivious to the chaos and destruction around him. He'd been in the communications hut since the landing ships were first spotted, trying vainly to contact the enemy, broadcasting the planet's surrender on every frequency. His panicked mind raced, trying to decide what to do. He couldn't understand. Why wouldn't they respond? Why wouldn't they accept the surrender? His people weren't warriors; they weren't a threat to anyone.

Now his worst fears were realized. The invaders weren't interested in surrenders or prisoners…they were here to slaughter the colonists. He walked across the village in a daze, only blind luck keeping him from being hit. He couldn't remember how long he wandered like that, but then the madness took him. That's when he first felt the rage, the drive to fight back, to kill the enemy.

He ran to the shed where the guns were stored, calling for those closest to follow. The storage building was a prefabricated metal structure 10 meters square. Tremaine had been heading around the corner toward the door, but the entire side closest to him had been ripped open by enemy fire, and he ran through the gaping hole. The shed had been ravaged by auto-cannon rounds, but the gun locker was untouched. He punched the combination into the locking mechanism, and the door slid open, revealing twenty light mag rifles stored in two neat rows. He grabbed them one at a time, handing them off to the villagers who had followed him into the shed.

Taking the last gun for himself, he ran out into the common. There were dead and wounded colonists everywhere, and the horrific sight fed his growing hatred. "To the mountains." He screamed as loud as he could, waving his arm and pointing north toward the looming peaks. "Run! Abandon the village! To the mountains, now!"

Tremaine gripped the rifle tightly and ran around the settlement, grabbing stunned colonists and pushing them toward the northern gate. "Flee to the mountains. We will regroup there." He repeated his entreaties as he ran back to the northern gate, pushing the terrified settlers through the narrow opening. Finally, when everyone still alive had fled, Ian Tremaine took one last look back at the dying settlement that had been his life's greatest achievement, and he ran across the plain toward the rugged foothills to the north where his people would make their last, futile stand.

Chapter 6

1st Division Headquarters
Camp William Thompson
Armstrong - Gamma Pavonis III

"Who the hell was it? The Caliphate? The CAC?" Erik Cain's voice was sharp, edgy. He was masking most of the rage, but he couldn't hide it all.

"We don't know yet, Erik." General Darius Jax stood in front of Cain, his bulk dominating the room as it usually did. Jax was meticulous as always, his uniform neatly pressed, looking like he'd just put it on. But he was tense, rushed, his body rigid. Something was very wrong; that much was clear. "General Holm sent me right over to tell you what little we know." Jax paused for an instant before continuing with a slight frown. "He didn't want this on the com yet."

Cain sighed forcefully. They'd all been operating carefully for the last year...ever since they'd uncovered the true extent of Alliance Intelligence's infiltration. Cain hated the spy service - he hated all of Alliance Gov - but his anger had reached a new and frightening level since the rebellions. He loved the Marine Corps. It had saved him; it had made him all he'd become. It was home, a family of brothers and sisters that operated, as much as anything, on trust. Now they were afraid to even use their own communications systems. The Corps had endured despite the plot to destroy it, but he wondered if they would survive the paranoia left in its wake.

"So what do we know?" Erik stood next to his silver metal desk, wearing his uniform pants and a gray t-shirt with the Marine Corps emblem on the left breast. His jacket was laying on a small table near the door where Cain had carelessly tossed it. It was late, though he'd still been working when Jax came running in. He motioned for the big Marine to take a seat, but he remained standing himself. "Go through it from the beginning."

Jax glanced at the chair Cain was pointing at, but he continued to stand. "Admiral Garret's people got a transmission on Commnet. It was a Priority Alpha distress call from a ship called the Northstar. She's a research and scout vessel attached to a support fleet en route to the Newton colony out on the Rim. Apparently she had some sort of malfunction and fell out of the fleet formation before making the final transit." Jax paused briefly, allowing Cain to absorb what he was saying.

Cain nodded. He was vaguely aware of Newton. The planet was far from rating a Marine garrison, but he still got reports on new settlements. Ultimately the Corps was responsible for defending them all. "Go on." He didn't snap at Jax, not exactly, but Cain wasn't the most patient of men either.

"She made repairs and passed through the warp gate, but shortly after entering the system she received a series of transmissions from the rest of the fleet." Jax's tone was somber as he continued. "The last of the signals carried Delta-Z protocols."

Erik was listening, but his mind was racing too, considering all of the possibilities. Newton was nowhere close to the borders with any of the other Powers but, of course, it would only take the discovery of a new warp gate, and the strategic map would be instantly redrawn. Cain himself had used such a newly located warp gate to surprise the Caliphate and seize the Gliese 250 system years before. It was a little soon after the peace to start paying attention to historians, but they were already calling that campaign the turning point of the war.

"There is no commnet station in Newton's system yet, so Northstar decelerated and transited back through the warp gate so they could transmit a report. Her captain is a navy vet, so he kept his cool and did what he had to do."

Cain sighed again, and he walked around the desk to his chair, sitting down forcefully and motioning again for Jax to take one of the guest chairs. "Whoever is hitting us picked a hell of a time. Another few months and we'd have had 1st Division better organized and up to 3 brigades."

Jax nodded as he reached out and turned the chair slightly. "It's a bad time for sure. But that's not the worst of it." He slid the chair closer and dropped his massive frame into it. "There's more."

Cain looked back with a pained expression. "For twenty years there's always been more." He leaned back in his chair and closed his eyes. "What is it?"

"The files Northstar transmitted have some details on the attack against the fleet." Jax hesitated, looking at Cain but not saying anything.

"What's wrong with you?" Erik looked quizzically at his friend and executive officer. "Speak up. What about the files?"

Jax took a breath. "Erik, the weapons that attacked the colony fleet are like nothing we've ever seen before." He pulled a data chip out of his pocket and placed it gently on Cain's desk. "You'll want to review everything on this chip very carefully. But make sure you're on a secure closed system. The general doesn't want any of this on the net." Jax's voice was tense, more so than Cain had ever heard it, at least when they weren't on the battlefield. He'd just seen the contents of the chip himself an hour before, and he was still a bit in shock.

"Stronger weapons?" Cain reached out and took the chip into his hand. He looked tense now too. Darius Jax was not easily rattled. He was one of the toughest of the hardcore, and seeing the expression on his face had Cain worried. "Talk to me, Darius."

"The missiles had three times the acceleration of our best, and they were a hell of a lot more accurate." Jax looked right at Cain as he spoke. "And the warhead yields were as high as six gigatons."

Cain leaned back again and let out a long exhale. "Well that's a problem." He rubbed his hand along his chin. "Are we sure about this data? We've seen our share of scams lately."

Jax stared grimly across the desk. "General Holm thought about that too, but every authentication checks out." He paused for an instant before continuing. "Of course it's still possible that this is some kind of misinformation, but it doesn't look that way." His eyes found Cain's. "We have to assume it's real until we can prove otherwise. And frankly, Erik, I'm not sure what the hell that means."

The two sat quietly for a long while before Cain broke the silence. "I guess it means we've got some problems, my old friend." He tried to force a smile, but only managed a brief grin. "It's bad enough if one of the Powers discovered a backdoor into the Rim. If they did, they can bypass most of our heaviest defenses and come at us through our soft underbelly." He fidgeted uncomfortably in his chair. "But if they've made some sort of major tech breakthrough as well, we're really in trouble."

Jax nodded, but didn't say anything. He just sat quietly and watched as Erik slipped the data chip into a reader. He had just started to play back the transmissions when Hector interrupted the silence.

"General Cain, I have General Holm on the line for you." Hector had been Cain's AI since he'd graduated from the Academy as a commissioned officer. The two had a somewhat strained relationship that nevertheless seemed to work fairly well. Hector had received a significant upgrade in his processing systems and databases when Erik had been promoted to general rank, but the AI's personality remained eccentric.

"Put him on speaker." Cain looked up from the portable reader he'd been using to view the contents of the data chip. "And lock the door. No one gets in here until I say so. Understood?"

"Yes, general." The AI's voice was calm and professional, but Cain could swear there was a hint of sarcasm in there somewhere. "I am quite certain my processing capability of 400 terabits per second enables me to understand a locked door." Ok, Cain thought, maybe more than a hint.

"Erik, is Jax there yet?" Holm's voice was clipped, tense.

"Yes, sir." Cain always got nervous when Holm sounded scared. "You're on speaker. It's just Darius and me here. Hector has the room locked down."

"Did Darius fill you in?"

"Yes, sir. I was just starting to review the transmissions, but I have the gist of the situation." Cain looked over at Jax, both of them wondering what fresh disaster Holm had to share with them.

The general didn't waste any time. "We got another transmission from Northstar on commnet." His voice was grim. "It carried a Delta-Z designation."

Cain and Jax just sat there, letting Holm's words sink in. Northstar had escaped the Newton system, and she should have been days ahead of any pursuit...not to mention well out of detection range of the enemy fleet. Holm didn't have any details yet, but they all knew it wasn't good.

"I want both of you over here immediately."

"Yes, sir." Cain started to get up. "We're on the way."

"Good. Holm out." The transmission terminated abruptly. General Holm had a lot of calls to make.

"I've got a transport outside." Jax gestured toward the door as he hopped out of the chair.

Cain grabbed his jacket off the table and followed Jax. "Hector, open the door." There was a metal on metal sound as the security bolt slid aside and the hatch opened.

Jax hurried through the door, ducking slightly as he usually did to clear the opening. Cain followed, but stopped abruptly. "Hector, contact Colonel Teller. Tell him to take operational command until I get back." Cain paused for an instant, thinking. "Tell him I want the division placed on alert. All units are to prepare to ship out immediately."

If they were at war, there was no time to lose. He took a quick breath and followed Jax through the main workroom and out into the quad.

James Teller got up on the wrong side of the bed. Actually, he'd jumped out of bed so quickly when he got Hector's message he almost took a header over his boots. The orders were suitably cryptic – take command of the division and put it on wartime alert. No explanation, nothing. Well, he thought, the

Marine Corps promised adventure, and so far it had delivered in spades.

He was at HQ now, sitting at one of the workstations in the main room. Hector had opened the C in C's office for him, but Teller wasn't about to sit at Erik Cain's desk, not under any circumstances. Cain had been an idol of his throughout his career and, while he managed to keep the overt hero-worship in check as the dignity of his new position demanded, he still had a healthy respect for anything to do with Cain, and that included the man's desk.

Colonel Prescott hadn't arrived on Armstrong yet, so Teller had been looking after the Canadian officer's brigade as well as his own. Prescott had resigned his commission when the rebellions started and returned to his adopted home on Victoria, with most of the Canadian regiment following his lead. A small colony almost out on the Rim, Victoria had been settled mostly by immigrants from the Canadian provinces of the Alliance. Bolstered by the arrival of so many Marine veterans, the planet was the first to drive the federal forces off-world. By the time of the armistice and Martian-sponsored peace, not a federal soldier or official was left on Victoria, and the planet had established a stable government and planetary army.

Having left the Corps to support revolution, Prescott found himself on uncertain ground with the coming of peace…that is until Major-General Erik Cain sent a communication personally asking Prescott to come back to the Corps and command one of his brigades. He jumped at the chance, gratefully accepting the appointment.

Cain had carefully chosen people he could trust for his key positions. Teller had been under his command for years, and Prescott was a tried and true revolutionary, very unlikely to ever work for Alliance Intelligence. Besides the trust issue, he felt he owed a debt of honor to his new brigade commander. The Canadian Regiment had been one of the units that broke through and relieved Cain's 1st Brigade on the Lysandra Plateau during the final battle on Carson's World. Prescott's troops, along with Angus Frasier's Highlanders, had suffered crippling losses during the bitter fighting, but they'd kept up the attack until they linked with Cain's survivors. It was the decisive moment of the battle...and of the war.

Teller was hunched over a workstation, reviewing orders of battle. The division wasn't up to strength yet, not even for its current two brigade organization. They were well-supplied, however, and more or less ready for action. Cain's orders had been to prepare for embarkation, and Teller was determined to see it done in record time.

Preparing an entire division for transport into a combat situation was an almost overwhelming task, especially when a good chunk of the top command was off somewhere, deep in conference. Teller was working with Hector; Cain had instructed his AI to assist in any way possible, and the quasi-sentient computer was obeying enthusiastically for once. "Hector, get me Major Brinn please."

"Yes, Colonel Teller." The AI's voice was professional and respectful. Teller had heard Cain complain about Hector before, but he himself had nothing but praise for the semi-sentient computer. Erik would have been pleased - and a little pissed - to know how well Hector had behaved in his absence. "Major Brinn on your com, colonel."

"Good evening, major." Teller glanced at the chronometer. "Actually, I suppose good morning is more appropriate. Barely."

"Good morning, sir." Brinn was trying not to sound half asleep, with limited success. The troops of 1st Division were mostly veterans, especially the officers. But none of them had been expecting an alert. The Powers were all at peace, and there had been no indication of imminent hostilities. "What can I do for you, sir?"

Teller took a short breath, feeling mildly guilty about the job he was about to dump on 1st Division's chief armorer. "The division is on full alert, major. I need you to do a full diagnostic check on the ordnance."

There was a brief silence. Hand-checking almost 10,000 suits of powered armor was a massive undertaking, and Brinn's team was understrength just like the rest of the division. "Yes, sir." Brinn paused for a few seconds, and Teller could hear the officer's breathing over the com. "Sir, I am very short of manpower. Is it possible to loan me some technicians?"

"Sorry, major." Teller wished he had the personnel. "We just don't have the bodies. The whole division is getting ready to bug out. There's just no one to spare."

"I understand, sir." Brinn was silent for a moment, but when Teller didn't say anything, he continued. "With your permission, sir, I will get started. We have a lot of work to do down here."

"By all means, major. Get to it." Teller cut the connection and glanced down at the screen on his workstation. The combat prep checklist was displayed. The first several items were highlighted in blue, indicating they were completed or underway. The rest of the list, which ran all the way to the bottom of the screen and scrolled off, was still red. "Hector, get me Captain Masters." It was going to be a long night, he thought. He scrolled down the list, all the way to the end. A very long night.

Cain was exhausted. They'd been there for six hours, and they had watched all of the transmissions three times. He kept hoping it would show something different if they ran it again, but it was the same every time. The colony fleet had been attacked with weapons far more devastating than anything the Powers had deployed before. The implications were sobering. Whatever Superpower possessed that technology could probably take on and defeat all the others. The entire balance of power on Earth was at stake, not to mention the newly won semi-independence of the Alliance colonies.

"I've never heard of anything with thrust capacity like that." Cain's voice was hoarse, and he practically had to shout to force out something audible. "Bigger reactors?"

"I'm afraid it's more complicated than that, General Cain." Colonel Thomas Sparks was the Corps' chief science officer. Head of the R&D team that produced the newest model fighting suits, Sparks was one of the most brilliant weapons designers who had ever lived. "The maximum yield of a fusion reactor cannot generate the thrust levels we see on these transmissions."

Sparks looked extremely uncomfortable, as if considering something he couldn't quite figure out. "There has to be another power source at work here."

"More powerful than a fusion reactor?" General Holm had been silent for a while, preferring to let his command team discuss the situation while he sat and listened. But now he spoke up. "What could that be?"

Sparks looked at the Commandant. "There's only one thing known to our science that could theoretically generate that much thrust." His voice was timid, as if he was suggesting something insane. "Antimatter."

"They'd been producing antimatter for 200 years now." Cain had started with a silent thought, but somehow he ended up blurting it out.

Sparks shifted in his chair and turned to face Cain. "Yes, general, that is true. However, there is a difference from the production of small quantities for research and…"

The door slid open, and Augustus Garret walked purposefully into the room, his boots clicking loudly on the hard metal floor. "Good morning, all." He looked harried, but of course they were all edgy and tired, and Garret was no worse than anyone else. He nodded appreciatively as Holm motioned toward an empty seat, and he walked over and sat down, dropping with considerable force into the chair. "I got here as quickly as I could. Perhaps you'd be good enough to catch me up." He paused, but just for an instant. "I've seen the transmissions."

Sparks leaned forward slightly, but he wasn't sure he should address the admiral's question himself. There was a lot of rank sitting at this table, including the commanders in chief of both the navy and the Marines.

"Colonel Sparks was just addressing the likely power source for the missiles we see in the transmissions." Holm had seen Sparks' discomfort, and he jumped in to make it easier for the colonel. "Please Tom, continue." He thought a little informality might ease the tension. There was a lot of stress in the room, and the last thing they needed was more, especially over something foolish like rank. Sparks' hesitancy was understandable, but not particularly helpful.

"Yes, sir." He glanced over at Garret. "I was just saying, admiral, that my only hypothesis for the power source is anti-matter. I know of no other way to generate the thrust levels we see in the transmissions."

"Could that also explain the yield of the warheads?" Garret was matter-of-fact, accepting the scientist's premise and moving on from there.

Sparks nervously cleared his throat. "Yes sir. That is a pos-sibility." His eyes wandered to Cain then back to Garret. "We have only been able to make very rough estimates on the mass of those missiles. We could build fusion warheads with yields that high, but they would be too big to be feasibly deployed. An anti-matter warhead would be able to achieve the same yield with a much lower mass." Sparks' mind was racing as he spoke, going over every detail he'd seen on the transmission. He was still thinking this all through, and he didn't want to make a mis-take. Not now. Not in front of those assembled here. "Never-theless, while it is theoretically possible to achieve a six gigaton explosion through different means, there is no other method known or hypothesized that could achieve those thrust levels."

Garret nodded, his expression grim. "So we are dealing with one of the Superpowers that has developed the capability to weaponize antimatter?"

Sparks' started to shake his head, but he decided that wasn't the way to disagree with a five star admiral. "Well sir, that would seem to be the case, but…" He paused, not sure if he should continue.

"Please go on, colonel." Garret's voice was friendly and informal. "We're all here to work on this together. Speak your mind."

Sparks still looked uncomfortable, but he nodded and con-tinued. "Well, sir…ah…as General Cain noted just before you arrived, we have been producing antimatter for 200 years." He shifted his gaze around the room as he spoke. "However, the energy requirement for creating even small quantities is prohibi-tive. Early 21st century methods were able to generate only nanograms, and the storage methods were crude and insufficient to preserve even such minuscule quantities for more than a few minutes." He took a breath and continued. "Two centuries of ongoing research have brought us to the point where we can generate a few hundred grams at a time and store them for a period ranging from hours to days." He paused for a few seconds, panning his eyes across the table. "A six gigaton detonation would require almost 100 kilograms of antimatter." He let that sink in before continuing. "If one of the Powers has developed the ability to produce and store that quantity, they have made a quantum leap...probably a thousand years ahead of where we are today."

"I see your point, colonel. It seems unlikely that one of the Powers could have achieved such an extraordinary breakthrough in total secrecy." Garret was looking at Holm, though he was speaking to everyone in the room. "Surely Alliance Intelligence..." Garret stopped abruptly, and his eyes shifted toward Cain. "Is it possible Gavin Stark is behind this?"

Cain returned Garret's stare. "I don't think so, admiral." Erik's reply was straightforward, matter-of-fact. "No one mistrusts Alliance Intelligence more than I do, but it just doesn't make sense. If Stark was so close to something so powerful, why did he take such risks during the rebellions? For that matter, why push the colonies so hard and precipitate the revolts when you were a couple years away from overwhelming superiority?"

Garret was about to say something, but Sparks spoke first. "I believe General Cain is correct." He noticed that Garret had been ready to speak, and he paused.

"Continue, Colonel Sparks." Garret nodded at the Marine scientist. "Please."

"Yes sir." Sparks glanced at Garret then turned to look out over the table. "In the first place, the Alliance lags badly in this type of research, making it highly unlikely that any branch of Alliance Gov is behind it." He paused for a moment, considering. "The Central European League is the leader by a large margin in antimatter research. In the almost inconceivable circumstance that one of the Powers developed this technology, it would be the CEL." The German-dominated League was a middling power measured by size or military strength, but its scientific community, and particularly its physicists, were without equal.

"Why would the CEL attack us?" Cain's voice was deeply skeptical. "And why out in the middle of nowhere? Even if they found a new warp gate leading to our frontier. Wouldn't they hit Europa Federalis first?" The CEL and Europa Federalis were bitter enemies, and no one doubted that a League newly armed with superweapons would settle that score before attacking anyone else.

"To be clear, General Cain, I consider it extremely unlikely that any of the powers has developed the technology we are discussing." Sparks was becoming a little surer of himself, more willing to interject his opinions forcefully. "I simply cannot offer any alternative scenario." He looked over at General Holm. "Sir, is it possible that the data is inaccurate or compromised in some way? Perhaps we are misreading the situation. All we truly know is that a small colony fleet was ambushed and destroyed." His eyes moved to Garret. "Perhaps these acceleration rates and warhead yields are the result of a scanning failure."

"Or a deliberate attempt to misinform." Cain's statement came out louder than he'd intended. "Perhaps this is more of Gavin Stark's trickery." He lowered his voice, his tone calmer, though there was considerable hostility just beneath the surface. "Maybe the whole thing is a setup."

Garret looked down at the table for a few seconds then up at Cain. "You might have something there, Erik." Since he'd been kidnapped and held hostage by Gavin Stark, Garret had become as paranoid as Cain. "It would explain a lot of things more plausibly than anything else I can think of."

"For all we know, the entire colony fleet was controlled by Alliance Intelligence." Cain was starting to convince himself he was right.

"But what's he trying to accomplish?" Jax spoke up for the first time. "I hate the SOB as much as you, Erik, but what does Alliance Intelligence have to gain by a stunt like this?" He looked around the room. "Why now? They can't be ready to make some kind of bold move...not yet. Even if he had something like this up his sleeve, wouldn't he wait until he was prepared to capitalize on it?"

"It might be some type of trap." Garret looked deep in thought as he spoke. "Maybe Stark's working with one of the other Powers." He looked like he'd bitten into something sour. "Do any of you think there's anything that piece of shit wouldn't do it if it served his purpose?"

"No." Cain answered first, with considerable gusto, though it was obvious everyone in the room agreed. "Which makes it even more important for us to respond. We need to know if this is more Alliance Intelligence bullshit." He paused, an uncertain look briefly flashing across his face. "And if it's not, we need to know what we're really up against. Whether Stark's involved or not, any enemy would benefit from convincing us they had achieved a major breakthrough."

"Put 1st Division on alert, Erik." Holm was leaning back in his chair, his right hand partially cradling his face, an instinctive response to the headache sawing through his skull. "We need to be ready for whatever we have to do."

"Already done." Cain flashed Holm a self-satisfied grin, a luxury he'd never have allowed himself before the upheavals of the rebellion. He and Holm had always been close, but it had been the two of them that had rallied the shattered Corps. Since then the last shreds of formality between them had fallen away, replaced by deep mutual trust and friendship. Holm was Commandant, and Cain would follow any orders his superior chose to issue. But the banter between them tended toward the casual, at least when there were no junior officers or troops around. "Colonel Teller has been prepping them since before I got here."

Holm smiled. "I should have known." He turned toward Garret, his grin fading as he did. "What are you thinking, Augustus?" His eyes darted back to Cain for an instant then to the admiral again.

Garret sighed. He'd spent the past year trying to stretch his available fleet units to cover the bare minimums. Now he was faced with putting together a new task force to counter a threat coming from the least expected direction. "I'm going to have the 18th Squadron at Farpoint scout toward Newton. They're the closest formation I've got." Garret paused for a few seconds and exhaled softly. He didn't like it, not one bit. The 18th Squadron was 3 fast attack ships and nothing else...if they found anything hostile it was probably going to be a suicide mission. "At least we'll get some reliable intel." He paused again. The young Augustus Garret had pursued glory with a relentlessness few people could comprehend. Now that longing was gone, and nothing but fatigue and duty had filled the void. He was tired of sending his people to die. "Meanwhile, I'll transfer what units I can from 1st Fleet to bring 3rd Fleet up to strength. The base at Farpoint can support a large formation, so once the transfers are in place I'll send 3rd Fleet there. If we're looking at a fight, we'll have a substantial force in place."

"What transport assets can you give me?" Holm had nodded while Garret was outlining his plan. The Marine Commandant obviously agreed with everything the naval CO had just laid out. "We'll need ground forces in the theater as well."

Garret looked down at the table briefly, considering the ships he could assemble. "We can move a brigade in the short term." He looked over at Cain. "If necessary, we can get the rest of 1st Division shipped out in another three months, four tops."

"With your permission, sir, I'll dispatch 1st Brigade immediately. They can be ready in less than a week." Cain had still been looking at Garret when he started, but his gaze shifted to Holm. He was making big promises for Teller and his troops, but he was confident they could make the deadline. Besides, it was unlikely Garret could have his transports ready that quickly anyway, so if they needed an extra few days, they'd likely have it. "I'd like to go with them, sir. They're going to be way out on the frontier. It's almost ten days each way on Commnet. Someone has to be onsite." Cain girded himself, half expecting an argument. Holm had been trying to restrain his protégé's most aggressive tendencies for years.

"I agree, Erik." Holm almost laughed when he saw Cain's surprised expression. "We just don't know what we're facing… either it's a trick of some sort, or one of our enemies has taken a massive leap forward in power." Cain had a bad habit of taking personal risks Holm considered unwise or unnecessary. But this time the Commandant agreed completely. "I need to have you out there. There are just too many variables. We have to have someone on the scene with unlimited discretion." He looked right at Cain. "That's you, Erik."

Holm leaned back in his chair and looked over at Jax. "Darius, you'll take charge of the rest of the division. I want you to put Prescott's brigade through its paces until he gets here. He's got less experienced units on average than Teller, and I want everybody ready for anything."

"Yes sir." Jax's response was sharp and decisive, as always.

"And Jax…I know 1st Division is understrength, but I'm going to divert the cadre for your third brigade to Angus Frasier's 2nd Division." Holm glanced quickly at Cain to get a read on his reaction. He expected an argument, but Cain surprised him by silently nodding his agreement. "But I'm going to do what I can to expedite bringing your divisional support units up to regulation strength. That should compensate somewhat, and it will give you a wider range of capabilities, especially when we know so little about the prospective enemy."

"I'll get more transport here ASAP." Garret was looking across the table in the general direction of the Marines. "If things get hot out there, we'll get the rest of 1st Division to the front…if I have to set up couches in the launch bays of the battleships to do it."

"And I'll get General Frasier to Armstrong to start getting 2nd Division shaken out." Holm's voice was firm, but his expression showed concern. "Hopefully he can get them in enough shape to take your place here." He was staring at Erik and, for once, the decisive General Holm looked like he could use a little reassurance. "After all, we still have to defend everything else."

"Angus Frasier is a good man, sir." Cain was happy to give Holm the support he needed, but he was speaking from the heart too. "He saved my ass on the Lysandra Plateau." Cain paused for an instant, recalling those hellish days on Carson's World. Frasier's Highlanders fought alongside Prescott's troops and broke through the enemy lines to relieve Cain's surrounded brigade...and they'd paid heavily to do it. "I can't think of a better man for the job."

The room fell silent, each of them considering the situation from their own perspective. Finally, Holm took a deep breath and stood up. "Well, we all have work to do, so I suggest we get moving."

The others started to rise and head toward the door. Garret walked around the table toward Holm. The two senior commanders spoke quietly as the rest of the officers present filed out of the door.

Jax and Cain stepped out into the quad, the sunrise just peeking over the mountains west of the camp. Jax waved for the orderly to bring the transport around. The two had been silent since leaving the conference room, but now Cain turned to his oldest comrade, his head arched up, blue eyes looking into those of the big man. He had an oddly calm expression on his face. "Well, my friend...once more into the breach."

Chapter 7

Committee Room
Combined Powers Excavation Site
Carson's World – Epsilon Eridani IV

"Dr. Hofstader, this committee would like to be lenient, but your actions are impossible to justify." Ivan Norgov sat in the center of a long table at the front of the room, his angular face betraying anything but a desire for leniency. "Frankly, I find it difficult to conceive of a worse breach of the Committee's trust." He leaned back in his chair slightly, making a moderate effort to suppress a self-satisfied grin. "And I cannot overstate the recklessness of your actions nor the danger in which you placed this research facility."

Hofstader sat silently in a smaller chair, one significantly less comfortable than the plush leather seats of the Committee. He faced the long, polished wood table, staring defiantly back at the Committee members who looked at him with varying degrees of disdain. The whole thing disgusted him…the bureaucracy, the pomp, the obscene luxury. The Committee table alone cost more than the salary of 20 research assistants for a year. Why, he wondered, do these fools care so much for all this nonsense? They are sitting on the most profound discovery in the history of mankind, and all they want to do is have meetings and write rules.

"I would also like to add that I am personally shocked at your conduct. Whatever your own inclinations, this Committee had already considered and rejected your repeated requests to accelerate the exploration timetable." Norgov's tone was scolding, his arrogance showing itself. "Yet you took it upon yourself to secretly enter sections of this facility that were newly discov-

ered and off-limits." Norgov glanced right and left at his colleagues on the Committee then back at Hofstader. "You compromised the safety of this installation and the entire research
team because of your impatience."

God, he loves the sound of his own voice, Hofstader thought
derisively. He had nothing but contempt for Norgov and all the
others like him. As far as he was concerned, people like him
had been holding back human development and advancement
for centuries. He had intended to remain quiet, but finally he
decided the only way to shut Norgov up was to say something
himself. "Dr. Norgov, I believe that you are mischaracterizing
the nature of my activity." Hofstader paused for an instant,
reminding himself to stay calm and keep his voice even. An
angry outburst wouldn't help him now. "I merely scouted a section of tunnel and confirmed the presence of a large particle
acceleration chamber. I did nothing further except to conduct
passive radiation readings."

"Dr. Hofstader, you are again leaping to premature conclusions." Adam Crandall was seated at the far end of the table.
The expression on his face was troubled, and his voice was gentle, almost sad. Crandall was pompous and unable to embrace
anything outside academic orthodoxy, but he lacked Norgov's
mean streak. He was upset at Hofstader's actions, but he also
knew the German was probably the foremost expert in antimatter in any of the Powers. It felt wrong to ban him from the
project, even if his actions warranted punishment. "I agree that
the evidence suggests such a usage for this facility, but we have
nowhere near the data we need to reach such a blanket conclusion. We must not sacrifice scientific validity for the sake of
enthusiasm."

Hofstader held back a frown. He couldn't stand Norgov,
but Crandall was different. The Alliance scientist was unques-
tionably a genius, however choked by procedure and protocols
his research might be. Norgov, on the other hand, was more
politician than scientist. Hofstader didn't think the Russian contributed anything of use to the research effort. "Dr. Crandall,
I understand that you take a more deliberative approach than I

often do." He was trying hard to sound conciliatory. "But that is why it is even more imperative that we move with greater urgency…so we can collect the data to meet your criteria."

The Alliance scientist was about to respond, but Norgov spoke first. Crandall had an uncertain expression on his face, as if he was considering Hofstader's words, but Norgov wore a scowl, and it was clear he had no interest in anything the German physicist had to say. "Dr, Crandall, Dr. Hofstader, your debate is tangential to the issue. The fact remains that a gross violation of the rules and a betrayal of trust has taken place." He turned his head to look down the table at Crandall. "The time for discussing proper research protocols is past. This Committee has already done that and made its decisions." His head moved back toward Hofstader, his eyes narrowed, face twisted into a disapproving frown. "Dr. Hofstader simply did not like the Committee's decision, so he ignored it."

Hofstader sat still, angling his head slightly to pan his eyes down the Committee table. You've lost them all, he thought bitterly. Some of them just want to slap you on the wrist, but none of them will stand up to Norgov. Fools.

Norgov continued, hardly taking a breath as he droned on. "I am personally astonished at the arrogance you have displayed in wantonly ignoring the directives of this Committee."

Hofstader sat quietly listening as Norgov continued. He wasn't really paying attention; his mind had wandered to other things, leaving the Russian's nasal voice a distant buzz in the background. As always, he was stunned how detached many researchers could be from reality. A lifetime in academia often created an inability to consider the real world implications of research. Hofstader had done some preliminary calculations on how much antimatter a planetwide factory could produce, and the results scared him to his core. His numbers were just short of a wild guess at this point, but he was confident they were at least reasonably close to accurate. The potential applications of so much energy were sobering…at least to anyone with the sense to consider them. The weaponry that could be created was terrifying.

Norgov was still talking when Hofstader drifted back from his own thoughts. "This is the greatest international scientific project ever undertaken by mankind, and its success will depend on adherence to a properly enacted series of protocols, not intellectual anarchy."

Hofstader could feel the frustration turning to rage. He knew Norgov was a pompous windbag, and he'd girded himself to sit and quietly endure the asshole's tirade. But there was a limit to what he could stand, and he'd reached it. His temper had often been a problem...he had very little patience for those he considered stupid or foolish. Now the anger bubbled out and he interrupted Norgov.

"Dr. Norgov, excuse me for cutting short your unceasing prattle, but I'm afraid it's the only way anyone else is likely to get a word in." Norgov was glaring at him, silent for once, with an expression that looked like it could bore through a plasti-steel bulkhead. "I exercised some initiative and conducted a brief exploration of a section of the facility before it was officially open. I did not removed or disturb anything; I simply examined a length of tunnel." He saw Norgov shift in his seat, and he raised his voice to forestall the Russian from interrupting him. "No harm was done, and I was able to substantially support my hypothesis. If you want to be a politician and a petty bully, why didn't you do it somewhere else, and leave the research to those who crave knowledge."

Norgov sat in his chair silent, his expression apoplectic. Hofstader knew he shouldn't have lost control of himself, but he really didn't think it mattered. Norgov was determined to banish him from the research team anyway, so why not let the pompous ass have it with both barrels? Hofstader almost had to force back a little smile. *I didn't even come close to unleashing both barrels on the miserable little prick*, he thought. *Maybe later.*

"Dr. Hofstader, you have only reinforced the finding of this Committee that you are undisciplined and unwilling to work within the framework established for the safety and success of your colleagues." Norgov's voice was a little wobbly. He was so angry he could hardly sit still in his chair. "It is with the deepest regret that I must put forward a motion that you be expelled from the research team and that your occupancy visa be revoked immediately."

If there was any regret in the Russian's voice, Hofstader couldn't hear it. He felt another rush of anger, but he controlled it this time. There was no point in arguing. This was a kangaroo court, and nothing he said was going to matter. He leaned back in his chair, silent but with a defiant expression on his face. He watched and listened as Norgov called the role. The others looked uncomfortable, especially Crandall but, as Hofstader expected, none of them would cross Norgov. The vote was 6-0 for expulsion.

Friederich Hofstader leaned back in his chair and looked one last time at the Committee members. Crandall and most of the others looked edgy and upset, and they tried to avert his gaze. But Norgov wore a big smile, and he stared right back at Hofstader.

Hofstader leaned back in one of the hard plastic chairs in the waiting area, Katrina sitting quietly across from him. He felt guilty about his assistant sharing his fate, and he'd tried mightily to get her exempted from the expulsion order and reassigned within the CEL team. He swore she was simply following his orders, and he thought for a while he'd convinced the Committee members, but Norgov intervened and quashed the whole thing. Hofstader was really starting to hate the Russian scientist. "One of these days, you spiteful piece of shit." He whispered quietly to himself. "One of these days."

The shuttle was scheduled to board in twenty minutes. They'd be traveling back to Earth on the regular transport and supply ship. The trip would be fairly comfortable, as much as space travel ever was. The ship would be almost empty, so they'd have their choice of cabins. But Hofstader still couldn't believe he was on his way back home. He'd spent thirty years studying antimatter, and he'd singlehandedly designed the most advanced trap for storing the precious and volatile material. No one on this planet – or Earth - knew as much about the subject as he did but, he thought bitterly, that didn't seem to matter as much as petty bullshit and politics. Of course, these fools are too busy writing rules and regulations to worry about actually conducting research.

The hatch slid open and Brad Travers ducked into the room. Travers had been with Hofstader and Katrina when they engaged in their controversial exploration, but he'd managed to keep himself out of the Committee's crosshairs. Epsilon Eridani IV was under the joint jurisdiction of all the Powers, but it had been the Martian Confederation that seized it from the Alliance and invited in the other Powers. While the Martians didn't retain any official preferential status, it would have been embarrassing for the Committee to take action against one of their scientists, so Travers' involvement had been kept quiet. He'd tried to intervene for Hofstader as well, but all his efforts had been unsuccessful. He'd even sent a transmission to Roderick Vance, but he wouldn't have a response until after Hofstader's ship had departed. He was sure Vance would be upset. The head of the Martian Security Department wanted the best research team possible in place on Epsilon Eridani IV, and without Friederich Hofstader it was definitely not the best team.

"Bradley…nice of you to drop by." Hofstader was genuinely pleased to see the Martian scientist. "Come…" He pointed to the chair next to him. "…have a seat. They're not very comfortable, I'm afraid."

Travers nodded and walked across the room. "Hello, Friederich." He turned briefly and nodded to Hofstader's young assistant. "Katrina." She nodded back and smiled sadly. Travers turned again and walked over to take the seat next to Hofstader.

"You have something to say other than goodbye, my friend." Hofstader was facing his visitor, speaking softly. "I can see it on your face."

"Friederich, just listen to me." Travers was leaning close to Hofstader, speaking very softly. "There is something I discovered that I haven't shared with anyone." That wasn't entirely true – he'd reported it to Roderick Vance, who had told him to keep it to himself until further notice. But he thought Hofstader should know, and he didn't have time to get approval from Mars. "I was conducting a number of scans myself several weeks ago…all unauthorized, of course."

Hofstader smiled. He was glad that there was one other, at least, who had no time for the Committee and its endless debates. "Go ahead." He was curious…he respected Travers and considered anything the Martian might have to say worth hearing.

"Friederich…" Travers paused and swallowed before continuing. "…this facility is not entirely dead." He paused, seeing the shocked expression form on Hofstader's face. "I have detected energy readings on two separate occasions."

Hofstader gasped, but he quickly caught himself and forced a routine expression back onto his face. He could hear his heart beating in his ears, but there was no way to know if they were being watched, so he tried to hide his excitement. Travers was a reliable source, and Hofstader took his words at face value. "What kind of readings? Are you sure it wasn't from our own equipment."

"Two brief pulses." Travers was also trying to look normal, despite his own tension. If anyone was watching, he preferred they thought he was just saying goodbye to Hofstader. "Definitely not ours. It's type of energy I've never seen before, which is why none of the other equipment picked it up. I was testing some experimental scanners designed to look for life signs. The scanner was a failed experiment, actually. A complete bust as far as detecting life forms. But it seems to pick up this type of energy."

Hofstader had a million questions, and trying to decide which to ask first had his head spinning. Travers reached over and dropped a data chip into his hand. "We don't have time now, Friederich." He was whispering, even more softly than before. "Every piece of data I have on the phenomenon is copied on this chip. Figuring out the source of this energy is more your area of expertise than mine." Travers paused as Hofstader slipped the tiny data chip into his pocket. "I am trying to recalibrate my scanner to increase its sensitivity. I only detected the two pulses, but perhaps there are more readings – weaker ones I was unable to pick up."

Hofstader had been silent while Travers spoke. Now he looked at his friend and colleague, his eyes wide with amazement. "Brad, have you considered the implications of this?"

Travers stared back, his eyes locked on Hofstader's. "Oh yes. I understand. You need to look at that chip immediately."

Chapter 8

Militia Training Grounds
Just Outside New Sydney
Adelaide Colony - HD 80606 VII

"Ragged…very ragged. Let's go; we're going to do it again."
Cooper Brown stood atop a framework metal tower watching
the militia below conduct their maneuvers. "We're going to do
this until you get it right." Brown was speaking into a micro-
phone that broadcast his voice across the muddy, rutted fields,
now covered with khaki-uniformed men and women. He could
have used the com, but he liked the style of the loudspeaker. He
felt it amped up the pressure on the troops, and right now that's
what he wanted.

Adelaide was a frontier world and, though settled less than
twenty years before and located far out on the Rim, it was well
populated. The planet was blessed with especially rich resources,
and before victory in the Third Frontier War gained several
choice Caliphate possessions, it was the only substantial source
of certain very heavy elements in Alliance space.

It was a barren world, scattered with small oasis-like patches
where humans could eke out a fairly comfortable existence, but
it was a paradise compared to the radioactive and toxic hells
where stable trans-uranic substances were typically found. Its
inhabitants were a hearty breed of adventurer, willing to brave
the rugged conditions for the chance to build a fortune.

Its settlers had come mostly from the Oceania state of the
Alliance, primarily Australia, and they quickly built a prosperous
and growing colony. Exports of the nearly priceless elements
had already repaid all of the costs of colonization and allowed
the residents to accelerate the growth of the plant's infrastruc-

ture. Adelaide had a small orbital space station, half a dozen satellites, and a moderate spaceport in the capital of New Sydney. It was the wealthiest and most populous world in the sector, and its residents took considerable pride in that fact.

The planet had a substantial militia as well, much larger and more powerful than typical for such a world...especially one located so far from any known enemies. Adelaide had become the destination of preference for Australian veterans mustering out of the Alliance forces and, during the purges following the end of the Third Frontier War, over 1,000 former Marines immigrated, including Major Cooper Brown.

Brown was a veteran of the final battle on Carson's World, where his battalion had continued its drive against the enemy despite 50% casualties and a critical lack of supplies. It had been a hard experience for the seasoned officer, who lost several old friends over those few days, and hundreds of his troops. When the downsizing came he took his benefits and retired, having decided he'd seen enough of war.

Though he came to Adelaide determined to live a civilian's life, he was a Marine deep in his soul. When the local government offered him a colonelcy and the command of the planetary militia, he accepted the post and gave up thoughts of becoming a miner. Leavened with so many discharged Marines, the Adelaide militia was formidable, far stronger than anything possessed by a comparable colony world.

When the rebellions came, Adelaide quickly declared its own independence and put its militia in the field to defend it. But the federals never came. The planet was too remote, too far out, and the Alliance Gov forces were hard-pressed dealing with the inner colonies like Columbia and Arcadia. The few federal officials who'd been present were interned and, when shipping became available, sent back to Earth.

Now Adelaide was part of the Colonial Confederation and, as such, it enjoyed a sort of quasi-independence. There were certain obligations to Alliance Gov, mostly in terms of tax payments and export quotas, and the navy and Marine Corps were responsible for its external defense. Otherwise, the inhabitants pretty much governed the planet's affairs as they wished, which suited the sometimes-cantankerous expatriate Aussies just fine.

The militia lost some of its best troops when the Corps put out the call for retired veterans to return to the colors. Brown himself considered an offer to come back to active duty as a colonel, but he still felt burnt out, and he decided to stay on Adelaide and continue commanding the local forces. He was still plying his trade, but the likelihood of serious battle seemed remote, and he decided that suited him just fine.

Even with half its veterans returned to active Marine service, the militia was a solid organization, still well-provided with experienced combat troops. Except for Brown's staff and a few small units, they were part-time soldiers, but the cadre's proficiency and morale was high.

He'd been working them hard ever since the first message came in on Commnet. The colony at Newton had been attacked by an unknown enemy and was presumed destroyed. Newton was much farther out on the frontier than Adelaide, but Brown had put the militia on alert anyway. Better safe than sorry and, in matters of war, much better to be needlessly prepared than caught unready.

The subsequent communications vindicated Brown's preparedness. Barrow was attacked and, a few weeks later, Wellington. Each colony had gone silent almost immediately after reporting approaching enemy ships. There had been no Alliance ships in Barrow's system when that attack took place, but a freighter had been inbound to Wellington. It was able to transmit scanning data showing the planet's satellites and orbital facilities being destroyed before the vessel itself was targeted. The last transmission carried Delta-Z protocols.

There was no longer any doubt...the Alliance was at war. The enemy was still unknown, though the general consensus was that one or more of the Powers had discovered a "backdoor" warp gate leading into the weakly defended Rim. Of greater concern was the apparent leap in weapons and propulsion technology. It was hard to project what would happen when an Alliance fleet engaged the enemy's forces, but it was a good bet things would get ugly fast.

Brown was more concerned with the enemy's ground capabilities. He had no data at all about any planetside fighting, but his mind had filled in the blanks. He'd been working his troops hard…too hard, perhaps. But he had no idea what they would have to face, and he was sure they needed to be at 110%.

"Back in line. We're going to do this all night until you get it right." Brown's amplified voice ripped through the air, and the 1st Regiment of the Adelaide Militia scrambled back into position in the deepening twilight.

"We're getting intel from the warp gate scanners, sir." Lieutenant Khan didn't take her eyes from the display as she reported. "We have ships inbound."

Captain Riley Calloway sat in his command chair rigid as a marble statue despite his repeated efforts to remain calm. Calloway knew his small squadron was a forlorn hope with little chance of survival. Admiral Garret hadn't had a choice when he'd ordered them here; Calloway knew that. The admiral had sent him a personal note, and he pulled no punches in it, either about what was at stake or their chances of coming back. Augustus Garret did not send his men and women to their deaths lightly, and Calloway wasn't about to let the admiral down. His ships would fight like hell, but their chances of victory or escape were nil. He knew that, and so did his crews. But he'd be damned if they were going to die for nothing. They had to get data back to the high command…much better data than they'd been getting up to now.

"Ensign Carp, run a diagnostic. Confirm that the sensor array is working properly." Calloway's squadron had been in the system for almost three weeks, and he'd used the time to set up a network of small scanners at each warp gate. He was determined to collect solid data no matter what. Carp sat behind and to the left of the captain's command chair. Calloway turned to look back, but his view of the ensign was partially blocked by a large plasti-steel conduit. The bridge of a fast attack ship was anything but roomy or comfortable.

"Yes, sir." Carp was a young officer, barely a year out of the Academy, but his answers were sharp and crisp. "Stand by for results."

Calloway couldn't help but wonder what kind of career Carp might have had ahead of him. He was an excellent young officer who showed every sign of developing into an outstanding leader one day. But fate had put him in the 18th Squadron and the 18th Squadron in the path of a terrible new enemy. Ronald Carp didn't have much chance of surviving to take a crack at that future. He was young and smart, but he was probably going to die in this system in the next few days. Calloway sighed quietly. Such waste.

"Captain, all scanners check out fully." Carp looked up from his display, his head tilted so he could see Calloway under the conduit. "The scanner array is up and operating, capturing all data." Of course, the warp gate was 243 light minutes from the squadron's position in Adelaide orbit, so the data they were receiving was more than four hours old.

The squadron had deployed a hundred tiny scanning devices at each warp gate. Calloway didn't doubt the enemy would be able to locate and destroy them all, but not before they sent back considerable information…data that could be crucial when the fleet was ready mount a serious defense against the invaders.

"Ensign Carp, I want you to monitor our communications. All incoming data is to be retransmitted to the Commnet station immediately."

"Yes, sir." Carp was moving his hands over his screen as he responded. "I'm sending transmissions every thirty seconds, sir." Carp paused slightly then continued. "Commnet is sending drones on twenty minutes intervals, captain." Another brief pause. "Any faster and the station will run out."

"Very well." Calloway scowled, thinking quietly to himself. Damn, you always overlook something. He'd have preferred drone launches every five minutes to mitigate the damage when the enemy managed to knock out the station. He hated to think of losing 18 or 19 minutes of priceless data his crews had paid for with their lives. He realized they'd had neither the time nor the cargo space to bring extra Commnet drones, but it was frustrating all the same.

"Lieutenant Khan, I want ongoing reports." He had a better look over to Kahn's workstation, at least one without any major obstructions. You got used to the cramped quarters on an attack ship…eventually. "Anything at all of note."

"Yes, sir." Khan was a bit older than Carp, old enough to have seen combat in the closing phases of the war and then later when Admiral Garret hunted down Gavin Stark's rogue ships. Calloway had high hopes for Carp, but the young ensign hadn't seen battle yet. Intelligence, courage, ability…they were all important, but there was no substitute for combat experience. No training, no lectures, no emphatic warnings could truly prepare a recruit for the realities of battle. Khan had seen those realities, and she'd come through it with distinction.

"We're getting transit reports, sir." Khan's eyes were glued to her screen as she spoke. "Looks like seven ships, sir." She paused slightly as she waited for the data to cross her display. "Yes, sir. Seven vessels. They all appear to be the same or similar class, approximately cruiser size, estimated at 40,000-50,000 tons."

"Very well, Lieutenant Khan. Carry on." Calloway leaned back in his seat. "Ensign Carp, order Stingray and Hornet to commence silent running protocols." The term was obsolete, a bit of a carryover from wet navy days. In space it didn't refer literally to noise; it meant no non-critical use of energy. "Use line-of-site laser communication only.

"Yes, sir. Laser communication only."

"Place Raptor on silent running as well." Calloway instinctively reached for the seat belt on the command chair. Silent running meant no unnecessary energy emissions…and that meant the loss of even the modest gravity-equivalent generated by the ship's drives. Capital ships could produce near Earth-normal gravity, or at least a reasonable facsimile, but the small attack vessels were lucky to generate one-third of that. On silent running they would lose even that - the ship would be a near zero g environment.

Calloway knew his tiny squadron didn't have a chance in a fight, but the longer a ship remained undetected, the more data it could collect and ultimately transmit. Perhaps, though it seemed a remote possibility to him, one of his ships might even manage to remain hidden and actually survive. If that happened, it wouldn't be Raptor…he'd placed his ship on point to get the maximum possible amount of scanning data as the enemy approached. Stingray was positioned behind the planet relative to the enemy's most likely axis of approach, and Hornet was hidden behind Adelaide's distant moon, over 600,000 kilometers out. Raptor was situated to allow direct line communication with each of the other ships.

Long-range scanners worked primarily by detecting energy emissions. A small ship like Raptor was difficult to target at any range when running silent. Calloway knew his ship would be all but invisible to scanners similar to his own at any range greater than 1,000,000 kilometers. Of course, he had no idea what kind of capabilities these enemy vessels had.

His ships' own ability to detect the invaders was highly dependent on the energy output of those vessels. His warp gate sensors were giving him great info now, positioned as they were in the immediate area of the transiting ships. In a Rim system like this there were typically only a few scanners deployed, while the warp gates leading to a major planet like Columbia were blanketed with detection devices designed to give extensive information on any invading fleet. But Calloway's squadron had laced the entry points into the system with clouds of portable scanner buoys; his people would have known if a mosquito had tried to fly through the warp gate.

Once the enemy ships wiped out his warp gate scanners – or cleared range of them – he'd lose contact for a while. Unless they blasted away with massive amounts of thrust there was little chance his ships would detect anything more distant than one light hour. Tactics then became a guessing game based on the last observed vectors and velocities of the ships.

"Scanning array under attack, sir. Forty-three percent of scanner buoys have stopped transmitting."

"Thank you, lieutenant." Calloway wasn't surprised, but he'd hoped it would take the enemy a bit longer. "Ensign Carp, continue recording and retransmitting all data."

"Yes, sir." Carp was monitoring his display closely, even though everything the captain had ordered would all be done automatically by the ship's AI. He was going to double-check it anyway and make sure everything was sent out properly.

It wasn't more than another minute before the incoming data stopped completely. The enemy had taken out all of the scanner buoys. Calloway took a deep breath and rubbed his forehead. It would have taken a normal fleet much longer to clear the area. Whatever these ships were, their short-range detection and targeting was spot on. Better than anything he had…better than anything the entire Alliance had.

"The last transmission has been forwarded to Commnet, sir." Carp sounded as steady as ever. "All scanning frequencies are silent now."

Calloway leaned back in his seat, looking out across his cramped bridge. Now it was a waiting game.

"How is the evacuation proceeding?" Cooper Brown stood outside the Capitol Building, enjoying the shade created by the structure. Capitol was a grandiose name for the modest building that served as the seat of the planetary council. The citizens of Adelaide were an independent sort, with a decidedly limited tolerance for heavy regulation, not to mention a profound unwillingness to pay higher taxes to fund the construction of monuments to government. The planet's administrators were expected to operate on a shoestring budget and, for the most part, that is what they did.

"Things are moving along. A little slower than I'd like, but we should be OK if we get another day." Jacob Meklin was the president of Adelaide, a position of limited power and responsibility most of the time, not unlike a small town mayor, but on a planetary scale. However, the Adelaide Constitution gave the president enormous powers in time of emergency, and now Meklin had invoked those provisions. Every resident of the planet was being evacuated to makeshift shelters, and detachments from the militia were out enforcing the mandatory order.

At some point in its long journey through space, Adelaide had passed through a cluster of heavy metal asteroids, several hundred of which impacted its surface. These collisions delivered the precious trans-uranic elements that were otherwise inconsistent with the planet's geology. The violent collisions had also destroyed the ecology of a planet that had once been an Earthly paradise, turning it instead into a marginally habitable world of windswept steppes and dusty deserts.

In their search for the priceless resources buried in the planet's crust, the mining operations had left an extensive network of tunnels burrowed deep below the surface, and these man-made caverns had now been converted to temporary shelters. Meklin had worked to have the shelters prepared as soon as word arrived of the attack on Barrow but, prior to the emergency declaration, he lacked the authority. The council was hesitant to commit the necessary resources until Commnet brought news of the invasion of Wellington. Then, later than Meklin would have liked, the plan was finally approved. Work began immediately, and the tunnels were structurally reinforced and stockpiled with supplies.

Now they had to get the people into the shelters before the enemy reached the planet. Unfortunately, they had no reliable estimate of how long that would be. An Alliance battlefleet could cover the distance in a little under four days at maximum thrust. But these enemy ships were a mystery. It had already been 2 days since they'd arrived in the system, and they had not yet entered detection range of Adelaide's early warning systems.

"It looks like we'll get that day." Brown was looking down at his feet as he spoke. "They'll probably be decelerating hard, which means we'll pick them up almost a day out anyway."

Meklin was staring off to the side, looking across the almost-deserted central square. "Yeah." His voice was somber, almost despondent. "And then what, Coop?" He turned his head to face Brown's. "We just wait in those holes until they seal us in or dig us out?"

"Then we fight like hell, Jacob." Brown had a soldier's outlook – he looked at a battle an hour at a time, not letting his mind wander too far into speculation. Survive the next hour first, then worry about the one after that. He knew as well as Meklin that they didn't have much chance, but the only alternative to what they were doing was to give up and meekly wait for death. After ten years in the Corps, that wasn't something that even entered Cooper Brown's thoughts. "They're going to have one hell of a time finding everyone in those tunnels. The superheavy elements will play havoc with their scanners." He put his hand on Meklin's shoulder. "And my people are going to give them hell, my friend."

Meklin smiled weakly. He didn't really feel any better. In truth, his spirit was broken and he'd just about given up hope. He'd do what had to be done – he was as much a creature of duty in his own way as Brown – but his morale was leaden. "Alright, Cooper." He tried to pump some energy into his voice, for Brown's sake if nothing else. "You can be sure we'll fight. We've got what weapons your folks could spare in the shelters already. Every man, woman, and child on Adelaide is a fighter now." In spite of his own foreboding, the defiant talk made him feel a little better.

"Good." Brown nodded, a grim smile on his lips. "Is the rest of the council in…" He stopped abruptly, holding up a hand to Meklin as he listened to an incoming message on his earpiece.

"They're here, sir." It was his aide, Captain Krantz, on the com. "Captain Calloway just flashed a message through the satellite. "His scanners detected all seven enemy vessels inbound, decelerating hard. Estimate arrival 16 hours, 20 minutes."

"Understood. Put all units on stage 3 alert. Brown out." He turned to face Meklin. "We've only got two-thirds of that day, Jacob." He paused an instant before continuing. "Enemy ships inbound. ETA planetary orbit, 16 hours, 20 minutes."

"Prepare to execute thrust plan Gamma in three minutes." Calloway's voice was a little strained, but not too bad for a man staring at 150 gigatons of warheads heading straight for him. "Weapons control, I want full countermeasures ready in 90 seconds." Like all fast attack ships, Raptor was lightly equipped with point defense. A small vessel, it simply didn't have the room a cruiser or capital ship did to store dozens of defensive missiles and rockets. The ship was equipped with a spread of ECM devices and anti-missile mines, but otherwise she had to rely on a few light lasers and her dispersed ordnance magnetic batteries. More commonly known as "shotguns," the turrets of the DOMB system were highly effective at short range.

"Thrust plan locked in." Her fingers moved across her board as she spoke. "Weapons control reports countermeasures ready, sir."

Calloway was impressed with Lieutenant Khan's focus, but he could hear the stress creeping into her response. She'd have to be a robot not to be scared now, he thought. "Very good, lieutenant." He'd ordered the crew to get into their acceleration couches five minutes before, and anyone who failed to obey that command was going to end up as so much strawberry jam. He was about to push Raptor to the limits of her ability, and that meant serious g forces. "Bridge personnel, prepare for thrust burn."

He glanced around the control center, watching the acceleration couches activate. Each of the chairs reclined, and heavy padding expanded, almost totally covering the seat's occupant. Calloway knew how it worked; it was a chemical reaction taking place, vastly increasing the volume of the material in the chairs. It was an ingenious system, which saved a lot of space over dedicated couches or convertible seats with storage areas for retractable cushioning.

He felt the pinch in his arm followed by the familiar bloated feeling as the drug increased his internal pressure and strengthened his cell walls. One day someone would figure a way for men to go into battle without feeling sick and half crushed to death, but for now this was the best they could do.

The ship's AI would fight most of this battle. Once Raptor's engines opened into a full burn, none of his crew would be able even to lift an arm to press a button or turn a lever. They'd be able to speak, barely, but that was all.

"Engage countermeasures." Calloway's voice was wheezy and forced, the side effect of the drugs that would keep him alive during the coming high g maneuvers.

"Engaged, captain." The voice of the AI was calm, unaffected by the drugs now making the crew of the Raptor feel like they had the flu and a hangover at the same time. "Launching ECM buoys now."

The ship shuddered slightly as the ECM devices were launched with considerable force. Calloway probably would have noticed if he hadn't been cocooned in his couch, but swaddled as he was he had to rely on the AI's announcement. The ECM buoys were small missiles that broadcast a variety of transmissions, all designed to confuse and delay the incoming missiles. Calloway had no idea if the enemy ordnance would be susceptible or not, but he'd find out soon enough.

"Launching interceptor mines now." The AI was following the plan Calloway had programmed in previously. The ship shuddered again, harder this time, as it launched its full spread of mines into the path of the incoming missiles. A variant of the DOMB system, the mines would explode when any missiles entered range, blasting out a cloud of small metallic chunks, presumably across the path of an enemy missile. It didn't take much mass to seriously damage a target moving at 5 or 10 percent of lightspeed. Even a projectile a few centimeters across could destroy a missile that impacted it.

Calloway gritted his teeth; he knew what was coming. When the ship's engines fired, Raptor would accelerate at maximum, heading off in a random direction, trying to confuse the missiles' targeting. It was hard to build enough velocity to escape, especially beginning at a standing start, but Raptor was going to do her best.

"Initiating thrust plan Gamma." The AI made the announcement a few seconds before the engines burned, giving the human crew an instant's warning.

Raptor shook wildly as its engines, which consumed almost

40% of its hull space, roared to life. Calloway felt the breath forced out of his lungs despite the protection of his couch and the relief provided by the drugs. It took most of his strength to breathe in and out. It was hard to think at all, and almost impossible to concentrate on anything. He was wondering, in a moderately confused state, just how much acceleration the ship's engines were generating.

"Now accelerating at 32.7 g." The AI's announcement answered his question. The computer was untroubled by the massive forces torturing the crew, and its voice was calm and even as always. Raptor was now accelerating at a far higher thrust than it was designed to endure. Its reactor was running at 125%, an overage so severe there was a real chance its containment could fail, with catastrophic results. Reactors were designed to scrag and terminate the reaction if a problem developed, but at this level of output, anything was possible. The engines were blasting well past their design specs, and Calloway knew they could also fail in a number of ways, most of which would vaporize his ship in an instant. The vessel's frame rattled and shook, enduring pressures far beyond what it was built to withstand.

Calloway lay in his couch, nearly crushed to death despite the padding all around his body. His thoughts were slow and hazy, but he tried to stay as focused as he could. He knew he was asking a lot of his ship, but it was the only way he could think of to try and survive…at least against this initial barrage.

The ship took off at an angle from the incoming volley, quickly building velocity. A number of the enemy missiles locked on to the ECM buoys, revectoring at 200g thrust to target the decoys. But almost half began to swing around and pursue Raptor. Stingray and Hornet were still powered down, hiding behind the planet and its moon. It looked like neither had been discovered yet…and that was how Calloway wanted it.

Raptor blasted toward Adelaide, as the pursuing missiles steadily closed the distance. Calloway still had a few tricks up his sleeve, but he needed to get closer to the planet, and he wasn't sure they were going to make it. It was going to be close…very close.

"Raptor Control…" He addressed the AI by its formal designation. "Go to 130% on the reactor and increase thrust level." That should get them there ahead of the missiles…that is unless one of the overtaxed systems failed and they briefly added a second sun to this system.

Chapter 9

C1 Headquarters Building
Wan Chai, Hong Kong
Central Asian Combine, Earth

"I would like to thank you all for coming on such short notice. The information I wish to share with you is far too sensitive for the normal communications networks." It was a small Asian woman speaking. She was stylish and impeccably dressed, though age was finally catching her, and she walked with a cane now. Her already small frame was frail and bony, but her eyes blazed with undiminished intelligence. She looked completely harmless, but such an assumption would have been extraordinarily erroneous. Li An was as harmless as a viper in a pile of leaves. A member of the CAC Central Committee, she had been the head of C1, the CAC's external intelligence agency, for forty years, and she was one of the most feared people on Earth, at least among those who knew who she was.

"Minister Li, I believe I speak for all present when I thank you for inviting us here and convening this meeting." Mahmoud Al'Karesh was Li An's counterpart in the Caliphate. The Chairman of State Security had less blood on his hands than Li An, but only because he was twenty years younger. "At the risk of speculating on the nature of your news, I believe we have all noticed some rather…shall we say…unorthodox activities on the part of the Alliance military."

Li An maintained her emotionless smile despite her annoyance at Al'Karesh's audacity. The Caliphate official was a guest, and in the CAC there was a code of conduct that was rigidly followed, at least on the surface. She could have written his boorishness off to ignorance, but she knew it had been deliberate.

Al'Karesh was perfectly aware of CAC customs, and his speculation on the likely reason for the meeting was a clumsy effort to
achieve a sort of dominance over the aged CAC spymaster. But
Li An had dealt with rivals far more intelligent than Al'Karesh,
and she simply ignored his rudeness. For the moment.

The CAC and the Caliphate had been bitter enemies during
the Unification Wars, but a shared rivalry with the Alliance had
ultimately pushed them together for almost a century of unin-
terrupted cooperation. The relationship had been beneficial
for both powers. The Caliphate had arguably achieved at least
a fleeting position as the strongest Superpower, and the CAC
had gained a solid hold on third place. There was a considerable gap between the top three and the remaining Powers, and
the interstellar struggle had largely become a dance between the
Alliance and the Caliphate-CAC bloc. The other Powers tended
to ally with either side as their interests dictated. Except for the
CEL and Europa Federalis, which continued to fight their own
century-long battle with only brief pauses along the way.

Now the Caliphate-CAC relationship had become strained.
After a promising start, the Third Frontier War had become a
disaster for the two allied Powers. The war left the Alliance as
the preeminent Power, with a level of dominance unseen since
the Unification Wars. That position had since been seriously
eroded by rebellions and internal strife but, by most accounts,
the Alliance still clung to the number one spot among Earth's
Superpowers.

The Treaty of Mars had ended the Third Frontier War. It
had also cost the Caliphate a dozen systems and a huge percentage of its resource production. The war had been over for seven
years, and the CAC was beginning to recover both economically
and militarily. But the Caliphate was still mired in a massive
economic depression, and its armed forces had only begun to
rebuild. The CAC had clearly moved into the number two position among the Powers, and the Caliphate had sunk to third…
and was struggling to keep from falling into the second tier.

Although the Caliphate and the CAC remained allies, considerable resentment had built up, and for the first time in a century

there was a real possibility of a realignment among the Powers. The diplomats had been working furiously, seeking whatever gain could be had. The CAC was particularly worried about any cooperation between the Alliance and the Caliphate, which would be a grave threat, especially since the Pacific Rim Coalition was almost certain to join any such lineup. That concern was the primary reason the CAC's master spy had called this meeting. Presenting the Alliance as a likely aggressor, whether true or not, was helpful to CAC diplomacy.

"Chairman Al'Karesh is quite correct as to my reasons for asking you all here." Li An looked out over her guests, glancing at each for an instant before continuing. "We have recently become aware of very alarming activity by the Alliance military. Our analysts have reviewed the data and, while it is clearly not normal, it does not seem to be conventionally consistent with pending military action against any of the other Powers." She took a short breath. "Candidly, we do not know what they are doing."

"I want to express my own gratitude to you for extending this outreach. I, too, have become quite concerned about recent Alliance activity. Their previously purely defensive deployments now seem to be undergoing a major reshuffling. We have no reasonable conclusions on the reasons for this as of yet." Igor Tankovich was the Director of the Russian-Indian Confederacy's spy organization...one of them, at least. The Russians had a history of cloak and dagger operations, and they employed several competing agencies. Bitter rivals for the most part, they tended to spend as much time fencing with each other as spying on external Powers. Tankovich was the head of GRU, arguably the most powerful and far-reaching of the competing organizations.

Li An smiled and nodded deferentially to Tankovich. He was the only person in the room older than her, though she had to admit he still looked pretty good, even if he had put on at least 30 kilos. In many ways, he was the most important to her of all those present. That fact had less to do with the Russian's abilities than with the realities of international power politics.

The Russian-dominated RIC was definitely in play, more so than any of the other Powers. Its position had leaned slightly toward the Alliance for many years, but the power realignment after the war had caused considerable concern in St. Petersburg.

She had spent an enormous amount of time since the war analyzing the relative strengths and positions of the Powers. There was going to be another war eventually; nothing had resolved the fundamental disputes between the nations. The Alliance had a massive frontier, with extensive access to unexplored space, but many of the Powers were becoming hemmed in, denied access to warp gates leading to new systems. Conflict was inevitable.

She was worried about the Caliphate, but only moderately. In the end, there was just too much bad blood between them and the Alliance. The two Powers, and their predecessor states before them, had been enemies for 200 years. Both governments had employed extensive propaganda campaigns, inflaming nationalist and racial hatreds to rally support for the fight. And the Alliance held a large number of ex-Caliphate colonies… holdings the Caliph wanted back. It was extremely unlikely the respective governments could overcome all of this and become allies, at least in the near term. In the end, the Caliphate would side with the CAC.

The German-dominated CEL and Europa Federalis were both essentially useless as allies. With the unending feud between the two, alliance with one meant war with the other. There was no gain to be had from pursuing either, so Li had discounted both in her analysis.

The South American Empire was barely clinging to Superpower status. Blocked off from access to new systems, its tiny collection of colonies wasn't enough to prop up its bankrupt terrestrial economy. The empire had sided with the Caliphate-CAC bloc in the last war, and they'd suffered massively as a result. They were unlikely to openly join any side in a new war, at least not until it seemed almost certain they were aligning themselves with the victors.

The Martian Confederation would never side with the CAC.

Li An had established a relationship with Roderick Vance, help-ing the Martian's chief spy in his manipulation of the Alliance rebellions. By his own admission, Vance even owed her a favor. But she didn't kid herself that there was any real chance of bringing the Confederation in any war alongside the CAC. Her efforts there would be to maintain neutrality and keep the Mar-tians out of any new conflict.

That left the RIC as the only significant Power really up for grabs. They had been marginally allied with the Alliance in the war, but their involvement had been half-hearted and limited to a few support units. If the Confederacy joined the CAC's bloc and provided its full support, it could make the difference in the next conflict.

"Igor, my old friend, you are quite correct. The Alliance activity is bewildering. I do, however, have two working hypoth-eses." She had known the ancient Russian for a very long time. Indeed, a lifetime ago the two had briefly been lovers. Li An had discovered Tankovich's weakness for Asian women, and she'd used it to her full advantage. The dalliance didn't long outlive the needs of her operation, however. Though she'd moderately enjoyed the Russian, Li An's sexual preferences ran more toward women than men. It was something she'd kept private over the years…the CAC was a conservative society, and it was particu-larly difficult for a woman to reach the heights of power. She didn't need her personal affairs being used against her. A few of her lovers with less than ideal discretion had been the victims of unfortunate accidents, but the secret had been largely kept. Even those who knew about it were afraid to cross the CAC's deadly spymaster.

Tankovich leaned back in his chair and looked across the room at Li An. His mind drifted back across the decades, fondly remembering his host's extraordinary seduction skills. She'd gotten the better of him on that operation, but he didn't care. It had been worth it. "I suspected that you would have some insight to offer. Are you prepared to share with us?"

"Of course, Igor. That is why I asked you all to come here." She looked around the table and took a breath. "Our first theory is that the Alliance has discovered a previously undetected warp gate leading from one of their Rim worlds to a strategically sensitive location elsewhere. As you are all aware, the Alliance used such a discovery to great advantage during the recent war." She glanced over at Al'Karesh as she delivered the pointed barb, repaying the Caliphate spy for his earlier rudeness. The Alliance had used a newly-located warp gate to seize the Gliese 250 system and, subsequently, a massive sector along the Caliphate frontier. She smiled almost imperceptibly as Al'Karesh squirmed. The Gliese affair was not a welcome topic of conversation in the Caliphate.

Li An continued, slowly moving her gaze from Al'Karesh to her other guests. "If this interpretation is correct, the Alliance military movements could, in fact, be aggressive in nature. They could be massing for a strike through this new warp gate, and that attack could come anywhere…against any of us." She paused, trying to read the faces of those assembled. "This is our primary hypothesis."

"We also have considered this." Al'Karesh sat rigidly upright as he spoke. Clearly, he was concerned about the possibility of the Alliance gaining another advantage by bursting out into a previously secure sector. "Do you have a proposed plan of action, or are we here to simply discuss obvious concerns?"

Li An looked back at the Caliphate official, but she refused to take the bait and become angry. "Yes, Chairman Al'Karesh, we do have a proposed course of action, but before I move on to that, we do have one other theory." She glanced away from Al'Karesh. She was a master at controlling her emotions, but sometimes it was difficult. She really couldn't stand the little shit. If he hadn't been the Caliph's cousin, she thought derisively, he'd be shoveling camel shit in some desert. "We believe it is also possible that the Alliance has discovered something of significant value on one of their frontier worlds. Perhaps a find similar to that on Epsilon Eridani IV."

A low murmur rose in the room. None of them had considered such a possibility, and the prospect of the Alliance discovering another ancient artifact deep in their own space was unsettling. The balance of power was in a precarious state already – a major Alliance technological advantage could shatter it permanently.

"This hypothesis is somewhat supported by the force compositions of the Alliance fleets. The naval units they are moving are decidedly second line formations. Perhaps they feel older vessels are sufficient to defend an important site deep in their own space." She paused, taking a short breath. "Nevertheless, we still believe the first theory is the most likely. They may be moving older ships simply because that is all they can spare and still maintain the border defenses on their inner colonies. With the losses they suffered during the recent rebellions, this is a decided possibility, if not a probability."

Tankovich leaned back in his seat. The furniture in the conference room was of the highest quality, but the chair creaked anyway under the Russian's massive weight. He had always been a big man, Li An thought, but now he's a fat man too.

"Assuming we concur on the likely reasoning behind the Alliance's moves, what are the CAC's intentions?" He paused, but before she answered he added, "And what would you have us do, my dear Minister Li? You did not call this meeting for nothing."

Li An looked out across the table, her expression a blank canvas. "I am afraid I am not at liberty to divulge what actions the CAC may choose to undertake on its own." She paused… it was time to try to sell her plan. "But I do have a proposal for joint action, assuming your respective governments are in agreement with us."

Tankovich shifted uncomfortably in his chair. The RIC was willing to listen to CAC entreaties, but if Li An was going to suggest a military alliance, she was moving far too quickly. The Russians tended to act cautiously – ponderously some said - whatever course they ultimately chose. He opened his lips to speak, but decided to remain silent. Li An knew all of that - he would wait and see what she has to say.

"I propose that all of our nations mobilize their space-based armed forces and deploy significant formations near our borders with the Alliance." She glanced methodically around the room, weighing reactions. "I want to be clear, we are not suggesting an attack on the Alliance…merely that we all apply pressure. The presence of significant forces in a position to strike Alliance targets will compel them to retain heavy garrisons. This will starve any offensive launched via a newly discovered warp gate." She paused as the others considered her words. "It is the least aggressive stance we can responsibly take. It does not require us to initiate any hostilities, yet it still serves our purpose. I do not believe any of us can afford to simply wait and see what the Alliance is doing."

The discussion continued for hours, and by the time her guests filed out of the room, Li An was confident she'd convinced them all. Whether or not they could persuade their faction-ridden governments was another question. She bid them all goodbye, all except Tankovich. She asked the Russian to stay.

"I wanted to have a little chat, Igor." She smiled at her aged colleague. "We both know the RIC has some significant choices to make in the future. I thought perhaps we could discuss some options." As she spoke, the door opened and a startlingly beautiful young Asian woman walked into the room. She was dressed impeccably, though her skirt was extremely short, almost scandalously so by the prudish standards of the CAC. "Ah, here she is. Igor, allow me to introduce my new assistant, Jia."

Chapter 10

Parnasus Desert
20 km South of New Sydney
Adelaide Colony - HD 80606 VII

"Keep digging, all of you." Sergeant Jake Clarkson wiped his grimy, sweat soaked forehead. The grizzled ex-Marine could have been plucked right from a war vid. Bald, with a nasty scar over his left eye, he looked like everyone's idea of the veteran Marine sergeant. "I know it's hot boys and girls, but it's going to be a damned sight hotter if those bastards land and we don't have these works done."

His troops had been digging all day. It was almost impossible to determine where the enemy would land…they could come down just about anyplace on the planet. But New Sydney was the biggest target by far, and Cooper Brown figured they'd land somewhere near the capital. And if they were going to hit New Sydney, they had a limited number of options.

The asteroid strikes that had damaged Adelaide's ecostructure also created an atypical geography. New Syndey had been built on one of the small, temperate oases, the only spots on the planet even marginally comfortable to human settlers. As with most of these small habitable zones, the area around New Sydney was almost entirely surrounded by mountains. To the east and west were jagged ranges, almost impassable to ground forces. That left the passes to the north and south as the only practical approaches…and the logical places for the militia to mount a defense.

Clarkson's com buzzed. "Sergeant, give me a status report." It was Captain Krantz. "The colonel wants an update."

"Yes, sir." Clarkson had 50 troops under him. Cooper

Brown had tried to make him an officer three times, but he'd refused the commission. Clarkson was at home close to his troops. He was a sergeant at heart, and he couldn't see himself as anything else. Brown respected his wishes to remain an enlisted man, but he gave him a lieutenant's billet and put him in command of a front line platoon anyway. "I estimate 18 hours to complete phase one fortifications."

"Very good, sergeant. You're running a day ahead of the units on your flanks." Krantz had expected good news – Clarkson was one of the best men they had. But he was still surprised how much progress 4th Platoon had made. It was always hot out on the rocky plains south of New Sydney, but the last two days had been unseasonably brutal. Krantz knew Clarkson had a lot of Marine vets in his unit, but he still didn't know how he kept them moving at the pace he did. "Keep up the good work. Krantz out."

Clarkson turned and walked back along the line where his troops were busily digging. How many of them, he wondered, would be alive in a week? He didn't know what was coming – not even Cooper Brown knew – but he had a bad feeling. He wasn't part of the high command, and he didn't have access to whatever meager intelligence Brown had, but his gut told him they were in big trouble…and it had never been wrong yet.

He'd match his militia against any raiding force…even enemy regulars in powered armor. He'd been in the field against every enemy the Alliance had fought, and he'd face any of them again if he had to. But there was something different this time. In spite of the heat and the almost unbearable sun, he felt a strange chill down his spine. Not even his iron discipline was enough to keep his mind from drifting…wondering what the next week would bring. His thoughts were dark, grim. What is coming here?

Raptor shook to her very core, and her reactor almost redlined half a dozen times…but she held together. The ship's AI and its small squadron of maintenance bots kept everything running as her straining engines continued to build velocity.

Riley Calloway lay in his acceleration couch, trying to cling to consciousness. His desperate maneuver was pushing his ship to the limit…and exposing his crew to g forces well beyond maximum sustainable levels. Calloway was hurt; he could tell that much. His shoulder was dislocated…or his arm broken. He wasn't sure. He could feel the pain, but it was abstract, fuzzy… his mind couldn't quite place the sensation.

If they survived this run they'd have fatalities. The part of his brain that was still functioning was certain of that. Suffocations, probably, and maybe broken backs and necks. There was nothing to be done about it though…if he hadn't engaged his crazy plan they'd all be dead already, vaporized by the massive detonations of the incoming missiles.

Those missiles were still gaining, but if Raptor held together for another half hour they would zip right past Adelaide's orbital station. It wasn't a true fortress, not even close, but it did have significant point defense batteries. At close range and firing on the flank of the missile volley, the shotguns and lasers of the station would tear into the enemy ordnance. Maybe – just maybe – it would be enough to get Raptor and her crew out of this mess.

Calloway and his people were out of the fight, at least this part of it. Raptor's AI and the crew of Adelaide's orbital station would determine the outcome now. Riley's last lucid thought was that it would be close. Then he drifted off into a dreamlike state. An instant later he was awake, and the crushing g forces were gone. The acceleration padding on his couch retracted, and he sat up…and lurched forward vomiting. Most of the rest of the bridge crew were doing the same.

A glance at the chronometer confirmed that an hour rather than an instant had passed. He could feel the cloudiness in his head receding, the result of the massive stimulant injection his couch's med system had just injected. His entire body ached, but his shoulder was something different entirely – it hurt like fire. He winced and reached his other arm instinctively to the injured spot as he looked around the bridge.

"Lieutenant Khan, damage report." The crew members were shaking themselves out and turning toward their control boards…all except Khan. She was lying motionless on her couch, her arm hanging limply over the side. "Lieutenant Khan?" Calloway was unstrapping himself from his couch as he called to her. "Sylvia?" Still no response.

He stood up quickly…and almost fell. He was still disoriented, and he had to grab for the arm of his chair to keep himself from collapsing. His shoulder was pure agony, but he wasn't thinking about that now. He staggered across the tiny bridge toward Khan's workstation. The medibot should have responded by now, he thought. It was only then his mind cleared enough to realize the extent of the damage all around the bridge. One of the main conduits had partially fallen, and it was hanging, still attached to the ceiling from one end. There was wreckage strewn everywhere.

"We were hit." He spoke to himself in a whispered tone. The damage was too heavy to be from the acceleration alone. He stumbled as he reached Khan and he grabbed the edge of her couch to stabilize himself. She was dead; he could see that immediately. The best he could tell, she'd vomited during the maneuvers, and under the tremendous pressure she'd choked to death. She was lying on the couch, her head tilted at an unnatural angle, still-open eyes staring lifelessly back at him.

Calloway turned away. He'd been in battle before, more times than he liked to remember, but he'd never gotten used to losing people. Especially bridge crew…they had a special relationship with the captain, almost like family. It didn't matter how many times he went through it – it hurt just as much every time. The suicide boats were small, and their tiny crews tended to bond more closely than those on the massive battleships.

"Raptor Control…report." Calloway turned to move back toward his chair, but as soon as he let go of Khan's couch his legs began to wobble. He staggered forward and grabbed one of the structural supports to stabilize himself before taking the last few steps. I shouldn't be this weak, he thought. Then he realized what it was…radiation.

"We are approximately 4.2 million kilometers from Adelaide. We are moving at a velocity of 0.009c on a heading of 194/76 relative to the planet." The AI's voice was a little off…the com system was functioning, but clearly not at 100%.

So, Calloway thought, the plan worked…at least partially. "Continue report."

"Raptor has sustained damage from two warheads. The primary effects are the result of a 4.5 gigaton detonation approximately 5.2 kilometers distant. Damage has been sustained to a number of systems. I will display a complete list on your screen. The crew has also received a harmful level of radiation exposure, ranging from 30LD to 85LD depending on location and shielding. Sickbay is non-operational, and only one medibot is functional. I have dispatched it to treat critical cases and administer anti-radiation therapy to the crew. I do not yet have casualty figures compiled."

"Engine status?" If they couldn't get the engines started again they'd just keep heading off into deep space. There was no one out here to come and rescue them. Calloway didn't relish ending his days frozen solid as the captain of a ghost ship, careening forever into the depths of the galaxy.

"The engines are currently shut down and undergoing repairs. I have begun a diagnostic check for damage suffered during the recent period of redline thrust output." The static on the comlink was getting worse. Calloway could make out what the AI was saying, but the interference and background noise were getting worse. "The reactor is currently operating at 10%, providing power to primary ship's functions only until I complete a maintenance diagnostic and review of its systems."

"Can you do something about the com?" Calloway had his hand pressing the earpiece into his ear. "It's really bad."

"The main internal communication system was severed in sector B2. I have temporarily rerouted traffic, but the secondary lines have suffered damage as well. I will attempt to clean up the audio and reduce the background interference."

"Very well." Calloway leaned back in his chair and winced as the pain in his shoulder flared up. He shifted to the other side, taking the pressure off the injury, and he pulled up the automated ship's log on his screen. He wanted to know just what had happened over the past hour while he was in his delirious stupor. He was amazed at what he saw.

Raptor had indeed raced past the orbital station as Calloway planned it, the enemy missiles close behind and gaining. The station's point defense tore into the spread, but the attack still left a group of missiles intact and on Raptor's tail…more than enough to bracket and destroy the small ship.

Then, an instant later, Stingray came around from the other side of Adelaide. She had almost no velocity, but her timing was perfect. She launched a spread of ECM countermeasures that drew most of the remaining missiles off on a vector leading away from both Raptor and the planet. Then her crew unloaded with their own lasers and shotguns, destroying most of the rest of the warheads. Only two detonated close enough to Raptor to have any effect, and just one of them was in the serious damage zone. Somehow, amazingly, Calloway's ship had survived the first round.

"We just got the final transmission." Cooper Brown sat on a folding chair in his makeshift headquarters. His legs fidgeted nervously as he spoke, and his boots scraped lightly on the rough stone floor. "Stingray was destroyed. They hit her with some energy weapon from almost double our own laser range. Hopefully she was able to transmit some data on it to Raptor before they finished her off." That information could be crucial to the war effort. It was the first serious data they had on the enemy's energy weapons and, once again, they were superior to anything the Alliance possessed. "They took out the orbital station and satellites with the same weapon."

Jacob Meklin's face stared back from the portable com unit, his expression grim. "Any word on Raptor?" Meklin's face bounced around the screen – he was walking down a corridor holding his 'pad as he spoke.

"We got a flash message from Captain Calloway. Raptor has heavy engine damage and he's had to restrict the reactor to 40% output. Apparently one of the containment chambers is cracked." Brown tried angling his head, but finally he couldn't take Meklin's face sliding all over his screen. "Jake, can you hold still for a minute? You're making me seasick."

Meklin laughed, briefly breaking the tension. "That's pretty impressive, wouldn't you say? Since there hasn't been a sea on this planet for forty million years." He stopped walking and leaned against the wall, holding the 'pad steady in front of his face. "Better?"

"Much. Thank you." Brown squelched his own short laugh. "Anyway, Raptor's decelerating, but with their present reactor and engine capabilities, it's going to be days before they can make it back." Any brief trace of amusement was gone from Brown's face. "The station's last report indicated one of the enemy ships had broken off. Projections strongly indicate a course to intercept Raptor."

Meklin was silent for a moment, but his expression confirmed he knew just what that would mean for Captain Calloway and his crew. "Hornet?"

"As far as we know, Hornet is still undetected. We can't be certain." The third ship in Calloway's squadron had been ordered to remain hidden and not to intervene in the battle taking place. Her mission was to stay intact so she could transmit data on the enemy ground forces once they landed – intelligence that General Holm and the Marines needed desperately if they were going to have a chance of mounting a successful defense against the invaders.

"Are your people ready, Coop?" Meklin's tone changed, became grimmer. It was bad enough thinking about the naval crews up there, but Cooper's militia were citizens of Adelaide. Those were Meklin's friends and neighbors up there in the trenches, waiting for God knew what.

"Yes." Cooper's voice was just as somber. He'd done everything he could, but he knew his forces had no real chance to win the fight that was coming. "We've got the approaches to New Sydney and Johnston covered. The troops are dug in and as ready as they can be."

"You're positioned to cover the shelters too then?"

"Yes. Most of the civilians are in the tunnels under the

Wings." The Wings were the two mountain ranges that flanked the capital of New Sydney. They were honeycombed with mining tunnels that had been hastily converted into shelters for the planet's civilian population. "Johnston and the other settlements are a side show. The main battle will be around New Sydney."

Mcklin sighed heavily. "Ok, we're sealing up the shelters now. After I sign off we'll be going silent." He paused for a few seconds. "Take care of yourself, Coop." There was a sadness in his voice he couldn't hide. He didn't expect to see Brown again.

"Good luck to you too, Jacob." Brown was no more optimistic, but he had put on his warrior persona. If he had a fight ahead of him – no matter how hopeless - he was going to think about winning, not worry about losing.

There was a sudden commotion down the corridor from Brown. "Major! We have landing craft inbound."

"Got to go, Jacob. It's showtime." He smiled one last time at his friend and cut the link. He looked around the small headquarters for a few seconds before grabbing his helmet and rifle. "Captain Krantz, take over here. I'm going to the surface."

Riley Calloway leaned back in his command chair, trying to find an angle that didn't make his shoulder hurt like hell. It was dislocated – badly – and the tendons and ligaments were torn to shreds. The medibot had set it crudely, but with Raptor's sickbay a pile of junk metal, there was only so much that could be done. At least the injections had offset the radiation dose he'd received. Between that and the stimulants, he was alert and aware. More aware than he wanted to be…at least with regard to the losses his people had suffered.

Raptor had been hit hard. She was limping along on one-third power, still decelerating so she could turn and head back toward Adelaide. She had twenty dead from her complement of 87, and many of the rest, including her captain, were wounded.

Calloway had watched Stingray meet her end. He couldn't help but feel the loss even more keenly since Captain Heinz had taken her vessel from the relative safety of its hiding place to save Raptor from the enemy missiles. Calloway hadn't been able to repay the favor…his ship was still zipping away from the scene, its damaged engines and reactor struggling to decelerate. It wasn't like the shattered Raptor could have done anything to save Stingray anyway, but it was hard to sit helplessly and watch friends and comrades die alone and unaided.

Stingray had done her duty until the very end, transmitting close in scanner reports to Raptor right to the last second. And that data was crucially important indeed. Stingray - and Adelaide's orbital facilities - had been torn apart by an enemy energy weapon…one with almost twice the apparent range of the heaviest Alliance lasers. The data had already been sent to the Commnet station for rapid transmission back up the line. The forces massing behind Adelaide needed to know what they would face. The 18th Squadron was on a thinly-disguised suicide mission, but eventually the Alliance would make a real stand someplace. Calloway's people had increased the chances for that battle to be a victory, and that gave him some comfort. If they were doomed men and women, he thought, far better to die for something rather than for nothing.

Raptor and her crew were likely to join Stingray very soon. Their scanners had detected one of the enemy vessels veering off in their direction. They'd survived the missile barrage, but they'd made a spectacle of themselves doing it. Calloway knew the chance of going silent and slipping undetected into the void was nil, and now he had his confirmation.

The enemy vessel was close enough to launch missiles, but it had not done so. Apparently they were planning to finish off Raptor with that energy weapon. Calloway didn't know if that was simply a tactical choice or if it indicated a limited supply of missiles, but he reported it anyway, sending another pulse transmission to the Commnet station.

They'd get a close look at that new weapon…far too close. Calloway set the ship's AI to record and retransmit data until the last second. That would be Raptor's final service, he was pretty sure of that. The ship was tactically ineffective; its weapons systems were all non-operational. All it could do now was share a view of its demise with comrades who might be able to use that information in some future battle.

"Ensign Carp, begin startup sequence for lifeboats Beta and Gamma." Raptor had four small escape pods for use in abandoning ship, but only two were still operational. "Program for overload." The ships had a capacity of 24, but he needed to get 33 people on each...everyone still alive on Raptor except himself.

Carp hesitated, turning briefly to look back at the captain. "Do it now, ensign." Calloway's voice was gentle, not the normal scolding he'd give an officer who dithered in executing one of his orders.

"Yes, sir." Carp's voice was tentative, but he turned toward the workstation and began entering the required program.

Calloway leaned back in his chair, deep in thought. The bridge, which had been quiet already, was utterly silent, save for the sound of Carp's fingers tapping on his board. I can do this last duty alone, he thought...I can give my crew a chance to survive. How much of a chance he didn't know. Even if they escaped detection, they'd be marooned in lifeboats behind enemy lines. But even a fleeting hope was better than none. A small smile crept across his face.

"Who the hell are these guys?" Lopez was a Marine veteran and one of the best men in the platoon, but he sounded scared...scared shitless.

"Cut the chatter, Lopez." Sergeant Clarkson was scared too, but he was still managing to hide it. "It's just another enemy. You getting picky all of a sudden?" Clarkson's troops were dug in along a 200 meter frontage. Their left flank was set on the fringe of the Eastern Wing, and their right was covered by 3rd Platoon...Lieutenant Mitchell's troops. Clarkson couldn't think of anyone he'd rather have there than Eva Mitchell. She'd won her sergeant's stripes fighting in Erik Cain's brigade on the Lysandra Plateau during the final battle on Carson's World. That was all anyone had to say about any Marine, even one who was retired now and serving in the militia.

"But sarge, they just keep coming!" Lopez was definitely

losing it…otherwise he'd have never had the guts to keep talking after Clarkson told him to shut up. "I blasted off half of one, but he's still up and shooting back."

Clarkson didn't answer, not right away. He was looking out over the field, watching the enemy troops move toward his lines. They were tough as hell, no question about that. The militia had good assault rifles, but they were next to useless against the enemy's armor. The heavy SAWs were the only thing that really hurt them…but even those mostly ripped off bits and pieces. Lopez was right…they just kept coming no matter how much damage they took. Were they drugged, impervious to pain? Clarkson's mind scrambled, trying to figure it out. He didn't think his people had taken out more than one or two completely.

He watched as a mortar barrage impacted all along the enemy frontage. The shot was perfectly aimed, and the entire line was engulfed in clouds of smoke and displaced earth. The enemy troops were thrown around and knocked to the ground, but Clarkson watched in stunned silence as every one of them got up and continued forward.

"That's the toughest powered infantry I've ever seen." He was muttering to himself, but the comlink was still open.

"You said it, sarge." Lopez again, still sounding shaky.

"Never mind, Lopez. Just keep up your fire." You careless asshole, Clarkson thought to himself, what the hell are you doing thinking out loud on an open comlink?

Suddenly he heard a scream, then another. His head snapped to the right to see most of 1st Squad staring down at the ground. Bragg and Cullen were dead. Their heads and a good chunk of their shoulders and chests were just gone. Enemy fire was still targeting the area, and the rest of the squad was crouched low, beneath the lip of the trench.

"Keep down…all of you." Clarkson was talking to the entire platoon, not just 1st Squad. "The enemy fire is damned accurate. If you show it to them, they're gonna blow it off. So pay attention."

He looked back over at 1st Squad. They were still standing around stunned, crouching to keep their heads out of view of the enemy. "Pull it together, 1st Squad. Get that SAW going." Bragg and Cullen had been the heavy weapon crew for the squad. "Keep up your fire."

Clarkson wasn't sure how much that fire really mattered. They'd taken down a couple enemy troops, that was true, but they weren't getting nearly enough…and these guys didn't seem to be fazed by losses. Whoever they were, they were fearless bordering on suicidal. Nothing seemed to slow their advance.

"Incoming!"

Clarkson was never sure who shouted the warning first, but he reacted immediately. "Everyone down…now!" He dove to the side, taking cover deep in the trench.

The first sound was faint…soft popping noises coming from above. Then the real explosions started. Small bombs were dropping all over the line, a significant number landing right in the trenches. The explosions were powerful…strong enough to collapse sections of entrenchment…not to mention obliterate any men and women unfortunate enough to be in the vicinity.

Clarkson was immediately on the com. His orders were clear…any new weapons or equipment were to be reported immediately. "Captain Krantz, Sergeant Clarkson here. Sir, we've just been hit by a bombardment from a new weapon system. It seems to be some type of cluster bomb. It's ripping us apart in the trenches."

"Very well, sergeant. Carry on." Krantz sounded harried, distracted. Clarkson figured he was getting reports from all over the battlefield.

"Sergeant, 3rd platoon's pulling back." It was Corporal Nance, another Marine vet. He was keeping his cool, but Clarkson could hear the fear in his voice. "Lieutenant Mitchell's dead, sir. They've got 60% losses."

Shit, Clarkson thought. He'd been determined to hold the position, but with 3rd Platoon gone, his troops would be bracketed between the mountains and the enemy on the now-open right flank. "Ok, platoon, we're pulling back by squads. Even squads, withdraw to the second line positions. Odds, maintain fire."

Clarkson's platoon withdrew in perfect order. He watched with pride as they executed the maneuver. It was a testament to his troops…and to him as well, though he didn't think of it that way. Thank God Colonel Brown had us dig these lateral trenches, he thought. He couldn't imagine any of them would have survived the murderous fire if they'd had to pull back in the open. He paused to take one last look before following his people. He heard the whistling sound again…another barrage of the cluster bombs. He dove, and his helmet came loose and clattered over the rocky floor of the trench. That's when it hit him…a chunk of shattered rock. He felt an instant of pain and then there was nothing but blackness.

"That is an order, Ensign." Calloway's voice was stern, resolute. He'd decided what he was going to do and, by God, it was going to be done. "Launch now."

Calloway was alone on the bridge. Every other live member of the crew was crowded into one of the two functional lifeboats. There were only 62 of them now – the destruction of the ship's sickbay had made caring for the wounded difficult at best, and another four of Calloway's people had died from their injuries…wounds they'd have easily survived if the required treatment facilities had been available.

"But sir, there's no reason for you to stay behind. Come down now. We'll wait for you." Carp was distraught, his voice pleading with his doomed commander.

"I have a job to do, ensign. Are you going to make it harder on me with your insubordination?" He hated coming down hard on Carp. He really liked the kid. Maybe, he thought, Carp will actually get out of this and have a shot at a real future. Maybe. "Now follow my orders, Ensign Carp."

"Yes, sir." Carp's voice was despondent…he was defeated. He didn't have it in him to disobey Calloway's orders. "Launching now, sir."

Raptor shook as the magnetic catapult launched her last functional lifeboat. Calloway was now alone on board, and his last means of potential escape was gone. He was committed to his plan, but now he felt a wave of fear and uncertainty. It was one thing to face grave danger, but Calloway was past that now. His last, fleeting chance at survival was gone. He was a dead man living a few final moments of borrowed time.

He fought the urge to call Carp and order the lifeboat to come back. He knew that wasn't an option…once launched, the escape craft didn't have the capability to dock again. Still, he could feel the panic building inside him, and it took all his will to fight it. Finally, grimly, he forced back the fear. He had a job to do and, by God, he was going to do it.

"Raptor Control…" Riley's voice was soft but steady. He had regained his composure. "…it's just you and me now."

"Yes, Captain Calloway. The lifeboats are safely away." The AI's voice was not entirely unemotional. It understood the situation, and it modified its audio output accordingly. "Now what would you like me to do?"

Calloway paused. He knew what he had planned, but that didn't make it any easier to actually do it. He'd ordered the lifeboats to run silent, and that meant their only velocity was that of Raptor, modified by the force imparted by the launch catapults. Firing their thrusters would be like sending out a signal flare at this range, and their only hope for survival was to remain undetected. Calloway was going to give them the diversion they needed. He was going to give them a chance to survive.

"Prepare to exert full thrust. Calculate optimal vector toward enemy ship." Raptor still had considerable velocity heading away from Adelaide. The thrust Calloway was planning would only modify that slightly, but it would put distance between Raptor and her lifeboats - the escape pods would continue on the original, unchanged vector.

"We have completed partial repairs to the engines, captain, however full thrust at this point would be extremely dangerous."

Calloway smiled grimly. Things were way past caution now. "Yes, I understand. Please execute nonetheless." He hesitated for a few seconds then added, "And please deactivate all reactor safety systems."

"In our present condition, at 100% capacity, a reactor failure is a virtual certainty." The AI modified its tone yet again, expressing extreme concern. "Without the failsafe systems operational, a thermonuclear explosion will be unavoidable."

"Yes, my friend." Calloway's thoughts were drifting, but he remained steadfast. "That is exactly what I want." The massive output of energy when Raptor exploded might…just might… provide the cover the lifeboats needed to remain undetected.

"Understood, captain." A few seconds of silence, then: "All systems are prepared, Captain Calloway." The AI would obey Calloway's commands, but in its processing core it was experiencing unfamiliar sensations. Its voice was steady – it was not human, and its auditory systems were not connected directly to the status of its primary thought routines. The quasi-sentient AI units were not true beings, but they were more than just computers. The system's loyalty to Calloway was absolute…it would do whatever he commanded and sacrifice itself in any way necessary for the mission or the preservation of the crew. But it did feel an urge for self-preservation. It was afraid.

Calloway looked around the battered wreckage of the Raptor's bridge, now empty save for himself. His mind wandered down the corridors of the vessel, silent and abandoned. He thought about his parents back on Terra Nova, and he felt a wave of guilt when his imagined his mother reading the notice from the navy. He'd sent those letters too many times, to too many loved ones. It is with my deepest regret that I must inform you of the death of…

He looked out at the bridge one last time, though his eyes were not seeing the battered control center…they were lost in time, imagining things and people long gone. Finally, he took a deep breath. "Engage."

Raptor's reactor roared into full operation, feeding power directly to the straining, tortured engines. Calloway was pushed back into his chair as Raptor thrusted at nearly 8g. It was nowhere near the maximum normal output, but it was all she could coax from her savaged engines.

The Raptor's captain lay in his chair, struggling to breath under the heavy pressure. Without the drugs and a properly

functioning acceleration couch, 8g was a lot of pressure to withstand. He lay there in a dream, his thoughts drifting, imagining
things he hadn't thought of in years.

Raptor's systems held for 93 seconds. It wasn't long, but it
was enough…enough to get her away from the lifeboats. When
the containment vessel in the reactor finally blew, AS Raptor
performed her final duty. For a few seconds she became a miniature sun, and with her destruction…and the death of her captain…she bought her crew a chance, however slim, of survival.

There was a white haze in front of Clarkson's eyes. He was
groggy, confused…and his head ached like someone had driven
a spike through it. He tried to get up, but his legs wouldn't
move. He eased himself back down and took a deep breath.
Slowly, steadily, the disorientation faded. The haziness pulled
away, leaving only the late afternoon sun in the sky.

At first he couldn't remember anything, but then he realized
where he was. He reached around frantically, trying to find his
rifle. He expected the enemy to be on him any second, but
finally he realized he was alone. The trench had been virtually
obliterated, and he was half-buried in the coarse brown Adelaide
sand.

He tried to pull his legs free, but there was too much weight.
He leaned over and started shoveling the dirt with his hands, and
finally he managed to claw his way out. There were bodies lying
half-buried all along the trench line…the bodies of his troops.
He stumbled to his feet and looked around for survivors, but he
didn't find any. Then he remembered – his people had carried
back their wounded when they retreated.

"Clarkson to platoon…Clarkson to platoon." He spoke into
the comlink, but all he could hear was static. "This is Sergeant
Clarkson calling any Alliance personnel." Still nothing. He
wondered if his comlink was damaged…or if there was just no
one left to answer.

He climbed up and looked out over the remains of the
trench. The field the enemy had approached over was empty…
all except for the bodies of the few attackers his troops had

managed to take down. He climbed up and out of the trench, sliding back down a few times before he managed to get a foothold and hoist himself out. His head was pounding, but he ignored it. He had a quest now…he was going to see who this enemy was.

He walked across the field, stopping every few steps to scan the horizon. Nothing. He was alone. The ground all around the trench line was torn to shreds…mostly the work of the enemy's cluster bomb weapon. Once he got out of the immediate area, the ground was in better shape, although there were craters all around where the militia's mortars had impacted, largely ineffectively.

Clarkson stumbled across the pockmarked field. He was weak and his throat burned with thirst, but he pushed himself forward. His SAW teams had taken down several of the enemy troops about half a klick from the trench line, and he walked out in that direction. He could see them lying just ahead in the dusky light, their bodies shattered by the heavy weapons fire.

He looked down as he reached them, and he froze in stunned silence. Then he dropped to his knees, hands furiously grabbing at enemy body parts, examining them closely. No, he thought, not body parts…these aren't soldiers at all – they're robots.

"What the hell?" Clarkson was talking to himself as he continued pawing through the debris. "Who sent these…things… here?" Clarkson was no expert on robotics, but he knew that none of the Superpowers had ever managed to produce automated soldiers that could replace humans. The AIs the Marines used were useful tools, but in the end it was the men and women that mattered.

Naval ships were often controlled by their sophisticated computer systems, especially when their crews were being crushed into semi-consciousness by the g forces experienced in battle. But even then, the strategies and overall guidance was in the hands of human officers.

On the ground, no robot constructed had ever been able to match the fluidity of movement and the effectiveness of human reflexes and instincts. A robot could be tougher or move faster, but one had never matched a well-trained human as a warrior. Until now.

Clarkson had seen these things in action. The way they moved, the smoothness of their maneuvers…they were the equal at least of trained human soldiers, and maybe better. And their equipment and technology was like nothing Clarkson had ever seen. He sat on the ground, surrounded by the wreckage of those few of the enemy warriors his troops had managed to take down. The sun was fading, but it was still hot, and his parched throat burned with thirst. His grimy, sweat-soaked body ached and his head was pounding. You've got to get up, he thought. You have to report this.

He struggled to his feet and turned to walk back toward the trench. He had no idea where to go – he didn't know where the battle had progressed after the enemy had pierced the defensive line. Maybe everyone was dead already…maybe each tortured step he took was in vain. But he had to try.

He stopped and looked back one last time, remembering the sight of those monsters marching across the field toward his position. A shiver took him despite the heat, and he closed his eyes and wondered – how are we going to fight these things?

"I want that alignment checked again, lieutenant." Captain Jacobs was tense. The refractor satellite had been Captain Calloway's idea, and it was a brilliant one. Positioned with line of sight to both Adelaide and Hornet, it was really just a large lens, angling direct laser transmissions from the planet to Jacob's concealed ship. Hornet was still running silent, hiding on the far side of Adelaide's moon. The satellite itself ran on very little power, and it repositioned itself with small jets of compressed air that were almost undetectable to scanners.

Jacobs knew that both Raptor and Stingray were gone, and he was dealing with a bad case of survivor's guilt. If all three ships had fought, and he had just been luckier, he could have dealt with that…such were the fortunes of war. But Hornet had been hiding while their comrades were out there fighting and dying. It was a hard pill for an officer like Jacobs to swallow. He poured his frustrations into doing the job he was given. He was there to transmit as much information back up the chain to the high command, and he was going to see it done no matter what.

"Refraction alignment checks out, sir." Lieutenant Mink was a little exasperated, but she was an experienced enough officer not to let it show. She'd checked the alignment three times in the last hour…and that was on top of the fact that the AI was monitoring it in real time. But she knew why the captain was being so relentless, and she understood. If the alignment was off by even a fraction of a degree, any messages from Adelaide would miss Hornet entirely.

They hadn't received a transmission in almost a day, and everyone's nerves were on edge. Adelaide had managed to send some data on the enemy ground forces, but nothing very detailed. The fighting had been going very badly, and no one knew how long the planet's defenders could hold out. They had retreated from their prepared defensive lines and were getting ready to mount a final defense of the shelters. That was the last Hornet had heard from the planet.

Jacobs zipped his jumpsuit all the way up, but he still shivered. It was cold on Hornet's bridge. He'd ordered the ship's reactor shut down entirely, and the life support and other vital functions were running at minimum settings using battery power. He was going to do everything possible to keep Hornet undetected.

"Sir!" Lieutenant Mink turned toward the captain. Her voice was high pitched, excited. "We're getting a transmission from Adelaide!"

"Very well, lieutenant." Jacobs felt the same excitement, but he didn't show it. His voice was calm and steady. "Relay to my screen, and retransmit immediately to Commnet."

"Yes, sir." Mink regained her composure. "On your screen now, captain." A brief pause, then: "Transmission to Commnet complete, sir."

Jacobs looked down at the screen, reading the reports. The news was grim. Adelaide's militia had been shattered. There were no reliable casualty reports, but best estimates indicated loss rates in excess of 80%. The survivors had fallen back to the shelters with the enemy in pursuit.

Jacobs looked up from the screen for a moment. It was the same story they'd been hearing since all of this began, but this time on the ground. An overwhelmingly powerful enemy with weapons and equipment beyond anything the Alliance possessed. Any hope that the enemy's advantage would be restricted to space combat had been dashed.

He glanced back at the reports. There was more data on the enemy ground forces. Finally, some good news, he thought. A militia sergeant had managed to escape from behind enemy lines, and he brought back a report and some video on the attackers. Jacobs read on, and he soon decided the news wasn't so good after all. My God, he thought, the high command has to have this information.

"Lieutenant Mink, retransmit this report to Commnet." He was still staring at his screen as he spoke. "I want redundant drones sent from the station." He paused and took a deep breath. "This information must reach Admiral Garret no matter what."

"Yes, sir. Transmitting again now."

Jacobs looked up again from the report on his screen and wondered about this sergeant. His information didn't say if he'd made it back or just gotten off a communication. He didn't know if the man was dead or alive, but he was pretty sure this new war had its first genuine hero.

Chapter 11

AS Cambrai
Approaching Planet Farpoint
Epsilon Fornacis System

Cain stood on Cambrai's observation deck, staring out at Farpoint. From this distance, the planet was a magnificent blue and white disk floating in the blackness. He was thinking quietly and, for once, not about battle or tactics. *How many times have I looked out at something like this without giving it a second thought?* It was easy to overlook the staggering beauty of space, especially when you were rushing from one desperate battle to another. One day, he thought sadly, maybe I'll have time to see – to really see – some of the wonders of this universe. "Someday," he muttered to himself. "But not today."

Erik was troubled. It had been bothering him more noticeably lately, but when he'd really started to think about it he realized it had been there for a long time. A growing weariness, a disillusionment. He had always been a fighter, and he'd be one until that bullet with his name on it finally found its mark. But it was different now. Never a teary-eyed optimist, he'd still managed to believe that when he climbed into his armor and hit dirt for yet another battle he was fighting for some better future. Now, however, that belief was fading. That future always seemed to be another maelstrom, another war…more death and suffering, more waste. Duty had become obligation…obligation to his comrades, to the colonists he defended, to all those Marines who'd remained behind on one of those many battlefields. He'd do what was expected of him, what was necessary. But inside there was a growing emptiness.

He had accepted Admiral West's invitation to ride aboard

Cambrai. His inclination, as always, was to stay close to the troops, but this time he decided he would be extraneous at best. Colonel Teller was more than capable of running his brigade, and Cain's presence on one of the transports could only undermine his authority. Erik wasn't here to do Teller's job or to give the impression he didn't trust the colonel. His purpose was to get a firsthand look at what was going on and to make strategic decisions on the spot.

He had known Erica West for years. She'd commanded one of the big Gettysburg class transports that carried then-Major Cain's battalion on several campaigns. She was a gifted tactician, though her years commanding troopships had threatened to set back her advancement as a combat commander. That is until Augustus Garret got a good look at her. Garret had a great nose for finding talent, especially when it was a bit unorthodox, and he put West on the fast track, leapfrogging her over a dozen officers with more seniority.

After the rebellions, he put her in command of the newly-organized Third Fleet, jumping her once again over a number of her colleagues. But Garret was sure of her ability...and her loyalty too, and that had become just as important a consideration. Since he had been kidnapped by Alliance Intelligence, Garret had developed a healthy level of suspicion – some close to him called it paranoia – and he was not about to give a fleet command to anyone he wasn't 100% sure about.

Unfortunately, Third Fleet had been put together from the scraps left after Garret organized First and Second Fleets. Its ships were older and, put together from whatever was available, its battle order was less cohesive. Cambrai was the only capital ship on the OB. She was the oldest battleship still in service... and she had been for some time. Transferred to the Strategic Reserve after the war, she'd been seized by Alliance Intelligence along with the other mothballed ships. Because of her age she'd been slated to be manned last, and she spent the entire rebellion in drydock waiting for a crew that never came. That had been her salvation – Garret's forces hunted down the other rogue ships, destroying them all in a bloody campaign. Afterward, he was grateful to find Cambrai still operational, and he ordered her recommissioned at once to help plug a hole in his battered fleet roster.

Stuck at Armstrong for the foreseeable future, with Compton tied down at Wolf 359, Garret had chosen West to lead an expedition that might very well turn into a heavy fight. She was shocked when he told her; she knew he had confidence in her, but she'd had no idea how much. Erik knew she was a little overwhelmed at the size of her new command and the uncertainty of the mission, but from what he could tell as a passenger, she had her people working like a finely tuned machine.

Cain took one last look through the observation window. A meter high and three meters long, the hyper-polycarbonate panel was a luxury not to be found on more modern vessels. Though the material itself was as strong as reinforced plasti-steel, the seams connecting it to the hull were a weak spot. Newer ships had dispensed with the observation decks, choosing greater strength over aesthetics. The beauty of space sacrificed to utility again, Cain thought wistfully, though he couldn't argue with the logic. Perhaps one day men would spend more time stargazing and less trying to kill each other but, he thought again sadly, that day was not today.

He turned and walked slowly toward the hatch. He'd checked with Teller earlier, and everything was under control on the transports. He really didn't have anything to do. He'd already reviewed all the new intel…twice. They'd lost two more colonies on the Rim. The report from Barrow was sketchier even than that from Newton, but they'd gotten excellent data from Wellington before the attackers took out the Commnet station. It was more of the same – overwhelmingly powerful weapons, missiles moving with unprecedented acceleration. It was looking less and less likely that this was some sort of ruse. Cain had spent a considerable amount of time trying to imagine comparably advanced ground weapons, but with no hard data it was a pointless exercise in science fiction.

The hatch slid open as he stepped out into the corridor. He turned toward his quarters then changed his mind and walked the other way, toward the gym. Might as well keep myself in shape, he thought. Even with the rejuv treatments, he didn't have the body of an 18 year old anymore. The years of constant stress and wounds were starting to take a toll in spite of modern medicine's best efforts. The stiffness he felt each morning told him that much.

He was about to enter the lift when his earpiece buzzed briefly. "General Cain…Admiral West here." Her voice was tense, edgy. "We've received another transmission. I think we should go over it. My conference room…ten minutes?"

"Yes, Admiral…that will be fine." Cain had to force back a sigh. It was bad news…almost certainly. The predictability of that was getting tiresome. "I'm on my way. Cain out." He flipped off the link and then he did sigh. Loudly.

The steward filled a glass with water from a small pitcher and set it on the table in front of Cain. He walked around the table and did the same for the admiral then he stood at attention. "Is there anything else, Admiral West?"

"No, that will be all, Crewman Smalls. Dismissed." Enlisted personnel of the lowest rank on a naval vessel were designated simply as crewman. In the old wet navy Smalls would have had been called seaman, but the sea had nothing to do with interstellar fleets, and spaceman had seemed a bit silly to the founding officers of the service. Non-commissioned personnel tended to advance to various Specialist and Technician grades that defined both their rank and their area of expertise. A modern spaceship just didn't need a lot of low-skilled crew. There were bots to swab the decks and load supplies.

Admiral West waited for the hatch to close behind Smalls. "Thank you for rushing right up here, Erik." She was a spit and polish type, quite unlike Cain in that regard, and she sat bolt upright in her chair. "There's been another attack."

Cain didn't look surprised. He'd just taken a drink, and he put the glass down in front of him. "I don't suppose that should come as a shock now, should it?" He leaned back in his chair and looked across the table. "So what are the grisly details?"

"It's Adelaide."

Erik looked back, and for the first time there was a hint of surprise on his face. "What do we know? They must have put up a fight, at least." The first three worlds attacked were undeniably soft targets, new colonies with no defensive capabilities to speak of. But Adelaide was different. "Cooper Brown commands the local forces there. I don't know him well, but I remember him from Carson's World." Cain paused, trying to picture Brown's appearance. He came up blank. When you fought in powered armor you got to know people without seeing their faces much. "He's a fighter."

West looked across the table, her face somber. "The 18th Squadron was also there." Her eyes drifted downward, looking at the table. "Admiral Garret ordered them to scout forward, and they ran into the enemy attack force near Adelaide."

She closed her eyes, only for an instant longer than a blink, but Cain noticed, and he understood. "All lost?"

West looked up, her eyes finding Cain's. "Yes. We presume so, though we only got two Delta-Z transmissions." She looked across the table at him, her expression pained. "The third ship..." She paused, trying to recall the vessel's name. "... the Hornet...she must have been destroyed so quickly the crew never got their final transmission out." West took a deep breath and continued. "But the squadron sent up solid intel before they were wiped out. We have much more reliable information now." She took another breath, exhaling hard this time. "And it's not good, Erik."

Cain hadn't been expecting any good news – he'd already pretty much written off the theory that the advanced technology was a hoax, and it looked like West was about to confirm his conclusions. "Do I look like a man who is expecting good news?" He managed a weak smile.

West let out a short laugh. "No, I don't suppose you do." Her levity quickly faded. "Anyway, we can now confirm a number of the things originally reported by the Northstar." She ran her hands over a large touchscreen built into the table. "The enemy missiles are indeed capable of producing thrust levels in excess of 200g." She briefly glanced up from the screen to look at Cain. "You can imagine the implications of this not just in terms of ordnance closing faster but also with regard to maneuverability. These missiles are able to execute vector changes much more quickly than our own. I hesitate to venture a guess on the numerical superiority we would need to have a chance of prevailing in any missile exchange."

Cain was silent for a few seconds. While he understood the problem and empathized with the naval officers who were going to have to deal with it, he couldn't keep himself from wondering what implications this new technology had regarding ground combat. Whatever those were, they were going to be his problem. His…and Holm's and Jax's and the rest of the Marines'. "How about the warhead yields?"

"A good portion of them were in the 3-7 gigaton range. Again, the same as Northstar originally reported." There was no surprise in her voice; neither she nor Cain had expected anything different.

"Antimatter." Cain was not a physicist, but six years of education during basic training plus all the courses at the Academy had given him enough of working knowledge to understand the potential power of antimatter weapons and drives.

West nodded. "It's the only thing that can possibly explain those thrust capacities. Not to mention the warhead yields." Her expression brightened slightly. "There is some good news as well…or at least potentially good."

Cain looked across the table expectantly. "Well, we could certainly use some. What is it?"

"There were two waves of missiles, and the second group exhibited sharply lower thrust rates." She paused, trying to decide how much of her conjecture she should share. "This is pure guesswork, but maybe they have a limited supply of the better weapons…the antimatter ones."

Cain nodded slightly, but he didn't answer right away. What she said made sense…antimatter was difficult to produce and store, and it was highly plausible that these ships only carried a certain amount. But his training, like West's, had repeatedly warned against relying on wild guesses. They needed hard data, and a lot more of it, before they could even begin to guess how much antimatter-powered weaponry these ships carried.

West looked at Cain, reading his mind. "I know, I know. I'm taking a leap here. But we have so little to go on, Erik. I'm afraid we're going to have to rely on our gut instincts in this fight."

Cain nodded slightly, but he was silent. He was looking across the table at West, but he wasn't seeing her – his mind was elsewhere.

West sat quietly for a minute, but when Cain remained lost in thought she spoke softly. "What is it, Erik?" She watched him for a few seconds, but when he didn't respond she added, "What are you thinking about?"

He hesitated another few seconds before his focus returned to her. "I was just wondering what kinds of ground capabilities these attackers are likely to have." He paused, but his eyes remained fixed on hers. "Whatever they are, I'm going to have to figure how to meet them."

"Yes." West spoke slowly, softly. "At least we have some intel on the space combat systems we're likely to face. We're totally blind on their ground forces." She leaned back in her chair, but her gaze didn't waver from his. There was something else on his mind; she was certain. "There's more, isn't there Erik?"

Cain shifted in his chair and took a deep breath. He stared at her wordlessly for half a minute before he said anything. "I was just thinking…" His voice was soft and calm, but there was an undercurrent there too. Concern, worry…maybe even fear. "It's looking like these weapons are real, and I have a hard time buying the fact that one of the Superpowers made this kind of advance in total secrecy."

She could see it in his eyes and hear it in his voice. He was afraid…and that scared her more than anything she'd seen in a career full of combat and strife. "No." She forced back a shiver. She was a veteran admiral, and she wasn't going to let herself be overcome by fear. But she'd never seen Cain so nervous. "I can't imagine how any of them could have managed that."

Cain looked right at her, his blue eyes wide open. "That leaves us with one other question." He sat frozen, barely even blinking. "Who the hell are these guys?"

Chapter 12

Western Alliance Intelligence Directorate HQ
Wash-Balt Metroplex, Earth

Gavin Stark sat behind his desk in near darkness, the only light in the room coming through the windows from the nearby towers. There was a glass full of very expensive Scotch sitting untouched next to him. He stared out at the Washbalt skyline, but he wasn't really seeing anything. His mind was focused on his recent frustrations, and his thoughts were dark.

The rebellions had turned into a complete disaster for Stark. It was bad enough to be forced into accepting the Confederation Agreement, but he had also seen all his carefully assembled military assets destroyed. The Marines had beaten off all his strike forces, despite being surprised and low on supplies. He'd underestimated those damnable Marines again, and he'd paid the price for his arrogance. Now the Corps was less accountable than ever before, though at least its power and combat readiness were reduced. The Marines would have their hands full protecting the Alliance colonies from the other Powers. Stark would have time to prepare before they became a major threat to him again.

Even worse than the situation with the Corps, Augustus Garret had aggressively hunted down and destroyed every ship Stark had managed to seize from the Strategic Reserve. Millions of tons of warships were destroyed and all the crews Stark had carefully assembled were wiped out. Garret had refused any surrenders or negotiated agreements…he'd outright forbidden any communications at all with the target vessels. Stark's kidnapping plan had backfired, and he'd turned the naval commander into a blood enemy and a raging paranoid. Augustus Garret had become more dangerous than ever, and now he was unpredictable as well. But just like the Marines, Garret's navy was struggling to cover its basic defensive obligations with its remaining force. Augustus Garret hated Stark, but he didn't have the time or resources to do anything about it right now. Again, Stark had time.

The Garret kidnapping had remained a secret at least, the admiral no more willing than Stark to publicize what he considered embarrassing carelessness on his own part. Garret had discussed the matter with General Holm and Admiral Compton, and they all agreed...without proof he'd just look like a madman making wild accusations.

However the loss of so many warships couldn't be hidden, and Stark had to answer a lot of questions from the highest levels. Only his massive storehouse of dirty secrets – and his willingness to utilize targeted assassinations – had enabled him to survive as head of Alliance Intelligence. One Senator in particular, who'd been determined to see Stark removed from his post and prosecuted, had gone missing without a trace. Stark smiled when he thought about the pompous windbag. No one was going to find the fool; that much he knew for sure.

But Gavin Stark wasn't one to brood over dashed hopes. He still had a number of plans, and he was determined to see them to fruition. But now he had another problem. Something was going on out on the Rim, and Stark had absolutely no idea what. Whichever power was attacking Alliance frontier worlds, Stark's organization was completely in the dark. How, he wondered, was it possible for one of the Superpowers to take such a quantum leap in technology without his people even hearing about it? He had spies and double agents everywhere...it just couldn't be.

Yet the reality was unavoidable. Sol was far back from the frontier worlds the enemy was attacking, and even Commnet took weeks to get a transmission through. But it was clear that the Alliance had a full-fledged emergency on its hands. Stark had to find out what was happening, and he had to do it immediately. But, for the first time in a very long time, Gavin Stark didn't know what to do. He was low on reliable agents, at least at the highest level. Jack Dutton had been his mentor and closest confidante, but the ancient spymaster had finally lost his long battle with age. Stark missed the old man's council and friendship even more than he'd expected. He was alone now, in a way he'd never imagined.

Rafael Samuels had proven to be a useful addition to the Directorate, despite the failure to bring down the Marine Corps. But he was off in the Dakota Foothills, managing the development of Plan C. That was far too important to interrupt. Plan C was the future...Stark wasn't going to allow anything to interfere with that. It would be his final revenge on those accursed Marines...and it would give him the tools he needed to seize total power.

Alex Linden had been his closest ally since Dutton's death, but she'd been off-planet for more than six months, trying to get intel on the restructured Marine Corps and navy. Alex was the sister of Sarah Linden, chief of staff of the Marine hospital on Armstrong...and the longtime lover of Erik Cain. Sarah believed her sister had died as a child, and Stark had planned to use a surprise reunion to get Alex into the inner circle of the Corps. It was a perfect setup for espionage, save for one inconvenient fact. Alex had run into Erik Cain on Carson's World during the war and, with her tremendous resemblance to Sarah, he was sure to remember. Stark thought of Cain as a stubborn, pain-in-the-ass jarhead, but he knew the Marine wasn't stupid. He had to be patient and wait for the right time to send Alex in. The time would come...indeed, he thought, it may have come already. It appeared Erik Cain was heading out to the Rim to deal with the mysterious attacks. With Cain gone, there was nothing to stop Alex from making contact with her sister...and then she would not only sabotage the Marine Corps...she would be in position to rid him once and for all of Erik Cain.

Rodger Burke was also deeply involved in Plan C. He was Number Seven on the Directorate, but Stark had promised him a position in the top three if he successfully shepherded his section of the plan to completion. He'd anxiously accepted, even though it meant virtual exile from Earth for years to come.

There were vacant Seats as well. Several Directorate members had made moves against Stark when he was at his weakest. But even with all his problems, he was too clever to fall into their traps, and three of the conspirators met with very unpleasant ends.

With his most capable people committed elsewhere and the Directorate otherwise nearly vacant, Stark was forced to look to other means to investigate this new situation. He still had Troy Warren, though Warren wasn't really a spy. An enormously successful Corporate Magnate, he'd bought his way onto the Directorate. Still, Stark trusted him as much as he trusted anyone, and there was no question that Warren was smart. Stark would find a way to use him.

He had to figure out which power was launching the attacks, and he had to do it now. He'd been thinking about it for days, and his mind kept working its way back to the CAC. They must have found something themselves on Carson's World, he thought. Stark couldn't imagine any other way for one of the Superpowers to leapfrog so far in technology so quickly.

He suspected Li An was involved. She had called a meeting of representatives from the RIC, the empire, and the Caliphate. She thought she'd kept the whole thing under wraps, but Stark had an informant there...one she would never have anticipated.

Mahmoud Al'Karesh was the Chairman of State Security for the Caliphate and a relative of the Caliph himself. He was also the mastermind behind a 30 year campaign of graft and theft so extensive that the Caliph would have his head if the true extent of it was ever discovered. Unfortunately for Al'Karesh, Gavin Stark had quite a little file on his escapades...enough to blackmail the Caliphate security chief into working for Stark, at least as an informant. Stark had refrained from asking Al'Karesh to spy on his own nation...he just wanted to know what the Caliphate knew about the other powers. And that included Li An's secret little meeting.

He hated the little midget, as he called her, but he had to admit that she was the closest thing he had to a rival. Brilliant, cunning, and as reptilian as he was, Li An was the enemy he

worried about most. If anyone slipped alien technology out
of Epsilon Eridani under his nose, it was probably Li An. And
now she was trying to persuade the other Powers to mobilize on
the Alliance's borders. The more he considered it, the more he
convinced himself she was behind the whole thing.

He reached out for the com unit and pushed the button for
his assistant's line. "Jamie, call Peter Hillman. Get him in here
immediately." Hillman was the chief of intelligence gathering
on the CAC.

"Yes, sir." Like all of Stark's assistants, Jamie Larken never
questioned the chief's orders; she just carried them out. The
fact that it was well past midnight meant nothing to Stark. Intelligence was a 24/7 business, and he expected his people to be on
the job whenever he needed them.

Stark leaned back and looked out over the skyline. "I don't
know what you're up to Li An, but I'm going to find out if I
have to burn every asset I have in Hong Kong."

General Isaac Merrick walked down the hall, his boots echo-
ing loudly off the polished marble floor. His uniform was impeccable – perfectly tailored and neatly pressed. It was the only
thing in his life that was as it should be. Merrick had been the
federal commander on Arcadia, charged with using any means
necessary to defeat the revolution and return the planet to its
status as an obedient colony. He'd fought a war and almost won,
but he'd refused to inflict institutionalized atrocities against the
rebels, as federal commanders had done on other worlds. He
was a soldier, not a butcher, and he knew he would make the
same choices all over again.

Unfortunately, in the wake of an embarrassing defeat, Alliance Gov looked for scapegoats, and Merrick's refusal to tor-
ture and murder civilians had been recast as incompetence and
weakness. There were even whispers that he had sympathized
with the rebels. Ironically, that had not been the case at all when
he'd been fighting on Arcadia, but in the aftermath of the conflict he'd come to look at things in ways he never had before....
thoughts that turned his entire way of life upside down and

forced him to question everything he believed.

His family was very influential, and they had expended the money and political capital necessary to save him from any serious problems. He kept his rank and avoided any official reprimand, but he knew he'd never again see a serious command or meaningful assignment. His career, both in the army and in politics, was, for all intents and purposes, over. He could remain a well-dressed figurehead, carrying some made up title and walking the halls of one army base after another, or he could retire and live comfortably and quietly on his family's resources. Or he could emigrate.

That last option was unthinkable to a member of the Political Class, especially one from a family as highly placed as Merrick's. But Isaac Merrick was thinking about it nevertheless...he was thinking about it very seriously.

He'd been unsettled since his return to Earth. At first he thought it was stress from dealing with the intense criticism, but all of that had passed by now, and he was as restless as ever. He'd seen things on Arcadia that had challenged everything he'd believed all his life. He had been disgusted with the casual brutality and ineptitude of many of his officers...all Political Academy graduates and members of the privileged class. He began to have serious questions about the system that created such people. At the same time he'd been impressed with many of the colonists he fought against. They'd had their share of closed-minded fools too, but their ranks produced some truly extraordinary people.

Merrick truly mourned for Will Thompson. The enemy commander had proven to be a capable and honorable opponent. The news of his death at the Second Battle of Sander's Dale had been greeted with laughter and derision at federal headquarters...but not from Isaac Merrick. The federal commander in chief spent the hours after the battle alone, locked in the office of his mobile command center, paying silent tribute to his fallen counterpart.

Merrick had always considered the Cogs inferior...the descendants of the lowest levels of humanity. But William

Thompson had been born a Cog in one of the most notorious slums in the Alliance, and he had become a better man than any of Merrick's peers. The same was true of Kyle Warren and Gregory Sanders...they all had a strength of character that Merrick found to be quite rare among his colleagues.

He wasn't sure emigrating was even possible. His family would go along; he was sure of that much. He was an embarrassment to them now anyway. But would he be accepted anywhere? It had been barely a year since the end of the rebellions, and less than two since he'd been in the field as federal commander on Arcadia. Could the colonists overlook that fact so soon and allow him in as one of them?

He opened the door to his office and walked to the desk. A glance at his screen confirmed he had no messages. Apparently being a supernumerary figurehead didn't entail much actual work. He sat down in his chair and turned to face the window. Work...that was another issue. What would he do if he emigrated? He wasn't enjoying being useless on Earth; he didn't expect to appreciate it any more as a colonist. But his only trade was soldiering. Was it possible to somehow to be a part of the colonial military establishment so soon after he was their enemy? He couldn't go to Arcadia; he was sure of that much. It was too soon, and the wounds were too fresh. Maybe another world. But where?

The Marines and navy had selected Armstrong for their new joint headquarters. Both organizations were rebuilding and frantically trying to expand the facilities they needed to become independent of Earth-based supplies and manufacturing. They needed skilled personnel badly, and Merrick liked the idea of being part of something dynamic and growing.

He'd met Erik Cain on Arcadia, when he surrendered to Kyle Warren and the rebel forces. Cain's troops had turned the tide and saved the rebellion, but the Marine general had remained virtually silent, respectfully leaving the negotiations to Warren and his officers. They had exchanged only a few words, mostly polite pleasantries, but Merrick had a good impression of Cain. Perhaps he could work with him somehow. He knew the Marines would never make him one of their own, but maybe he could be a consultant or planner of some kind.

He looked out at the afternoon sun dancing off the pine trees. It was a beautiful day, early spring and just a little chilly. He sat there staring through the window, and the enormity of what he was considering hit him. Leaving Earth...it was almost inconceivable. Yet that is just what he was planning. He knew it would be a one way trip. Those who emigrated where rarely permitted to return, at least not for permanent residency. As a disgraced member of the Political Class, he almost certainly would not be allowed back. He'd be ostracized even more by his peers for his choice to leave Earth. If he went, he went for good.

He sat there for hours thinking as the dappled sunlight gave way to dusk and then to a clear, crisp, starlit night. Finally, he hoisted himself out of his chair, his joints and muscles stiff and aching from the long day spent sitting. His choice was made. He would go to Armstrong.

Chapter 13

1st Division HQ
Iron Gate Valley, North of Landing
Farpoint - Epsilon Fornacis III

It was a beautiful day, sunny with a gentle breeze. Men had colonized Farpoint because of the six warp gates in the Epsilon Fornacis system – the magnificent climate was just a bonus. Few worlds man had discovered offered the kind of paradise Farpoint did, and that made it easier to coax colonists out to what was then the very edge of the frontier. Several decades of expansion had pushed that line much farther out, to the extent that Farpoint was not really even a Rim world anymore. The changes in the map of occupied space had rendered the name obsolete and a little silly, but the locals wouldn't give it up.

With the practicality common to Rimworlders, the original settlers had unimaginatively named their first settlement Landing. Built on the site where the first colony ship hit ground, it had grown from a small cluster of huts into a true city, at least by colonial standards. Farpoint, with its half dozen transit points, had become the primary hub for new colonization efforts and commerce with the resource worlds on the frontier. And the navy base was the largest in two sectors, charged with the defense of the entire Rim.

Farpoint Base had once hosted an entire fleet supported by a reinforced brigade of Marines, but the gains made in the Third Frontier War had eliminated most enemy threats to the Rim. The Alliance outer colonies now bordered only unexplored space, and the forces stationed at Farpoint had been steadily reduced until only token contingents remained.

Now, however, the base hummed with activity once again.

Admiral West's Third Fleet had arrived and, if her second line
vessels were old and past their prime, they still represented the
largest force Farpoint had seen in a generation. Sections of the
station that had been long closed were now reopened, and Farpoint's extensive orbital defenses were fully active. The system's
massive scanning array was operating at full power, searching for
any incursion through one of the warp gates.

On the planet itself, the lush valley north of the capital was
now an armed camp. Colonel James Teller's 1st Brigade had
arrived with 3rd Fleet, and their encampment stretched over 10
square kilometers of rolling grasslands. In the center of this
small, bustling city, Erik Cain sat outside his headquarters structure, staring down at a large 'pad set on a folding table.

Cain had been having difficulty focusing on tasks with his
usual intensity. His mind wandered, often to things and people
he hadn't thought about for years. He was troubled, and it was
weighing heavily on him. His skills were still there, and his devotion to duty, but something of the motivation that had once
driven him was gone. He felt lost.

But now he was getting ready to send his Marines into
harm's way, and his thinking was razor sharp. Nothing was more
important to him than the lives of his men and women, and he
was grimly determined to do everything in his power to prepare
them for this new ordeal. He felt deep in his gut that many of
them wouldn't survive what was coming. Perhaps most. More
ghosts to haunt him in the night.

The 'pad displayed the map of local space on the Rim, with
large circles representing solar systems, connected by thin blue
lines denoting the warp connections that made transit between
them feasible. The whole thing looked like a bizarre glowing
spiderweb, but Cain saw it for what it truly was...a battlefield.

"Providence, Taylor's World, Cornwall, and Lancaster...
they're all along the approaches from enemy-occupied space."
Cain was pointing at the map as he spoke. "They could hit any
of them...maybe all of them." He looked up at his companion.
"Conventional tactics say we need to garrison them all."

James Teller glanced from the map to Cain and back down

again. "That means no more than a battalion on each...not if we're going to leave anything in reserve on Farpoint." Teller stared intently at the map, as if the situation would change if he looked hard enough. The circles representing solar systems were color-coded. Red for those that had already fallen to the enemy, orange for the four threatened worlds Cain had just discussed, blue for Farpoint, and yellow for everything else.

Cain didn't answer right away. He continued to stare at the map and, finally, he extended his finger toward one of the large orange circles. "Cornwall. That's where we need to be." He looked up at Teller. "They may hit everything, but I'd wager anything they definitely come at Cornwall. Look at the warp gate layout."

Teller looked down and scanned the 'pad. All the threatened systems had multiple warp gates, but other than Cornwall, they mostly led in circles, connecting to the other worlds right on the Rim. Cornwall was the most direct route into the heart of the Alliance...it was a primary target for any enemy bent on invasion. "Are you saying we leave the other worlds undefended and focus on Cornwall?" Teller glanced quickly back at the 'pad and then back up at Cain. "They can get to Farpoint without Cornwall, you know. Providence to Six Rings to Norris Station to Point Luck to Stanchion to Farpoint."

Cain took a deep breath and stared at the map. "Yes, but that route leads through four essentially uninhabited systems. And the trip between warp gates in Point Luck is over 30 light hours. It's a long way around, and if they go that way we'll have plenty or warning and a lot of useless real estate we can give up while we prepare a defense." He paused and took another breath. "But if they take Cornwall, they're two transits away from here on a direct line."

"What about the civilian populations?" Teller asked the question, but his voice was somber. He already knew the answer.

"There aren't many civilians on those worlds...and letting our forces get chopped up piecemeal isn't going to save one of them. We have no idea how large this invasion force is, but if we don't stop them somewhere out here, we'll be fighting them on Columbia and Arcadia and the other Core Worlds. Then you'll see civilian casualties." He hesitated for a few seconds. "I've already discussed this with Admiral West. We're going to concentrate our forces to defend Cornwall. Meanwhile, she's mobilized the extra transports and every civilian vessel we can get our hands on. We're going to evacuate the other planets."

Teller looked back at Cain, his expression doubtful. "You think we'll have time to get them all off?"

Cain sighed. "No. Probably not. But we'll get some of them. Maybe most of them...as I said, there are no large populations on those planets." He stared back at Teller. "And that's more than we'd do trying to mount hopeless defenses on all the threatened worlds." Cain hated the idea of leaving civilians undefended, no matter how small the population. It was a calculus of his profession he detested. But there was no choice. Dividing his troops to cover all four planets might make him feel better superficially...if he could work himself into enough denial. But he knew it would be futile in the end, and Erik Cain hated futility. If his men and women were going to fight and die against a vastly superior enemy, they were going to do it where their deaths might have some meaning. If they could get more data on the enemy and hold him up for a while they would help their brothers and sisters who would fight the next battle.

Teller didn't entirely agree, though he did see the cold logic in Cain's plan. But he knew his commanding officer well enough to be sure there was no point in trying to change his mind. Besides, Cain was just about the only person alive that John Teller trusted without reservation. "What do you want me to do, sir?"

Erica West sat in her office and stared down at the screen of the com unit, a stunned expression on her face. "You want me to do what?"

Erik Cain's face stared back at her on the small display. His expression was resolute. "You heard me the first time." He forced a grim smile. "I want you to pull your forces out of the system after you drop Teller's people on Cornwall."

"Erik, I need to mount a defense. I can't just give them the system." She stared back at him incredulously. "And I can't abandon your people there!"

"Erica, think for a minute." Cain was trying to be gently persuasive – he knew he'd react the same way to a similar request. "You know you can't win the battle, and if you fight it will be over in a couple days…if not hours." He paused for an instant, thinking of what he wanted to say. It wasn't easy telling a respected colleague she had no chance in a fight. "Their ships are faster, their weapons are longer-ranged. If you let yourself get sucked in you won't be able to get away. My people will be alone anyway, and we won't have Third Fleet waiting in the wings."

"I don't know, Erik. It doesn't seem right." Her voice was somber; she knew her fleet didn't have a real chance, especially not at Cornwall. At least at Farpoint they had the bombers and fixed defenses of the base and the enhanced detection grid. But in Cornwall it would just be her aging ships. She was realizing Cain was right, but she still couldn't reconcile herself to turning tail and leaving the Marines on their own.

Cain paused uncomfortably. After all these years he'd never gotten used to the small delay in ground to orbit communications. "Hear me out, Erica. I have a plan." He took a breath. "I want you to fight at Cornwall…just not on the enemy's terms."

West looked back with a confused expression on her face. "What do you have in mind, Erik?"

"Take a look at your map." He hesitated a few seconds, giving her time to pull up the information on her display. "Cornwall's system has three warp gates. The enemy will be coming through the one from the Banshee system. We'll be going in from Olympia." He glanced down at the map display then back at the com. "Take a look at the one from XR-3."

There was a considerable pause then West looked back up at the com. "But XR-3 is a dead end, and an empty one at that. There's not even an asteroid there, much less a planet. What could we possib…"

"But look where it is relative to Cornwall." No one had ever called Erik Cain a patient man. He'd started to interrupt almost immediately, but the communications lag had allowed West get out a few more words.

She stared down at the display again, her fingers moving to expand the view of the Cornwall system. She was confused for a few seconds, but then she realized what Cain was talking about. Warp gates were almost always located in the outer reaches of solar systems, far beyond the orbits of any planets. But the warp gate connecting Cornwall with XR-3 was an anomaly…it was less than 15 light minutes from the planet.

"You want me to hide in XR-3 and then bushwhack them." She smiled as she finally understood what Cain had in mind. "That's brilliant, Erik." She allowed herself a small chuckle and added, "I thought you were a ground-pounder. You after Admiral Garret's job now too?"

Cain returned the smile. "No, thank you. My own is quite enough. But this is an infantryman's plan. My people can hold out longer on the ground than your people can in space facing an enemy that can out-thrust and out-shoot you." A wicked smile crept onto his face. "If my people dig in, those bastards will have a hell of a time forcing us out, futuristic robots or not."

West's smile faded into a concerned look. "Erik, please tell me you're not planning to go down to the surface on Cornwall." When he didn't answer she continued, "Because General Holm would have a stroke if he knew you were even considering it."

Cain was still silent. He honestly didn't know what he was going to do. There was no justification for him leading those troops himself. He was the overall theater commander, and he knew Jax and the second half of the division would be embarking any day to reinforce him. He had responsibilities far beyond the tactical command on Cornwall. But he still wanted to go. Deep down he knew the mission was futile. They might gain intel, and they might slow the enemy down, but there was no way they were going to beat them. Not on Cornwall. And Erik Cain wasn't sure he had it in him to send thousands of his men and women to their deaths while he stayed behind. Not again.

He looked into the com, at Erica West's troubled expression, but all he said was, "Cain out."

Chapter 14

Kendall Peninsula
Just North of the Dover Archipelago
Planet Cornwall - Zeta Bootis B IX

Cornwall was an ocean planet. Less than 10% of its surface area was land, and much of the single major continent was covered with low-lying tidal marshes. The primary occupied area was a stretch along the mountainous east coast where a series of plateaus and rocky islands provided dry land for habitation. It was some of the most defensible ground James Teller had ever seen. His troops had turned the position into a series of interlocked strongpoints and heavy weapon emplacements. He wasn't sure they had a real chance in the battle about to begin, but he was damned sure they'd sell their lives dearly.

The high command on Armstrong had approved Cain's plan to concentrate his forces on Cornwall, leaving the other potential target planets virtually undefended. Admiral Garret ordered Erica West to pull her fleet back and wait…just as Cain had suggested. She was to ambush the enemy forces at her own discretion.

General Holm sent one other message. He ordered Erik Cain not to lead the forces on Cornwall directly, and he did it in terms so clear and incontrovertible that even Cain couldn't twist, interpret, or deliberately misunderstand the command. Holm had known Cain for a long time, and they were almost like father and son. There hadn't been a doubt in Holm's mind that his protégé would want to hit ground with those troops going in, but he wasn't going to allow it. Apart from his personal feelings, there was no way he could afford to lose Cain now, not facing a war they didn't even understand yet.

Holm was stuck on Armstrong, managing the mobilization effort and keeping an eye on the other Powers. The CAC and Caliphate were massing on the border, which was a nightmare scenario for the Alliance right now. Worse, there were signs the RIC was also moving forces forward. The Russian-Indian Confederation and the Alliance didn't have a lot of shared border, but the last thing Garret and Holm needed was more area to cover.

Cain had reluctantly obeyed Holm's order, but he'd pushed it to the limit, accompanying the expeditionary force to Cornwall's system and directing the landing from orbit. Finally, he boarded the fast attack ship Condor for the journey back to Farpoint, leaving Teller in command of the six battalions of crack Marines dug in on the planet.

Teller stood on a rocky bluff looking out over the jagged peninsula. Once the planet's main population center, it was now deserted except for his troops. Admiral West had used every civilian ship she could commandeer to evacuate the civilian population, at least all those she could cram into the space available. The action would save lives, and it also freed the Marines from worrying about defending civilians. They could focus solely on the battle at hand, which they knew was going to be a fight to the death.

They'd been on Cornwall for over a month, and Teller had begun to wonder if they had guessed wrong on the enemy's next move. But then he got the communication relayed from the warp gate scanners…enemy ships inbound, at least a dozen. Admiral West had seeded the space 1,000,000 kilometers out from the planet with scanner buoys, so Teller had several hours' warning before the enemy ships moved into orbit. His troops were suited up and in position before the first landing craft entered the atmosphere.

The enemy was vastly superior technologically, that much was certain. But they hadn't yet run into a force as large as Teller's, and they hadn't faced powered infantry either. They'd still have the edge in firepower, but not by the margins they'd enjoyed against the planetary militias. Maybe…just maybe,

Teller thought, we've got a chance.

He started down the path toward his command post. There were enemy landers coming down all over the peninsula and the adjacent archipelagoes. It was showtime.

Lieutenant Erin McDaniels watched the approaching enemy forces on her visor display. There were a lot of them - her people were going to have a hell of a fight on their hands. A tiny smile crept onto her lips as she watched. But we have a few surprises for them first, she thought.

"Enemy vanguard approaching initial targeting range, Lieutenant McDaniels." She'd instructed her AI to monitor the enemy's progress and make regular reports.

"Thank you, Mystic." Like most officers, McDaniels had named her virtual assistant. Enlisted personnel had AIs too, but they were basic models designed to help with suit operations and simple tasks. The officers' units were full-blown quasi-sentient units with considerable capabilities...and distinct personas as well. Hers was relatively straitlaced, generally just following her instructions without comment. Some of the other officers had units with more colorful personalities.

"Get the missile teams on the com, Mystic." McDaniels was in charge of a heavy weapons detachment. It was a regimental asset and a captain's billet, but 1st Brigade was stretched thin for officers, and she'd been bumped up from her platoon to take command.

"Yes, lieutenant." A brief pause. "You are on the comlink, lieutenant." Mystic's voice was female, fairly high-pitched. It could get a little annoying at times. McDaniels had been meaning to have the AI reprogram it, but she'd never gotten around to it.

"McDaniels to missile teams. Enemy forces approaching. All teams, lock on to your chosen targets and prepare to commence firing." The hyper-velocity missiles were going to come as a big surprise to these bastards, she thought. The militias they've been fighting didn't have anything remotely like them.

The HVMs were a new weapon, developed near the end of

the Third Frontier War. Powered by nanotech nuclear reactors, the launchers fired multiple warhead missiles at extremely high velocities. The Marines knew the attackers were hard to kill, and the HVMs were among the strongest and deadliest weapons they had to throw at an enemy.

She watched the blips on her display moving closer. The enemy first line was coming up over a ridge. She knew exactly where she wanted to catch them…just past the crest. "Missile teams…fire!"

She watched the weapons fire, her visor set on Mag 2. The HVMs left a glowing trail in the dusky darkness. She had four teams, and each of their missiles split into one primary and six secondary warheads. The entire line below the ridge erupted into a maelstrom, rock and debris flying everywhere amid the billowing flames of the detonations. The HVMs were great for ripping apart the landscape, and they tore huge chunks from the shattered ridge.

It was hard to get a read on how badly the enemy's first line was hurt, but she wasn't about to let up on the fire now. The HVMs had a short window of effectiveness before the enemy would be too close. "Missile teams reload." An unnecessary command, she knew. Her people were veterans, and they were already halfway through the reloading process. She cranked up her visor to Mag 10, trying to get a close look at the ridgeline, and she flipped the comlink to internal communications only. "Mystic, I want your analysis and a damage assessment as soon as possible."

"Yes, lieutenant. I am compiling data now." The AI's voice was a bit higher pitched than normal, showing some stress. It was all a construct of course…whatever the AI was "feeling" did not directly impact its auditory routines, as humans' fear or tension affected their voices. Mystic varied its voice and speech patterns in accordance with its analysis of McDaniels, and it had determined that the lieutenant responded better to a feeling of camaraderie in stressful situations. The AI responded by imitating a shared tension and fear in battle. Some officers preferred an AI that sounded like a rock no matter what was going on, but not McDaniels…at least not according to Mystic's analysis.

She flipped back to the open com. "Missile teams, fire!" Another round of warheads slammed into the ridgeline, plumes of flame and shattered rock rising against the darkening sky.

"Enemy casualties projected at 10-20." Mystic was reporting data as it became available. The AI was receiving input from all the scanning devices in the detachment and compiling its analysis as new information came in. "Attacking forces still advancing."

McDaniel's swallowed. That was a surprise…or maybe not. She'd picked her position carefully, and she was sure it would be an ideal killing zone. Any enemy she'd ever faced would have been annihilated. But these things were still coming.

"Autocannons, fire at will. Pick your targets and take them down." The enemy's lead elements were inside the minimum range of the HVMs, and her heavy auto cannons were the next line of defense. "Missile teams, continue firing." She had no idea how many enemy troops were still coming over that ridge, but she wasn't going to slack off anywhere.

"Incoming fire, lieutenant." Mystic announced the barrage an instant before McDaniels saw it on her display.

"Incoming!" She knew she didn't have to alert the detachment – when Mystic warned her, all of her troop were getting the same notification from their AIs. But it made her feel like she was doing something. She ducked her head down and waited, the sound of her heart beating loud in her ears…she knew what was coming.

She'd been worried about the enemy's cluster bomb weapon. The reports from Adelaide were far from complete, but the bombs had proven to be extremely effective against troops in entrenchments and fortified positions…just like the ones her force occupied now.

McDaniels had her speakers set to pump in the outside noise, and she heard the popping sounds the reports spoke of… the small explosions that broke the shells into dozens of tiny, but powerful, warheads. Her troops were positioned along a row of rocky foothills pockmarked with large outcroppings and small, natural fissures. It was virtually a natural trench line, constructed of solid rock. But the enemy warheads landed all over, falling into the gaps and behind the rock walls her troops were using for cover.

She had her comlink set to an open line, and she could hear the screams as her people were hit. The visor display rapidly updated her on status – Mystic was tied into the med systems of all her troopers' suits. It didn't take long to realize her people were getting torn apart. *The accuracy of that enemy weapon is uncanny*, she thought as another round began impacting all across her line.

"Mortar teams. Open fire…silence those batteries." She knew it was probably futile. From the intel she had, it didn't seem that mortar rounds hurt these guys much. But she had heavier ordnance than the line units, so she figured she might get lucky. Besides, she didn't have a better solution. She wished they had some airpower, but they hadn't had the time or transport capacity to bring ground-based air units to Cornwall…and with the fleet bugged out they didn't have any atmospheric craft tended from orbit either.

Her heavy autocannons were taking down enemy targets, but the incoming barrage was wreaking havoc on her crews' effectiveness. *We're hurting them*, she thought grimly, *but not enough*. She was going to have to pull back.

"Missile teams, cease firing and retire to secondary position. Autocannons, maintain fire." She breathed deeply, the oxygen-rich mixture of her suit's air helping her to maintain her alertness, holding back the growing fatigue. She was glad she had mostly veterans. There were few things harder on morale than part of a unit holding firm while the rest is retreating. But she couldn't lose her HVMs, and if she waited any longer she would.

The enemy was getting closer, and the cluster-bomb bombardment stopped. *They don't want to hit their own people*, she thought. Of course, she corrected herself, *they're not people at all…are they?*

She pulled her mag-rifle up and glanced over the lip of the rocky wall. Her heart was pounding in her chest and she could feel the droplets of sweat making their way down her bare back, despite the optimal temperature inside her armor. I've never been this scared, she thought, struggling to maintain her composure. "Those aren't people at all coming. They're machines." She spoke softly, inaudibly to herself. Mystic heard, of course, but the AI knew McDaniels was talking to herself and didn't respond.

McDaniels and her people had faced tough enemies before, but this was different. There was a relentlessness to these machines that was like nothing she'd seen before. A human enemy, even an elite veteran, had the same weaknesses and doubts you did. He might fight to the death, but he wasn't immune to fear. Even veteran units broke. They fatigued. They fell back. But these things just kept coming, even when half of their bodies were shot away.

She felt a jolt of adrenalin as one of the robots came into her field of fire, and it pushed the fear back momentarily. She opened up with her mag-rifle, firing on full auto, raking the thing. An appendage got torn off...she wasn't quite sure whether she should call it an arm. The things had four of them, whatever they were.

She saw that at least five of her Marines were also firing at the thing, and slowly they took it apart...piece by piece. Still it came forward, returning their fire and taking out two of her people. Finally, under the sustained fire of the Marines' nuclear-powered mag-rifles, the thing stopped moving. She didn't know if it was completely destroyed or not, but it was down and it wasn't shooting anymore. But at least six others were moving into her field of fire.

"Detachment, prepare to fall back. Autocannons move to secondary line. Everyone else, hold and provide covering fire." She wasn't sure how much covering fire would accomplish against these things...they didn't seem to pay attention to fire at all. I've got to give the autocannons a couple minutes, she thought...I can't lose them. She knew it was going to cost her casualties, but she had to salvage her heavy weapons. "Pick your targets, people." She took a deep breath. "We've got to hold them for two minutes." She focused her eyes forward and opened fire again. It was the longest two minutes of her life.

James Teller stood on a rocky bluff overlooking the sea. Enemy cluster bombs were beginning to drop near his position...close enough to get his attention, but not a real problem. Not yet. We've got to complete the withdrawal, he thought. Most of the brigade – what was left of it at least – was retreating to the offshore islands. The Scorpion Archipelago was even more defensible than the rocky coastal areas where they'd been fighting for the past four days.

His forces had been driven almost completely off the peninsula, though for the first time the enemy had been made to pay heavily for the ground they'd gained. A few of his units had even managed to launch locally successful counter-attacks, though the gains were short-lived. Overall the entire battle had been a fighting retreat. The Marines had bled the enemy, but they hadn't been able to stop them.

He knew he should have moved back long before – the command post had already been relocated to Blackrock Island, and he was 30 lightyears from his replacement. But he had two companies covering the retreat, and he just couldn't bring himself to leave with them still engaged. He figured General Cain would have scolded him and ordered him back to the command post, but then Cain wasn't there. Besides, he'd seen Cain in action and had a pretty good idea what the general would do in his situation. Teller was in charge and completely cut off from the chain of command...the decisions were his to make. And he wasn't leaving until his last two companies were on their way.

He looked down at the shore. Most of the barges had pushed off, headed for Skarn Island, 3 klicks out to sea. Skarn was the first island in the archipelago, and the most rugged. His reserve units had spent the last three days turning it into a virtual fortress. The retreating Marines would occupy all of the islands, but the big fight would be for Skarn. If they couldn't hold that, they didn't have much chance on the others.

"Companies A and C, this is Colonel Teller." He spoke

deliberatively and firmly but, in truth, he was a little shaken up by the capabilities of these enemy war machines. It was bad enough dealing with it in the field here and now, but the thought of the CAC or Caliphate fielding power like this across Alliance space was terrifying. "Begin withdrawal by odds and evens…100 meter intervals."

They'd already been badly hurt. He could tell that much from his tactical display. He couldn't even guess how many would make it down to the shoreline…probably not many. The bombardment was getting heavier…and closer…and he ducked behind a large rock outcropping.

Though they had been driven from position after position, his people had managed some successes too. They had inflicted heavy losses on the enemy, and they had collected massive amounts of data – video, scanner readings…even salvaged parts of destroyed robots. It would be invaluable to the high command in studying the enemy…assuming he could get it to them. But that was out of his hands. It all depended on Admiral West.

Teller knew the basics of the plan, but he had no idea if and when West would actually attack. For that matter, he had no idea what ships the enemy had in orbit and around the planet. The orbital scanners and satellites were the first things to go, and with them Teller lost his eyes.

It looked like the retreating companies had casualties over 50%, but at least they were close to the beach. With any luck they'd all be of the mainland in 20 minutes. "Keep it moving, Marines!" Teller was walking down the winding path to the shoreline as he shouted into the com. "I want everybody on the beach in ten minutes."

"Captain Wallace, commence firing." Teller had put mortars on six barges, turning them into makeshift gunboats. The mortars hadn't been very effective weapons against the enemy troops, but they did shake things up and churn the ground. Teller was just hoping to buy a few extra minutes to get his people offshore, and he figured some shell craters and smoke might help.

"Yes, sir." Wallace's response was nearly simultaneous with

the sounds of mortar rounds flying overhead.

A few seconds later the shells began hitting all along the enemy line. Teller knew they weren't taking out too many enemy troops, but knocking them over and tearing up the ground would be enough to let him get his rearguard out. He hoped.

Erica West lay strapped in her acceleration couch, the heavy polymer padding tight against her body. She was trying to stay focused, but at 20g it wasn't easy. The drugs strengthened the cell walls, increased blood flow to the head and extremities, and relaxed the muscles to prevent injury. They were also mildly hallucinogenic, an effect that was amplified by the high pressure.

West had bristled at every day spent hiding in the empty XR-3 system. She knew the Marines had to be catching hell on Cornwall, and she hated herself for abandoning them there. She was just following the agreed-upon battle plan, but that didn't make it any easier.

Now she was going to do something about it. She'd taken a chance by sending in probes to scout out the enemy deployments. She accelerated the drones in XR-3, cutting thrust just before they entered the warp gate. The tactic required extremely accurate coordinates to calculate the correct insertion angle and insure that the probes were on a post-transit vector heading toward Cornwall. Once out of the warp gate, the probes ran silent, sending point to point laser communications to a relay satellite positioned adjacent to the warp gate.

Now Third Fleet was heading toward the warp gate at .05c. West had her ships imitate the drones, accelerating hard as they approached the transit point. Thirty seconds before Cambrai entered the warp gate she felt the sudden relief as 20g of pressure suddenly ceased. Her chair's control system injected meds to counteract the drugs in her system, and it gave her a double dose of stimulant. She was just sitting up, slowly, painfully, when Cambrai entered the warp gate and exited into Cornwall's system.

"All units have completed transit and are on silent running, Admiral." West had instructed her AI to confirm the fleet's post-transit status. The crew was still recovering from the effects of the acceleration, and these first few seconds were too crucial to trust to her disoriented officers...managing the fleet for the first few minutes post-transit was a job for the AIs. It was vital that all her ships remain undetected as long as possible. If Third Fleet could get close enough before the enemy knew they were coming, they just might have a chance.

"Very well, Athena." West had reached back to ancient mythology for a name for her AI. "Status of scanning grid?" Before she'd withdrawn her fleet, West had seeded the area around Cornwall with scanner buoys and other detection devices. The grid was heavily shielded with ECM in the hopes that one or more of the devices might avoid detection, giving her data on the enemy strength and deployments.

"I am picking up laser transmissions from three of the scanner buoys, admiral." The buoys had been programmed to send information by direct point to point laser communication. Unless an enemy ship happened to cross the beam, they shouldn't have picked up anything. Normally, laser communication was used between ships that knew each other's precise locations, but at this range the lasers' beams had widened to several thousand kilometers. It was diffused and harder to detect, but as long as one of West's ships was in the cone, they would get the transmissions. A laser communication at this range was sharply limited in the data it could carry, but West was only interested in basic coordinates right now.

"Very well. Send a plot of the enemy deployments to my display." There was a knot in her stomach. It was time...now she'd see what her people had to face. They'd bugged out of the system before the invading fleet arrived, and they had no reliable information on enemy strength. Until now.

"And Athena...set up a fleetwide com line. Direct laser communication only." Setting up a spiderweb of laser links connecting the flagship to the rest of the fleet was a complex job. Third Fleet had 62 ships deployed over a billion cubic kilometers of space, and calculating the optimal pattern of lasers was a computer's job. "I will address the fleet in 15 minutes." She wanted a look at the data first. West tended to be honest with her people, and she wanted to let them know what they were up against. Whatever it was, they were going in…the Marines had been fighting and dying on Cornwall for over two weeks. She'd be damned if she would just abandon them…no matter what the odds.

"Yes, admiral. Preparing communication links now." Athena's voice was soft and soothing. West tended to get very focused in battle situations, and over the years her AI had adjusted its demeanor to offset her tension. Athena had made the adjustments slowly, and West never realized how her AI had conformed itself to her needs. "The enemy deployment data is on your display."

West looked down at the screen, and she almost gasped with excitement. The enemy had 14 ships in orbit and around the planet. It could have been worse, she thought. It could have been much, much worse. She looked up from her screen, panning her eyes across Cambrai's bridge and whispered softly to herself. "Maybe we have a chance."

"Get those autocannons set up NOW!" McDaniels' voice was hoarse, her throat raw from shouting. Skarn Island had become an inferno, a manifestation of hell for the Marines desperately trying to hold out on its rocky slopes.

She still had all six of her autocannons, but most of them were on their second crew, and one of them was on its fourth. Casualties had been heavy, and the enemy had been targeting the weapons teams in particular. The regular mag-rifles of the Marines could take down one of the battle robots, but it took a lot of concentrated fire to do it. The HVMs and heavy autocannons were a much bigger threat, and the enemy had adjusted its fire priorities accordingly.

McDaniels had abandoned her mortars – they were more or less ineffective anyway – and turned the crews into replacements for the autocannon teams. She'd lost two of her four HVMs. She could replace lost crews, but there was nothing she could do about missile launchers that were blown to bits. She hated to think of her people as more replaceable than equipment, but in the cold mathematics of the Battle of Cornwall, they were. There was time for self-loathing later…if she ever got off this miserable planet. For now all she cared about was keeping the maximum amount of fire on those things.

McDaniels was a cold realist - most of her colleagues would say a pessimist - and she generally expected things to get worse rather than better. Her years of combat experience had only confirmed that point of view. But even she was unprepared for what happened next.

"Lieutenant! What the hell is THAT?" It was Sergeant Jones, but he only beat the rest of the section leaders by a few seconds.

She saw it too. The enemy robots were fearsome adversaries, two and a half meters tall, with four large appendages bristling with weapons. But the thing she saw now froze the blood in her veins. It was close to four meters tall and jet black. Its legs were wider than an armored Marine, and its massive body supported six huge arms.

McDaniels was transfixed, but only for a few seconds. "HVMs, target that thing. Now!" She tried to keep her voice calm, but she didn't quite manage it. She took a deep breath, forcing back the urge to turn and run. She was having a hard time dealing with these things. She'd faced enemies before, and she'd always been afraid…anyone sane was afraid in battle. But this enemy was different. There was a coldness, a relentlessness about them. A human enemy was frightening enough, but at least you knew he felt the same things you did – fear, pain, uncertainty. But that equilibrium was shattered here. She didn't think these foes had any of those weaknesses. And these new monstrosities were like some nightmare conjured up from the darkness.

She saw two HVMs impact just in front of the thing, and she watched in horror as it lumbered forward through the maelstrom. It looked untouched, its jet black exoskeleton showing no signs of damage. "Fire again! Autocannons, open fire on the enemy front line." Her voice was rougher this time. She didn't know what to do, and the stress was pushing her to the breaking point. Her people couldn't leave…not yet. Colonel Teller had personally positioned her detachment here. The rest of the line was pulling back, and it was her job to cover that retreat. If the enemy got past her now they'd hit the retiring units in the flank and slaughter them. No, she thought, we're not going to let that happen.

"HVM teams. Reduce spread pattern to minimum dispersion." She was regaining her composure, at least a little. She knew her people had to be near the end of their endurance, and the last thing they needed was to think their CO was losing it. "We need to score a direct hit." The HVMs were designed to split into seven separate warheads just before impact. The default setting was to spread them as far as possible to create the largest target area. With the dispersal settings on minimum, they had a better chance for one of the warheads to actually hit the enemy. The kinetic energy from a hyper-velocity missile was substantial…maybe even enough to hurt this monster.

She watched as her teams fired another shot, and her heart leapt as one of them scored a direct hit. One of the secondary warheads slammed into the massive robot and exploded into a billowing fireball. A ragged cheer went up on the comlink. Usually she'd scold her people for the indiscipline, but this wasn't a normal situation. Besides, her own voice had been one of those among the cheers.

She cranked up her visor to Mag 10 to get a good look, and she could feel her limbs go cold as she watched the thing walking out of the billowing smoke. It was damaged at least, that much she could tell. One arm was gone and another was hanging loosely, apparently inoperative. But it still came forward, and it began to return fire, raking her line with rapid fire hypervelocity rounds of its own.

The heavy projectiles slammed into the ridgeline, shattering the rocks and showering her people with smashed chunks of stone. She had three people down almost immediately. Then it was five. Then six.

"Down. Everybody get low…now!" The command was

unnecessary. Half the detachment had hit the ground on their own…and the other half were running to the rear. It wasn't a rout, not exactly. But her unit was broken, and she knew it. If she didn't pull back now and regroup she'd lose them all.

"Withdraw to secondary positions." Oddly, the impending failure of her unit's morale bolstered her own. They needed their CO, now more than ever, and something deep within her rose to the occasion. "Let's move it, people. I want everyone in good order." Her survivors filed back through the ravine leading to the rear. Teller had chosen this position well, and the line of retreat was shielded from the enemy by the mountains. She maintained her own position, counting off to make sure that every one of her Marines who was still alive had pulled back. Then she took one last look over the rock wall at the approaching enemy. The monster was still advancing…and in the distance she could see three more of them coming up over the ridge. She shivered and turned to follow her troops into the ravine.

"All ships…activate Plan Theta-1…now." Admiral West's transmission broke the radio silence the fleet had observed since re-entering the Zeta Bootis system. There was no time to set up another laser transmission grid, and it didn't matter anymore anyway. Third Fleet was about to send 200 missiles at the enemy armada…and there was no way that was going to remain undetected.

The ships shuddered as they emptied their external missile racks, jettisoning the used cradles and repositioning to fire from their internal launchers. They were launching from point blank range, closer than West had ever seen missiles deployed. She'd come back to Cornwall to bushwhack the enemy, and by God that's what she was going to do.

It had taken an iron will to wait this long to launch. She hadn't known if the fleet could get this close undetected, but she knew they didn't have much chance to win the fight unless they did. So she staked everything on stealth…and now she would reap the reward.

"Mystic, put me on with the bomber crews." Third Fleet had only one capital ship, the ancient Cambrai...and it had only 12 bombers in its launch bays. It was a pitiful strike force, but she needed every bit of firepower she could get, and the 48 men and women of her bomber wings were set to launch. Not many of them expected to return, but they knew the situation, and they were ready to go.

"Connection established, admiral."

"You all know the gravity of the situation." Her voice was somber, emotional. "The fate of Third Fleet...and the thousands of Marines fighting on Cornwall...depends on us hitting the enemy hard and fast. We're not going to get a second chance, so I need each of you to stay focused. Get in close, launch your torpedoes, and then get the hell out of there." She paused, taking a deep breath. She didn't think any of them were going to survive, but everyone needed at least a little hope...and she need to convince herself she wasn't sending them to certain death. "Good luck to you all, and my deepest thanks for your courage and steadfastness." She leaned back in her chair and closed her eyes. "Mystic...issue the launch order."

Cambrai bucked as her magnetic catapults launched the strike force. The vector was straight ahead...every unit of Third Fleet was heading directly at the enemy. The bombers fired their thrusters accelerating ahead of the fleet, following close behind the missile volleys. The naval battle for Cornwall had begun.

Teller closed his eyes for a minute and took a deep breath. The stimulants were great at keeping you focused and alert...for a while. But eventually there was a price to pay. He felt strung out and sick, and he didn't have time for that now. "Grant, give me another stim. A double dose."

"Colonel, you are already beyond the maximum dosage for this 24 hour period." Teller's AI spoke with a low, gravelly voice. It had modelled its audio output for compatibility with its user, but Teller could never figure out why it had selected such an odd voice.

"I understand that. Give it to me anyway." He felt the pin-prick in his arm as the AI obeyed his command. Teller didn't have time to worry about consequences…he needed to be 100% right now.

His people had fought for every inch of ground, but this was their last stand. They'd made the enemy pay for Skarn Island, but they hadn't been able to hold it. Some of his frontline units were below 20% strength. He was consolidating shattered companies now…trying to put together combat-worthy formations to maintain some sort of battle line.

They'd island hopped down the archipelago, but Cavin Island was the last substantial piece of dry land to defend. The area around his command post was crowded with wounded. They were coming in faster than his medical staff could handle them. His troops had made herculean efforts to evac all their wounded, but he couldn't know who'd gotten left behind in the chaos. He had no doubt there were wounded Marines trapped behind the lines, waiting for the enemy to slaughter them. He closed his eyes tightly as he thought about it. It was one of the Corps' most sacred creeds…not to leave anyone behind. But on terrain like Skarn Island it was almost impossible to find a wounded Marine if his suit transponder was knocked out.

Teller had never really expected to win the battle. But now his people faced the end of their tenacious defense, and he found himself wracking his brain for some way…any way… out. The thought of seeing his brigade wiped out completely was just too much to take.

As bad as the total casualties were, the losses among the officers were worse. The overwhelming power, the cold relentlessness of this enemy had worn down the morale of his troops, even the veterans. The officers found themselves having to rally units that had never wavered before, and they lost heavily in the process. His reorganizations were moving the survivors up two, sometimes three echelons.

He'd just put Erin McDaniels in charge of 1st battalion. Major Greives was dead, and Teller had already taken the two surviving captains to head up other battalions. McDaniels had more experience than any of the lieutenants in the battalion…

besides, she only had 23 people left in the heavy weapons detachment anyway. Teller folded her people into the remnant of the battalion and put them back on the line. They were positioned along the west coast of the island…right where he expected the final attack to come.

He put his final report into the log, including McDaniels' battlefield promotion to captain. He downloaded it into two digger-drones and set them to burrow beneath the rocky ground of Cavin. Maybe someday the Alliance would fight its way back to Cornwall…and then they would know how 1st Brigade had fought and died.

"Colonel Teller!" It was his aide, Captain Walsh. "Lieutenant…I mean Captain…McDaniels reports she is under bombardment from enemy cluster-bombs.

"Understood. All units on alert." Teller stood there and took a deep breath. Time for the final battle, he thought grimly. Then he deployed his mag-rifle and walked up the path toward the front lines.

Third Fleet's missiles were accelerating at almost 50g… straight into the enemy ships. Launched from knife-fighting range, they closed the distance in a matter of minutes. The targeted ships fired their thrusters, trying to build some velocity to maneuver, and they began to deploy anti-missile defenses. But the incoming weapons had been launched at such close range, and with such high intrinsic velocity, the response was only moderately effective.

West watched on her screen as the ship's AI reconstructed the entire battle area from the transmissions sent back by the missiles. The enemy ships launched large torpedoes in the directions of the heaviest missile concentrations. West knew they would break into a spread of mines that would explode in the path of the oncoming warheads. The Alliance had a similar weapon, though its effectiveness was inferior to some of the alternative systems, and it had fallen into disuse.

"If that's the best they have to put up against our missiles…" She was speaking softly, mostly to herself, but she stopped short when she got the data on detonations. The explosions were massive, over 100 megatons...from each of the tiny mines. The massive patchwork of explosions destroyed dozens of missiles outright, and massive bursts of gamma radiation fried the control mechanisms of others. More than half her missiles were taken out in a few minutes.

"They must be antimatter warheads," she whispered under her breath. They only launched a few of those torpedoes, she thought...I wonder why. A larger spread could have wiped out her entire missile barrage. "Athena, I want all data on the enemy's anti-missile defenses logged on two drones." She wondered, was this another weapon the enemy possessed in inexplicably short supply? Admiral Garret would want to know.

"Yes, Admiral West." The AI's response was immediate, as usual. "Drones are activated and receiving data now."

"I want them launched one minute before we enter the enemy's energy weapons range." Of course they didn't know the enemy's range for sure...they were working on the sketchy data that trickled back from the ships fighting in earlier battles. Destroyed vessels and dead crews, she thought somberly.

"Yes, admiral. Launch sequence is already pre-programmed."

West's eyes went back to the display, watching her surviving missiles close on the enemy. They were moving at a very high velocity, making vector changes a slow and difficult process. But Third Fleet had caught the enemy almost stationary, and West had plotted her missiles perfectly. The target ships lashed out with anti-missile energy weapons similar to the Alliance's lasers, but longer-ranged. Their fire was accurate, but over 20 of West's missiles closed to detonation range.

The enemy ships were caught in the firestorm, some of them taking damage from multiple detonations. Right behind the nuclear maelstrom of the missile volley came Cambrai's 12 bombers, bearing down on their targets at .08c. Half of them were destroyed by the point defense, but the others closed on the damaged ships.

The Cambrai's bridge erupted in shouts and cheers as one, then a second bomber hit a damaged enemy ship with plasma torpedoes. The vessel shuddered and exploded into a massive fireball.

"Scratch one bogie!" It was Lieutenant Polk, her junior tactical officer. The outburst showed a lapse of discipline, but West let it go. She'd almost loosed a rowdy cheer herself.

Then another bomber hit one of the enemy ships, and both of them vanished in an enormous explosion. West sat back in her command chair and took a deep breath. She hadn't been sure they'd be able to destroy any of the enemy ships, and now she watched in astonishment as two more erupted into miniature suns.

"Admiral, we got them with antimatter missiles on some sort of external rack system." Polk's voice was still high-pitched with excitement, but he'd regained his composure. "We caught them flat-footed, sir."

West suppressed a smile. She couldn't believe their luck, but the battle was far from over. "Athena, implement damage control plan Zeta-2." They were about to enter range of the enemy's energy weapon.

"All personnel secure helmets now. Secondary life support systems active." The announcement was being heard on every ship in the fleet. West knew they were going to take it hard from the enemy particle accelerators, and she didn't want to lose anyone because of carelessness. If a section of a ship lost atmosphere, the Zeta-2 protocols would save lives.

"Entering maximum previously detected enemy firing range." The ship's AI gave the warning. No one knew the actual effective range of the particle accelerators – all they had was the sketchy data from previous engagements.

West leaned back in her command chair. She always felt claustrophobic with her helmet on. People used to tell her she'd get used to it, but 30 years into her career she still hated it. Of course she hated the idea of choking on vacuum more. She was just about to ask Athena for a status update when Cambrai shook wildly. The lights on the bridge flickered briefly and the ship shuddered again.

"Real-time damage reports, Athena." West was stepping on

Captain Johansen's toes. Running Cambrai was her flag captain's job – managing the fleet was hers. But West had always been a bit of a control freak, and she and Johansen had made their peace on the issue. Besides, Cambrai was her only capital ship, an enormous component of Third Fleet's firepower. It rated some attention from the admiral.

"Landing bay Alpha destroyed, hull integrity lost in sections 14 through 18, primary reactor control circuit offline…backup has engaged and is functioning." West's AI was ratting off the damage reports as they were compiled. "Casualty estimates unavailable."

They may not have an estimate yet, but West knew some of her people were dead…and a lot more were wounded. And she knew it would get worse. The fleet's high velocity would close the distance to laser range quickly, but until then they had to run this gauntlet.

Cambrai shook again…it was a hit near the flag bridge and one of the structural members crashed to the floor a meter from West's chair. Her head snapped around, but she quickly saw that none of her people were injured.

"Sixty seconds to laser range." Athena gave West the notification, but she didn't need it. The firing solutions were all locked into the ships' AIs. "Diamondback and Falcon destroyed by enemy fire."

West's shoulders slumped. The two attack ships were the first ones she'd lost. She knew the fleet would suffer losses, but that didn't stop it from hurting. Captain Marne skippered Falcon…Marne had been part of West's staff until she'd put him up for his own command. Now he was gone. He wasn't the first friend she'd lost, but it never seemed to get easier.

She stared straight ahead, and her eyes were like death. "Athena…relay to all ships…." Her brow was furrowed and her fists were clenched. "Fire."

Teller crouched behind a large outcropping, heavy hyper-velocity rounds impacting all around. His lines were broken at four points, maybe more. He was losing track of things in the growing chaos. The enemy was coming at them without a break. The Marines had taken down a lot of the battle robots, including a few of the big ones they'd dubbed Reapers, but the enemy units kept coming despite their losses.

Teller was proud of 1st Brigade. They'd fought like demons, despite crippling losses and crushing exhaustion. But he knew they were done. The battle robots attacked day and night…no fear, no doubt, no fatigue. His troops were exhausted, and their morale was broken. They were low on ammunition and they'd been in their suits non-stop for almost two weeks. Human endurance had a limit, even for veteran Marines. And they had reached it.

He knew what would happen. His wavering lines would crumple, and the enemy would pour through and wipe out his troops. This was an enemy that didn't communicate, didn't pause. They'd slaughtered helpless colonists on the other worlds; they would massacre his people too. James Teller had never considered surrendering in all his years as a Marine, but if it had been an option now he'd have taken it. He was as broken as his troops.

He didn't hear the sounds at first – the battlefield was too noisy, and his attentiveness was worn down. But when he poked his head above the rock to get a look at the enemy, he saw their position erupt in flames. Then he saw the strike craft angling up after their attack run.

The comlink burst into chaos as Marines up and down the line began cheering. At first Teller was confused, but then it dawned on him. Admiral West. She must have defeated the enemy fleet. Was it possible?

He was still watching when another wave of fighters swooped down and unloaded on the enemy line. His morale soared. Then his comlink buzzed with an incoming transmission.

"Colonel Teller…this is Admiral West. Sorry it took so long, but we're here to get your people out."

"I've never been so glad to hear someone's voice, admiral. Thanks for the assist. It came none too soon." Teller was still in shock. Maybe they would actually get out. "I assume congratulations are in order…you must have had a good fight up there."

The delay was longer than normal for surface to orbital transmission. Cambrai must have been farther out, beyond Cornwall orbit. "Thank you, colonel. We control local space for the moment." She sounded exhausted, Teller thought as he listened. "But we can't hold it. I've already sent my worst damaged ships back toward the warp gate, and we've picked up enemy ships inbound. I'm sending down the shuttles. Hopefully the airstrikes bought us some time, but whether they did or not, we need to get your people out of there. Now."

"That works for me, admiral." Teller took a deep breath and let out a long exhale. "We're ready to get the hell off this rock."

"Leave everything behind, James. I just want your people on those ships. We're barely going to make it out of the system ahead of the enemy as it is. Probably." She paused then added, "So please…move as quickly as you can. If we don't start blasting in 20 hours, none of us are getting out of here."

"You have my word on it, admiral. Teller out." He switched the comlink to transmit to the acting battalion commanders. "Attention all personnel. We're getting off this shithole. I need all units to fall back in an orderly fashion." He turned to walk back to the command post as he spoke. "We're going to evac the wounded first, but everyone needs to be on a shuttle in 18 hours…because in 20 the fleet will be under full thrust heading for home, and anybody not on a ship is screwed. You'll be receiving specific embarkation instructions shortly. In the meantime…"

He never heard the cluster bombs coming in. The ground erupted all around him, and his last memory was flying through the air and landing against the rock wall. He felt the pain…all over his body…then nothing as the suit flooded his system with painkillers. For a few seconds he heard the hissing from the breaches in his armor and felt the slickness of blood all over. Then there was just the blackness.

Chapter 15

Conference Room
AS Lexington
Outer reaches of Alpha 327 System

Cain walked swiftly to the briefing room, his dress uniform for once a model of crisp perfection. His shuttle had just docked a few minutes earlier. He knew he was the last one to arrive, so he'd come right to the conference room, without making any stops. His staff would see to his baggage. He thought what an odd journey his life had been, and he wondered if he'd ever get used to things like having a staff. Certainly life was simpler when he had less rank and fewer perks. He wondered, was I happier then?

He was deep in thought as he strode down the corridor, and he barely noticed at first that he had reached the door. The two Marine guards flanking the entryway snapped to attention when they saw him. They had that awed look in their eyes. Cain knew it was admiration, but he still hated it. He wanted to take them aside and tell them the truth...that he'd gotten these stars and medals sending thousands of wide-eyed young recruits like them to horrible deaths. But he just nodded and shook himself out of his self-indulgent musings.

He walked through the door and stopped just inside, stiffening to attention and raising his arm to salute. He had two platinum stars on each collar, but the rank gathered in the room was almost overwhelming.

"Let's skip the formalities, Erik." Holm's voice was the same as ever, though there was something else there, possibly a little more fatigue. "We don't have any junior officers here to perform for."

"Yes, sir." Cain smiled. "It's good to see you, general." It had been half a year since the two had been together.

"It's good to see you too, Erik." Holm sighed softly. "I wish the circumstances were less dire, but then we never seem to get that, do we?"

"No sir." Cain smiled darkly. He glanced around the table. Admirals Garret and Compton were seated next to each other. Garret was at the head of the table with Holm to his left and Compton to his right. "Admiral Garret, Admiral Compton." Cain nodded as he spoke, thinking it was an informal way to greet two fleet admirals.

"Erik." Garret nodded back with a warm smile. The two had known each other by reputation for years, but they'd formed a friendship after Cain led the team that rescued Garret from Gavin Stark's prison. "It's good to see you as always."

Compton nodded as well. "That goes for me too, Erik. I know things have been rough out on the Rim. You and Admiral West have borne the brunt of it so far, I'm afraid." Compton and Cain had been part of the cabal of officers that effected Garret's release and intervened for the rebelling colonists. Since then they hadn't seen much of each other, but the trust and mutual respect remained.

Colonel Sparks sat next to General Holm. The Corps' chief science officer and engineer nodded as well, and Cain returned the gesture. Erik was anxious to see what Sparks had to say. His people had sent back a lot of video and other evidence… including some actual bits and pieces of the enemy combatants. They'd paid heavily for it all, and Cain hoped Sparks and his team got good use out of it. If the Alliance was going to win this war, his people were going to need some help from the boys in the labcoats.

As Cain walked to his seat he noticed two other men sitting at the opposite end of the table. One he recognized immediately. "Mr. Vance, I'm surprised to see you. I hope you've been well." Roderick Vance was the head of Martian Security. He'd helped Cain in the mission to rescue Admiral Garret, and later he'd provided clandestine assistance to the rebellions.

"Indeed I am well, General Cain." His face was unreadable, as always. "I wish better circumstances had renewed our acquaintance." He gestured toward the man at his left. "Allow me to introduce Friederich Hofstader. Mr. Hofstader is the leading physicist in the CEL."

Cain was impressed. He was no scientist, but he knew that the leading physicist in the CEL was probably the top expert in the world. The Central European League was considerably ahead of the other powers in researching antimatter and subatomic particles, though the Alliance arguably had bragging rights on uncovering the mysteries of the warp gates. "It's a pleasure to meet you, Mr. Hofstader." Cain had no idea what a CEL scientist was doing at the meeting – and with Roderick Vance, no less - but he figured he'd find out soon enough.

"Thank you, General Cain. I assure you, your reputation has reached us in Neu-Brandenburg. It is an honor to meet you." Hofstader was tall and thin, with sandy blond hair partially mixed with gray.

Holm looked over at Cain. "How is Jim Teller?"

Erik's expression turned grim. "I think we salvaged enough of him for Sarah's people to grow back the rest." He paused, sighing softly. "He's got a rough recovery ahead of him, but I think he'll make it. He's in medical stasis now…he really needs the facilities on Armstrong."

A sad look crept across Holm's face. He'd seen too many good men and women chopped up on the battlefield. How many, he wondered, can one man endure? "He's a good man. A tough man. He'll pull through."

"I want to give him his star when he gets out of the hospital." Cain stared over at Holm. "He's earned it."

"I already approved it, Erik."

Cain forced a tiny smile. "Thank you, sir."

Garret stood at the end of the table and cleared his throat. "Well now that we are all here, I'd like to get started." He paused for a few seconds until Cain sat down. "We all know we are facing a crisis the likes of which we've never seen. None of us have all of the information, however, which is why I called this strategy meeting. When we leave here, each of us will be fully apprised regarding our combined analysis of the situation." He looked at Erik. "General Cain, let's begin with a report from the front."

Cain had just taken his seat, but he put his hands on the arms of the chair and hoisted himself back up. His eyes paused on Vance and Hofstader for a few seconds. He wasn't accustomed to giving military briefings with foreign nationals in the room, but he figured Admiral Garret knew what he was doing. "Thank you, admiral." He glanced around the table. "As you already know, we mounted a significant defense on the planet Cornwall in the Zeta Bootis system. We committed most of 1st Brigade to the battle, under the command of Colonel Teller." Cain glanced briefly at Holm. "Admiral West positioned her fleet in the adjacent XR-3 system, hoping to take advantage of the warp gate positioning to ambush the enemy armada."

Garret interrupted. "According to Admiral West's report, that was your idea, Erik." He let out a brief chuckle. "Am I going to have to give you a set of navy stars to go with those gaudy Marine things?"

Cain started to reply, but Holm beat him to it. "Don't go poaching my people Augustus." He glanced over at Cain. "Besides, you have no idea how much of a pain in the ass he can be."

Cain smiled and looked at Garret. "I appreciate the offer, sir, but I'll always be a Marine, I'm afraid." He paused for few seconds then continued, "Seriously, sir. Admiral West and I may have worked on the plan together, but she executed it...and brilliantly, if I may presume to judge naval tactics."

"You may. I've only had time to partially review her report, but it appears our good Admiral West pulled off somewhat of a tactical masterpiece." Garret nodded for Cain to continue.

"Colonel Teller's forces were very hard-pressed, but he was able to engage in a series of fighting withdrawals, taking advantage of the terrain." Cain's voice was becoming grimmer as he spoke...he'd seen the full casualty reports. "His tactics were perfect." He paused, looking down at the table for a few seconds. "Unfortunately, he was badly wounded during the final stages of the battle. We are hopeful he will survive, but he faces a long recovery."

Cain was restless, and he was having a hard time standing still. The endless parade of dead and mangled friends had worn him down. For the first time, he wasn't sure he could face it again... he didn't know how he'd send another group of his brothers and sisters into the meatgrinder. One thing he did know...if he sent another force into battle, he was going with them.

"Admiral West's forces took the enemy fleet utterly by surprise, and she was able to win a complete victory...though not without cost. Third Fleet suffered considerable losses, and Cambrai was damaged." Cain glanced at Compton and Garret. "She feels she can conduct field repairs and keep the ship in the line." Cambrai was West's only capital ship...without her, Third Fleet would be a bad joke as a fighting force.

"Admiral West is being reinforced, Erik." It was Compton this time, but Cain knew he spoke for Garret. The two of them had been friends since their days in the Academy. "She's getting two more capital ships, including Princeton." Princeton was one of the newest ships in the fleet, a Yorktown class battleship with more firepower than West's entire force.

That's good news, Erik thought. Two more battlegroups would make a huge impact on Third Fleet's preparedness, even with the recent losses. "I'm very glad to hear that, sir. I'm sure she's going to need them."

"Yes, I'm sure she will." Garret this time, his expression grim. "I wish I could send her more, but we've got huge problems on our other borders."

Cain had heard that the CAC and Caliphate had mobilized, but he didn't think he should go off on a tangent. Garret would address it, he was sure. "Admiral West's victory gave us temporary control of the space around Cornwall. Her intervention came just in time to save Colonel Teller's survivors, and she was able to evacuate them under fire and escape from the system before enemy naval reinforcements could arrive."

"How bad were 1st Brigade's losses, Erik?" Holm asked, but

he didn't sound like he really wanted to know.

Cain knew he should have included the casualty figures in his report without being asked, but he didn't want to think about it, much less discuss it. "Colonel Teller's forces suffered 2,695 casualties out of 4,411 engaged…61%."

The room was silent for a minute, as everyone present considered what Teller's Marines had been through. All for an unimportant world they had no real hope to hold. But the Corps had to get a measure of the enemy's ground capabilities, and the job had fallen to Teller and his people. They were Marines; they did what they had to do.

Cain broke the silence, mostly because he wanted to distract himself from thinking of Teller's casualties. "We were very successful, however, in collecting data on the enemy ground forces…including a considerable amount of debris from destroyed enemy combatants."

"Yes, we've already begun inspecting it all, General. It is fascinating." Sparks scientific enthusiasm got the better of him. Normally, he'd have never spoken out in a room full of such high-ranking officers.

"Is it fascinating, colonel?" Cain was pissed, and it was obvious from his tone. "Did you have to wipe the blood of our people off it all before it became fascinating?"

"Erik…" It was Holm. He felt the same way Cain did, but he knew Spark's comment came from dedication to his work, not indifference to the suffering of the Marines in the field. Sparks had spent his entire adult life designing equipment to make Marines safer in battle. "I'm sure Colonel Sparks meant no disrespect to Colonel Teller and his people."

Sparks looked at Cain, a panic-stricken expression on his face. "General Holm is right, sir. I meant no offense. It's only that the sooner we can understand this technology the sooner we can get your people the weapons and equipment you need for this fight." Sparks' voice was tentative and cracking, but he managed to get it all out.

The anger drained from Cain's face. "I'm sorry, Tom. I know how much you've contributed over the years." His eyes locked on Sparks' as he spoke. "We're all on edge...that's all." Cain knew he was more than just on edge, but this wasn't the time or place to discuss it.

"Thank you, sir. I truly meant no disrespect." Sparks nodded...then he stayed quiet and sat very still.

Cain looked out at the assembled officers. "That's about it. We're doing everything we can to fortify Farpoint. We've got a lot to work with there...the base, the orbital facilities. I don't know if we can hold it or not, but we can give them a hell of a fight." He paused to see if anyone had questions, but no one said anything. "It is possible the enemy could bypass Farpoint, but extremely unlikely. It's a long way around, and it would leave the forces at Farpoint in their rear." He glanced at Holm, then Garret. "Militarily, both Admiral West and I agree that an attack on Farpoint is almost a certainty."

Garret took a deep breath. "I agree, Erik. Elias, Terrance, and I already discussed it. We're 100% behind your decisions." He leaned back in his chair. "Do you have any other observations you want to add before we move on?"

Cain stood silently for a few seconds, thinking. Finally, he looked back at Garret and said, "Yes, admiral." He paused again, putting his thoughts together. "Admiral West and I had a conversation about the enemy's pacing." He hesitated again. "I mean the time between campaigns. It seems slow to us, sir."

"What do you read into that, Erik?" Garret had been thinking the same thing, but he wanted Cain's read on it.

"It could be anything, sir. We just don't have the data to develop an informed theory." Cain paused. He knew Garret wanted a better answer than that. "But if I had to guess, sir, I'd say they have some kind of logistics issue." He paused again then added, "If this is one of the other Powers, maybe they have a long route back to their own space."

"I agree with you, Erik." Garret had come to the same conclusion. For some reason it was taking the enemy a long time to resupply and move on to the next target. That was the one real piece of good news they had.

Cain moved to sit down, but he stopped and straightened

himself. "There is one more thing." Everyone looked up, waiting for him to finish. "As you know, it appears that the enemy... their ground forces at least...are entirely composed of automated units. Robots."

"Yes, the evidence from the fighting on Cornwall seems to confirm that." Holm wasn't sure where Cain was going. "Beyond the obvious concerns about the technology employed, do you think this is tactically relevant?"

Cain looked uncomfortable. "Sir..." He hesitated, clearly not wanting to finish what he'd started. "Sir, I spoke with a number of officers who were engaged on Cornwall." He stopped again.

"Yes, Erik?" Holm coaxed him to continue.

"Well, it's just this...and I mean no disrespect to Teller's people...my people. But they were shaken up."

"Of course they were shaken up." Compton had a confused look on his face. "After what they'd been through? Anyone would be a wreck."

"Cain looked over at Compton then back at Holm. "Yes, that's true...but this was something...different. The battle robots are so hard to kill...and they are completely relentless. They just keep coming...they don't break, they don't feel fear. My people are just plain scared of these things. I mean beyond the normal fear of combat." He paused again. He hated suggesting his Marines couldn't face the Devil himself and laugh in his face, but he felt this was important. "This enemy is getting in my peoples' heads like nothing I've ever seen before." Another uncomfortable pause. "I'm concerned about the long term morale effects in this war."

Holm stood up slowly. "Thank you, Erik. I know everyone here appreciates your insight." He knew how hard it was for Erik to say what he had said. In 20 years, Holm had never known Cain to admit his people might not be able to take on any enemy. "I want to review the overall strategic situation, but first I think Colonel Sparks should update us all on the current status of research into the new technologies we are facing." He turned to face Sparks. "Colonel, if you would."

Sparks jumped to his feet. He was the junior man in the room by far, and his faux pas with Cain had only increased his tension. "Yes, General Holm." He paused for an instant and cleared his throat. "As all of you know, our forces in the field have been fighting against an enemy with significantly more advanced technology than we currently possess. Our operating theory has been that one of the Powers has achieved some sort of broad-based breakthrough, though it is almost certain there is some other factor at work. The technology we have seen appears to be centuries ahead of us based on normal rates of advancement. Whatever Power is behind this, they must have found something…an artifact or something similar…that allowed them to leapfrog us. I'm afraid my people don't have any more insight in this area."

He took a step back from the table and slid his chair aside. "We have, however, done considerable work in categorizing the enemy capabilities and developing possible systems and weapons to at least partially counter the disparity our forces face." He scooped a small controller off the table and hit a button. The large viewscreen along the wall activated.

"As you can see, we have listed several basic areas that constitute the bulk of the of the enemy's advantage over our forces. First, they appear to have developed the ability to produce and deploy antimatter in useful quantities. This allows them to build warheads considerably more powerful than our largest thermonuclear weapons, with a lower mass and, consequently, better maneuverability." He punched a button on the controller and the screen switched to a series of tables comparing energy output from fusion and antimatter explosions. "The advantage of more powerful explosions in ship to ship missile combat are obvious. With their generally superior targeting capabilities, the enemy is able to get its more powerful warheads closer to our vessels, putting us at a very significant disadvantage in a missile duel. Additionally, it appears that some of their missiles utilize antimatter fueled drives, allowing them to achieve thrust level far in advance of our own weapons."

Sparks paused for a few seconds, allowing everyone to digest what he had said. "In reviewing the data from Admiral West's recent battle at Cornwall, we have identified another apparent use of antimatter by the enemy. Indeed, this may be the more tactically significant issue. They appear to have developed a defensive torpedo that scatters tiny mines across the path of incoming missiles. We have employed similar weapons in the past, however we have been constrained by the yield we can achieve relative to the mass of the individual mines." He clicked the controller again, and the image on the screen changed to a graphic displaying relative weapons yields.

"The enemy mines appear to produce approximately 100 megatons of explosive force. For us to achieve a similar yield would require a device with a total mass in excess of 17,000 kilograms. By comparison, only 2.5 kilograms of antimatter are needed to produce the same yield. With reasonable use of nano-technology, I would project that the total mine, including containment and propulsion systems could have a mass under 300kg." He looked back from the screen toward the table. "The implications for blanketing an area with enormous coverage of anti-missile warheads are obvious."

The room was silent. The staggering power of antimatter weaponry was a sobering realization. Most of those present knew at least the basics of everything Sparks had said, but it was still a shock to see it laid out not as theory, but as a straightforward analysis of weapons that had actually been employed in battle.

Garret broke the silence. "Colonel, what are your thoughts on countering this advantage? However powerful the enemy's weapons are, we need to find a way to defeat them."

Sparks looked over at Garret. "Yes, sir. I'm afraid it is virtually impossible for us to deploy our own antimatter weapons. I am at a loss as to how one of the Powers could possibly generate enough energy to produce meaningful quantities of antimatter. It is well beyond our current capabilities."

He shifted his glance from Garret down the table. "Containment is another issue. We have no idea how to safely store weapons-level quantities of antimatter on an ongoing basis. We can keep research quantities stable for a limited time, but we don't even have a clue how to store large amounts…and certainly not in a ship or other mobile location. However, there is some good news. Our first potential advantage is not a technological one at all…it is logistics. As General Cain touched upon, an analysis of the combined data strongly suggests that the enemy has a constrained supply of antimatter weapons. Perhaps they can only produce a limited amount, and this could mitigate our disadvantage, at least somewhat. Nevertheless, in every weapons category, it appears they have a conventional system as well. These are generally far more advanced than our own comparable systems, though the disparity is far less than it is with the antimatter weapons."

Sparks hesitated nervously before he continued. "If you will all indulge me in what I freely admit is pure guesswork, I believe there is another factor that we should consider."

"Please, colonel. Go on." Holm nodded as he spoke.

"Yes, sir." He hit the button on the controller again, and a schematic appeared on the screen. It looked like a rough engineering diagram of the superstructure of a space ship. "The enemy seems to utilize an external weapons deployment system not unlike our own missile racks. Their setup is substantially larger and more complex, however." He paused and took a breath. "It is my opinion that they utilize this system for all of their antimatter weapons and that their doctrine requires full deployment of that ordnance before entering into the effective zone of any opposing weaponry."

Garret leaned back in his chair, and odd smile on his face. "You weren't kidding about guesswork, were you?"

Sparks felt his stomach clench. "I'm sorry, admiral. I just thought…"

"Relax, colonel." Garret's smile widened into a full-fledged grin. "I happen to think you are correct." He turned to face Compton. "Admiral West's experience seems to add validity to this theory. She apparently caught the enemy by surprise with antimatter weapons still bracketed to their hulls. It appears that a number of vessels were destroyed by their own secondary explosions. What do you think, Terry?" Garret was the only person in occupied space who called Fleet Admiral Terrance Compton Terry.

"I agree." Compton didn't hesitate. "In fact it would explain the apparent disparity in the damage levels it took to destroy different enemy ships. According to West's data, the ones that didn't get vaporized by their own antimatter warheads took a hell of a lot more pounding before they went." He paused with a crooked smile on his face. "It almost reminds me of the old wet-navy stories. Catching an aircraft carrier with bombs stacked on the deck."

"Of course the problem is getting close enough unde- tected." Garret's smile morphed into a thoughtful expression. "Erica West took advantage of an anomaly in the system lay- out...something we won't be likely to have again." He rubbed his hand over his mouth as he thought. "I'm not sure how we can replicate that."

Compton leaned back in his chair, but he remained silent. It was Tom Sparks who worked up the courage to jump back into the exchange. "Sirs, I may be able to offer some insight that may be useful in that regard." He paused, eyes shifting back and forth between Compton and Garret.

"By all means, colonel." Garret looked up expectantly.

"Well, it appears that the enemy weapons are quite suscep- tible to our ECM...strangely so, in fact. To the extent we have been able to calculate it, our ECM success rate in the engage- ments to date is higher than what we achieved in the Third Frontier War. If this is new technology being deployed by one of the other Powers, I am at a loss to explain this." He hesitated, then added, "Perhaps some of their new technology interferes with their electronic systems in some way. Or maybe they had to sacrifice their ECM and ECCM suites to make room for the new tech." He didn't sound convinced.

"I apologize for interjecting, but I believe that Dr. Hofstader has some insights that I think you should all hear at this time." Roderick Vance hadn't said a word since he'd greeted Cain. "Indeed, this is why I brought him here to this meeting."

Vance was a Martian and a spy...not the most likely candidate to enjoy the trust of the men sitting in the room. But he'd proven to be a loyal ally, and he'd followed through on every promise he'd made them. If he thought it was important, they wanted to hear it.

"Please, Dr. Hofstader," Garret responded immediately. "If Mr. Vance feels it is important, we shouldn't delay."

Hofstader rose slowly from his chair. He wasn't easily intimidated, but the last few months had been bizarre to say the least. Expelled from the scientific mission on Epsilon Eridani IV, just before be boarded his shuttle he was handed a data chip with some extraordinary information...evidence he'd used to develop a theory so shocking, he'd at first been hesitant to share it even with his assistant. Then his transport was intercepted by a Martian warship and he was escorted off and taken to a meeting with none other than Roderick Vance. Now he was in a conference room with the top commanders of the Alliance military. Hofstader didn't care about nationalities...not now. If what he theorized was correct, it transcended borders and nations. If he was right, mankind was at an historic juncture. And in grave danger.

"Thank you, Admiral Garret." His voice was clear and steady. With everything that had already happened, he was beyond being nervous about addressing a few officers, however highly ranked. He'd settled into an odd sort of calm. "As you all know from my previous introduction, I am a physicist. My primary fields of research are antimatter and sub-atomic particles." His eyes moved around the table as he spoke. "I was assigned to the research project on Carson's World to study the alien artifact that was discovered there."

He took a step back from the table, which gave him a better view of everyone as he spoke. "I developed a theory that the structure on that planet was actually far vaster than indicated by preliminary investigation. In fact, I believed it to be planetwide, extending all the way down to the core. Unfortunately, the committee in charge of the expedition had imposed very rigid rules regarding the pace of research and exploration."

A momentary flash of anger gripped Hofstader – he was still bitter about the Committee and its actions in expelling him. "I took it upon myself to conduct unauthorized explorations in which I was able to confirm – to my satisfaction, at least – that my initial hypothesis was correct. The structure was a massive antimatter production facility, drawing on all of the planet's seismic and volcanic activity for power."

"That must be the answer." There were rumblings from everyone present, but it was Terrance Compton who spoke first. "One of the Powers must have successfully infiltrated the facility and learned enough to mimic the technology."

The others started to all speak at once, but Vance put up his hands. "Gentlemen, please…your indulgence. Dr. Hofstader has much more to share with you, so I ask you all to refrain from jumping to conclusions."

"Thank you, Mr. Vance." Hofstader shifted his feet nervously. What he had to tell them wasn't easy. "I'm afraid, Admiral Compton, that it is quite out of the question that any of the Superpowers are behind this invasion force you are facing." The room went silent. "Apart from the extraordinary implausibility of any nation of Earth successfully adopting this level of technology so quickly, the production of antimatter in the quantities we have seen deployed would require power generation facilities beyond anything possessed by the Powers. Constructing something on the order of the machine on Carson's World would take us centuries, even if we understood the technology, which we most profoundly do not."

"Well, Dr. Hofstader, I can assure you that we are actually being attacked. I have the dead Marines to prove it." Cain hadn't intended to sound as hard-edged as he did, and he softened his tone. "What is your explanation?"

Hofstader took a deep breath and looked over at Cain. "Well general…that is where the data provided to me before my departure from Epsilon Eridani IV comes into play. We had been proceeding on the assumption that the machine on Carson's World has been long dead but, as it turns out, that is not entirely true." Every eye in the room focused on him. "One of Dr. Travers' instruments recorded two separate bursts of an unidentified form of energy. None of our normal detection devices were capable of picking it up. My belief, which admittedly lacks supporting evidence at present, is that we are dealing with a form of dark energy…something entirely different than anything we have encountered." He paused for a few seconds and swallowed hard. "And I believe that it was some kind of alarm or distress call."

The room erupted, everyone shouting at the same time. Admiral Garret stood up and pounded his hand on the table. "Please, please. Let's not lose our composure, gentlemen." He turn his head toward Hofstader. "Am I correct that you are suggesting that we have been fighting the race that built the machine on Epsilon Eridani IV? That we have made first contact?"

Hofstader looked extremely uncomfortable, but there was a confident look on his face…almost defiant. "Well, Admiral Garret, I wouldn't state it exactly that way. However, yes, I do believe we are facing a force that has responded to the distress call we undoubtedly activated during our research efforts." He took another breath. "And as such, we could indeed be dealing with that very race…or their servants or successors."

The room was silent for a long while. Everyone present sat quietly, deep in thought. Finally, General Holm asked, "Dr. Hofstader, I find your theory compelling, but it is a lot to accept… especially with so little evidence. Yet you seem to be quite confident in your determination. May I ask why?"

"I had considerable doubts, general…before I arrived here." Hofstader looked over at Sparks. "I believed I was correct, but I very much wanted some form of corroborating evidence. And I got that here, courtesy of Colonel Sparks."

Sparks looked surprised. Whatever Hofstader had been able to determine, he had no idea what it was. "Me?"

"Yes, colonel. You were kind enough to allow me to examine some of the battle debris General Cain's people sent back… and it was extremely enlightening." He panned his eyes down the table. Everyone was staring at him intently. "Among the wreckage are some pieces of the larger robots…the ones your people call 'Reapers.' A portion of their exoskeleton appears to be constructed from a specific alloy, one that exhibits a number of odd properties, not the least of which is a strength several times that of the reinforced osmium-iridium polymer combinations used on your own powered armor."

"I'm afraid I'm not following your logic, Dr. Hofstader." Garret's expression showed confusion.

"I have seen that alloy before, admiral..." Hofstader looked directly at Garret. "...in certain crucial conduits on the machine on Epsilon Eridani IV."

The room was silent. Hofstader's findings were far from outright proof, but it was all starting to make sense. Each of those present gradually came to the realization that the German scientist was right. They weren't fighting a rogue Superpower that had managed an unexpected technological breakthrough... they were fighting the ancient race that built the facility on Carson's World.

Cain felt a coldness, and a tightening in his stomach. He wanted to think it was surprise or tension...but he knew better. It was fear. Cain had been in some of the most horrific battles ever fought, and he'd come through all of them. But the thought of facing the builders of Epsilon Eridani IV was almost overwhelming. That mysterious race was piloting starships when men were learning to hunt with sharpened sticks. It was a prospect not unlike going to war with the gods.

Chapter 16

Emir's Palace
City of Izmir
Planet Bokhara – 109 Piscium II

Kemal Raschid listened to the petitioners, but his patience
was nearly at its end. Hearing the entreaties of petty lords
squabbling over mining claims was tiresome, and if they troubled him much longer, he swore to himself, he would render a
judgment neither of them would like.

Raschid's family on Earth was very powerful, his father one
of the Caliph's Pashas, the highest ranking of all government
officials. The family was fabulously wealthy and highly respected
in the Caliphate. But Ahmed Raschid was a man of insatiable
appetites, and he had a dozen wives and mistresses who had
given him many sons. Kemal was the youngest of these, and
though he was also the most capable, all he could hope for on
Earth was a life of comfort and dissolution while the eldest of
his brothers succeeded to the family's power and titles.

For most citizens of the Caliphate, a life of even minimal
comfort was an elusive dream. But for Kemal it was a curse, an
existence without purpose. His mind was too strong, his spirit
too powerful to spend his days sitting uselessly alongside the
fountains in the family gardens.

He besought his father's aid - that is when the old man had
time for his youngest son, which was rarely. The two had discussed a place in the Caliph's army, but the officer corps of
the Earth-based forces had become a dumping ground for surplus sons of petty noble houses. The army that had shaken the
world in the Unification Wars had atrophied during a century of
terrestrial peace, and father and son agreed such a commission

was beneath the dignity of the Raschid.

The offworld forces were vastly more capable than the Earth-based army, but there was no place among the slave-soldiers of the Janissary Corps for the son of a highly-placed family. The Janissaries were backed up by the picked levies of the lords who ruled the colony worlds, again leaving no career path for an Earth-based nobleman.

But Kemal could not be content to aimlessly walk the halls of his father's vast palace with nothing more to occupy his thoughts than what he would eat for the evening meal or which of his women he would take to his bed that night. Finally, in his desperation, Kemal looked to the one place where superfluous younger sons could hope to wield power…space…the frontier.

The Caliphate's colonies were, for the most part, estates contracted out to noble lords who agreed to pay certain taxes and a percentage of production to the Caliph. Convincing members of the nobility to leave behind the pleasures of Earth for the danger and hardship of founding a colony was difficult, and the Ministry frequently resorted to blackmail and coercion to secure enough "volunteers." But Kemal needed no prodding, and his father's influence obtained for him the position of emir on the newly discovered planet Bokhara. Most of the nobles who emigrated to found colonies were granted only the title of Subashi and the mandate to govern a world, or portion of a world, on behalf of the Caliph. But as emir, Kemal's power was nearly total; he was the absolute ruler of the planet, save only for his fealty and obligations to the Caliph.

Fifteen years had passed since Kemal left Earth, and though his wealth would have allowed him to travel back and forth freely, he had never returned. The journey was long - over six months each way – and Kemal was busy building a world.

His energy had produced results. Calling Izmir a city was a bit of a stretch perhaps, at least by Earthly standards. But it was well on its way to deserving that status and, with 25,000 citizens and a bustling spaceport, it was a major metropolis out on the frontier.

Kemal had come to Bokhara a wealthy man already. Even

the small sum allocated to a youngest son in a family as wealthy and prominent as the Raschid was a vast fortune. But now the planet itself had begun to add to his wealth. Most of the Caliphate's colonies were backward, with a disinterested and decadent nobility ruling over the lower classes. These worlds produced only raw materials, shipping them back to Earth for processing. Kemal demanded more. Bokhara produced gemstones, some of the rarest and most valuable in human-occupied space. But Kemal did not ship raw stones back to the markets of Earth. The gems Bokhara exported were already cut and polished, and often used to create exquisite jewelry that sold for premium prices, swelling the coffers of Kemal Raschid.

In every area, the resources of the planet were fully exploited. The lower classes of Bokhara were poor and oppressed, as they were everywhere in the Caliphate, but the planet's prosperity filtered down, making the life of a Bokharan peasant much more bearable than those elsewhere. As the demand for labor grew, Kemal allowed more immigration, mostly workers bonded to ten years' service to pay for their passage. Kemal's rule was firm, and sometimes harsh, but it was also fair…much more so than in most places, and he was popular with the masses.

The Caliphate had lost the Third Frontier War badly, and it had been forced to surrender a number of resource-rich colonies to the hated Alliance. Yet even this was to Kemal's advantage, as the demand for new colonies to replace the lost production was acute. In addition to its planetary resources, Bokhara's system boasted something else of great value – two warp gates leading into unclaimed space.

The Caliph was so desperate to replace the lost colonies with new worlds, he did something that had never been done before…he granted a lord power over more than one world. Kemal Raschid had been given vice-regal authority over two new planets discovered in one of the adjacent systems, with the proviso that he agree to develop them with his own resources. He anxiously accepted and initiated plans to settle the first of these almost immediately. Kemal had even been excused from the recent mobilization order, freeing 500 of his Spahi petty nobles from military service to assist in the colonization effort.

Now Kemal himself prepared to visit his new fief. At the spaceport, the shuttles had been launching for days, ferrying people and equipment to the orbiting fleet. An armada of ships, mostly transports, but some gunboats as well, had been assembled by Raschid to support his new interstellar dominion. The ships were mostly older surplus hulls but, old or new, fleets were expensive, and this one had strained even the vast resources of Kemal Raschid.

Kemal wordlessly waved his hand. It was a signal that he was finished listening to the petitioners. Hamid, his chamberlain and major domo had entered through the side door of the audience chamber.

"My lord, your shuttle awaits you." The chamberlain stood respectfully in the doorway. His uniform was utilitarian, crisp and clean in sharp contrast to the intricate décor of the palace. When Kemal had first arrived on Bokhara he had imitated the pomp and ceremony of his father's domicile, including antique period costumes for the staff. But years of hard work and a focus on the profitability of his estate had instilled a new appreciation for practicality.

"I am ready, Hamid." Kemal walked toward the door, the chamberlain moving quickly out of his way. "It is time for me to see what these new worlds have to offer."

Red Crescent moved across the front of the warp gate. The ship was thrusting at half a gee, altering its vector slightly to position itself to drop the next scanner buoy. The solar system, dubbed Zon 111 by the Caliphate, not only had two useful planets, it had a warp gate leading into uncharted space.

Zon 111 was far from any hostile borders, but Kemal was a cautious man, and he intended to take no chances. That warp gate probably led farther out into the galaxy, but it was always possible that the chain of warp lines looped back to an enemy world. The Caliphate had lost the war in no small part because the Alliance found a previously undiscovered warp gate that turned a once secure sector into a warzone. So Red Crescent was out here to put a detection grid in place. Once that was active, anything coming through the gate would trigger an alarm.

Captain Mustafa was bored. A veteran of the Caliphate's navy, Mustafa had been in some of the largest battles ever fought. He'd mustered out during the purges after the war. It was better to retire in good standing, he thought, than to stay too long and become a scapegoat for defeat. He'd gotten a few civilian jobs, but trade among the Caliphate's colonies collapsed after the war, and they were still recovering slowly. When Mustafa received Kemal's offer to captain one of his new ships he gladly accepted.

"Scanner reading, captain." First Officer Fawaz looked up from the display screen and turned toward Mustafa. "Energy emissions from the warp gate."

Mustafa's head snapped around. "Confirm readings."

Fawaz turned toward his control board, but before he could do anything the ship's klaxon went off. "We have something transiting in through the warp gate, captain." His voice was shaky. Fawaz wasn't a military veteran; his career had been on freighters and survey vessels.

"Activate deployed scanners." Mustafa's military reflexes were a little rusty, but they started coming back. "I want all possible data on whatever comes through that gate."

"Ship transiting now, captain." Fawaz stared at his screen and froze.

"What is it?" Mustafa stared over at his stunned first officer. "Now, officer, Fawaz!"

Mustafa's rebuke shook Fawaz out of his shock. "Ah...sorry sir. According to preliminary scans the vessel masses approximately 70,000 tons." He turned back toward the captain, his face white as a sheet. "What ship that large could be all the way out here?"

Mustafa ignored the question. He was wondering the same thing. There were warships that size, certainly, and even larger. Freighters too. But not usually out on the extreme frontier. "First Officer, send a communication. Demand the vessel identify itself." Mustafa sat on his chair rubbing his chin. "And power up the laser battery." Red Crescent wasn't a warship, but it carried a double turret of light lasers.

"Yes, sir. Identity request transmitted in all languages, sir." Fawaz glanced down at his board. "Laser turret activated and ready, captain."

"Prepare a burst communication to Kemal's Sword." With a lack of modesty universal in his family, Kemal had named his flagship after himself. "Transmit from my communicator."

Fawaz worked his controls. "Ready, sir. You may begin at any time." A brief pause then: "No response from the unidentified vessel, captain. Scanners indicate significant power buildup." Ships suffered a short period of disruption after a warp transit. It wasn't usually tactically significant...unless a defender was sitting right on the gate, like Red Crescent was. Normally, battle-fleets positioned themselves farther back, which gave them a wider range of options to react to an invading force.

Mustafa flipped on his communications headset. "This is Red Crescent with a priority communication for Emir Kemal." It would take six hours for the transmission to reach Kemal's ship. Whatever was going to happen in the next few minutes, Mustafa and his ship were on their own. "We have an unidentified vessel that has just transited into the system. Estimated mass of 70,000 tons. Intent and origin unknown." Mustafa felt like he should say more, but he didn't know anything else. Not yet.

"Officer Fawaz, repeat the communication demanding identification."

"Yes, sir." Fawaz moved his hands toward his board. "Sir... detecting massive energy buildup in..."

Red Crescent shook wildly. The lights went off, the bright illumination of the main system replaced by a dim glow from the battery-powered backups. There was a groaning sound and then another shudder, the metal spine of the ship breaking. Mustafa knew immediately that his ship was dead. He didn't know what had hit them, but whatever it was, it was enough to kill Red Crescent with one shot.

"Sir, the reactor has shut down." Fawaz was near panic.

"Life support on minimal operation. Hull integrity compromised. Secondary explosions."

"Get Engineer Nassar on my com." Mustafa was staring down at his own display as he barked out the order.

"Engineer Nassar is dead, sir. So are both his technicians." Fawaz was almost incoherent with fear. "What are we going to do?"

Mustafa leaned back in his chair and closed the visor on his helmet. I don't know what to do, he thought grimly. He knew there was no way to save the ship.

Red Crescent tumbled again as it was torn apart by a second blast. The bridge shook wildly as it lost hull integrity and its atmosphere was quickly sucked out into the vacuum. Mustafa saw a large chunk of a conduit hit Fawaz, beheading the first officer in the process...just before the captain was sucked through a large gash in the hull.

Mustafa had his survival suit on with his helmet secure, and by some miracle, he was pulled unhurt through the opening in the hull. He was floating in space...actually he was moving at over 150,000 meters per second, the intrinsic velocity of Red Crescent when we was ejected. He couldn't feel anything...just a calm sensation. The enemy ship was close by the standards of space warfare, but it was far too distant for him to see with the naked eye. He saw only the mangled hull of his own ship...and the black curtain of space, pin-pricked by the stars.

His survival suit wasn't powered armor. He didn't have a nuclear reactor to energize it, just a few small batteries. He knew he had six hours, maybe seven before he ran out of power. He would die then, though it would be a close race between suffocation and freezing. Unless, of course, he'd gotten a truly massive dose of radiation. Then the end would be quicker and he would die in agony, wracked with pain and choking on his own vomit.

I'll just have to see what happens, he thought with an eerie calm.

"I want full power now, captain. We must reach the warp gate before that ship can fire on us." Kemal was strapped into his acceleration couch on his self-named flagship, suffering terribly. He was not a navy man; he had no experience with the g forces that ships' crews underwent during battle…or when fleeing. He'd thrown up at least three times, all over his expensive silk outfit. His present state was considerably beneath the dignity he customarily considered his due, and he was in a foul mood.

Kemal's Sword had been a hunter-killer, the Caliphate's answer to the Alliance's fast attack ships. The ship had been obsolete and posted to the mothballed reserve for years, but in the post-war scramble for cash, the navy sold it off, along with two dozen other ancient vessels. When Kemal bought the ship, he replaced the military grade reactor with a standard commercial one. The naval reactors were simply too expensive to operate and maintain, and they required an engineer with a much higher rating to keep them safely functioning.

The commercial reactor was enough to operate the ship normally, but its acceleration capped out around 15g. It was enough to make Kemal uncomfortable, but it was woefully inadequate to escape from an enemy accelerating at 30g.

"Yes, my lord." The captain sat at one of the workstations on the bridge, since the normal command chair had been converted for Kemal's use. "With my lord's permission, I will take personal charge of the reactor's operation. Perhaps we can coax 110% or even 115%." Captain Essa had been an engineer in the navy before he'd moved up to command rank. His naval career had been promising, but his family were retainers of the Raschid on Earth, and he resigned from the fleet to accept the command of Kemal's flagship. He'd been reluctant to leave his naval posting, but the lesser nobility in the Caliphate were highly dependent on their sponsors, and offending one of the Raschid would have been a betrayal to his family.

"Yes, yes." Kemal's head ached like nothing he had ever felt before, and his patience was at an end. He couldn't understand how the veteran spacers could put up with this discomfort so often. "Whatever you feel is best. Just get us through that warp gate." Kemal was afraid too. If they didn't make it to the gate on time, they would die. This unidentified ship had already blown most of his little fleet to plasma, and he knew Kemal's Sword had no chance in a fight.

Essa stared down at his board, speaking softly into his com to the ship's computer. He'd have preferred to be down in engineering handling the reactor at close quarters, but moving around in a ship at 15g wasn't practical…and cutting thrust, even for an instant, was unthinkable right now.

Kemal leaned back in his couch trying to remain quiet despite his urge to cry out. The pain was getting worse…he was sure of it. He got his confirmation a minute later when Essa announced he'd managed to get the thrust up to 17g.

Kemal lay back, focused almost entirely on his distress. But in the back of his mind there was a spark of lucidity, a thought and a feeling of urgency accompanying it. We have to get back and report. The Caliph must know about this.

Chapter 17

Critical Care Unit 3
Armstrong Joint Services Medical Center
Armstrong - Gamma Pavonis III

Sarah Linden was leaning over the med-capsule, her face a
mask of concentration. She had her top team waiting – she'd
gotten word days before that James Teller was on his way to
Armstrong, badly wounded and in medical stasis. She knew
Teller well; he was one of Erik Cain's top officers…and Cain
was Sarah Linden's longtime companion and lover.

"Oh, James. Just look at you." She muttered softly to herself as she looked down at Teller's mangled body. She'd known
exactly what to expect; all the data on the patient's condition had
been sent to her long before the transport docked. But it was
still always a shock to see a human being – especially someone
you knew – so gruesomely mutilated.

Her focus was total, but the back of her mind drifted
through the years. She'd met Erik when he was brought to her
at this very hospital, wounded at least as badly as Teller, and possibly worse. Cain had been exposed to an enormous amount of
radiation, and he was so weak he could barely turn his head. But
he recovered, and it wasn't long before he became a nightmare,
terrorizing the entire med staff. Except her. He'd had a crush
on her from the day he regained consciousness. At first she
thought it was cute…he wasn't the first Marine who fell for her
after she'd put him back together. But then she began to realize
there was something different about him. She'd never been able
to explain it, even to herself. But the two of them were kindred
spirits of a sort. She couldn't keep a tiny smile from her lips
as she thought back. It had been more than fifteen years, and

nothing had changed. War and duty put distance between them far more often than they wished, but nothing dampened their feelings for each other.

"OK, Andrea, let's get him into surgery right now." Sarah was a pleasant, soft-spoken woman in most situations, but when she was dealing with the wounded she ordered her people around as imperiously as Cain did on the battlefield. Sarah was fanatically dedicated to her job, and she'd saved thousands of Marines over the years. She'd always sympathized with Erik about the demons he faced. Her successes, at least, got up and walked out of the hospital. His victories were as bathed in blood as his defeats, and the ghosts that haunted him didn't seem to care if they'd died in a battle won or a battle lost.

"No significant radiation exposure, right?" Andrea Tuscan was one of her younger doctors, still in surgical training. She was smart as hell, and Sarah had taken her on as a protégé of sorts.

"No." Sarah was staring at the med-unit's readouts, confirming what she already knew from the advance transmissions. "He's in bad shape, but it's all just physical injuries." She'd still never had a patient who'd been exposed to as much radiation as Cain had been...at least not one who'd survived. He'd managed to get caught in the open with his armor breached just about as close to a nuclear detonation as a human could be and still survive. Literally. She'd had to regenerate almost every internal organ to replace those destroyed by the radiation. She'd flushed his circulatory system at least ten times, but finally she managed to repair all the damage. He still had some residual effects – she'd treated him for various cancers three times since then. But that was easily cured, a minor inconvenience at worst.

"Surgery unit C." The med-unit moved under its own power, the medical AI following Sarah's verbal instructions and directing the hulking, coffin-like capsule. It made a soft hum as it worked its way slowly down the corridor. Sarah followed, reading the display at the end of the unit. There wasn't much to monitor – the machine was breathing for Teller, pumping his blood, providing nourishment and hydration. He was arguably really dead, the machinery preserving what was left of his body so the medical team could treat his injuries and revive him.

The surgical team was waiting in the unit. Teller would be in surgery for hours. Sarah and her people would repair whatever they could, and they would harvest the tissue grafts they needed to grow replacement organs for those damaged beyond repair. Teller would remain in medical stasis while his new organs developed, and then Sarah would transplant them into his body. After that was completed he would be revived and go through the agonizing process of regenerating an arm and both legs. Then, after some physical therapy, he'd be as good as new. If all went well, he'd walk out of the hospital in six months, maybe seven.

"Seal off unit." The doors to the surgical theater closed at Sarah's command. There was a high-pitched whine as the atmospheric system sterilized the room and everything in it. "Prepare to open med-unit." Sarah took a deep breath and looked over at her team. "Ok people, let's get started."

Sarah sat in her office exhausted, still wearing her blood-soaked scrubs. Teller had been in surgery for twelve hours and, despite a few complications, he'd come through fine. Her people were catalyzing the regeneration tanks now…in another few hours they'd begin growing perfect replacements for Teller's left lung and his liver. The rest of his organs hadn't been as badly damaged, and they'd been repaired during surgery. Teller would remain in medical stasis until Sarah completed the transplants. Then she'd have a conscious patient to deal with.

Marines were tough to deal with under the best of conditions, but the ones like Cain and Teller were particularly difficult to handle. Men and women cut from that cloth don't respond well to infirmity or inactivity. Teller didn't have Cain's rebellious streak or his fiery temper, at least. She knew she'd been spared the worst of Cain's fury when he was her patient, and she shuddered to think how hard he'd have been on a doctor he wasn't falling in love with.

Right now she wanted to sleep. More than anything. Just the

thought of her waiting bed was enough to make her weep. But there was work to do. A lot of it. Teller didn't arrive on Armstrong alone, and Sarah had a legion of his shattered Marines to deal with. Her staff had been working through the night, getting the worst cases into surgery. Sarah Linden took her responsibilities seriously, and she wasn't about to lose any Marine who managed to get to her hospital. She would make damned sure of that. If it meant no sleep, so be it.

At least on Armstrong she had the resources to properly treat everyone. She'd commanded more than one field hospital where that hadn't been the case. She closed her eyes as her thoughts drifted back to Carson's World during the war. They'd been forced into old mining tunnels to avoid the shelling. The wounded came in faster than her people could handle, and they ran out of everything – med-units, drugs, monitors. There were wounded men and women everywhere…laying on the cold stone ground for lack of even a cot. It was a painful memory – she'd lost a lot of Marines there, men and women she could have saved with the right equipment and supplies. The waste of it all was hard to take.

She'd come the closest she ever had to resigning after that nightmare. She'd never told Erik, but she'd actually filled out the forms. But something kept her from submitting them. Everyone she loved was in the service, and if any of them was wounded, she wanted to be there. But it was more than that… she realized resigning would be a futile gesture. Those broken and bleeding bodies would still be there and, without her efforts, more of them would die. Leaving would be too selfish. It would be abandoning her duty, her purpose.

She forced her mind back to the data on the screen. She had far too much work to sit and daydream, and she rubbed her bleary eyes and focused on her display. Her nightmares would still be there when she had time for them.

"Colonel Linden?" She was reading through the case reports when her assistant's voice came through the com. "There is a visitor for you. She's at the outer gate. She doesn't have credentials, so the guards won't let her through."

Sarah looked up from her screen, wondering who could be looking for her at this hour. Everyone she knew was in the Corps or the navy, and they'd have been admitted without a problem. "I'm swamped here, Kim." Her tone was tense; she was annoyed at the distraction. "See what it's about and take care of it."

There was a brief pause. "Umm...I think you might want to handle this yourself, colonel."

Sarah exhaled hard, her impatience growing. "I'm busy here, captain." She almost cut the line, but she paused. Captain Quinn wasn't one to waste her time, especially when she had a hospital full of wounded to deal with. "What is it all about?"

"Well, colonel...your visitor's name is Alex. Alex Linden." Another pause. "She says she's your sister."

Chapter 18

Hall of Nations
Lunar Neutral Zone
Luna, Sol III

Vance was sore. Every square centimeter of his body hurt. Man wasn't supposed to endure crushing acceleration and deceleration without a break. But it had been essential for him to get back to the Sol system and to do it as quickly as possible. This wasn't just a problem the Alliance was facing – it was a threat to all mankind.

He'd left Garret and Holm and the rest of the Alliance military leaders believing there was probably something to Hofstader's theory, but he himself had no uncertainty...he was absolutely convinced the German scientist had figured it out. Mankind had achieved first contact with another intelligent race, and it had turned out to be a disaster as bad as anything depicted in an old science fiction vid. They hadn't taken the conversation to its full extent during the conference on Lexington, but Vance had done it in his own mind...mankind faced the very real possibility of extinction.

He had never been happier he'd committed the resources to develop the Torch. They were small ships, with almost no armor or defensive systems, but they were fast...faster than anything else built by man. The ships represented a breakthrough in nanotech systemization and reached a new level of thrust to mass ratios. And Vance had pushed it to the max the entire trip, thrusting over 40g most of the way.

The Torch's force dampening chambers were a step above a normal acceleration couch. They kept the crew alive, even at 40g, but it wasn't a lot of fun floating in ectoplasmic goo, with a

hose snaked down your throat forcing air into your lungs. Especially not for days on end. A lot of people couldn't handle it,
and half the crew had needed a heavy dose of anti-psychotics to
bring them back to reality.

He'd left the Alliance officers one of the ultrafast speeders
for their own use. It was a major breech of national security
to leave a top secret advanced system in the hands of another
power, but Vance knew it was no time for such considerations.
Who cared if the Alliance stole some tech when they all faced
destruction from outside? If the Superpowers couldn't learn to
work together, man's worlds were likely to become graveyards,
the wind whipping through the haunted ruins of lifeless cities.

Vance was unemotional and straightforward...not all at susceptible to periods of introspection and self-doubt as most of
those he met were. But he couldn't help wonder how he'd ended
up in the forefront of all this. His family had been one of the
first to settle on Mars. His great-grandfather had led the second
colonization expedition, and his grandfather had been a hero
of the independence movement. As a young man, the spoiled
heir to a wealthy family, his plans had been limited to managing
the family's far-flung business interests. But when his father
died suddenly it fell to him to take his place – both as a Council
member and the head of Martian Security.

The Martian Confederation, while it had some features of a
republic, was, for all intents and purposes, an oligarchy ruled by
the oldest and most important families operating through the
High Council. And that council had always included a Vance.
Roderick hadn't wanted the responsibility, but it was his duty
to the family as well as the Confederation, and he accepted it
without question.

That had been three decades past, and now Vance was part
of the council's leadership, one of the three or four individuals
who effectively governed the Confederation. He'd first taken
a leading role when he launched the effort to aid the Alliance
colonies during the rebellions, and the enormous success of that
endeavor had cemented his role as the most trusted member of
the Council. Now he'd sent a report with the most momentous

and dangerous news in human history, and the other oligarchs had reacted by voting him extraordinary powers to deal with the crisis. For all practical purposes, Roderick Vance was the temporary dictator of the Martian Confederation.

He'd already issued a blizzard of orders, sending a battlefleet and a heavy regiment of Marines to support the Alliance forces. Now he had to convince the representatives of the Superpowers to put aside their disputes and join to together to face the new enemy. He expected it to be the most difficult task he'd ever attempted...and the most vital.

He stood at the entry to the Hall, clad in the dress uniform of the Martian Guards. He was the ceremonial unit's honorary colonel and, as such, he was entitled to wear the spectacular dress reds at diplomatic affairs. He had called the meeting, and though the Powers would be equally represented, Vance was the host. He would greet each of the diplomats himself, his nearly-eidetic memory packed full of personal details on each. With enough prep work, even charm could be manufactured. He hoped it would be enough.

Vance was very methodical, prepared to wait as long as it took to achieve his goal. But his legendary patience had been sorely tested at the summit. For three days he'd listened to pompous gasbags recite tired old grievances. He was grateful, at least, to have escaped some of the legendary problems of past diplomatic congresses. He'd managed to sidestep such foolishness as arguing over table length or seating arrangements – though he had the feeling the escape had been a close one. The politicians and diplomats never seemed to tire of their own voices, he thought, though Vance himself certainly did.

"Ladies and gentlemen, with all due respect, we have discussed many matters not germane to the topic at hand." Vance was trying to cling to his patience and civility. He had to suppress a momentary grin when he imagined how Erik Cain or Augustus Garret would handle the crowd. He was pretty sure Cain's solution would involve a crack platoon delivering a fairly blunt message. "I understand profoundly the importance of these pre-existing issues, but we are now faced with a grievous threat to all of humanity. The time for conflicts among ourselves is past. We must join together, and we must do so immediately and without reservation, lest we all be destroyed."

Vance could hear the diplomats still arguing among themselves. He'd gone over the transmissions sent from the destroyed Alliance ships and colonies, and he had listed and explained the enormous technological advantages of the enemy. They had listened, and he'd seen fear in their reactions, but he'd been unable to get the agreement he needed. Finally, he reached into his pocket and retrieved a small controller. With a click he activated the room's giant viewscreen. He'd saved one last bit of evidence…video sent back by Teller's troops on Cornwall, footage of the advance of the massive battle robots the Marines called "Reapers."

The room fell silent, every eye upon the terrifying images on the screen. None of them had ever seen anything like these monstrosities moving relentlessly forward, firing a massive array of weaponry as they did. It was like a nightmare unfolding on the giant screen, and it mesmerized everyone present.

"That is what we are facing, ladies and gentlemen." Vance spoke loudly, his voice grim. "That is what is coming here." He paused to let that sink in. "If we do not defeat this enemy, we will be fighting those things on Columbia, Persis, Shanghan." He made sure to list important colonies of the major Powers. "We will be facing them on Earth."

Vance's last statement hit everyone like a sledgehammer. Earthbound elites and diplomats tended to think of the colonies as separate from the home world, more expendable. They were important for their resources, yes, but not the same as Earth. But Vance had plunged right into the unthinkable… the fact that nothing would stop this enemy from moving into the Sol system…from sweeping it clean of human life. Indeed, the situation at Sol was even worse from a military perspective. The Powers fortified their colonies, but the Sol system itself was demilitarized. Only the Martians had any appreciable orbital defenses. Earth would lay open and prostrate before an invader.

"We have all had our differences, our disputes." Vance's voice boomed out loudly, the echo bouncing off the high ceilings and reverberating throughout the room. "Yet cooperation is not impossible. Faced with imminent apocalypse, our forefathers forged the Treaty of Paris and ended almost a century of war on Earth." They weren't Vance's forefathers – his family had already emigrated to Mars – but he made the point nonetheless. "We can do the same thing now…to set aside our struggles and unite to avert Armageddon."

Vance stood silent and looked out over the assemblage. Slowly, tentatively the debate began again, and in a few minutes Vance realized he'd succeeded. There would be hours of discussion, he knew, but in the end they would agree. It was the only option. Vance would have his Grand Alliance.

The ship was almost ready to set out. Another hour and the refueling would be complete. The Torch was barely a ship; it was really a few cabins perched on top of a fusion reactor and four powerful engines.

Vance sat in the embarkation area waiting to board. He was seated in a hard plastic chair, enjoying a few last moments of the light lunar gravity. Soon enough he'd be squeezed into the force dampening chamber, something he was dreading. The crews had taken to calling the Torch's innovative new system the "womb," a term Vance had to admit was, at least superficially, fairly descriptive.

The trip would be hard, especially so soon after his breakneck voyage back to Sol. But there was no choice, no time to spare. Vance had been successful and had secured the agreement he'd come for. In the true style of politicians, the delegates had argued for some hours on what to call the partnership. Vance had put forth the name Grand Alliance, but the other Powers objected to the name's similarity to Western Alliance, feeling it implied superior status for that nation. Coalition, confederation, and league were rejected for the same reason. Vance's negative opinion of people was reinforced when the squabbling ambassadors wasted precious hours seeking a word that none of the

Powers used in their names. But finally they agreed to Grand Pact. Vance thought it was a cumbersome name, but he was just glad to have the issue settled.

He knew his creation was imperfect. Despite the agreement, despite the real possibility of extermination that forged it, he was sure the Powers would play games. They would fight the invaders together, but they would jockey for position, each trying to insure it ended this war in a favorable position. Greed and stupidity would win out even over fear. But it was the best he could achieve, and it was a damned sight better than nothing.

He wondered how the various military establishments would fare under the Pact. The soldiers were less likely to debate and scheme and argue over details than the politicians and diplomats. He was sure of that, at least. But there were other issues...distrust, anger, old hatreds. How well would Cain's Marines fight alongside Caliphate Janissaries? Would CEL grenadiers and the Chasseurs of Europa Federalis be able to put aside a century of hatred and war?

Vance didn't know the answer, but he suspected the survival of the human race would depend on it.

Chapter 19

Conference Room
AS Lexington
Outer reaches of Alpha 327 System

The conference had been going on for hours. It was the second time they'd met in the wastes of the Alpha 327 system. Alpha 327 was an unremarkable star with two barren, useless planets. But it was midway between Armstrong and Farpoint, making it the ideal location for strategy meetings.

Since they'd met a little over four months earlier, everything had changed. The enemy was methodically occupying the minor colony worlds along the route to Farpoint. That was tactically helpful, allowing more time to fortify Farpoint, but it was tragic as well. Those planets had small populations and, while the navy had evacuated as many people as it could, there were still colonists left behind. It tore at Cain to leave anyone unprotected, abandoned to die at the hands of a ruthless alien enemy, but there was nothing he could do. Any small forces he could have deployed to those worlds would have been wiped out; in the end they wouldn't have saved a single colonist. He simply couldn't afford to fritter away his strength on small, futile defense efforts. Once again, the cold math of war was clear. Cain knew he was right, but that didn't make it any easier to live with himself.

The attack on the Caliphate and the release of Hofstader's findings reduced the tension between the Powers. The diplomats had been working overtime since Vance left Luna. Slowly, grudgingly, they all came to realize they were facing something that transcended their mutual distrust and territorial squabbles... they came to realize they faced not just defeat, but the possible extinction of the human race. The Commnet communications from Luna reached Alpha 327 before Vance's ship, so Admiral Garret had to update the Martian on what had transpired since he'd left the summit.

The establishment of the Grand Pact and the receding threat of war between the Powers allowed Garret to reinforce Admiral West's Third Fleet. Positioned around Lexington was an armada of warships, all bound for Farpoint, and behind them, a flotilla of transports carrying part of Angus Frasier's 2nd Marine Division, welcome reinforcements to back up the battered 1st Division.

Cain was listening to Vance's update. He was in the same chair he'd occupied four months earlier, the only real difference being the larger crowd…and the third star on his collar. Lieutenant General Erik Cain had just assumed command of the reactivated I Corps. It was a formation more formidable on paper than in reality. Teller's 1st Brigade was shattered, and the survivors had pulled back to Armstrong to regroup and reinforce. That left Prescott's 2nd Brigade and the below-strength divisional support assets under 1st Division's new CO, Major General Darius Jax.

Angus Frasier's 2nd Division had mobilized, but could only field one combat-ready brigade. Designated 3rd Brigade, it was on the way to Farpoint, led by Frasier himself. General Gilson was overseeing the final training and organization of Frasier's 4th Brigade on Armstrong.

"The vote has been confirmed. The Grand Pact is in effect." Vance had recounted the council on Luna, bringing some perspective to the messages Holm and Garret had received via Commnet. "The Powers are united against this threat."

"So we're just supposed to let enemy…excuse me…Caliphate and CAC forces free access through our space?" Cain was the first to speak up, and he made his doubts clear. "The last thing we need is having to worry about untrustworthy forces in our rear."

"General Cain…" Vance knew he would have to combat this type of feeling among the Alliance officers, and he thought

addressing Cain formally would lend gravity to the point. "…
you better than anyone know what we are facing. Your forces
will not be able to defeat this enemy without help." He paused,
staring at Cain, but trying to gauge Holm's and Garret's expressions in his peripheral vision. "You need more allies, general,
and the only ones available are former enemies."

Cain was silent, but he didn't look convinced. Intellectually
he knew Vance was right. But he still couldn't reconcile himself
with the whole idea. How was he going to make peace with all
the ghosts…brothers and sisters who were killed by the very
people he was now supposed to welcome as allies?

Vance sighed softly. He was frustrated, but he also knew he
couldn't understand the difficulty of what he was asking…not
like these men and women. Vance was a manipulator and the
head of an intelligence agency. He was accustomed to bartering
with enemies and using whatever resources he could put to his
advantage. Besides, the Martian Confederation had managed
to remain mostly neutral in the wars between the Powers. They
had better relations with some nations, certainly. But the deep
hatreds weren't there.

He looked at Holm…then at Cain. The Alliance had fought
the Caliphate in space for over a century…and before that the
precursor powers had battled on Earth for almost 100 years.
Holm and Cain had watched friends blown apart…they'd held
comrades in their arms as they drew their last breaths. And
many of those friends had died at the hands of Caliphate forces.
Now they were supposed overcome two centuries of hatred to
welcome the detested Janissaries into their ranks. The logic of
the plan was unassailable, but men's minds work on more than
pure analytics. Vance knew his Alliance friends would have a
hard time accepting the Pact…but he was confident they would
recognize the necessity and learn to work with their old enemies.
Reasonably confident, at least.

Garret cleared his throat…loudly enough to get the attention of the room. "In any event, other than Mr. Vance's Martian
forces, it will be some time before the rest of the Powers can
get any substantial units to the frontlines." He paused, looking

first at Holm and Cain and then at Vance. "I suggest we focus first on matters with relevancy in the immediate future." Garret was trying to sidestep the issue for now, but he knew it wouldn't be that long before they had to deal with it. The other Powers were already mobilized, with substantial forces positioned on the borders. Any day now, Garret might have to allow a CAC or Caliphate battlefleet to sail right past his defenses. That wasn't going to be an easy day.

Holm took his cue from Garret. "I'd like to hear from Dr. Hofstader and Colonel Sparks now." He glanced at Garret briefly then at the two scientists. "I think it would help us all to be up to speed on the technology aspects of this fight." His eyes fixed on the German physicist. "Dr. Hofstader, would you be kind enough to bring us up to date on your research?"

Hofstader took a deep breath and slid his chair back. He stood up and looked around the table. "Certainly, General Holm." He paused, thinking for a moment about where to start. His mind was always active, darting wildly from one topic to another. But these people were depending on him to give them clear guidance, not an outpouring of disorganized thoughts. He wasn't in a lab now…he knew his insight was a key component in learning to defeat this enemy. In determining if humankind would survive.

"Thank you, Admiral Garret." Hofstader looked haggard. He'd been working almost around the clock for months now, and the exhaustion was beginning to show. "I would like to begin with the energy we detected in the transmissions from Epsilon Eridani IV. Although I cannot confirm this with absolute certainty, I now am totally convinced we are dealing with a form of dark energy." He paused, trying to decide how much detail to offer. He tried to remember he wasn't talking to a panel of theoretical physicists. "This energy is undetectable to our normal scanning devices. In fact, we originally picked up the signal by accident when my colleague Dr. Travers was attempting to detect signs of life."

Vance was looking at Hofstader as the scientist spoke. Travers, he thought, had been doing a lot more than Hofstader knew.

But that wasn't something they needed to discuss, at least not yet.

"We hypothesized that there may have been numerous prior transmissions that our detection devices were simply unable to intercept. Indeed, I just received a Commnet transmission from Dr. Travers. It was extremely cryptic…I'm sure he didn't want to say too much on Commnet, but I believe he has been able to detect further signals."

"He has." Vance had to fight the instinct to keep his mouth shut. Travers was one of his people as well as a gifted scientist. Normally, Vance would be cautious about flaunting that connection. But he'd just lectured everyone on the need for cooperation, and he figured it should start with him. That Commnet transmission to Hofstader had also included a heavily coded message, one intended for Roderick Vance. "I have received a communication from him as well. He has detected four additional transmissions, though he has been unable to locate the source."

"The transmitter could be anywhere…even the core of the planet." Hofstader's eyes had widened when Vance mentioned the additional signals. "I believe that the type of signal we are dealing with would move through the rocky mantle of the planet as easily as through deep space." He looked from Vance toward Garret and Compton. "I also theorize that this energy can be used to send a signal directly through a warp gate."

There was a stir in the room. No energy form yet detected could pass through a warp gate. The Commnet system was the fastest way to send a message, with transmissions traveling at lightspeed across each system before being downloaded into drones and sent through the warp gates.

Hofstader took a breath and continued. "I am sure you can see the implications of faster transmission." He paused and swallowed. "Perhaps less immediately obvious is the enormous amount of power required to send a message through multiple solar systems without retransmission. Once again, we are dealing with a technology that is likely centuries ahead of us…if not millennia.

The German physicist paused and looked around the room again. He'd always been a maverick scientist, willing to go with his hunches rather than spend months or years endlessly running proofs, but now he was speculating wildly, and even he was uncomfortable with the level of pure guesswork in what he was reporting. But he knew there was no choice...if the men and women fighting and dying on the frontier couldn't stop these things, this enemy would cut through the heavily populated areas of human-occupied space. They would attack Earth and spread death through the great cities of the Powers. He imagined neatly-arrayed columns of Reapers marching down the Kurfürstendamm and laying waste to the Institute. Human civilization – if not the entire human race – would cease to exist.

"Dr. Hofstader?" It was Admiral Garret who pulled Hofstader from his haunted daydream.

"Yes, admiral. Please excuse my distraction." Hofstader was startled, and he pushed aside the nightmarish thoughts. "I... ah...would also like to review the strange metal used in the exoskeletons of the larger battle robots... the ones we have been calling Reapers." The name, initially used by Teller's exhausted troops to refer to the largest of the enemy combatants, had stuck. The smaller units were called simply battle robots...or just 'bots. "As I stated at our last meeting, I noted that this same alloy was found in several areas of the Epsilon Eridani IV complex. I have now completed a deeper examination of the material, and I have some insights...some highly speculative ones... which I would like to share."

He moved back a step from the table and pulled the control unit from his pocket. "I believe this alloy contains a lattice-like structure of dark matter, which serves to strengthen the metal and also to make it far more resistant to certain forces." He flipped the switch and the viewscreen activated, displaying a large diagram showing the theorized composition of the metal in question. "We unfortunately know very little about dark matter, so my ability to even guess at the characteristics of this material is minimal." He looked over at Holm and Cain. "For now, I would simply assume that it is very, very tough, and it will take your strongest weapons to damage it." He paused and glanced at Garret. "I also believe it is likely that this material is used to some extent on their spacecraft, possibly the hulls. I would expect it to be highly resistant to laser fire though, again, that is a pure guess on my part."

Garret and Holm both leaned forward and looked at Hofstader, but Garret spoke first. "Do you have any insights into how we should attack this metal? Any weaknesses or vulnerabilities?"

Hofstader frowned. "I'm afraid, admiral, that all I can offer now is the suggestion that you bring as much force to bear against it." He sighed softly. "I know that is not terribly helpful."

"No, I'm afraid it's not." Garret smiled briefly...the whole thing seemed like a sort of gallows humor.

"I have been researching it, but you have to understand, we have barely been able to confirm the existence of dark matter. The ability to secure or produce a large quantity and to manipulate it in a manufacturing process is utterly beyond us." He paused, then added, "Indeed, a strict interpretation of our network of theories suggests that this type of usage is not possible."

"I guess that book needs to be rewritten." Cain leaned back in his chair, half-lost in thought.

"Indeed, general. I suspect much of what we believed we knew will be subject to significant change." He paused, rubbing his chin. "We will be researching this for decades...centuries, probably."

"Assuming anyone is left alive to study it, you mean." Holm was fidgeting in his chair, trying to get comfortable. That was becoming more difficult for him with each passing year. The rejuv treatments slowed aging, but they didn't seem to do anything for old wounds. "I'm afraid we're going to be needing some help from you and your people in a much shorter time frame."

"I assure you I understand fully, general." Hofstader wasn't an intellectual snob, but it was sometimes frustrating dealing with non-scientists. Some of them seemed to think you could drop a chunk of silicon in the ancient Roman forum and, three months later, they'd have a working fab producing integrated circuits. His academic colleagues frustrated him too, with their slow pace and rules and constant delays. But research did take time, no matter how many guns were pointing at your head. "We are doing everything possible to aid the war effort. Neither I nor anyone on Colonel Sparks staff have been out of the lab for more than a few hours of sleep every couple days."

Holm softened his tone. "No one is suggesting anything to the contrary, doctor. We already owe you a great deal for the insights you have provided. Without your data indicating the invasion was external, we might still be facing imminent war with the CAC and Caliphate." He looked down at the table. "We're all just frustrated." Another pause. "I'm afraid I don't react very well to not knowing what to do."

"That is entirely understandable, general." Hofstader wasn't about to criticize anyone for being on edge. He was terrified himself, and plunging into his research 20 hours a day was the only thing that took his mind off of it. He hadn't thought of the Marines being subject to the same fears as him, and realizing that the great military heroes of the Alliance were also scared wasn't helping his own state of mind. "We do have some information that is useful in the short term." He glanced over at Sparks. "The colonel's people are working on some equipment that will certainly help."

"Colonel…" Holm looked over at Sparks. "…perhaps you could report now." He glanced back over at Hofstader. "Though please interject, doctor, if you have anything to add at any point."

Sparks stood up a little too forcefully, and his chair slid away from the table. He reached behind himself and pulled it back. "Thank you, General Holm." Sparks was reflexively straightening his uniform. The meeting was casual, but he was still uncomfortable with all the rank present. "Dr. Hofstader is correct. We have utilized much of his work, as well as the data sent back from the battlezones, and we are working on several systems that can probably be put into the field in the short term."

He reached down to the table and picked up his own controller, pushing the button and bringing a schematic of a spacecraft onto the screen. "First of all, we feel quite confident that the enemy vessels carry their anti-matter weaponry in exterior harnesses not unlike our missile racks." He clicked the controller again, and the display changed to a close up of the ship's hull. "Everyone needs to understand there is an enormous amount of conjecture in what we are able to tell you today. This is a conceptualization of the most common type of enemy ship, which we are calling the Gargoyle for reference purposes. These vessels mass approximately 68,000 tons, about the displacement of one of our cruisers."

He clicked again, bringing up another image, a view of the same ship from a different angle. "Notwithstanding the size of these ships, they appear to have firepower well in excess of one of our Yorktown class capital ships. Indeed, it is likely they have several times the effective strength, though the technology difference makes straight-line comparisons difficult." Ships weren't really in Spark's area of responsibility, but the joint naval-Marine research team was reporting to him, and he was presenting all of the data to the high command.

"Despite the strength of these ships, we have identified a number of potential vulnerabilities." He clicked the controller again. The display showed a complex schematic with icons and vector arrows all over it. "This is a diagram of the missile attack on Raptor near Adelaide." He turned to look at the screen. "I know it's a little hard to read, so I will get right to the point. The enemy seems to be quite susceptible to our ECM systems...far more vulnerable than one would expect considering the technological advantage they enjoy."

He clicked again, and a chart listing percentages appeared. "These are the estimated percentages of enemy missiles successfully diverted from the targeted ships in every engagement for which we have data." He hit the controller again, zooming in on the chart. "You will note that ECM effectiveness exceeds 35% in every circumstance, and ranges as high as 61%. Further, if we look only at our first line warships and remove the match-ups involving civilian and local craft, the minimum percentage is 46%. Comparable rates of ECM interception when facing Caliphate or CAC vessels are in the mid-teens."

"Do you have an explanation for this disparity, colonel?" Terrance Compton was flicking his eyes back and forth between the display and Sparks.

"Only an educated guess, sir." He glanced over at Hofstader. "Dr. Hofstader and I have discussed it, and we feel it is likely nothing more than the fact that our electronic systems and frequencies differ from the ones they use and any that they have faced before. The Alliance and the CAC and Caliphate know each other's weapons and systems very well, but we are new to this enemy." He paused, waiting a few seconds to see if there were any questions. "This is a lucky break for us, and we need to use it to the maximum advantage while it lasts." His voice became grimmer. "They will undoubtedly adapt at some point."

"It's a damned lucky break, considering the power of those missiles." Garret leaned back in his chair rubbing his forehead. "Nelson, send the yeoman in with some analgesics." He looked around the room. "Anyone else?" Most of those present nodded or raised a hand. "Nelson, make that a dozen doses." Nelson was Garret's virtual assistant. The AI's code had been wiped clean as part of Gavin Stark's plot to kidnap Garret during the rebellions. Nelson had managed to get a last message out to Admiral Compton, and he'd hidden a copy of the kernel, the primary component of his synthetic personality, in the transmission. After he was freed, Garret had ordered the AI reconstituted. The result was only a moderate success. The new system was very similar to the original Nelson, but Garret could tell the difference…it just wasn't the same. The AIs weren't human, but Garret still felt like he'd lost a friend.

"In order to press this advantage, I have had my team working on some enhancements to our existing ECM suites." Sparks paused when the door opened, and the yeoman came in carrying a tray. The steward walked around the room, offering a small tab of tablets and a glass of water to each person seated at the table. Most of the room's occupants took them.

Sparks waited until the door closed behind the yeoman. "As I was saying, we have developed some new features for our ECM suites, including a randomization routine that varies signals and frequencies." He took a breath and wished he'd taken one of the painkillers. "We hope this will delay the enemy's efforts to adapt to our ECM. The modifications are relatively easy to make, even in the field. I can have a team ready to ship out to Third Fleet in a week. We can upgrade Admiral West's ordnance on station at Farpoint."

Garret's expression widened. "Good work, colonel. I didn't expect anything deployable so quickly. Let me know what transport resources you need for your team." He knew West was going to have a massive fight on her hands at Farpoint, and he wanted to get her any support he could.

"Thank you, sir." Sparks looked at Holm, who nodded. Sparks was a Marine, and he reported to Holm, not Garret. "A small transport will be more than sufficient. It is mostly a programming change. The hardware upgrades required are minimal."

"Send your orders back to Armstrong. I will have a vessel prepared for your people." Garret paused then added, "I will also authorize any materials they need. Have them present their manifest, and they will be able to requisition whatever they require.

"Thank you, admiral. I will send the directive as soon as we are finished here." Sparks was looking right at Garret. "We are also working on a new system, but it is not currently ready." He glanced around the table. Every eye was on him. "We have preliminary designs on an ECM missile. Essentially, the missile mimics one of our vessels – power output, communications traffic…everything."

He could see the questioning looks. "The purpose is to trick the enemy into expending their anti-matter weaponry while still out of range. Our examination of the enemy's behavior in combat indicates that their tactical protocols call for deploying their heavy anti-matter ordnance at long range. Our studies further suggest that their forces are indeed supply-constrained with regard to anti-matter weaponry." He paused and looked around the table. He could see from the expressions that they knew where he was going. "If we are able to convince the enemy our ships are closer than they are, we may be able to take the anti-matter weapons out of the equation." Another pause. "Remember, these are not just the large warheads...we also believe they have anti-matter drives, which explains the massive thrust capacity of the enemy's initial volleys."

"If that system is effective, it will go a long way to giving us at least a fighting chance." Garret glanced over at Compton, who nodded. "This system needs to be prioritized." He looked back at Sparks. "Just let me know what you need, colonel." Garret paused, looking into the Marine engineer's eyes. "Anything."

"Thank you, sir. I believe we are nearly finished with the design. After that is ready we will produce testable prototypes." Sparks took a breath. "I'm afraid my normal facilities are not set up to manufacture ship to ship weaponry." Anticipating the next question he continued, "With luck we may be able to deploy the system in four months."

"Thank you, colonel." Holm had a sledgehammer pounding through his skull. He'd taken the analgesics, but he'd be damned if he could tell what good they were doing. "I understand you are also working on some things for our Marines on the ground." He was happy to share his engineering wunderkind with the navy, but his people needed help as well.

"Yes, general." Spark's voice perked up...developing systems for ground combat was his specialty. We are working on a number of moderate upgrades, mostly focused on increasing the impact power of our weapons. These things take a lot of punishment, and we need to be able to dish it out." He clicked the controller again, and the screen displayed small schematics of the primary Marine weapon systems. "We are working on increasing the impact velocity of our mag-rifles as well as developing a weapon that delivers a larger projectile. We are also working on a series of small upgrades to our other systems."

He looked back at Holm and then to Cain. "There is one

other research project I would like to present. It was pre-existing in another form, but we were able to build on that prior design work to rush this to a prototype." He clicked the controller again, and the screen displayed a monstrous suit of armor. More than armor. It had the shape of a fighting suit, but it was over three meters in height and massively broad across the midsection. There were SAW-sized autocannons built into each arm and hyper-velocity missile launchers mounted on each shoulder. "Meet the Obliterator…our next-generation heavy armor."

Everyone in the room stared at the screen. There was a long silence, and a tiny, self-satisfied smile crept onto Sparks' lips. It was Cain who spoke first. "That is truly impressive, colonel. Is it realistic? Or just something conceptual?"

Sparks' smile widened. "It is very realistic, general." He looked at Holm then back to Cain. "In fact, we have built ten of them."

There were a few gasps in the room. "You mean this actually exists?" It was General Holm this time. "I was aware of the enhanced armor research project…I assume that is what you built on…but this is quite a leap from where we were on that."

"Yes, sir." Sparks wiped the smile off his face. He was a little nervous – he'd exceeded his authority in going right to production. "As you know, sir, we backburnered the project. The proposed armor was simply too expensive and would have required too much additional training before deployment. Against our projected potential adversaries at the time, we determined the same resources could produce greater battlefield power with our existing weapons." He paused then added, "In other words, we could get a section of normal Marines in the field for every enhanced suit…and the section was more effective."

He glanced quickly at the naval officers then back to Holm and Cain. "Once I saw the footage of the enemy's Reapers I knew our tactical needs had changed. We have to have something to match those monsters." He clicked the controller, bringing up an enlarged schematic of the heavy armor, with arrows and small captions describing each system. "I upscaled the suits – the original ones were considerably smaller than this

– and I added a second reactor. The extra power allowed us to load the thing with high-impact weapons…just what we need to take the enemy robots down."

"It looks extraordinary, colonel." Cain's eyes were focused on the screen. "When can I have them?"

Sparks cleared his throat. "I wish it was that simple, sir."

"What do you need?" Cain finally turned away from the display to look at Sparks. "I'm sure General Holm will give you whatever resources you require."

"Yes, sir, I understand that." Sparks shuffled his feet nervously. "But it's not just a question of resources. In order to get the prototypes built, I skipped all kinds of preliminary testing. There is no way we could put Marines on the battlefield in these suits until we conduct extensive field tests." He shifted his glance to Holm – Cain's impatient stare was making him tense.

"Additionally, the men and women using these suits will require extensive training. You will note that, unlike our normal armor, these units are much larger than the Marines who will wear them." Sparks hesitated, trying to decide how to explain. "Operating one of these suits is quite unlike wearing standard armor. The relationship between the moves of the user and what the suit does is considerably different. It's sort of like walking on stilts…on steroids. The arms have the same issue."

"How quickly can we train someone for this?" Holm's question was right to the point. Cain looked like he might argue, but Holm knew Sparks was right. Putting untrained Marines in these suits in battle wasn't an option. He might just as well shoot them in the head.

Sparks was silent for a few seconds; he could only take a wild guess how long it would take a Marine to become proficient in the new armor. "Well, sir, under normal circumstances, I would say at least a year…possibly 18 months." Cain looked like he was going to interrupt, but Sparks continued first. "But I believe we could cover the basics in four months, perhaps five." He glanced over at Cain, who still looked unsatisfied with the answer. "I just don't see how we can get anyone even remotely battle-ready in less time."

"Ok, colonel." Holm spoke quickly, mostly to forestall Cain from arguing pointlessly. Cain was the best Marine Holm had ever met, and he thought of him like a son. But there was no question…he was a pain in the ass sometimes. His stubbornness and impatience were almost legendary in the Corps, and Holm had experienced it firsthand many times. "I will give you a blank check to proceed. This project is priority one - we need these in the field as quickly as possible."

"Yes, sir." Sparks started to sit, but he snapped back to attention. "Sir, there's one other thing."

"Yes, colonel?"

"Well, general, we were able to build these prototypes on Armstrong, but I don't see any realistic way of producing them in quantity anywhere except Earth." Sparks looked toward the display. "There simply aren't production facilities on any of the colony worlds for something like this." He paused. "And that's going to add a lot of transit time getting them to the front."

The room was quiet for half a minute. It was Cain's voice that broke the silence. "Cheer up, colonel." His voice was grim. "The front may be a lot closer to Earth by then."

Chapter 20

Alliance Intelligence Facility Q
Dakota Foothills
Western Alliance, Earth

Gavin Stark was impressed. He'd only visited the facility once before, when it was still under construction. Plan C was top secret, possibly the most confidential operation in the history of Alliance Intelligence…and Facility Q was the most important part of the whole thing. Stark himself was too high profile, and he didn't want to draw attention to the abandoned wastelands of the Dakotas, where he'd built Q and where work now proceeded ceaselessly toward the completion of his master plan.

The facility itself was underground, deeply buried and heavily shielded. Indeed, to any observer, the location would appear to be nothing but the outer pastures of a large cattle ranch. Of course, the steer were owned by Alliance Intelligence, and the cowboys herding them were heavily-armed agents. Occasionally a drifter would wander onto the land and end up reprocessed as cattle feed.

The complex was massive, one of the most expensive undertakings in history. Getting it built in secret, and hiding the costs in the government budgets, had been Stark's masterpiece. His plan had been brilliant and his execution flawless, but it had also taken a torrent of bribery, blackmail, and assassination to make it happen. When the false accounting finally collapsed in on itself, the Alliance government would be bankrupt and the economy would probably implode. But Stark didn't care. He expected to be in power by then and, without the troublesome politicians interfering, he'd turn the Alliance into the dominant

Superpower...and those arrogant colonists into pliant and duti-
ful citizens. The economic chaos would actually aid his coup,
and a few years of depression and famine would be useful to
reduce the surplus population. There were far too many Cogs,
in his estimation, and a reduction by half would be welcome.

"Dr. Zenta, your work appears to be proceeding according
to schedule. I must congratulate you." Stark stood in the small
conference room, staring out through a large glass wall at the
cavernous chamber beyond. There were large metallic tanks,
thousands of them, lined up in neat rows.

"Yes, Mr. Stark. We have been most fortunate in that we
have avoided any major delays." Zenta was a short man, with a
bald head and a large crooked nose. There was an intensity to
the scientist that made even Stark uncomfortable. "The prototypes have been moved into phase three. Director Samuels has
begun his work with them already."

"Good, good." Stark had to suppress a smile. "The prototypes are, of course, expendable. I want them thoroughly
tested." Plan C was Stark's ultimate scheme, a vast project
designed to settle his scores...and gain for him the absolute
power he craved. It had been underway for some time – and it
would take years more to bring it to fruition, but he had resolved
to be patient. His past plans had been thwarted largely because
he had moved too soon. Now he would make sure everything
was prepared. When C was fully launched, those cursed Marines
and miserable colonies basking in their new liberties would pay
the price...just as the gutless bureaucrats in Washbalt would.

"I assure you, Mr. Stark, that every aspect of the plan will
be thoroughly tested before the units are released." Zenta was
the mastermind behind the science of Plan C, though he had no
idea of the full extent of Stark's intentions. Zenta was out to
prove his theories and breakthroughs to the world, and he had
gratefully accepted Stark's sponsorship to make that a possibility. Stark had seen the practical applications immediately, and
he'd spared no expense to make it all happen. Of course, in
Stark's plan, Zenta did not long outlive his usefulness. Gavin
Stark was a big believer in cleaning up loose ends.

"Very well, doctor." Zenta was an egomaniac, and Stark knew it. It was time to pump him up. Stark wanted the scientist's total focus, at least until he had completed his part of the plan. "You are to be commended. Your scientific breakthroughs are nothing short of miraculous." Stark smiled, though on him it was unnatural and a bit unsettling. "We will shake the world with your discoveries, doctor." Stark turned to leave, and once his back was turned to the scientist, his small smile expanded into a wide grin. Yes, he thought…we will shake the world. And beyond.

"I will be at the ranch for a couple days." Stark made a face. "As few as possible." He'd purchased a small ranch near the facility for his personal use. It was a secondary cover. He was pretty sure he'd traveled here in secrecy, but just in case there was a leak he wanted a backup explanation. It wasn't at all uncommon for government officials of his stature to have opulent vacation homes, often in remote locales. Stark himself could think of few reasons to leave Washbalt unless it was on necessary business, but it was eminently believable that the Alliance's spymaster sought solace riding horses at his ranch.

Rafael Samuels towered above Stark. He'd always been a big man, but he'd gotten fatter over the years. He was wearing a black uniform, a gaudy thing trimmed with silver shoulder lace and buttons. The army for which it was designed didn't exist yet, but Samuels had spent his entire adult life in the Marine Corps, and he wasn't comfortable thinking of himself as a civilian. Stark didn't really care if Samuels wanted to prance around in an overdone dress uniform, though he thought the whole thing was a little silly.

"Perhaps some rest is what you need, Gavin." Samuels had never been invited to call Stark by his first name. He'd heard Dutton doing it, and he'd just followed the old man's lead. Stark indulged it. Samuels was a weak man, and now that he was no longer a Marine, he was a bit lost, haunted by regrets and doubts. Stark was more than willing to let Samuels believe he was a trusted confidante if it helped get the job done. When everything had played out, perhaps he would allow Samuels to enjoy a little power, though more likely the ex-Marine would be a loose end that had outlived its usefulness. And Gavin Stark didn't like loose ends.

Samuels had been troubled, but he was starting to come around. He'd been immensely depressed in the aftermath of the plot against the Corps. Samuels had been a reluctant participant in that unfortunate affair. Once he was exposed as a traitor he was committed...he couldn't even fool himself into believing there was a way back. The cold hatred of the Marines affected him deeply, and he regretted his actions. Stark sensed he was in danger of losing his new tool, and he continued his subtle manipulations, whispering in Samuel's ear, shaping the thoughts of his somewhat dim-witted accomplice.

Stark had initially lured the Marine commandant slowly into treachery. Samuel's act had been the darkest betrayal in the history of the Corps, but it hadn't started that way. In the beginning, Stark had offered only redress for grievances. Samuels hadn't considered the ruthless methods Alliance Intelligence would employ to secure his rise – he only wanted the position and respect he felt he'd been wrongfully denied. He was shocked when he realized what Stark's people had done, and he'd almost exposed them. But the human mind is capable of enormous rationalization, and Samuels realized he couldn't blow the whistle on Alliance Intelligence without exposing his own role in the whole affair. He teetered on the edge for a while, considering sacrificing himself to stop Stark's plans then and there. But in the end he chose his own survival, his own prosperity. The commandant's chair was right there, beckoning to him...all he had to do was keep his mouth shut.

Later, when the true scope of Stark's plans became apparent, Samuels had another moment of doubt. But he was too deep in; there was no way for him to escape...not without being destroyed in the process. Once again, Samuels felt guilt and uncertainty, but not enough to sacrifice himself. He went along with Stark and became the most hated Marine who'd ever lived.

"I find rest too stressful." Stark's voice was businesslike. "I spend the entire time wondering what incompetence is going on in my absence." He was staring down at a 'pad, reading a series of figures. "It appears you have done quite well so far, Rafael."

Samuels smiled. "Thank you, Gavin. I am fully prepared for the next phase." He'd been plagued by doubts, but over time he'd become more resigned to his choice. He knew he could never go back to the Corps, and the certainty of that had closed in on him. First it was frustration, so bad it almost paralyzed him into inactivity. But gradually it turned to resentment...until he blamed the Marines themselves for their stubborn hatred.

Stark's eyes bored into Samuel's. "Rafael, I cannot express how crucial the next five years will be. Your role is absolutely essential." He paused, largely for effect. He knew exactly what he was going to say. "I need you. I am counting on you more than anyone else."

Samuels smiled again. Stark grinned back, but his thoughts were derisive...what an imbecile, he's easier to manipulate than a child.

Stark turned to leave, but Samuels spoke first. "Gavin?"

"Yes?"

"What about the situation on the frontier?" Samuels sounded concerned, uncertain.

Stark turned back to face his companion. "What about it?"

Samuels looked confused. "Shouldn't we be doing something?"

Stark stared back with an expression so cold Samuels felt a chill down his whole body. "Let the colonists and those thrice-cursed Marines deal with it. They wanted their independence. Let them choke on it." Stark's features morphed into a smile so feral it was almost inhuman. "Perhaps this enemy will do our work for us. The Marines...and the forces of the other Powers...will be decimated in this new war. They will be in ruins... just as we are about to strike."

"But what if they can't hold this new enemy back?"

Stark turned and started to walk away. "Yes, it will be all too easy. And then we will have the power."

Samuels stood there as Stark rounded the corner. He tried to suppress a shiver, but he couldn't. The head of Alliance Intelligence didn't seem to care that all mankind was threatened with destruction. He was starting to doubt Stark's sanity.

Chapter 21

Conference Room
AS Lexington
Outer reaches of Alpha 327 System

The second day of the conference had been as grueling as the first. Garret wanted to get through as much as he could while he had everyone together. They'd be sending reports back and forth on Commnet, but that was mostly one-way communication, with responses taking days or weeks to come back. There was just no substitute for the interaction of a face to face meeting, especially when they were working through problems and planning on this scale. He had the best military minds in the Alliance in the room – and a few of the top scientific ones as well. He wanted to get the best out of it before he sent them all on their way.

"I'd like Admiral Winton to report now." Garret glanced over at Holm, who nodded his agreement. "He has some insights on the enemy's logistics that I think are very interesting." He looked over at Winton. "Admiral?"

Winton stood up slowly, straightening his uniform as he did. "Thank you, Admiral Garret." Winton was the senior logistics officer in the navy, responsible for the vast supply operation that kept its battlefleets in action. "My staff has been studying the available data on the enemy's operations, and we have developed several theories that have considerable relevancy to the tactical situation."

Winton stepped back from the table. "The first issue involves the transport and weapons capacity of the enemy ships. As you all know, the largest vessels yet encountered are approximately comparable in mass to our own cruisers." He pressed the controller, bringing up an image of a ship. "Because of the technical superiority of the enemy, these vessels have substantially more firepower than our largest battleships, despite a mass less than one half as large." He looked around the table. "We've already discussed this. But we haven't examined the enemy's capability for carrying and supporting ground forces."

Cain's head snapped up. He had zoned out a bit when the topic had been naval combat, but the mention of ground fighting woke him from his daydreams. Cain was tired to his core. He missed Sarah; the separations were getting harder to take. It was tough to concentrate, to focus on what had to be done. He had to force himself to participate where years before he'd have been chomping at the bit.

"We have no idea how the enemy's command and control functions, but it is clear that all or most of their ground combat units are robotic." Winton reached down to the table and grabbed his glass of water. "This has serious implications with regard to the logistics of ground warfare." He took a quick drink and cleared his throat. "Specifically, the enemy is likely able to transport vastly more ground troops per available ton than we are. Humans require food and other supplies. Our ships are required to have acceleration couches for every Marine and crewmember onboard. We need gyms and mess halls and other support facilities. They require none of this. Indeed, the battle robots are likely kept on racks or some other form of storage system." He looked at Holm and then Cain. "I estimate they can carry up to ten times the number of ground troops we can in the same space."

"This may explain why we have not been able to identify any dedicated troops transports." Garret glanced over at Compton. "Perhaps they don't need them. They have room enough in each of their warships for a strike force of robots."

Compton leaned back in his chair and nodded. "What do you think, Jack?"

Winton set his glass down on the table. "I agree completely, Admiral Compton. I think that is a highly likely scenario. We can be sure it will be very difficult to estimate the size of the enemy's ground force reserves from an analysis of fleet units present. It is also likely they can deploy far larger numbers than they have to date. If Colonel Teller had defeated the enemy on Cornwall, it is very possible they could have simply landed another strike force as large as the first. Or not. Or twice as large. We just don't know."

Holm sighed, a little louder than he'd intended. "We've never had to fight a war where we know so little about the enemy. We're just going to have to take our best guesses and move based on those."

Winton was nodding as Holm spoke. "I agree, general. My best guess is that the enemy has ground capability we haven't seen yet. And if those ships are also heavily automated that frees up even more space."

"Well, all we can do is keep our guard up." Garret wanted to move the meeting along. "We're already committing everything we can scrape up anyway." He looked over at Winton. "Let's move on to any other insights, Jack."

Winton cleared his throat. "Yes, admiral. I think we can say with a reasonable degree of confidence that the enemy is experiencing some sort of logistical problem. Our analysis of the enemy hulls suggests that they can carry more anti-matter weapons than we have seen used…even restricting these to external mounts only. It certainly looks like a shortage to me. Whether it is an overall lack of sufficient ordnance or a transport problem in bringing it to the front, we don't know. It is possible that both conditions exist. But, at present, the enemy seems to have sharply limited supplies of their most powerful weapons."

"That will make Colonel Spark's ECM drones even more useful. If their supplies are low already and we can trick them into expending what they do have, we may be able negate the antimatter weapons entirely." Compton was speaking to everyone, but he was looking at Garret.

"At least once or twice." Garret's voice was distant; he was deep in thought as he spoke. "They're not stupid, we can be sure of that much. It would be foolish for us to believe we can deceive them repeatedly." He was looking out across the table, but he wasn't focusing on anyone. "Though I would like to discuss some thoughts I have on the enemy's tactics." He turned toward Winton, his eyes clear and focusing again. "Before me move on, do you have anything else to add, Jack?"

Winton thought for a second. There was one other thing on his mind, but he wasn't sure if he should bring it up. "Well… there is one more subject I wanted to broach." He was clearly uncomfortable.

"Go ahead, Jack." Garret slapped his hand lightly on the table. "Whatever you have to say, just say it."

"Well, sir. The evacuation plans…they are drawing off a significant percentage of our transport capacity. And now we've been talking about moving people off Sandoval and the other worlds along the enemy's path."

"What are you saying, Jack? That we should leave those civilians to die?" Admiral Compton looked incredulous.

"No sir. I am not saying that at all." Winton was a little nervous. He didn't like being cast as some cold-hearted mathematician sacrificing lives as if he were moving numbers on a spreadsheet. But he knew they just couldn't ignore the problem either. "What I am saying is that you may find yourself fighting the enemy without missiles or trying to defend worlds with understrength ground units." Winton hadn't intended to end up as the one advocating leaving colonists behind to be slaughtered, but they had to discuss this issue. If they lost this war for lack of weapons and troop transport, the civilian casualties would be astronomical. Possibly the entire human race.

"I'm sorry, Jack." Compton's voice was apologetic. "I didn't mean that the way it sounded." He stared silently at Winton for a few seconds. "It's just hard to compare saving lives to carting missiles."

"We're going to have to compare them if we want to win this war." Garret's voice was firm. "There is no point pretending otherwise. We're going to requisition every civilian craft we can get our hands on and do everything possible to get as many people as possible off these worlds." He looked around the table, cold determined eyes staring at each individual present in turn. "But the war effort has priority. It has to."

He slid back his chair and stood up. "People are going to die in this fight. This isn't the kind of war we've fought before... petty squabbles over new resource worlds. This is a war for survival, plain and simple. Everybody in this room needs to realize that right now. We are not going to rip into each other because we're angry and frustrated that we had to leave civilians behind so we could supply our troops and ships. Of course we're upset...but taking it out on each other isn't going to accomplish anything." The volume of his voice was increasing. He wasn't yelling, not exactly. But he was making his point forcefully. "We are going to have to cooperate with...to trust... old enemies. We are going to have to be coldly realistic in everything we do...even if that means pulling troops off a world and leaving the civilians behind." He slapped his hand down on the table, harder this time. "Because the only thing we can't do... the one truly unthinkable thing...is to lose this war."

The room was silent for a long moment. Garret had done what he had to do, said what needed to be said. He and Holm were technically equals in the joint military establishment, but Garret was older and had served longer at command rank. He was informally considered the overall commander...by Holm as well as everyone else. It had been his responsibility to address head on the concerns that were eating away at them all. They were all scared, and everyone knew that. That last thing they needed was to be at each other's throats besides.

Garret could see it in the faces around the table - he'd made his point. He gave them all another few seconds to consider what had been said. "I trust that we are all on the same page now." He stepped back behind his chair and started walking slowly around the room. "I will assume from the silence that we are in agreement. If we can move on now, I'd like to discuss some tactical issues. General Holm and I have reviewed every engagement in excruciating detail, and we have developed a few useful insights."

"First, while the enemy's technology is vastly superior to our own, their tactics are decidedly mediocre. At least to the extent we have seen to date." He was walking slowly back and forth along the table as he spoke. "Admiral West's attack was a brilliant maneuver. Nevertheless, even factoring in the surprise the admiral achieved, the enemy seemed to be exceptionally non-reactive…as if the audacity of her plan was difficult for them to comprehend. Admiral Compton and I have gamed the scenario several times. Against a strong opponent, Admiral West's fleet would have gained a considerable edge, but she would never have managed to hit with her missile barrage while antimatter weapons were still mounted. Certainly not multiple times."

"So what are we saying?" Cain had been quiet a long time, but now he spoke out. "That these…whatever they are…are vastly ahead of us technologically, but behind us in tactics? Isn't that a dangerous assumption for us to make?"

"You're right about one thing, Erik." Garret stopped his pacing and looked over at Cain. "We can't assume anything. But we still have to look for whatever advantages we can find. And this enemy seems hidebound…inexplicably unimaginative when it comes to battle strategy."

"Think about it, Erik." Holm now, turning to face Cain as he spoke. "Look at Teller's reports from Cornwall. The enemy's tactics were simplistic. They pushed his people back because of their tech advantage, not because they outfought him. If you look at that battle, Teller fought rings around them…it just wasn't enough to overcome the superior firepower and damage resistance of the enemy."

Garret was nodding as Holm finished. "General Holm is correct. On land as well as in space, there is a decided lack of creativity and initiative on the part of the enemy. They attack… they are relentless, but their tactics are basic, simple."

"Perhaps they simply don't have the experience your people do." It was Roderick Vance, who hadn't said a word all day. "Think about our history. We are a detestable species in some ways." Vance didn't get up, but he straightened in his chair and slid in closer to the table. "We have been fighting and killing each other since the dawn of history. The Unification Wars almost destroyed the Earth, so we exported our conflicts, and now we fight in space." He turned to face Holm. "Tell me, general, how many years of total peace have your people seen in the last 20 years? 30?"

Holm shook his head grimly. "Not many." He looked back at Vance. "Are you suggesting that these beings are not violent by nature?"

"Clearly they are capable of extreme violence. I'm not in position to state anything specifically...none of us are. All I am saying is there are many reasons why they may lack the proficiency in war that we take for granted." Vance's voice was calm, his poker face unreadable. He wasn't trying to hide anything from these people, but a lifetime's habit is hard to shake. "Perhaps they are united as a species and do not fight among themselves. They could be utterly dominant in their primary sphere, and they may have been so for a very long time. Maybe they haven't faced an enemy in centuries...or millennia...or ever. Possibly we're the only other intelligent species they've encountered. We can't know...we can only observe and draw conclusions."

"Mr. Vance is correct." Garret gestured toward the Martian industrialist/spy as he spoke. "All we can do is utilize whatever we can to obtain any advantage we can get. We've got the most experienced combat officers in the Alliance in here. The people in this room are going to create the strategies that win or lose this war. We need to use anything we can. And for now, what we know is the enemy seems to employ ritualized, inflexible tactics both in space and on the ground." He panned his eyes across the table. "Use that."

Garret turned and walked back toward his seat. "That just leaves us one more topic to discuss...the strategic plan going forward. General Holm and I have prepared a broad course of action that we'd like to share with you now." He looked over at Holm. "Elias?"

Holm stood up, a little slowly perhaps, but he'd been sitting all day and his old wounds had stiffened up. "Thank you, Augustus." He turned to look down the table. "I'd like to introduce our tactical plan." He scooped a controller off the desk and pressed a button. The screen displayed a stylized two-dimensional map of solar systems and connecting warp gates. The stars were small circles in a variety of colors. He pressed again and three of the star icons began shimmering. "Sandoval, Garrison, Samvar...three crucial systems, which from now on we will call the Line." He paused, looking out across the table. "This is where we make our stand."

There was a long pause. "Sir...pulling back to those systems means abandoning another dozen colonies." Cain was staring at the map as he spoke. "Isn't that a big concession to make?" He was also thinking that they'd never be able to evacuate all the colonists from that many systems, but he kept it to himself. Garret had been right – they were all upset about the civilian casualties, and beating each other up about it wasn't going to help anything.

"We need two things, Erik. Time and a defensible bottleneck." Holm pressed another button and the screen zoomed in on the highlighted stars. "These three locations are just such a bottleneck. The warp paths from all known enemy incursion points must pass through one of these systems to reach the rest of human-occupied space." He pressed the button again and the map zoomed back out. "There is no similarly defensible spot anywhere between these stars and the heart of occupied space. And Sandoval has a warp gate to Garrison, and Garrison has one to Samvar, so we'll have goo interior lines...we'll be able to easily shift reserves."

"If I may interject, since Samvar is a Caliphate colony, it also makes this a joint defensive effort. That can only aid us in fostering cooperation between the Powers. If the Alliance and Caliphate can work together to face the enemy, the other Superpowers will fall into line." Vance hadn't intended to involve himself into the discussion of tactics, but he took the opportunity to address cooperation again. He was still worried about how well former enemies could work together. Old hatreds and prejudices could end up dooming the entire human race.

Holm nodded to the Martian. "Mr. Vance is correct. Cooperation between the Powers will be essential. Regardless of our past disputes, none of the Superpowers can defeat this enemy alone." He looked at Cain. "I know it will be difficult... for me no less than anyone else...but we must work together."

He glanced over at Sparks. "We also need time...time to build fortifications, time to get some of Colonel Sparks' new systems into action. By choosing a defensive line this far back, we are likely to get it. As Admiral Winton noted, the enemy appears to have logistical problems. We're going to exacerbate those. We're going to stretch out their supply line and give them a massive fight when they're far from their support."

He turned and glanced at the screen. "And that space we give up will buy us time too. The enemy has been slow to advance after each engagement. If their behavior continues according to pattern, they will methodically occupy each system along the way. That time is priceless to us. We're bringing up allied forces and even towing orbital fortresses from nearby systems. Every week or month we get makes those three systems stronger."

Cain still looked concerned. "I can't argue with the logic, sir." He was staring at the display, but in his mind the star map extended offscreen...into the heart of the Alliance. "We will be gambling heavily on our ability to hold at your Line. If the enemy gets past us, they're going to run wild through our core systems." He turned and looked back at Holm. "We won't be talking about thousands dead...it will be millions."

"And billions if they reach Earth, Erik." Holm spoke softly, barely loud enough for everyone to hear. "But that doesn't change the fact that we need to choose someplace to make a stand." His eyes bored into Cain's. "Do you really think penny-packet defenses of outer colony worlds is the way to do that?"

Cain was silent for a moment. He knew Holm was right...in fact, he liked the basic tactics behind the plan. But he hated to give up ground. He'd spent his formative years as a command officer fighting to take back real estate lost early in the war. He didn't like it then, and he didn't like it now. But he realized there was no option. "I agree, sir."

"I'm glad, Erik. Because you've got the shit job...you and Admiral West." Holm's tone became darker, sadder. "We need time, and you're going to have to buy it for us. And I don't expect it to be cheap." He took a deep breath. "You have to hold Farpoint for as long as you can. Every extra day increases our chances to win this war. To survive."

Cain stood silently, looking back at Holm, his mind lost in thought. Erik had never chased glory…he'd never really cared about it. The medals, the fame, the awards…they'd mostly made him uncomfortable. For him the Corps was about camaraderie, about being part of a brotherhood. About fighting for something better, something more worthy than the hell he'd come from. When he was young he had believed in that…he'd believed it with his heart and soul. But now he looked to that place his resolve had come from and there were only doubts. A lifetime of war, and what had changed? A legion of slaughtered friends and what had it gotten them? Another war? A never ending cycle of suffering and death?

He felt himself trying to push through the doubts, the dark thoughts, and answer the general. But it was hard…difficult in a way that was new to him. It wasn't fear…though he was afraid…afraid of pain and death, afraid that he'd never see Sarah again…afraid of the judgment on his soul for the masses of faithful troops he'd led knowingly to slaughter. But this wasn't fear. It was exhaustion…a fatigue deep inside him. Maybe, he thought, there is a limit to the butcher's bill one man can endure.

"Erik?"

Cain could hear Holm's voice through his daydream, and he pushed back the grim thoughts, slowly, painstakingly clearing his mind. "Sorry, general." Erik Cain was a creature of duty, and he knew he would never retreat from that. He would find a way… somehow. "We'll hold them off, sir. Admiral West and I will give them a hell of a fight."

"I know you will, Erik." Holm could see Cain was struggling with his inner demons. No man had been more on the forefront of the Alliance's struggles for the past two decades than Cain. And no one knew Erik Cain like Holm did, save for Sarah Linden and perhaps Jax. "I'm counting on you." He walked across the room and put his hand on Cain's shoulder. "There is no one

I trust more."

Cain forced a smile. "Thank you, sir." He looked into the general's eyes and hop'ed his weakness didn't show in his own. "You can count on me, sir." But there was still doubt in his mind...and something else. A coldness, something he'd never felt. Is this a premonition, he wondered...is this what so many other warriors have felt? Perhaps this is my last battle...maybe death is finally catching up to me. He wondered if that wouldn't be a blessing of sorts, but he quickly suppressed those thoughts. He tried to put it out of his mind and focus on the work to be done, but the cold feeling was still there, hanging on the edge of this thoughts.

Chapter 22

Critical Care Unit 3
Armstrong Joint Services Medical Center
Armstrong - Gamma Pavonis III

"You are doing very well, James." Sarah Linden gave Teller a sweet smile. "You're a much better patient than Erik. I think there are still a few staff members here who draw nasty little cartoons of him."

Teller smiled. It didn't hurt. He was still getting used to things not hurting. For almost four months, every move he made was accompanied by excruciating pain. "There are a few Marines who do the same." Teller surprised himself – he hadn't realized he felt well enough to make a joke. Actually, he thought, you'd have to look far and wide in the Corps to find anyone with anything but reverent respect for Erik Cain. And that included James Teller.

"I'm clearing you for limb regeneration." She maintained her smile, but a little look of sympathy crept onto her face.

"So you're saying I shouldn't get used to being out of pain?" Teller winked at her. "I'll be fine, doc. I'm a Marine. We don't even feel pain." Limb regenerations were notoriously excruciating, and most anesthetics and pain relievers were off the table - they interfered with proper nerve growth. The pain was so bad that many patients needed psychiatric counseling to get over it once their new arms and legs were grown.

She let out a small laugh. "I don't know. I've had some big tough Marines in here, and I'm pretty sure they could all feel pain." Her smile faded. "You'll get through it, James. I won't lie to you and tell you it's not a struggle, because it is. But when it's done you'll be good as new." She paused uncomfortably. "I'm not going to be here during your regen. I'm heading to Sandoval to set up a forward hospital. Admiral Garret and General Holm are setting up a defensive line against the enemy invasion." Her voice was becoming sadder. "We both know there are going to be a lot of casualties. That's where I belong."

"Don't worry, Sarah." He'd miss the personal attention he was getting from Armstrong Medical's chief of staff, but he knew the Marines – and the naval crews – up there on the line needed her a hell of a lot more than he did. "You took great care of me." She'd seen him through the crisis, bringing him out of medical stasis and putting his guts back together. Now she had pronounced his internal systems fully recovered...though she hadn't proven it by giving him solid food yet. "I'm sure your team can slap two legs and an arm on without too much trouble."

"Yes, they can." She smiled once more. "You take care, James." She leaned over and gave him a light kiss on the cheek. "I wouldn't want you telling Erik I didn't take good care of you."

Teller smiled back and watched her walk away. Take care of yourself, Sarah, he thought. Things are likely to get hot up there.

Merrick walked down the street toward the Marine command center. He didn't see much ahead, just a ramshackle group of modular buildings. It was all part of his re-education. The Marines had relocated their headquarters to Armstrong, but they'd poured most of the available resources into equipment and training for the combat forces. More tooth, less tail. General Holm and his officers clearly felt supporting their troops was more important than fancy offices for the brass. On Earth it would have been the opposite. The soldiers might be armed with sticks and stones, but the top generals would have a palace for their HQ.

He had no idea what to expect. He was already far from familiar ground. Even traveling alone was new. He'd been born to a powerful political family, and he'd entered the army as a major. As long as he could remember, he'd been surrounded by servants and aides. Now it was just him. He was a little lost, but the self-sufficiency felt good too. He was beginning to realize that, for the first time in his life, he was happy.

He'd gotten a message through to Holm, offering his services in any capacity the general may want. He checked into the Armstrong Hotel and waited. He'd been there two days when he was instructed to report to General Gilson at Marine HQ. Perhaps she was going to discuss ways he could contribute to the war effort. Or maybe she was going to arrest him and charge him with war crimes on Arcadia. Whatever it was, he'd find out soon enough.

He walked up to the guard station. There was a small booth situated about a meter in front of the perimeter fence. The guard post, the fencing…it all had a temporary look to it, as if it were thrown into place as quickly as possible. "Isaac Merrick to see General Catherine Gilson."

The guard was dressed in neat gray fatigues with corporal's insignia on his arm. There was a sharpness, an alertness to him that Merrick had never seen in his own troops. These Marines, he thought, are crackerjack troops. He was glad he'd only had to face a small, scratch-assembled force of them on Arcadia. They'd torn his units to shreds anyway.

"Yes, Mr. Merrick. She's expecting you." The guard was polite, but Merrick noticed he'd said "mister" and not "general." Merrick had resigned his commission in the army, but as a retired officer, he was entitled to be called by his rank. He wondered if it was a deliberate snub. If so, was it aimed at him or just at the terrestrial army? "The private will escort you there, sir." The guard motioned toward a light transport. Another Marine, in an equally spotless uniform, stood at attention next to it.

"Thank you, corporal." Merrick turned and walked over to the vehicle. He pushed aside his uncertainties. The guard probably didn't even know who he was. The private pressed a controller in his hand and the transport's bay door opened. Merrick nodded and stepped inside.

The vehicle was a standard battle transport, but the inside had been fitted out to make the passengers a bit more comfortable. Though its accommodations were laughable by Earth standards, it was clear that Gilson had sent the best transportation she had. He leaned back in the borderline comfortable seat and waited as the private buttoned things up and boarded the driver's compartment.

The ride to Gilson's HQ was short…no more than five minutes. The hatch opened as soon as the vehicle stopped, and the driver turned and said, "This is General Gilson's office, sir. Just go through the main door; they are expecting you."

Merrick walked up to the entry. There was no guard, but as soon as he stepped within a meter of the door, the security AI addressed him. "Please identify." Merrick smiled. A general's headquarters on Earth would have a half dozen guards standing around in dress uniforms. He was really starting to admire the sleek practicality of these Marines.

"Isaac Merrick to see General Gilson."

"Enter, General Merrick." The AI's database, at least, had Merrick's proper title.

He walked through the door. He'd taken about ten steps when a Marine with captain's bars on her shoulder came walking down the corridor.

"General Merrick, I'm General Gilson's aide, Captain Holder. Welcome to Marine Headquarters." She stopped a few meters from Merrick. "If you'll accompany me, I will take you to the general."

Merrick nodded and followed Holder. Gilson's office was just off the main corridor, about fifty meters from the entrance. The general was standing outside her office, barking orders to several officers. Gilson was a tall woman, with a short, spiky haircut, blond with a few wisps of gray. She was attractive, but her style was quite severe. It was clear she was a Marine first. Merrick knew she was in her early sixties, but with the rejuv treatments she looked about forty. When she saw Merrick and Holder approaching she turned to face them.

"General Merrick…welcome to Camp Basilone."

"Thank you, General Gilson. It is my great pleasure to be here." Merrick was a little relieved. Gilson's demeanor was a bit stark, but he had a feeling that was just her personality. He didn't think there was a war crimes trial in his future, at least.

"General, let's go into my office. We have much to discuss." Gilson motioned for Merrick to walk through the door. "I've invited one of my key officers to join us."

Merrick nodded and stepped into Gilson's office. Standing on the far side of the room was a tall Marine wearing a crisp set of gray fatigues. He turned toward the door.

"Hello, General Merrick. Welcome to Armstrong."

Merrick noticed the single platinum star on each collar first... then he focused on the face. The recognition was immediate.

Gilson was standing behind him. "General Merrick, I believe you already know Brigadier General Kyle Warren."

Merrick looked like he'd seen a ghost, but only for an instant. "General Warren. I'm glad to see you well." Warren had led the rebel forces on Arcadia after Will Thompson was killed. Merrick had surrendered the remnants of the federal army to Warren.

"I'm glad to see you well too, general." Warren had a pleasant expression on his face, not quite a smile, but enough to relax Merrick. "It will be good working with you and not against you."

"You can stay in my quarters while I'm gone. Just order up anything you need. I've programmed my household AI to follow your instructions." Sarah still couldn't believe Alex was alive. The two had been inseparable as children, close even for sisters. The whole family had been tightly knit and happy. Until the 14 year old Sarah caught the eye of Presley Quinn, the son of one of the Alliance's most powerful senators. That had led to a catastrophic sequence of events, which destroyed the family and left Sarah a fugitive, scraping out an existence in the urban wastelands. She'd believed her sister to be dead all these years...up until the moment she'd walked into Sarah's office four months earlier.

"Can't I go with you?" Alex bore a striking resemblance to her older sister. Her hair was a little paler blond, without the reddish tint of Sarah's. She was a bit taller as well, but only a centimeter or so. "I just found you."

Once she'd gotten over the initial shock, Sarah had burst into tears, joyous at finding her baby sister alive and well. The two had been joined at the hip since, and Sarah had spent every hour she wasn't in the hospital catching up with her sister. They didn't discuss their father and mother...or the tragedy that destroyed the family. That was too painful. But they talked about everything else.

Alex spoke in great detail about an entirely fictitious life, one she'd assembled carefully before making contact with her sister. It ended with her joining a colonization expedition to Wellington...and being evacuated before the enemy attack destroyed the planet. She'd had to modify the manifest of one of the freighters involved in the evac, retroactively adding herself to the passenger list, just in case anyone checked. That had been easy enough...more difficult had been playing the role of the loving sister. Alex hated Sarah...she'd hated her for years. She blamed her for her parents' death, for the hell she'd lived through...the horrific things she'd had to do to survive. She even blamed her sister for creating the cold, scheming viper she herself had become.

"I'm sorry, Alex." Sarah's voice was firm, but conciliatory. "The navy is evacuating as many people from Sandoval as they can. It's far too dangerous for you to go there. Especially after you just escaped from Wellington."

In truth, Alex Linden wouldn't have been caught dead on a miserable speck of dust like Wellington. But it was a good cover. "I can take care of myself. Maybe I can even help."

"I'm sorry, Alex. It's just not possible. Admiral Garret would never allow it." She reached out and took her sister's hand. "Stay here where it's safe. I'll be back. One of these days Erik will be back too, and you can finally meet him."

"I can't wait." Alex's sweet little grin hid her deathly cold thoughts. "I'm so anxious to meet your Erik after hearing so much about him." She decided to give up on trying to get to Sandoval. Enough people here knew her as Sarah's sister, and that should open the door for her to do some significant snooping. Patience was essential in her business. She knew she had to wait for her moment. One day she would meet Erik Cain…then she would take Gavin's revenge. And after that she would take her own. Oh yes, she thought, we will settle our affairs soon, my dear sister.

Chapter 23

AS Broadsword
Outer Particulate Cloud
Near the Canis Minoris Warp Gate
Gamma Trianguli Australis System

Kristen Jarvis grabbed one of the white towels and wiped her face. It wasn't easy to get a good workout at zero gravity, but the sweat running down her neck was pretty strong evidence she'd managed it. Broadsword's captain wrapped the towel around her neck and made her way to the zero grav shower. She'd been working out twice a day – everyone on Broadsword had been. She was doing everything she could to keep the crew mentally and physically sharp.

The 11th Squadron had been on station for almost two months, running silent in the far reaches of the Gamma Trianguli Australis system. That was a long time to endure zero gravity, minimal life support, and cold food. Jarvis was particularly concerned about keeping her people busy and focused. Her crew was mostly green…new recruits fresh from training. All of her officers except for the XO were on their initial postings out of the Academy. Even she was on her first command mission, plucked from her berth as tactical officer on a cruiser to captain Broadsword. Fast attack ships were very different from cruisers and capital ships, and she was still going through an adjustment period. The suicide boat commanders usually came up organically through that branch of the service. But Admiral Garret had been able to get new attack ships off the production line a lot faster than larger vessels, and there weren't enough experienced crews to go around.

Gamma, as the crew had taken to abbreviating the system's

name, was a fairly worthless piece of real estate. It had three planets...two gas giants and a single rocky world so devoid of useful resources it had been bypassed by every colonization expedition in the fifty years since it was discovered.

What Gamma did possess, however, was a particularly dense cloud of dust, gasses, and small asteroids, coincidentally located very close to one of its two warp gates...the one leading deeper into the Rim. The one Admiral West expected the enemy to burst through on their way to Farpoint.

Jarvis didn't know when – or if – the enemy would arrive, but she was determined that her people would be ready. Their mission was a simple one, at least on paper - ambush the enemy warships right after they transited. With luck they might catch them with antimatter weapons deployed on their external mounts...and if they did they might be able to pick off a ship or two and wear down the forces headed for Farpoint.

After the attack they would head out into deep space, trying to escape before the enemy could hit them back. They wouldn't have any velocity to start, but they'd be heading in a vector opposite the enemy's. Any ships detached to pursue her vessel would have to decelerate first and then re-accelerate in the right direction. It gave her a chance, at least, to get away. And if she didn't, any ships that split off to chase her tiny craft would be pulled away from the Farpoint attack force. That wasn't a par- ticularly attractive option for Broadsword's crew, but she could see the tactical effectiveness of the overall plan.

She was just about to climb into the shower when Broad- sword's klaxon sounded. Damn, she thought...that couldn't have waited ten minutes? She pulled herself back to the chang- ing area and slid back into her combat suit. The new naval suits were fairly comfortable and snug-fitting, very unlike the bulk- ier things in use when she'd served on her first ship. But with the helmet on, the suit could keep a person alive, even in deep space...at least until the batteries wore down.

Jarvis sealed up the suit, all except for the helmet. She felt grimy and uncomfortable – she'd worked up quite a sweat dur- ing her workout, and the cold air of the ship had just made things worse…clammy and uncomfortable. If this was the enemy coming in-system she could be in this suit for weeks, and this was no way to start that kind of marathon.

It was always difficult to get around in zero gravity, but she had enough experience to make her way quickly to the bridge. Most of her crew were having a tougher time navigating the mag-boots and handholds. They'd all manage, but she didn't kid herself – working at zero-gee degraded the crew's performance.

She made her way slowly forward – the bridge was just down the main corridor from Broadsword's tiny gym. She still wasn't used to the cramped quarters on the fast attack ship. It's not that cruisers were spacious – no spaceships were – but Broadsword was a tenth the size of her last posting. The suicide boat crews were typically subjected to psych screening to cull out those least suited to working in such close proximity, but since the rebellion Admiral Garret had been without the luxury of such considerations. He was strapped enough getting his ships crewed, and some of the old luxuries fell by the wayside. Jarvis felt a touch claustrophobic herself – she suspected she'd never have passed the old screening.

She pulled herself through the hatch onto Broadsword's small bridge. "Ensign Garravick, report." The control center of the ship consisted of her command chair and four small workstations. The ceiling of the tiny room was crisscrossed with conduits and other obstructions, giving it a jumbled, unfinished look.

"Energy emissions from the warp gate, captain." Garravick was fresh out of the Academy, but he sounded sharp.

This would be his first time in battle…it would be the first time for most of Jarvis' people, and she was watching them all closely. She'd tried to get her best read on them, but she knew she couldn't be sure how they'd perform under fire until they faced the enemy. Most captains would put their most experienced officers on the bridge, but Jarvis had four fresh grads manning her workstations. She could keep an eye on them here…she wanted the few seasoned people she had keeping watch over the rest of her green crew.

"Very well. Monitor the scanning net." The squadron had deployed a web of scanner buoys around the warp gate. "All crew to the couches." They should all be in their positions already – she'd had a standing order for crew members to report to their acceleration couches when the klaxon sounded. But they were inexperienced, and she wanted to make sure. She didn't want to lose anyone because they were slow getting set for acceleration.

"Yes, captain." A brief pause. "All crew members report they are in their couches.

Good, Jarvis thought. So far they're all on the ball. "Advise Engineer Hinkle to prepare for crash reactor startup. They'd been keeping the reactor offline, only starting it up every three or four days to charge the batteries. Fusion reactors had multiple levels of safeguards, but a crash start was risky...it had to be done just right or the reactor could be damaged. Or worse.

"Yes, captain. Engineer Hinkle reports he is read..." Garravick turned his head quickly from his screen to face Jarvis. "Enemy vessels entering the system!" He was still under control, but she could feel his tension amp up. "Two Gargoyles... no, three." The designation Colonel Sparks and his team had given the larger enemy vessels had stuck.

Jarvis could feel her own stomach clench. She was always tense in combat, of course, but this was worse. There was something different about this enemy...something haunting. "Have Broadsword Control plot an intercept vector." The ship's primary AI would handle the calculations and execute the engine burn to build the necessary velocity. Jarvis and her crew would be cocooned in their couches getting squeezed half to death.

"The enemy is coming in hot...velocity 0.7c." Garravick had turned back to his workstation, and his eyes were fixed on the screen. "More vessels transiting now, captain."

Good, she thought. Broadsword was positioned back from the warp gate, which gave her enough room to maneuver in for a shot. The enemy ships would have a hard time reacting...even with their higher general thrust capacity. Seven percent of light-speed was fast...and it would take a long time to meaningfully alter that vector. Broadsword would have her chance…as long as the ECM let her get close enough. "Launch ECM missiles. Crash start reactor."

Broadsword lurched as her six multi-section ECM devices launched. They would spread out and divide into ten components, each broadcasting electronic signals comparable to a ship of Broadsword's class. Instead of one target, the enemy would have to find Jarvis' ship among 60 fakes.

"Missiles away, captain." The dim battery-fed lights on the bridge suddenly brightened as the reactor started up and fed power into the ship's circuits. "Engineer Hinkle reports reactor up and running at 100%." A slight pause as Garravick listened to the engineer's report. "No problems…reactor is functioning normally."

"All crew activate acceleration couches." She leaned back and winced as her couch injected the drugs into her arm. She'd flinched a little, and the needle had gone in at a painful angle. Her couch expanded and wrapped around her snugly, just as she started to feel the sluggishness from the drugs.

"Crew secured, captain." Garravick sounded a little more ragged than before. The drugs did that to everyone. The injections helped humans survive forces they were never meant to endure, but it came at a cost.

"Broadsword control…execute attack plan Alpha."

Jarvis lost her breath for an instant as Broadsword's engines blasted at 20g. She knew the AI would choose the optimum target, and at 20g, Broadsword would quickly build velocity. If the ECM decoys confused the enemy enough, Broadsword would get into range and empty its weapons into the target. If not, the ship would get sliced to pieces by the enemy particle accelerator beams.

"Enemy firing their energy weapon." Garravick was struggling to speak under the 20g pressure, and he sounded a lot more afraid than he had before. "Captain…it looks like they're targeting the ECM units!"

Good, she thought, but it was still a lottery. The enemy would have time to target ten ships, maybe twelve before Broadsword fired. The ECM missiles were well-designed…they even carried a small warhead to simulate a ship's destruction. But even if the enemy bought into them entirely, it was still a dozen 1 in 60 chances they'd target Broadsword before she fired. And Jarvis and her people wouldn't know until it happened. There was nothing to do but lay there half-crushed and wait to see if they survived.

"Captain, scanners report multiple antimatter explosions." Garravick's fear temporarily gave way to excitement. "It looks like Wolfhound took out a Gargoyle!"

"Good for you, Joann." Jarvis spoke softly to herself, smiling the whole time. Joann Grissom was Wolfhound's skipper… and one of Jarvis' oldest friends. Another transfer from the cruiser service, Grissom and her team had executed their attack run perfectly.

Jarvis was counting off the seconds. She knew roughly when they'd be in range. It was a useless exercise, but at least it kept her mind occupied. In the end, she was a bit slow. She was still counting down from 30 when the bridge lights dimmed and all of Broadsword's power diverted to the plasma torpedoes.

"Firing now." Broadsword's AI calmly announced. The ship shook wildly as it ejected the massive plasma bolt and again a few seconds later as its array of short-ranged rockets launched.

The lights dimmed again as the ship's AI executed the escape protocol, diverting all power to the straining engines. Jarvis winced a little as Broadsword's acceleration increased to 28g. They were on a vector almost opposite that of the enemy fleet. If we're lucky, she thought, they won't bother to pursue us. We're hardly worth the effort.

"Broadsword Control - damage assessment." It was a struggle to get the words out at 28g. Jarvis knew she'd set up a good shot; now she wanted to know how they'd done.

"We scored a direct hit, captain." The AI's voice was even and methodical. "It appears that we inflicted moderate localized damage to the enemy vessel. They seem to have jettisoned their antimatter ordnance before our attack hit."

Damn, she thought…looks like Joann won the big honors.

She was sorry they hadn't taken out the enemy vessel, but at least Broadsword's attack had stripped it of its heaviest weaponry. If the talk of enemy logistical problems was true, they might not be able to re-arm before they hit Farpoint. In that case, her people had probably saved a lot of their comrades' lives.

They'd done what they could for the fleet...now they were working for themselves. She closed her eyes and tried to force herself to remain coherent while the AI flew the ship. Now, if they just leave us alone, she thought hazily, maybe we'll make it out of this.

She started to drift in and out of awareness, and she didn't hear the AI when it announced that one of the enemy ships was decelerating and beginning a vector change.

Chapter 24

The Battle of Farpoint
Phase One – Naval Engagement
Epsilon Fornacis System

Third Fleet was arrayed for battle just past the orbit of the ninth planet, positioned to intercept an attack from either of the two Rimward warp gates. It appeared to be Third Fleet, at least, though most of the vessels were phantoms, creations of almost two hundred ECM drones positioned around less than twenty actual ships.

Admiral Sam Clark sat in the command chair of the cruiser Sussex. His mission was simple, at least in theory…trick the enemy into launching its antimatter ordnance and then get the hell out of there. He didn't think the first part would be all that simple in practice…and the last was likely to be nearly impossible.

Clark didn't know which warp gate the enemy would use to attack, so he'd had to position his forces to cover both. It could have been either – the invaders had occupied the systems on the other side of both of them. Now his question had been answered. Enemy ships had transited from the gate to Nu Ophiuchi, and they were bearing down on his "fleet," coming in at 0.04c.

"They're launching, sir." Barrett James was Clark's tactical officer. "Massive salvo incoming." A brief pause. "Missiles accelerating at 205g, sir."

Good, Clark thought. Those had to be the antimatter weapons. Hopefully it was all of them. "Very well, commander. All ships, full evasive maneuvers now. We've done our job; now let's get the hell out of here." Clark leaned back in his couch as the system activated and enveloped him. The rest of his staff was doing the same. Captain Wren would be engaging Sussex's engines any time now, and the ship's AI would do its best to get them out of this.

"Attention all personnel. Prepare for high g maneuvers in three zero seconds." Wren's deep voice boomed from the ship's com system. They'd prepped their escape well, placing counter-measures drones all along the projected lines of retreat. The missiles that didn't go after phantom ships would run into a deep defensive belt before they closed on Clark's actual vessels.

"Admiral...we have energy readings from the Delta Ursae Minoris warp gate." James' voice was alarmed. "Ships transiting, sir."

"Damn." Clark was whispering to himself. He'd planned for an enemy attack from either warp gate, but he hadn't expected them to launch a coordinated assault through both. It was a notoriously difficult operation, one Alliance tacticians found almost impossible to execute. But this enemy seemed to have a communications system that could transmit right through warp gates, making it much faster than the Alliance's Commnet. Maybe that allowed them to coordinate disparate task forces.

"We have four Gargoyles transited so far and ten Gremlins." The smaller enemy vessels had been dubbed Gremlins. No one was sure who had first come up with the name, but it had become standard. "Five Gargoyles...six....wait...something else, sir...it looks like..." James went silent, staring at his screen with a stunned expression.

"What is it?" Clark instinctively tried to look over at James, but it was a futile effort strapped into his couch. He waited a few seconds, but there was still no response. "Commander James...report immediately." Clark, like most flag officers, had a decided lack of patience...especially in the middle of a fight.

"Sorry, sir..." The tactical officer pulled out of his distraction, but his voice was distant, preoccupied. "Sir, we have a new enemy ship type...estimated mass 650,000 tons."

The bridge was silent. Clark lay back in his couch trying to imagine the enemy vessel...three times the tonnage of the

Yorktown class battleships that were the pride of the Alliance navy. And stuffed with technology centuries more advanced than anything found on one of the Yorktowns. The implications were overwhelming. If that thing was loaded up with anti-matter weapons, Third Fleet didn't have a chance.

"Enemy fleet number two is on a course to rendezvous with the first force…" There were a few seconds of silence as James rechecked his calculations. It wasn't easy concentrating at 20g. "…approximately ten light minutes from Farpoint."

"Very well." The best laid plans, Clark thought to himself. Even if he'd gotten the first enemy force to launch all its anti-matter ordnance, this second group probably had enough to take out West's ships at long range. He had to do something.

"Commander James, all ships are to prepare to cease thrusting and await a new course."

"But admiral, our retreat vectors are carefully calculated. If we're off by so much as a fraction of a degree we'll miss the ECM corridor." James didn't add that if they missed the prepared defensive array they had very little chance of surviving the pursuing missiles.

"I'm aware of that, commander." Clark's voice was icy. He had fought back an instant of doubt, but he knew what he had to do. What his people had to do. "Now carry out my orders."

"Yes, sir." James sounded suitably chastised…and scared as well.

"Sussex Control, calculate a fleet attack vector to intercept the second enemy force." Clark's resolve was firm.

"How do you want the fleet to approach, admiral?" The AI's voice was calm and professional, quite unaffected by the intense pressure of 20g thrust or the enormous danger posed by Admiral Clark's new plan.

"Directly at them." Clark sounded strangely calm for a man ordering his force to make a suicidal charge. "We're going right down their throats."

Erica West stared straight ahead with an intensity that could have bored through solid plasti-steel. After months of preparation, it was time. Finally she would give the enemy a real fight. If they wanted Farpoint, they were going to have to take it from her.

Her defense in depth strategy had paid off, delaying the enemy attack forces and forcing them to expend ordnance. She would soon find out if the enemy's logistical problems were as severe as the high command thought.

She was trying not to think about Sam Clark and his people. She wasn't sure they were all dead – at least she wanted to believe some of them might have survived. If they were alive, she wouldn't know. Their only hope was to run silent and pray the enemy lost track of them.

She sighed softly. The operation had been as carefully designed as possible. West was determined that it not be a suicide mission, and she'd meticulously planned the task force's escape route. But she hadn't planned for the enemy to come in through both warp gates.

One thing she knew for sure…alive or dead, Sam Clark was going to get the Navy Starburst. It was the highest decoration a naval officer could be awarded, and she just wished she had something even more meaningful to honor the bravery of her second-in-command and his crews. Somehow, Clark's ships had gotten close enough to the second enemy task force to induce at least some of the ships to launch or jettison their antimatter weapons. She had no idea how he'd done it, but from the flood of Delta-Z signals, it hadn't come cheap. In the aftermath of her successful ambush at Cornwall, it appeared the enemy was closely following its antimatter protocols. It remained to be seen whether Clark had stripped the entire enemy fleet or just a portion of it, but West was grateful for every antimatter warhead expended in deep space instead of fired at her fleet.

Third Fleet had been reinforced, its OB strengthened by the addition of two capital ships, including one of the Yorktown class behemoths. By all rights she should have transferred her flag to Princeton, but Cambrai had served her well, and she wasn't going to abandon the old girl now. It just didn't seem right somehow. For better or worse, Third Fleet would be led from the most ancient battleship in the navy.

"Enemy fleet has passed previously identified launch zone for anti-matter powered missiles." West had instructed her AI to advise her on the attacker's progress. It was highly redundant – West herself was monitoring the enemy's status more or less constantly.

"Thank you, Athena." West preferred to work directly through her AI. It was quicker and more efficient, and her staff was used to being bypassed. Some officers, older ones in particular, liked a more traditional workflow, barking out orders to their tactical and comm officers, who then worked through the AIs. She thought that was hidebound and inefficient, but a lot of flag officers felt it kept their staffs sharper and more engaged.

West glanced down at her screen, which displayed a projected plot of the enemy fleet. They were decelerating hard, and her scanners were easily picking up the massive energy output. She didn't know the detection capability of the enemy vessels – that was one piece of the puzzle the Alliance didn't have – but her ships were putting out a lot less energy, and they would be harder to pick up.

"Athena, execute Alpha launch."

"Executing, admiral." Farpoint's orbital fortresses supported several wings of fighter-bombers, and now the bay doors opened and 90 of the sleek attack craft launched.

"Prepare for Beta launch. All crews to the launch bays." West's three capital ships carried another 54 bombers. They were scheduled to launch when the fortress-based squadrons were two light-seconds out, giving them time to accelerate and match course and velocity. West wanted her attack craft going in as one big strike force. They all had enhanced power cells, increasing their range and allowing her to launch them before the missile volleys. They had a job to do, one a bit different than usual…but no one had ever accused Erica West of adherence to orthodoxy.

Commander Greta Hurley leaned back in her acceleration couch and double checked her ship's status. Princeton's strike force commander was set to lead the combined bomber wings…144 attack craft in all. Hurley was a veteran bomber pilot with years of service. She'd fought in Admiral Garret's massive victory at Gliese 250 during the war and two dozen other engagements. She'd been in more than one battle where fewer than half the bombers that launched came back, but this one was different…she knew that much. This time she wasn't sure any of them would make it back. And if they did, they probably wouldn't have any place to land anyway. There weren't too many illusions in the fleet about what they were going to face.

Third Fleet's morale was surprisingly good - that was Admiral West's doing. She'd shuttled around, speaking to the various ships' crews in person and reminding them how important this fight was. She'd realized the waiting would be the hardest part, and she had resolved to do whatever was necessary to help her people stay ready. Even a jaded veteran like Greta Hurley was affected by West's inspiring leadership.

Now Hurley lay in her couch awaiting the final launch order. After months of preparation, training, and waiting, it was almost time. Her crews were ready, she was sure of that. This mission was like none she'd ever flown. When Admiral West first suggested it, Hurley had been doubtful, but now she was completely convinced…certain that West's plan was brilliant. It would be difficult, but if her people could pull it off it might make a big difference in the battle.

The status light on her screen switched to yellow, indicating the launch order was imminent. She switched her com to the force-wide frequency. "Alright people, let's activate our couches and prepare for launch." She settled back in her own couch and whispered to her AI, "Activate."

Hurley closed her eyes, as she usually did just before a launch. It was a personal habit she'd picked up over the years. She felt the pin-prick of the injections and the pressure around her body as the AI triggered the chemical reaction that expanded the cushioning of her couch into a heavy cocoon that nearly enveloped her body. She was scared; she couldn't deny that to herself.

She didn't really expect to return, not from this mission. But she knew her duty…and she wasn't about to let Admiral West down.

"Good luck, people." She pushed back the fear…she wasn't about to be weak when her crews needed her. "Let's go get those bastards."

She lay there quietly, waiting for the bomber to launch. Everything was in the hands of Princeton's battle computer now. A few seconds passed, perhaps half a minute…then the status light flashed green and she felt the pressure of rapid acceleration as the magnetic catapult blasted her ship out into space.

The mag catapults gave the bombers enough velocity to quickly clear Princeton so their own engines could safely fire. A bomber launch was a jerky affair…the pressure of the catapult followed by a few seconds of free fall as the ship cleared the danger zone around the mother ship, then the intense g force as the bomber's engines fired at full thrust.

"Ok people, let's get this right." Her wings from the capital ships were linking up with those from the orbital fortresses. The AIs had all the course changes locked in, but she still wanted her people alert and aware. They had an unorthodox mission and a formation none of them had flown before. They'd practiced it twice, but that was all they'd had the excess supplies for. Hurley would have liked another 3 or 4 exercises before the real deal, but the pair of dry runs would have to do.

The intense pressure from the acceleration made it difficult to concentrate on anything, but Greta forced herself to focus on the plotting screen. It looked like her ships were falling perfectly into position. She knew the AIs would handle the maneuvers with precision, but this mission called for perfect formations, and it was her job to make sure that happened. All the external ordnance bolted onto the bombers was dragging down maneuverability, and if there was a mistake in the calculations, she wanted to catch it immediately.

She leaned back and closed her eyes for a few seconds. She really needed another stim to counteract the sluggishness of the pressure equalization drugs, but she was going to wait until they were a little closer to their objective…maybe 30 minutes.

Another hour, she thought. In another hour we'll know if the plan worked.

"All ships…launch." Erica West sat up in her command chair. The fleet had ceased its acceleration and the relief – plus the double dose of stimulants she'd just taken – cleared her head quickly. The entire fleet was arrayed for launch, and on her command 68 ships flushed their external racks, sending almost 300 missiles hurtling toward the incoming enemy fleet.

"All vessels report externally mounted ordnance launched." Athena was simply reporting what West could see on her status board.

"Prepare to launch internal missiles. All ships to execute on my mark." Athena was relaying West's orders to the entire fleet. West worked closely with her staff when she was planning an operation, but they were mostly spectators during the battle itself. At least the early stages…before plans started to fall apart and the improvisation began.

"Launch first wave." Unlike the externally mounted weapons, which could be fired all at once, the rate of fire of internal missiles was constrained by the number of launchers available. Ship types had various numbers of reloads, so a fleet firing all its ordnance would do so in successive waves, each of diminishing size as different vessels exhausted their magazines.

Cambrai shook as her launchers sent 6 missiles toward the enemy fleet. West's flagship carried 48 missiles internally, so she could launch 8 waves. Princeton, her newest and most powerful capital ship, had 12 launchers, and 120 missiles in her magazines, allowing for 10 full strength volleys. All told, Third Fleet was sending almost 700 thermonuclear weapons toward the enemy.

"All ships report second wave missiles loaded, admiral." Athena was coordinating all communications from the fleet to the admiral.

"Launch second wave." West leaned back in her chair and lightly gripped the handholds as Cambrai shook again. More missiles on their way to the enemy. This was the biggest attack yet made against one of the enemy's fleets. But there was no ambush here, no massive edge. She wondered how many of her weapons would get through. Would it be enough?

"Ok people, get ready for the first drop." Greta Hurley was sitting bolt upright. The bombers had cut their acceleration two minutes before, and she was out of her cocoon and jacked up on stims. "I want precision work here."

Her squadrons were arrayed in four lines, set about five light seconds from each other. The bombers began releasing anti-missile mines, dropping one every 50 seconds. The bombers in each wave were offset from one another so the mines were dispersed to cover an area of approximately 20 cubic light seconds.

The enemy had launched its missile salvoes, and they were plotted exactly as Admiral West had predicted...and the minefield the bombers laid was right in their path. The mines would detonate when their internal AIs deemed they had the maximum damage potential. They would scatter a field of smaller bombs, each of which would explode, creating a cloud of small projectiles in the path of the incoming missiles. With the velocity of the enemy volley, a chunk of metal the size of a grain of rice was enough to destroy a missile.

"Waves 1 and 4, prepare for anti-missile runs." Hurley was in the second wave. Her group and the third line were outfitted for normal anti-ship attacks. The 1st and 4th had been armed with shotguns, and reprogrammed for anti-missile runs. It was a new idea...as far as Hurley knew, bombers had never been used this way. But Admiral West knew her ships would take devastating losses from the enemy particle accelerators before they were able to respond with their own lasers...if she was going to have any chance at all she had to win the missile duel. Admiral Clark and his people had stripped away the enemy's antimatter weapons. Now it was up to Hurley's detached bombers to weaken the enemy's barrage of nuclear missiles, lightening the load on Third Fleet's close in point defense.

She leaned back in her couch, extending her arm to receive the injections. Her group was going to make a minor vector change and accelerate full all the way down the throat of the enemy. Her boats had the new ECM suites installed, but she had no idea how much protection that would offer against the enemy point defense. Regardless, though, her group was going right at the enemy ships.

"First and fourth waves decelerating and preparing for missile interception, commander." It was Jarrod Kynes on the com, her XO and the leader of the anti-missile group. "Good luck to you, Greta." Kynes' people had a chance of survival, at least. They could return to the fleet after their runs were complete and, with luck, there would still be someplace to land. But no one was fooling themselves about the casualties Hurley's group was likely to take. They were going straight into the maw of the beast with nothing to protect them save for an untested ECM suite and the grace of God.

"Full damage control procedures...all ships." West was staring intently at her plotting screen. Her multi-layered missile defense had exceeded her most optimistic hopes. The bombers had raked the enemy salvo, destroying missile after missile. Twenty of them got too close to nuclear detonations and were lost, but over 50 had survived. Now they were frantically trying to get out of the path of the incoming enemy fleet. Low on fuel and ordnance, they wouldn't stand much chance against the enemy's point defense.

The incoming missiles passed through the minefield next, and then into the range of the fleet's ECM. Finally, West' ships unloaded with the full effect of their own point defense, taking out most of the few missiles that remained. Barely twenty were going to detonate in proximity to the fleet. They could still do a lot of harm, but it could have been much, much worse.

"All ships report prepared for impact, admiral." Athena's steady voice was a welcome touch of calmness to West. Even veteran spacers found it difficult to sit and wait to see if a 500 megaton warhead detonated close enough to vaporize their ship.

"I want live damage updates, Athena." West leaned back in her couch, subconsciously bracing for any hits Cambrai might suffer.

"Yes, admiral." There was a brief pause before Athena started rattling off updates. "Shenandoah reports extensive damage. Her reactor is out, but Captain Walsh advises she expects to have power restored in 30 minutes." Another short silence, then: "We've lost contact with Quebec, admiral. Scanner reports indicate she was bracketed by multiple detonations."

West grimaced. Quebec was a light cruiser, not one of her most powerful ships. But it still hurt to imagine the vessel as a twisted, irradiated wreck holding its place in formation, dead along with its crew. "Keep reporting, Athena." West wasn't sure she really wanted to hear every grisly detail, but it was her job to know what was going on with her fleet.

"Brace for impact." Cambrai's central AI made the shipwide announcement. West reached out and grabbed the handholds on her couch just as the vessel began to shake wildly.

Chapter 25

Committee Room
Combined Powers Excavation Site
Carson's World – Epsilon Eridani IV

Ivan Norgov had no idea what was happening. He'd heard the alarms, and before he'd been able to find out what was going on, the explosions started. Norgov was a bully, but that didn't mean he had any real courage. He was the head of the Committee and, as such, he had a responsibility to all of the scientific personnel in the facility. It was a duty he failed to execute.

Two armored Marines pulled him from his hiding place in one of the storage rooms and brought him to the Committee room. He was shaking with fear, and his legs kept giving out. It didn't matter – the Marines easily carried him into the room and put him in one of the hard, uncomfortable chairs facing the Committee table. There were at least a dozen more Marines in the room, all wearing jet black fighting suits, and a lone, unarmored figure sitting in the center chair of the Committee table…Norgov's chair.

"Welcome, Dr. Norgov." Friederich Hofstader tried to maintain his poker face, but he was enjoying this whole thing far too much, and a tiny smile forced its way out. "The expression on your face is reason enough for the long journey I have taken."

Norgov stared back, his mouth open in amazement. There were several popping sounds as the Marines retracted their helmets. The shocked Russian scientist looked around the room in stunned silence.

"I'm reminded of an old saying…now how does that one go?" Hofstader leaned back in the plush leather seat. "Oh yes… payback is a bitch." He stared directly at Norgov and smiled.

"Though one could argue that such a phrase is simply common sense now...wouldn't you say?"

Norgov tried to speak, but he mostly just stammered an unintelligible babble. He was in shock, unable to form any coherent thoughts. He was also terrified. Being dragged around by armored troops was a new experience for him.

"Come, come, Ivan...you can do better than that." Hofstader's cold stare bored into the Russian's hapless eyes. "I've never been impressed by your scientific ability, but I know you're literate." A shadow of anger passed over Hofstader's face. "Indeed, you were quite talkative when you expelled me from this facility. I thought you'd never shut the hell up then."

"Friederich, please." Norgov spoke slowly. He was shivering and looking down at the floor.

"I could remind you of how you responded to my own entreaties." Hofstader was glaring at Norgov, but the Russian continued to look away. "You pompous, miserable piece of shit. You wouldn't even let Katrina remain on staff." Hofstader's voice was getting louder. He had a lot of anger toward Norgov. He'd intended to control it better, but sitting there looking at the whimpering fool his hostility got the better of him.

"Friederich, you don't understand." Norgov was pleading. He looked nervously at the armed Marines lined up along the wall. "I only did what I thought was right."

Hofstader stood up and stared at Norgov with withering intensity. "I don't understand? I don't understand?" He was trying to get a grip on himself, but his fury was in control now. "Listen to me you arrogant, useless asshole. I was right. Thanks to you we have lost months of research time here. Meanwhile, the beings who built this place have returned. They have returned, and they are massacring every human being they encounter. Colonies have been destroyed. Thousands of military personnel have died. Better people than you are being killed every day, and for months we have failed to exploit my discoveries here while you played your political games."

Norgov was silent, slumped miserably in his chair. He tried to respond, tried to look up and meet Hofstader's gaze, but he didn't have the strength to do it. He stared at the floor, tears running down his face.

Hofstader looked at the pathetic creature with disgust. Norgov wasn't worth his time…he realized that. He had important work to do here. He was as much a part of the war effort as the Marines on the front lines…and those men and women were counting on him to get them something they could use in the fight. He laid a small 'pad on the Committee table. "This document is signed by Fleet Admiral Garret, General Holm, and Roderick Vance. I appoints me military governor of Epsilon Eridani IV, with full and sole executive power."

Hofstader looked down at Norgov, but the Russian didn't say anything. "Where are my manners? I'd like to introduce you to Major Hank Taylor, from the Martian Confederation." He pointed toward one of the Marines. "Major Taylor and his Marines are here to enforce my authority over this facility. You will note that the document appoints me military governor over this entire planet. This research operation is now under my sole and complete control."

He walked around the end of the table, still staring at the hapless Norgov. "You are to be expelled from this facility. You and every scientist here who cares more about politics and petty power struggles than unlocking the scientific mysteries on this planet. You will all be held in custody until a ship can arrive to return you to Earth." Hofstader's eyes narrowed, and he stared into Norgov's. "Though I have authorized Major Taylor to shoot you if you cause any trouble."

"Brad, I'm glad to see you." Hofstader smiled as Bradley Travers walked into the room. "I think I owe you for a little behind the scenes help." Hofstader didn't know for sure that Travers worked for Roderick Vance's intelligence outfit, but he'd gotten a pretty good idea there was more than a passing relationship between the two.

"It's good to have you back, Friederich." Travers walked across the room and extended his hand. "You had no idea how right you were about the urgency of this research project.

Maybe we can get something done now. Something that might help in the fight."

Hofstader shook Travers' hand. "We'd better. I haven't seen the enemy in action, but I've been through enough video and spare parts to keep me up nights." He paused. "And I've talked to some of the people who have faced them." He looked right at Travers, his expression grim. "If we're going to win this fight…survive this fight…we're going to have to find something useful here."

Travers nodded. "Have you sent for everyone you need?"

Hofstader nodded. "Yes, Mr. Vance was kind enough to lend me one of his Torch transports. They should be here shortly, hopefully within a week." Hofstader had put together a list of scientists…his choices, not the selections of political cronies. He'd always hated the political games that suffocated academia, and his feelings were only compounded when he saw Garret and Holm and their people in action. For the first time he saw what could be achieved by the best people working together with no agenda but success. He was going to emulate that on Carson's World. He had to. For all the effort and courage of the troops fighting the war, Hofstader knew in his gut they didn't stand a chance. Not unless he could unlock some of this technology.

Chapter 26

Battle of Farpoint
Phase 2 – Ground Assault
Iron Gate Valley, North of Landing
Farpoint - Epsilon Fornacis III

Cain sat quietly, nursing a headache and paging through the OB for I Corps. He had some first class troops under his command; that much he knew for sure. But it was a ramshackle organization, thrown together from whatever forces could be assembled.

He had half of 1st Division, mostly 2nd Brigade plus some of the support units. The rest of the division had fought under Teller on Cornwall. Most of them were dead, and the rest were regrouping on Armstrong. Cain suspected it would be a considerable time before the brigade would be combat ready again, if ever. Fighting this enemy seemed to affect even veteran Marines in a way he'd never seen before. The engaged units had suffered a considerable amount of psychological distress and battle fatigue among the survivors.

Cain himself had recruited 2d Brigade's CO back into the service. James Prescott had been drawn deeply into the rebellion on his adopted world of Victoria, something he'd thought marked the end of his Marine career. But the Corps ultimately declared for the rebels, and when General Cain offered the Canadian officer a pair of eagles and the command of one of his brigades, he gratefully accepted.

Jax was Prescott's immediate superior, which worked out well. Both Cain and Jax trusted Prescott to work without a lot of supervision, and that freed up Jax's time. The big Marine was wearing two hats, commanding 1st Division and serving as I

Corps' XO. Darius Jax was Cain's oldest and closest friend. The two had been through hell and back together…several times. For the first time in a very long time, Erik felt he needed someone to lean on, to back him up and help him get through the fight that was coming. For him, that was Jax.

I Corps had half of 2nd Division as well. Erik had first met Angus Frasier on Carson's World, when the stubborn Scot drove his regiment of Highlanders through the enemy lines to relieve Cain's 1st Brigade on the blood-soaked Lysandra Plateau. When General Holm asked Cain his opinion on a commander for 2nd Division, Cain gave him one name…Frasier's.

Frasier's force was a mixed bag. Units like the reformed Highland Regiment were crack troops by anyone's measure, but the division had a significant number of green formations as well. They'd left the completely raw 4th Brigade on Armstrong to continue training under General Gilson, but there had been no way to field even a single brigade without including some inexperienced personnel.

Erik had a few unfamiliar units rounding out I Corps. Linus Wagner's regiment of Martian Marines had landed the week before, courtesy of Roderick Vance. Cain had never seen the Confeds in action, but he knew they were elite troops…and the Martian weapons and equipment were second to none.

He had less welcome reinforcements too. Tac-commander Farooq and his Janissaries had arrived two weeks earlier. Erik understood what was at stake, and he knew the Alliance couldn't hope to win this war alone…but that didn't make it any easier for him to accept his old enemies as friends. Farooq had been courteous and respectful, and he'd placed himself unreservedly under Cain's command. But Erik still didn't like it. Working with the Janissaries felt wrong…somehow disloyal to the thousands of his men and women who'd died at their hands. And he didn't care how much talk there was about joining forces and facing the common enemy – he just didn't trust them.

"So has the glory of corps command gone to your head yet?" Jax was smiling as he walked up from behind. "Could you have imagined back on Columbia that you'd be wearing General

Holm's hat one day?"

Cain turned to face his friend and second-in-command. "I wish we had that outfit now." Holm had been the commander of I Corps during the closing stages of the Third Frontier War. It had been a veteran formation through and through, honed during years of combat. Cain's corps had its share of seasoned troops, but it wasn't a match in numbers or experience for the formation Holm had commanded. The force reductions after the war and the savagery of the rebellions had taken a serious toll. Erik wondered how many Marines from the old I Corps were still with the colors…how many were still alive. He figured it wouldn't be hard to find out – Hector could probably tell him immediately. But he decided he didn't want to know. His own mental calculations told him the number would be depressingly small.

"We've still got some good people, Erik." He looked out over the sea of modular structures that stretched for kilometers in every direction. A lot of them were empty. Admiral West had been fighting the enemy invasion fleet for days now, and I Corps' frontline units had suited up and deployed to their defensive positions. Cain knew the enemy landings could come at any time, and he wasn't going to get caught unprepared.

"That we do, my friend." He looked up at Jax, squinting at the bright sun above the big Marine's head. "But not enough. Have the PRC troops disembarked yet?"

"Yes, they're mustering in the quad." Jax walked the rest of the way over to Cain and sat in one of the empty chairs. "We're loading up the civvies now. That will be just about all of them, except for the volunteers. I can't believe we got them all off-planet."

"This group will be lucky if they can make it out of the system." Third Fleet had done a tremendous job fencing with the superior enemy forces, but West's survivors weren't going to hold out much longer. Cain had been waiting for word that the enemy had taken out the remnants of the orbital fortresses and commenced their landing. The transport crews were trying to get the civilians loaded up, but they were as likely to get blown away in space as to escape.

"I do have one surprise for you, though." Jax's smile widened.

"I hate surprises." Cain frowned. "They're usually trouble." He looked over at Jax, his head tilted to avoid the sun glare. "What is it?"

"It, my dear General Cain, is me."

Cain spun around. Standing behind him was an Asian man of moderate height, fully armored with his helmet retracted.

"Aoki!" Cain smiled, for the first time in days. "I had no idea you were leading this force." He got up and walked over to the new arrival. "Welcome to I Corps."

"Thank you, my friend." Aoki Yoshi had been the PRC's liaison officer during the war, and he'd accompanied then-Major Cain's forces for a full campaign. The two had stayed in touch, but Cain hadn't actually seen Yoshi in years. "It is good to see you again."

"Why don't you head over to your billet and dump that armor and come back here for dinner?" Cain glanced back at Jax. "Our food service leaves a bit to be desired, but I'd wager Jax and I can pull rank and scare up a few burgers and cold beers."

Yoshi was the son of a diplomat, and he'd spent most of his childhood in the Alliance. While he was there he'd become fond of the food, particularly hamburgers.

"That sounds perfect." He nodded and started to turn. "Give me an hour to get my troops situated."

"We'll be right here whenever you're…"

"General Cain!" It was Captain Santos, a member of Cain's staff. He was running over from the HQ hut. "We've just received a communication from the orbital fortresses. They are under attack."

Cain turned to face Santos. "Any word from Admiral West?"

"No sir. The last report is that Cambrai suffered heavy damage and Third Fleet is retreating. The admiral may be…"

"Let's not bury Admiral West until we have some facts, captain." Cain turned toward Aoki. "Well, my friend, I'm afraid we'll have to postpone those burgers and beers - at least until after the dance."

The battle had been raging for six days. Cain had been dealing with his inner demons recently, but he pushed aside the doubts and dove into the job at hand. He'd abandoned the rest of the planet, creating one large defensive perimeter around Landing. That line redefined the concept of defense in depth. For weeks he had scoured every inch of the position, directing the placement of mines, choosing locations for heavy weapon emplacements, and managing the digging of trenches. He placed line after line, each one stronger than the last. The troops saw him everywhere, and his legend grew among the rank and file.

Cain's plan wasn't pretty; it wasn't elegant. He contrived to turn every centimeter of the battlefield into a killing zone. He was going to fight a battle of annihilation with the enemy. If they wanted Farpoint, they were going to have to take it one bloody meter at a time.

The first line, covered by minefields and extensive heavy weapon strongpoints, had held for three days. Finally, the enemy massed its Reapers and punched through, suffering heavy losses in the process. His front pierced, Cain ordered his forces back to the second line. The forward units had paid heavily for those three days of resistance, and most of the deployed companies were under 60% strength. Casualties among the officers were even worse, as high as 70% in the hardest-hit formations. The Marines fought like madmen, but the relentlessness of the enemy sapped their morale. Even veteran units wavered under the incessant attacks, and the officers were compelled to rally their troops, exposing themselves to withering fire in the process.

The second line had held for three days also, but now it was broken in at least four places, and the troops were retreating. The fallback from the first line had been orderly, but now the Marines were breaking, and crack units were retiring in disorder. Cain paced nervously around his command post, resisting the urge to run up to the line, as if his will alone would rally the troops and send them back at the enemy.

He turned abruptly and looked at another armored figure standing about five meters behind him. "Aoki, I need you to get your troops up to the front." He was looking at a tactical display on his visor. "Hector, transmit this map to Colonel Yoshi immediately."

"Yes, general." For once the AI simply acknowledged and obeyed. Cain never realized that Hector's sometimes sarcastic personality had developed in response to the AI's evaluation of his own emotional needs. Sparring with his personal assistant relaxed Cain, though he himself never realized it. But Hector knew what Cain was up against this time.

"Aoki, do you see the deep valley northeast of Landing?"

The PRC officer hesitated for a few seconds as he got his bearings on the map. "Yes, general. I see it."

"I want you to lead your regiment through that low area. I think you'll be in cover there. Try to get around the enemy and hit them on the flank and rear." It was a bold plan...a risky one. Against the enemy's firepower, the conventional move would be to feed reserves into the prepared defenses. But Erik Cain was anything but conventional.

"Yes, sir." Yoshi's voice was eager...he hadn't seen any action yet, and he was anxious to get into the fight. Yoshi was as wildly aggressive as Cain, and his troops hadn't faced the enemy yet. That was one reason Erik chose the PRC force for the attack. His Marines had fought the enemy for six days, and their morale was eroding. They would attack if he ordered it, but they'd hold back...he knew that. He would lead his troops to the bitter end here, but Cain wasn't fooling himself...his men and women, even the most seasoned veterans, knew they couldn't win this fight. He knew it too, but it wasn't in him to give up.

He still had the Janissaries in reserve too, but he couldn't bring himself to trust them. When he walked through their camp...when he met with Tac-Commander Farooq...all he could see were enemies. He realized intellectually his close-mindedness could endanger his plan and cost him any chance at victory. His rational mind saw the situation clearly, but it didn't prevail. Twenty years of war and thousands of dead Marines exerted a hold on Cain that he just couldn't break, not even with unassailable logic.

"With your permission, general, I will prepare my forces to move forward."

"Go ahead, Aoki." Cain paused, feeling the regret he knew wouldn't stop him. He was sending the PRC troops...he was sending a friend...on an attack he knew couldn't succeed. He was hoping to disorder the enemy and delay their advance...and get them out in the open. He had no illusions that Yoshi's attack could do more than that. And when the enemy regrouped, the PRC troops would have a hell of a time getting back into the defensive perimeter. Cain had a lot of guilt from the years of bloody battles that had cost so many lives...but once he was on the field, victory was the only thing that mattered. He'd push his troops mercilessly and ignore any losses. There would always be time for guilt after the fight was over. "And Aoki?"

Yoshi had started to trot toward the PRC camp, but he stopped and turned to face Cain. "Yes, general."

"Hit them hard." Cain hated himself even as he said it. "Don't hold anything back."

"We'll hit them, Erik. Don't you worry about that."

Lieutenant Sato leapt over the edge of the rocky wall, the troops of his company following close behind. Colonel Yoshi's orders were explicit. They were to advance at full speed to their objective and to stop for nothing. They'd worked their way around the enemy flank without being detected, but the surprise wouldn't last long...and Yoshi wanted to make the most of it.

Attacking this enemy was difficult. The battle bots were highly resistant to damage, and it was hard to efficiently employ the heavier SAWs and HVMs when advancing. Though the PRC troops hadn't faced the enemy before, Colonel Yoshi understood the problem, and he'd crafted his attack plan accordingly.

There was a low ridge running across the PRC frontage, perpendicular to the enemy line. It was not a major terrain feature, really just a ripple in the ground, but it was enough to provide decent cover for a firing line. It was a perfect spot to deploy the heavy weapons and enfilade the enemy position. But Sato's troops had to cross 2 klicks of open ground to get there. They could do it, he was sure of that, but it would cost. The PRC troops carried shells similar to the Caliphate's "smoke" rounds in their mortar teams. The shells, spread a chemically-laced, radioactive steam across the field, not only impairing visibility, but wreaking havoc with scanners and other detection devices. It was frequently used to cover advances, but Yoshi was holding his back. He didn't want to do anything to alert the enemy. He even forbade firing until the troops had reached the new position.

Sato ran forward, zigzagging slightly to take advantage of the contours of the ground. Even "flat" terrain had dips and folds that offered some degree of protection. The enemy was heavily engaged on this sector, pushing hard against the Marines' third line. Unlike the first two layers of defense, this line was manned by units with a high proportion of green troops, and they were starting to give ground. It was a perfect time to hit the enemy flank.

Sato's troops got about halfway across the field before they were targeted. A detachment of the standard battle bots responded first, swinging around and firing high-velocity rounds at the advancing PRC forces. Their fire was extremely accurate, but Sato had his troops running forward in a zigzag pattern, making them harder to target. Still, he lost at least 10% of his force in just a few seconds...then the cluster bombs started coming in.

"Damn," he muttered under his breath. "These things react faster than anything I've ever seen." He'd known his troops would take fire going in, but he didn't expect the cluster bombs. He didn't understand how they could reposition their batteries so quickly. Now he had to make a choice...order his troops to hit the ground and crawl the rest of the way...or make a mad dash for the cover of the ridgeline. The losses would be high if they just ran forward, but Colonel Yoshi's orders were explicit.

"Run to the objective." He'd flipped his com to the unit-wide frequency. "Let's go! Move!" He started running himself as he gave the order. He focused on a section of the ridge and ran toward it, trying hard to ignore the incoming fire. It only took about 30 seconds to get to the ridge, but it was the longest half-minute he'd ever experienced. He made one last push off his legs and dove forward behind the spiny rock outcropping, his outstretched arms driving into the damp clay ground.

"All personnel, commence firing. Heavy weapons teams set up. I want you shooting in three zero seconds." Getting some fire laid down was his number one priority. Number two was checking the casualty reports. His AI was tied in with the transponders on the suits of his troops. Theoretically, he knew who was alive, who was dead, who was wounded...even who was overly stressed. In practice the data was of limited accuracy. Dust and radiation interfered with the transmissions, and damage to a trooper's armor could knock out the medical reporting system. Sato's best guess was that 25% of his people were down. That was bad, but it could have been worse. They'd just dashed across 2 kilometers of open plain against a technologically advanced and ruthless enemy. He tried not to think about the fact that they'd probably have to go back over that same ground.

His troopers were already firing, and one of the SAWs was active as well. They were enfilading the enemy at close range, causing considerable disorder as the robotic units moved to change their facing to meet the attack. They were scoring a lot of hits, but the PRC mag-rifles were weaker than the Alliance models, and it took a number of direct hits in a vital area to even damage one of the battle bots. The PRC heavy weapons, on the other hand - the autocannons particularly - were the best produced by of any of the Powers. They delivered a very heavy projectile at an extremely high velocity – the perfect combination to take on the enemy robots.

Sato saw the bots start to go down as his SAW teams came online. He only had four, but they were raking the enemy flank with withering fire. For a few minutes his people had the edge, blasting away at an enemy struggling to change frontage. But gradually the intensity of the return fire increased. The enemy's cluster bombs started dropping all along the ridge, savaging not only Sato's troops, but the entire PRC line.

Sato's company was deployed on the extreme left of the position. His orders were to hold here at all costs, and continue to pour fire into the enemy. The PRC right was swinging around like a door, attacking the enemy from the rear. Colonel Yoshi was there, leading the assault himself. Sato focused on his position, but he couldn't help but think of those troops continuing to advance, pressing the attack right onto the enemy. The battle bots were terrifying. They seemed almost impervious to damage, at least from regular small arms. And they ignored losses. They continued whatever they were doing, regardless of casualties. The last survivor of a unit fought with the same relentless determination it began with.

He'd never approached a battle expecting the other side to cut and run, but now he realized how much of his courage and his morale hinged on the subconscious knowledge that the enemy could be broken. That if his people were just a bit more steadfast than their adversaries they could win the day. It was overwhelming knowing that if you destroyed 99% of the enemy, the survivors would keep coming…that they would claw at you with their last appendage until you put every one of them down.

Sato looked out over the plain and watched his company's fire tear into the enemy. His people were wreaking havoc right now, but he couldn't help but wonder what would happen when the enemy reorganized and counter-attacked. If the enemy broke through Sato's people they'd get between the rest of the PRC force and the main Alliance line. Yoshi's attack would turn into a blood-soaked disaster.

Sato pulled his rifle up over the edge of the ridge and started firing. We're not going to let that happen, he thought grimly.

"Aoki's people are getting killed, Erik." Jax was standing right next to Cain, though on the com it would have sounded the same if he'd been100 klicks away. He was edgy, and he sounded it. "You need to give them the recall order."

Cain stood unmoving, staring off in the direction of the

PRC forces. He couldn't see them at this distance, but he knew what was happening there…he knew it all too well. "They will hold." His voice was icy, frozen. Erik spent a lot of his spare time worrying about his troops and brooding about the ones he'd lost, but once he was on the battlefield he was as cold as they come. He knew what it took to win…or to hold out longer if victory wasn't an option. And he let nothing interfere with that. As the years passed he had become almost a robot himself when the battle was raging. He'd pay for it later…he'd pay with guilt and doubt and self-recriminations, but on the field he'd spend however many lives it took to accomplish the objective.

He wasn't so sure what that objective was anymore. He'd created the most nightmarish set of defenses imaginable, doing everything he could think of to repel the enemy. His troops had inflicted enormous casualties on them, wiping away entire sections, but the survivors just kept coming…and the orbiting fleet continued landing replacements. He'd never thought his people could win, not really. But now he was sure…they were fighting a hopeless battle. But if his entire corps was going to be destroyed, he was damned sure going to take out as many of these cursed machines as he could. And that meant Aoki's people stayed where they were…at least for a while longer.

Jax fidgeted in his armor, wanting to argue but knowing it was futile. The two were closer than brothers, comrades in some of the most horrific battles men had ever fought. But this was the one area where they differed, and the only thing they ever argued about. Jax could never embrace the brutal mathematics of war. Not the way Cain did.

"I'm worried about the western flank too, Erik." Jax changed the subject. There was no point arguing with Cain, especially on the battlefield; he might just as well debate a brick wall. "What if the enemy manages to get through those mountains? I really think we need to garrison that area."

Cain was focusing all his strength where he could hurt the enemy. The western approaches were covered by the Iron Hills, a low range of mountains that were extremely rocky and virtually impassable. "How are they going to move a significant force through there?" Cain was annoyed. He knew Jax was upset with him over the PRC troops, and now he felt his XO was venting his frustration by picking at his decisions. His head pounded, despite the two doses of analgesics Hector had administered, and he was in no mood for pointless debate. "We need those troops elsewhere, Jax. It's that simple." He'd normally never disregard Jax's opinions, but he was tired and frustrated and his temper was short.

Jax sighed softly. Erik is being reckless, he thought. He's so focused on lashing out at the enemy he's taking chances he shouldn't be. "Don't you think we should post something there just in case? The Janissaries are still unengaged."

Cain snapped his head around toward Jax. "Do you really want them loose right now out of our sight?" He paused, trying unsuccessfully to take the annoyed tone out of his voice. "I'm sorry, Jax. I just don't trust them. How many of our friends and comrades have they killed?"

Jax didn't answer. He'd been worried about Cain for some time. He knew his friend was troubled…they all were after recent events. The bloodbaths of the Third Frontier War had been closely followed by the cataclysm of the Rebellions. The schemes of Alliance Intelligence and the treachery of General Samuels had been too much. It had worn them all down. Cain still handled troops in the field brilliantly, but his paranoia and anger were starting to get the better of him, clouding his decisions. He was taking gambles he'd never have considered a few years earlier.

"I'm going to send out the air assets against the enemy fighting the PRC troops. They're out in the open right now, totally exposed." Cain was looking down at a large 'pad laying on a small folding table. He had two small air-attack squadrons, but he'd kept them hidden, waiting for the right opportunity to inflict some damage. Admiral West had deployed atmospheric fighters to cover the evacuation of Teller's troops on Cornwall, and she'd found that the enemy's anti-aircraft fire was devastating. Her wings had managed to hold back the enemy while 1st Brigade was evac'd, but they'd been virtually wiped out in the process. Barely one in five returned.

Now, Cain was launching his own squadrons, and he didn't expect them to fare any better. But they were armed with one of Sparks' new weapons, and this would be its first deployment. If it lived up to expectations, it could inflict massive damage on the enemy forces. It was more cold math – 24 two-man aircraft against the damage they could inflict.

Jax nodded, a pointless gesture in battle armor. He knew the pilots would take heavy losses, but he had to agree…Cain had created an ideal opportunity for the air strike.

"You're all set. Launch when ready."

Captain Jacoby could barely hear the gravelly voice of his crew chief over the noise of the engines. He looked down from the cockpit and returned the chief's thumbs up gesture. He could feel the shaking as the reactor in the VTOL craft fed power to the engines.

The strike fighters of the 11th squadron rose slowly, in perfect formation. They were all veterans of the Third Frontier War, the pick of the Corps' air wings. The normally lithe fighters handled sluggishly – they'd been stripped of their usual armaments and loaded with Sparks' new weapon. The plasma bombardment system was huge, almost too big to cram into a fighter.

Jacoby swore under his breath as his fighter pulled to the right and he had to compensate. These first-generation PBS devices had been rushed into use – they weren't properly balanced, and it took considerable effort to fly with a payload heavily weighted to one side. Jacoby was glad all his crews were veterans.

Despite the difficulties, his fighters fell swiftly into attack formation and blasted toward the enemy positions, with Captain Crill's squadron alongside. They were deployed in three successive lines, formed up to bombard the enemy forces now counter-attacking the PRC troops.

The strike fighters dove at the enemy formations, evading the heavy anti-aircraft fire as well as they could carrying their massive payloads. Jacoby was senior to Crill, so he took command of the entire strike. His fighter was in the lead, and he bore down on a heavy concentration of enemy 'bots. He was going to drop the PBS directly on top of them. "All pilots, follow my mark. We're going right down their throats. I know the AA fire is heavy, but I want these things dumped right on top of those SOBs."

It only took the fighters a few seconds to complete their attack run, but the enemy hyper-velocity rounds tore into them, taking down almost half their number before they reached the drop points. Jacoby managed to avoid the incoming fire, but Crill's plane was hit and erupted into a fireball.

"Damn." Jacoby saw Crill's plane destroyed on his scanner. The two had served together several times, and they'd always gotten along well. He didn't have time to brood, though...he was over the drop point. "Release." He'd chosen to eyeball the drop rather than have the plane's AI handle it. As soon as the PBS was away he arced into a steep climb, trying to clear the fire from the ground.

The PBS units split into half a dozen sections, each one a nuclear reactor that instantly superheated a large volume of condensed gas. The resulting plasma struck ground targets over a wide area. The effect was similar to ancient weapons like napalm or fuel air explosives, but the PBS was orders of magnitude more powerful. It was the strongest non-atomic weapon ever deployed by man, and it swept huge sections of the field clear of the enemy. Even the Reapers were obliterated when they were caught in the intensely hot clouds of plasma.

Jacoby circled his fighter around, giving himself a view of the field as he headed back to base. It was a vision of hell; for a few seconds it looked like a miniature sun had crashed to the ground.

The surviving fighters formed up behind Jacoby, and the nine of them, all that remained of two veteran squadrons, made their way back, leaving the wreckage of the enemy line behind them.

Cain had planned the strike perfectly. Yoshi's troops suffered grievous casualties, but the strike fighters had caught the main enemy force out in the open, and Spark's new plasma weapon had been a total success and had inflicted massive losses. Cain fed in reserves and ordered the previously wavering third line to attack the now totally disordered enemy. The Marines were able to engage small, scattered survivors at favorable odds, inflicting more casualties and splitting the enemy line in three places.

For the first time in the war, the surviving enemy units pulled back to regroup. The battle was far from over, and Cain knew the enemy would land more troops and renew the attack. His assaulting forces were exhausted, and he had no reserves to pour into pressing his advantage...at least none he would use. The Janissaries were still unengaged, and Commander Farooq had requested permission to advance. But Cain steadfastly refused, and the enemy retreated and temporarily broke off the engagement.

Cain knew it wouldn't last, but he savored it anyway. Even a fleeting victory was a victory. Throughout the lines, the Marines' sagging morale soared. The enemy could be beaten back after all.

Chapter 27

Battle of Farpoint
Phase 3 – The Breathrough
Iron Hills, Northwest of Landing
Farpoint - Epsilon Fornacis III

"We've got something coming." Lys Daniels was crouched behind a large rock outcropping looking out at a massive wall of granite. "I have intermittent readings from the other side of this formation." Daniels and her squad were scouts. General Cain had decided the small mountains northwest of the capital were impassable to a major force, but General Jax had sent her people anyway...just to be sure. Maybe that caution was paying off.

"I'm getting it too, sergeant." Corporal Farnum was a little farther forward, at the base of the rock face. It was 100 meters of sheer granite...almost perfectly vertical. "But how could any unit hope to get over this. It's at least 30 klicks to get around."

Daniels tried to recalibrate her scanners. It was no use... there was some mineral in these rocks that was interfering with her readings. She took a deep breath and thought quietly...how am I going to scout out the other side of this thing? Finally, she flipped on the squad-wide com. "Alright everybody, listen to me. We've got to get someone over this cliff and see what is on the other side." She paused, thinking she could almost hear the groans of her troopers. "Farnum, Varick...I need you to scale this thing and report." The choices weren't random. She'd quickly reviewed her unit roster...Farnum and Varick were the most experienced with this type of terrain. Both had served on Granicus during the war, and that planet was one giant mountain range.

"Yes, sergeant." Farnum looked up at the cliff. The scout

armor had some functionality for traversing rugged terrain, but this was really a job for specialized climbing gear…which they didn't have.

Farnum stared up the cliff as she began slowly climbing. This is something I might have done for fun, she thought… under much different circumstances. Farnum was a climber, at least when she was able to wrangle a leave long enough to indulge her hobby. But scaling a cliff in battle armor was a different matter, one with advantages and disadvantages. She was certainly stronger in her fighting suit, but she was heavier as well. And she didn't have the touch and the dexterity that was so essential to climbing.

The scout armor had some useful tools, even if it lacked a full suite of specialized gear, and she found it wasn't as difficult to reach the top as she thought it would be. She climbed up over the lip and reported back to Daniels. "Sergeant, I'm… ah…we're up top." She saw Varick pull himself up onto to the rocky ledge just as she started to speak. "Scouting the other side now."

"Excellent, corporal." Daniel's was looking up, but she lost sight of them as soon as they stepped away from the ledge. "Report anything…even if it's just a feelin…"

"Sergeant!" It was Farnum, and the veteran Marine sounded almost panicked. "There are enemy bots on the other side of this spur. Hundreds of them…thousands. About 7-8 klicks to the west."

Daniels could feel the breath sucked from her body. She couldn't understand why the enemy was massing so much strength on the other side of a huge wall of rock, but she knew it couldn't be good. She knew she had to report this immediately. "1st Division HQ, this is Sergeant Daniels, 3rd Scouting Section." She paused, almost amused at the audacity of what she was about to say. "I need to speak directly with General Jax immediately."

The battle was raging again. Cain had launched a series of sledgehammer blows, first with the PRC flank attack, then the air strike, and finally with the advance of the entire line. For the first time in the war, an enemy force retreated, leaving the field to the Marines.

But the respite didn't last, and neither did the morale boost. The enemy set up a defensive perimeter, one Cain's troops dared not attack, and they started landing reinforcements. The ships came in for days, bringing thousands of battle robots to the surface. The scouts had reported entire units of the feared Reapers, as well as several other types of larger bots.

Cain's fleeting victory had clearly triggered some type of tactical re-evaluation by whomever – or whatever - was commanding this force. The enemy responded to the elevated threat level by landing an army far more powerful than the original invasion force. Cain sat and grimly read reports detailing larger and larger enemy forces massing against his lines. He knew it was over…and so did his troops. Unexpectedly, as the prospects of survival vanished, the Marines' faltering morale stiffened again, morphing into an odd acceptance and a grim determination to sell their lives dearly. The pride of the Corps surged through the psyche of the battered and exhausted men and women in the trenches. One by one and in groups they swore silently…they would not give in to the fear...they would face these things and show them what Marines were made of.

It began with a report from Hector. "General Cain, I am receiving reports from the front line scouts." The AI's voice was calm and even. "The enemy is advancing."

So it begins, Cain thought. He knew the enemy wouldn't stop once the assault had commenced. The robots didn't get tired, they didn't feel the pain of wounds…they would just keep coming until all of Cain's people were dead.

That had been two days before. Now they'd been fighting nonstop for 48 hours. The Marines held grimly, but human endurance has its limits, and exhaustion was taking its toll. Cain knew it wouldn't be long now…when the enemy broke through somewhere, things would collapse quickly.

He was just about to move forward and get a closer look at the front when Jax broke in on his com.

"Erik, we've got trouble."

Cain sighed. There was always trouble. But Jax sounded shaken up, and that made Cain's stomach clench.

Daniels scrambled up the rocky terrain, trying to work her way around the massive wall of stone. Generals Cain and Jax had sent her 3 more sections of scouts, along with orders to inspect every centimeter of the mountain range. The enemy was massing on the other side, and they wanted to know why. If there was a tunnel or pass through the mountains they'd missed, they had to find it.

She was over ten klicks from where she'd left Farnum and Varick, but she hadn't seen a thing. Not a crack in the massive rock wall nor a serviceable path leading up and over. She couldn't imagine how the enemy forces massing on the other side expected to pass through. But they weren't there for nothing, and it was her job to find out how they planned to attack.

She extended an arm, steadying herself as she climbed up and over a large, jagged rock. She turned to look back and see how the rest of the squad was managing when a blinding light flashed across the sky. An instant later the ground shook violently and a shock wave took her and slammed her into the face of the mountain.

She wasn't badly hurt, but she was dazed and had trouble trying to get up. Her visor had gone dark, minimizing the damage to her eyes, but she still couldn't see anything but spots. Her suit was damaged but still functional. She could feel the med system giving her multiple injections. One, at least, must have been for the radiation...her detector was showing a nearly lethal exposure to gamma rays.

She pulled herself up enough to sit against the rock wall. To the south the sky was obscured by a massive cloud of dust and debris. "Scout sections, report." There was a long silence, at least half a minute, but then she started to get a few responses. They all reported the same thing, a massive detonation of some sort. Some of them were wounded and all were dazed. But most of her units failed to report. "Corporal Farnum? Report."

Nothing. "First Section? Corporal Farnum? Private Varrick. Report immediately." But there was nothing on the com…just silence.

"What the hell was that?" Cain snapped at Hector as he pulled himself back to his feet. He'd hit the ground when he heard the blast, but the area around HQ was only showered with dirt and small rocks.

"Based on observable data, I would hypothesize that a matter-antimatter annihilation event occurred." The AI paused for an instant as it collected additional data. "Preliminary radiation readings support this conclusion."

"Location of ground zero?" Cain was panning his head around, confirming there was no significant damage around the headquarters area. "Display on my visor."

Hector activated Cain's visor projection system, displaying a tactical map of the surrounding area. A flashing red dot marked the best estimate of the blast location. "This is a projection only, general. More data will be required for a precise determination."

Cain stared at the map and froze. The flashing dot was in the center of the Iron Hills…the mountains he'd called impassable. "Hector, get me General Ja…" He didn't get any further before he was interrupted by Jax's incoming communication.

"Erik, we've got a big problem." Jax sounded shaken up. "I've got Sergeant Daniels on the line. Sergeant, I need you to tell General Cain what you just reported to me"

"Yes sir." Cain didn't know Daniels personally. She was one of the scouts, a good one by all accounts, but he'd never spoken with her before. "General Cain, sir…it looks like the enemy mined the rockwall with some kind of extremely powerful explosive." Daniels' voice was hoarse, and she was breathing heavily as she spoke. She sounded like she was in pain. "Sir, the entire formation is gone, and there's a 300 meter gap through. There are enemy troops marching toward the opening."

"Jax, we've got to get that gap plugged." Cain remembered Daniels was still on the line. "Thank you, sergeant. Maintain your position and await further orders."

"Yes, si…" Cain cut the line before she could finish.

"I'm going to scrape up what reserves I can, Jax, and take them over there." Cain was making a mental list of the unengaged troops he had available…a very short list. "We need to block that gap before they get through and out in the open."

"Erik, that's crazy." Jax's voice was firm. He was going to dig his heels in on this one. "You're the commander in chief… you can't go running up into the mountains. I'll do it."

Cain opened his mouth to argue, but he knew Jax was right. He also knew that Jax had warned him about an attack from the mountains days ago. This emergency was his fault…it was his own carelessness, and he hated to send his friend and second in command to clean up his mess. "Ok, Jax." His voice was downcast, defeated. His duty wouldn't allow him to abandon the rest of the corps. He would have to let Jax do his dirty work.

"Hector, I want every unit not currently engaged to report to General Jax immediately." It wasn't going to be more than 1,500 troops, maybe 1,800.

"What about the Janissaries, Erik?" Jax sounded a little tentative.

"Do you really want them behind you in this situation?" Cain was nothing if not stubborn – in his prejudices and grudges as well as in duty and loyalty. "No, I just don't trust them. You take the available reserves, and I'll pull some of the lightly engaged battalions out of the line to reinforce you."

"Ok, Erik." Jax sounded like he wanted to argue. He didn't like the Caliphate troops any more than Cain did, but there were over 2,000 of them, elite veterans all, and they were just sitting there staring at each other. "Whatever you say." He sounded annoyed. "Don't worry…I'll plug that gap."

"I know you will." Cain started moving forward toward the main line. He was going to hand pick backup units for Jax. "I know you will," he repeated.

Chapter 28

Battle of Farpoint
Phase 3 – The Retreat
Pilgrim River Valley, Northeast of Landing
Farpoint - Epsilon Fornacis III

"General Cain…it's Admiral Compton. How the hell are you guys doing down there? We're here to get your people out."

Cain couldn't believe what he was hearing. He'd spent the last hour pulling troops off the line to reinforce Jax's defense at the gap, and he was on the far edge of the right flank when the signal came through. The last thing he'd expected was anyone coming to the rescue. He knew Admiral West's people had fought like demons, but once ships were damaged, out of weapons, and low on power there wasn't much they could do. Cain had wished the best for the retreating survivors, and he fervently hoped Erica West was one of them.

But now he had the second in command of the Alliance navy on his com. "Admiral Compton, sir…it's good to hear from you. This is unexpected."

"You can thank your friend, Admiral West. She kept insisting she'd detected a shortage of ordnance in the enemy fleet and that a rescue mission was feasible." He paused, just for a second. "I don't know how she convinced Admiral Garret to risk Second Fleet to try it."

"Admiral West is alive then?" Cain was glad to hear it. Erica West was a good officer…and a good friend. "We didn't know whether she'd made it or not."

"She barely made it. She's in rough shape, Erik. But she wouldn't let us put her in the infirmary until Admiral Garret agreed to make a try to get your people out." His voice became lower, more serious. "But we don't have time to catch up now. We just fought our way in, and by damned if she wasn't right... they seemed to be out of almost everything. They pulled back, but I doubt we can hold this space long." He hesitated and then added, "Besides, if my scanning reports are accurate, it looks like we got here none too soon."

"No joke there, sir." The exhaustion came through in Cain's voice...and the relief. He hadn't expected any of his people to escape, and now salvation was at hand. "Things are hot down here."

"Alright, Erik. I'm sending out some strike wings to support your people...they're loaded up with Colonel Sparks' PBS weapons." Compton knew those pilots would be running a deadly gauntlet, but he'd asked for volunteers, and every strike fighter crew in Second Fleet stepped forward. "Hopefully, that will take some of the pressure off of you. I'll be sending shuttles down shortly. But you're going to have to manage the withdrawal yourself."

"I'm on it, sir."

The fire was intense. Jax had a row of SAWs in cover behind the rubble spanning the entire gap. They were taking a fearsome toll on the enemy, especially the standard battle bots. But plugging the hole had already cost his force heavily. He'd had about 1,600 when he started, and Cain had sent another 1,000. But there were barely 800 left now...and the heavy weapons were on their fourth and fifth crews.

He climbed up on a jagged spur of rock, notching his visor to Mag 30 to get a good look for himself. Jax could see the enemy massing a force of Reapers to punch through his thin line, and he knew he'd never be able to stop them. But he had to delay them...buy some time. The withdrawal was going fairly well, by all accounts, but if the enemy sliced through his forces they'd be in the staging areas in half an hour. That would turn the retreat into a bloody nightmare.

He didn't like the Janissaries any more than Cain did, but now he was wishing Erik had agreed to deploy them. Former enemies or no, he needed more firepower, and they were the only fresh troops left in I Corps.

He barked out a series of commands, repositioning his SAWs for maximum effect, and moving the remaining HVM teams onto a ridge of higher ground behind the main line. They were just minor adjustments, but he needed everything he could get if he was going to repel the next attack. That was something he had to do…whatever the cost.

He pulled up his mag rifle and took up a firing position on the line. They needed every shot they could get. "Ok, people, we're holding here no matter what. Remember, you are Marines, and no enemy is going to push us around!" He was always amazed at the morale effect a little trash talk could muster.

A fighting withdrawal was one of the most difficult operations to execute, but I Corps was pulling it off. Compton's atmospheric fighters had savaged the enemy lines…everywhere except in the gap where Jax's people were barely hanging on. The confines there were too tight, and the planes couldn't maneuver. Besides, in those mountains they couldn't safely target the close in enemy formations without a major risk of hitting Jax's troops too.

The fighters paid as heavily as Cain and Compton had expected, but without their sacrifice, no one would have gotten off Farpoint. The other heroes of the withdrawal were the Janissaries. Commander Farooq finally convinced Cain to send his men in, and they held the line while the rest of I Corp's exhausted people made their way to the waiting shuttles.

Despite the carnage and the confusion, they'd gotten a lot of people off-planet already, and the remaining units were embarking now…all except the rearguards. I Corps had suffered heavily in the Battle of Farpoint, but it wasn't going to be wiped out after all. Cain allowed himself a moment of satisfaction. Every one of his people that survived was a cause for celebration.

The Marines – and their allies – had fought with grim determination, and they'd hurt the enemy badly, inflicting thousands of casualties on the technologically superior robots. Cain felt pride too, though he knew the elation would be fleeting. Once he was safely evac'd to Second Fleet he'd begin to review the casualty reports, and the guilt and doubts would move to the forefront. But for now he still had a job to do, and it was time to get his rearguards falling back on the evac area.

He had Hector connect him to Jax's direct line. "Jax, I need you to start pulling your people back. We've got most of the corps evac'd, and the rest of the rearguard isn't going to hold for much longer."

There was nothing…no response, only silence. "Jax, do you read?" Still silent. "Jax?" Cain switched to the command frequency for Jax's force. "Jax, do you read me?"

There was a response this time, after a brief pause, but it wasn't the voice Cain was expecting. "This is Major Killian, sir." As soon as Cain heard the major's voice he knew something was wrong. Terribly wrong. "General Jax was hit a few minutes ago." There was another pause, and Cain's stomach clenched and he felt the breath sucked from his body. "He's dead, sir."

Chapter 29

Orbital Station 2
Planet Sandoval
Delta Leonis IV
"The Line"

Cain stood on the observation deck in his dress blues. The occasion was a somber one. Marines die, they were used to that. But it still hurt to lose one of their own.

They were gathered to bid farewell to a hero of the Corps. Lieutenant General Darius Jax had survived some of the most horrific battles in human history, but finally one of those fights had claimed him.

Cain could never quite piece together exactly how Jax fell. He was leading the rearguard, holding the enemy at the gap while the rest of 1st Corps conducted a fighting withdrawal. By most accounts, it was one of the Reapers that hit him. Cain didn't know if his friend had died right away or lingered in pain and fear. But there was no doubt he was dead...his people had carried him back, and Cain had seen for himself.

I Corps barely made it off-planet, and they'd lost heavily in doing it. In the end it was the Janissaries who held off the enemy while Cain's exhausted people boarded the shuttles. Commander Farooq finally convinced Cain to deploy his forces, and his men fought grimly, holding the line at every point until they were the only ones left on Farpoint. By the time they boarded they'd lost 80% of their number...and Erik Cain had changed his opinion on old enemies.

It fell to Cain to give the eulogy. Jax had been his best friend, his comrade in arms through a lifetime of war. They had been closer than brothers. There was no one Cain trusted more than he had Jax…indeed, there were few he trusted at all, and the loss of his faithful companion had wounded him deeply, in ways he would let no one see. He dreaded speaking publicly about his friend – Cain was one to mourn silently. But Darius Jax deserved a tribute, and it was his obligation to his lost comrade, one he took seriously.

Cain was a legend in the Corps, and his Marines would follow him anywhere, but Jax had been different. He was a legend in his own right, but he had also enjoyed a special relationship with his troops. Cain was respected and revered…almost worshipped by the Marines he commanded. They would follow him anywhere without hesitation, but he was too coldly analytical, too insular for them to truly love. But they had loved Jax. He had been one of them, an enlisted man with stars on his collar. Among themselves, his Marines had called him Sarge, even as he rose ever higher in the ranks. It was the highest compliment those grizzled veterans paid anyone.

"We are gathered here to pay our respects to a man I had the immense honor of calling my friend." Cain's voice was soft, his tone mournful. "Lieutenant General Darius Jax came to the Corps, as so many of us have, from the lowest levels of Earth society. He took the opportunity offered him and he became a Marine…one to make all of us in the Corps proud."

Cain looked out at those assembled. General Holm, sitting in the first row, staring straight ahead with the grim discipline that made him who he was. But Erik could see in his eyes the grief tearing him apart. Sarah, her face red and raw from her tears, sitting silently, not quite able to look directly at Erik as he spoke. Admirals Garret and Compton were sitting at respectful attention and, in the back, leaning uncomfortably, was Admiral West. She was still in considerable pain from her partially healed wounds, but she'd checked herself out of the infirmary and insisted on attending.

"I met Darius a few days before Operation Achilles, and we served through that campaign together." Achilles was the failed invasion of Tau Ceti III, one of the worst debacles the Corps had ever endured. "During that fiery trial, he and I forged the foundations of a trust and a friendship that would carry us through some of the darkest places men have travelled." Cain's mind drifted back over the years, to worlds visited and battles fought long ago.

"Darius Jax spent his life fighting for a better future, for one where liberty is valued and preserved, where mankind can have another chance at freedom." Cain said the words, but in his heart he knew he didn't believe them anymore. That future they fought for was always another war, always more death and suffering. Now that never-ending cycle had claimed his friend. "He gave his life in that fight, so that future generations can know a better life than the one he was born into."

Erik looked at the back of the room, where many of Jax's Marines were gathered. They were hardened warriors, most of them, veterans of a dozen campaigns, but there was not a dry eye among them. "I'm not sure my friend ever knew his troops called him Sarge…" He forced a smile for the men and women lined up along the rear wall. "…but I am sure he knew how much they loved him…how much we all loved him. And I know that knowledge was one of the great joys of his life."

He looked back again, giving Jax's Marines his own silent tribute. "My poor skills are inadequate to describe the emptiness left by the loss of this great warrior, this excellent man. I could speak for hours about my friend Darius, about my comrade General Jax…but instead I will utter the one thing I know for certain he would have wanted me to say. Darius Jax lived and died for the Corps. He was a Marine."

Cain was finally alone. It had been hard to give the slip to Sarah and General Holm. They knew how much Jax's death hurt him, but after all the years they still didn't understand him…not completely.

He looked through the small porthole at the glowing blue sphere 50,000 kilometers below the station's geosynchronous orbit. He had never been to Sandoval before, but by all accounts it was a beautiful world. Now it would become a battlefield.

Cain had his pain and guilt about Jax, more than Sarah or

the general could ever know. But all that was locked away, deep down. It had taken a colossal effort to suppress it all, but he just couldn't face it now. He'd deal with it someday, but not today. The war wasn't over, and he had his duty. Duty had ruled his life, and that wasn't going to change now. He couldn't think of a worse tribute to his fallen friend than to let grief and guilt keep him from the fight.

There would be time to mourn, time to face his guilt...if he survived the war. When that day came, he thought, it might tear him apart. There might not be much left of Erik Cain, the man. He wasn't sure he cared...he suspected there wasn't much left of him anyway. It was his fault Jax died, at least that's how he saw it, and he didn't know how he would ever reconcile with that. If he'd garrisoned he mountains...if he'd sent in the Janissaries sooner. So many ifs. Was it arrogance, carelessness? Or was he just used up, no longer able to handle the burden of command?

He pushed back the doubts, and the self-hatred too. Erik Cain the Marine had a job to do and, as always, that came first. Personal pain and loss would have to wait. There was only one thing that was important now, one thing that demanded the best he could give. Everything he had left would go into the fight... body, blood, soul. He owed that much to Jax.

In his mind there was one mantra, one cause. The Line must hold.

Crimson Worlds Series

Marines (Crimson Worlds I)

The Cost of Victory (Crimson Worlds II)

A Little Rebellion (Crimson Worlds III)

The First Imperium (Crimson Worlds IV)

The Line Must Hold (Crimson Worlds V)
(July 2013)

Also By Jay Allan

The Dragon's Banner

www.crimsonworlds.com